FABIUS BILE
PRIMOGENITOR

JOSH REYNOLDS

BLACK LIBRARY

For Sylvie, who keeps me going.

A BLACK LIBRARY PUBLICATION

First published in 2016.
This edition published in Great Britain in 2017 by
Black Library,
Games Workshop Ltd.,
Willow Road,
Nottingham, NG7 2WS, UK.

10 9 8 7 6 5 4 3 2 1

Produced by Games Workshop in Nottingham.
Cover illustration by Lie Setiawan.

A CIP record for this book is available from the British Library.

ISBN 13: 978 1 78496 620 1

See Black Library on the internet at

blacklibrary.com

Find out more about Games Workshop
and the world of Warhammer 40,000 at

games-workshop.com

Printed and bound by CPI Group (UK) Ltd, Croydon, CR0 4YY

It is the 41st millennium. For more than a hundred centuries the Emperor has sat immobile on the Golden Throne of Earth. He is the Master of Mankind by the will of the gods, and master of a million worlds by the might of his inexhaustible armies. He is a rotting carcass writhing invisibly with power from the Dark Age of Technology. He is the Carrion Lord of the Imperium for whom a thousand souls are sacrificed every day, so that he may never truly die.

Yet even in his deathless state, the Emperor continues his eternal vigilance. Mighty battlefleets cross the daemon-infested miasma of the warp, the only route between distant stars, their way lit by the Astronomican, the psychic manifestation of the Emperor's will. Vast armies give battle in His name on uncounted worlds. Greatest amongst his soldiers are the Adeptus Astartes, the Space Marines, bioengineered super-warriors. Their comrades in arms are legion: the Astra Militarum and countless planetary defence forces, the ever-vigilant Inquisition and the tech-priests of the Adeptus Mechanicus to name only a few. But for all their multitudes, they are barely enough to hold off the ever-present threat from aliens, heretics, mutants – and worse.

To be a man in such times is to be one amongst untold billions. It is to live in the cruellest and most bloody regime imaginable. These are the tales of those times. Forget the power of technology and science, for so much has been forgotten, never to be re-learned. Forget the promise of progress and understanding, for in the grim dark future there is only war. There is no peace amongst the stars, only an eternity of carnage and slaughter, and the laughter of thirsting gods.

PART ONE

THE PRODIGAL

CHAPTER ONE

Dead-Alive

Oleander Koh strode across the dead city, humming softly to himself.

The dry wind scraped across his garishly painted power armour, and he hunched forward, leaning into the teeth of the gale. He relished the way it flayed his exposed skin. He licked at the blood that dripped down his face, savouring the spice of it.

Oleander's demeanour was at once baroque and barbaric. It was fitting, given that he had left a trail of fire and corpses stretching across centuries. His power armour was the colour of a newly made bruise, and decorated with both obscene imagery and archaic medicae equipment. Animal skins flapped from the rims of his shoulder-plates, and a helmet crested with a ragged mane of silk strips dangled from his equipment belt, amongst the stasis-vials and extra clips of ammunition for the bolt pistol holstered opposite the helmet. Besides the pistol, his only weapon was a long, curved sword. The sword was Tuonela-made, forged in the secret smithy of the mortuary cults, and its golden pommel was wrought in the shape of a death's head. Oleander was not its first owner, nor, he suspected, would he be its last.

Unlike the weapon, he had been forged on Terra. As Apothecary Oleander, he had marched beneath the banners of the Phoenician, fighting first in the Emperor's name and then in the Warmaster's. He had tasted the fruits of war, and found his purpose in the field-laboratories of the being he'd come to call master. The being he had returned to this world to see, though he risked death, or worse, for daring to do so.

He had been forced to land the gunship he'd borrowed some distance away, on the outskirts of the city. It sat hidden now among the shattered husks of hundreds of other craft, its servitor crew waiting for his signal. There was no telling what sort of defences had been erected in his absence. And while he'd sent a coded vox transmission ahead, asking for permission to land, he didn't feel like taking the risk of being blown out of the sky by someone with an itchy trigger-finger. The few occupants of this place valued their privacy to an almost lunatic degree. But perhaps that was only natural, given their proclivities.

His ceramite-encased fingers tapped out a tuneless rhythm on the sword's pommel as he walked and hummed. The wind screamed as it washed over him. And not just the wind. The whole planet reverberated with the death-scream of its once-proud population. Their delicate bones carpeted the ground, fused and melted together, though not from a natural heat. If he listened, he could pick out individual strands from the cacophony, like notes from a song. It was as if they were singing just for him. Welcoming him home.

The remains of the city – their city – rose wild around him, a jungle of living bone and wildly growing hummocks of rough psychoplastic flesh. The city might have been beautiful once, but it was gorgeous now. Silent, alien faces clumped on wraithbone walls like pulsing fungi, and living shadows stretched across the streets. Eerie radiances glistened in out-of-the-way places and tittering, phosphorescent shapes skulked in the broken buildings. A verdant madness, living and yet dead. A microcosm of Urum, as a whole.

Urum the Dead-Alive. Crone world, some called it. Urum was not its original name. But it was what the scavengers of the archaeomarkets called it, and it was as good a name as any. For Oleander Koh, it had once simply been 'home'.

Sometimes it was hard to remember why he'd left in the first place. At other times, it was all too easy. Idly, he reached up to touch the strand of delicate glass philtres hanging from around his thick neck. He stopped. The wind had slackened, as if in anticipation. Oleander grunted and turned. Something was coming. 'Finally,' he said.

Gleaming shapes streaked towards him through the ruins. They shone like metal in the sunlight, but nothing made of metal could move so smoothly or so fast. At least nothing he'd ever had the misfortune to meet. They'd been stalking him for a few hours now. Perhaps they'd grown bored with the game. Or maybe he was closer to his goal than he'd thought. The city changed year by year, either growing or decaying. He wasn't sure which. Perhaps both.

The sentry-beasts were low, lean things. He thought of

wolves, though they weren't anything like that. More akin to the sauroids that inhabited some feral worlds, albeit with feathers of liquid metal rather than scales, and tapering beak-like jaws. They made no noise, save the scraping of bladed limbs across the ground. They split up, and vanished into the shadows of the ruins. Even with his transhuman senses, Oleander was hard-pressed to keep track of them. He sank into a combat stance, fingers resting against the sword's hilt, and waited. The moment stretched, seconds ticking by. The wind picked up, and his head resounded with the screams of the dead.

He sang along with them for a moment, his voice rising and falling with the wind. It was an old song, older even than Urum. He'd learned it on Laeran, from an addled poet named Castigne. 'Strange is the night where black stars rise, and strange moons circle through ebon skies... songs that the Hyades shall sing...'

Prompted by instinct, Oleander spun, his sword springing into his hand as if of its own volition. He cut the first of the beasts in two, spilling its steaming guts on the heaving ground. It shrieked and kicked at the air, refusing to die. He stamped on its skull until it lay still. Still singing, he turned. The second had gone for the high ground. He caught a glimpse of it as it prowled above him, stalking through the canopy of bone and meat. He could hear its jagged limbs clicking as it moved. His hand dropped to his pistol.

Something scraped behind him. 'Clever,' he murmured. He drew the bolt pistol and whirled, firing. A shimmering body lurched forward and collapsed. Oleander twirled his sword and thrust it backwards, to meet the second beast as it leapt from its perch. Claws scrabbled at his power armour, and curved jaws snapped mindlessly. Its eyes were targeting sensors, sweeping his face for weakness. Oleander stepped back and slammed the point of his sword into one of the twisted trees, dislodging the dying animal.

He prodded the twitching creature with his weapon. It was not a natural thing, with its gleaming feathers and sensor nodes jutting from its flesh like spines. But then, this was not a natural world. The sentry-beast had been vat-grown, built from base acids, stretched and carved into useful shape. Idly, he lifted the blade and sampled the acrid gore that stained it. 'Piquant,' he said. 'With just a hint of the real thing. Your best work yet, master.'

Oleander smiled as he said it. He hadn't used that word in a long time. Not since he'd last been here. Before Urum's master, and his, had exiled him for his crimes. Oleander shied away from the thought. Reflecting on those last days was like probing an infected wound, and his memories were tender to the touch. There was no pleasure to be had there, only pain. Some adherents of Slaanesh claimed that those things were ever one and the same, but Oleander knew better.

He kicked the still-twitching body and turned away. Something rattled nearby. The sentry-beasts made no noise, save for that peculiar clicking of their silvery carapace. More of them burst out of the unnatural under-growth and converged on him. Foolish, to think there were only three. Excess was a virtue here, as everywhere. 'Well, he who hesitates is lost,' he said, lunging to meet them. There were ten, at least, though they were moving so swiftly it was hard to keep count.

Beak-like protuberances fastened on his armour as he waded through them. Smooth talon-like appendages scraped paint from the ceramite, and whip-like tails thudded against his legs and chest. They were trying to knock him down. He brought his sword down and split one of the quicksilver shapes in half. Acidic ichor spewed upwards. He fired his bolt pistol, the explosive rounds punching fist-sized holes in his attackers.

All at once, the attack ceased. The surviving sentry-beasts scattered, as swiftly as they had come. Oleander waited, scanning his surroundings. He'd killed three. Someone had called the others off. He thought he knew who. He heard the harsh rasp of breath in humanoid lungs, and smelled the rancid stink of chem-born flesh.

Oleander straightened and sheathed his sword without cleaning it. 'What are you waiting for, children?' He held up his bolt pistol and made a show of holstering it. 'I won't hurt you, if you're kind.' He spread his arms, holding them away from his weapons.

Unnatural shapes, less streamlined than the sentry-beasts, lurched into view. They moved silently, despite the peculiarity of their limbs. They wore the ragged remnants of old uniforms. Some were clad in ill-fitting and piecemeal combat armour. Most carried a variety of firearms in their twisted paws – stubbers, autoguns, lasguns and even a black-powder jezzail. The rest held rust-rimmed blades of varying shapes and sizes.

The only commonality among them was the extent of the malformation that afflicted them. Twisted horns of calcified bone pierced brows and cheeks, or emerged from weeping eye sockets. Iridescent flesh stretched between patches of rank fur or blistered scale. Some were missing limbs, others had too many.

They had been men, once. Now they were nothing but

meat. Dull, animal eyes studied him from all sides. There were more of them than there might once have been, which was something of a surprise. Life was hard for such crippled by-blows, especially here, and death the only certainty. 'Aren't you handsome fellows,' Oleander said. 'I expect you're the welcoming party. Well then, lead on, children, lead on. The day wears on, the shadows lengthen and strange moons circle through the skies. And we have far to go.'

One of the creatures, a goatish thing wearing a peaked officer's cap, barked what might have been an order. The pack shuffled forward warily, closing ranks about Oleander. It was no honour guard, but it would do. Oleander allowed the mutants to escort him deeper into the city. While he knew the way perfectly well, he saw no reason to antagonise them.

Their ranks swelled and thinned at seemingly random intervals as the journey progressed. Knots of muttering brutes vanished into the shadows, only to be replaced by others. Oleander studied the crude heraldry of the newcomers with some interest. When he'd last been here, they had barely known what clothes were. Now they had devised primitive insignia of rank, and split into distinct groups – or perhaps tribes. Perhaps the changeovers were due to territorial differences.

Whatever their loyalties, they were afraid of him. Oleander relished the thought. It was good to be feared. There was nothing quite like it. The beasts who surrounded him now were more human-looking. They were clad in purple-stained rags and armour marked with what might have been an unsophisticated rendition of the old winged claw insignia of the Emperor's Children. It amused him.

They likely had more in common with the men they aped than they could conceive. Both were far removed from their creator's intended ideal.

His amusement faded as the palace at last came into sight. Its delicate tiers stretched gracefully up towards the blistered sky. Chunks had been gouged out of its curved walls, to allow for the addition of multiple power sources, rad-vents and gun emplacements. It was akin to a beautiful flower, encrusted with a bristling techno-organic fungus. Rubble had been cleared from the broad avenue leading up to the main entrance. A crude shanty town, built from debris, had sprung up around the outer walls of the ancient structure.

More than once, he saw what could only be barbaric shrines, and statues decorated with articulated bones and offerings of stitched skin and gory meat. Mutants chanted softly to these statues, and he heard the words 'Pater Mutatis' and 'Benefactor' most often. The Father of Mutants. He wondered whether the object of such veneration was pleased by the acknowledgement, or annoyed by its crudity.

Unseen horns blew a warning, or perhaps a greeting, as Oleander and his escort moved along the avenue. The wind had picked up, carrying with it the ever-present screams of the ancient dead, as well as the barks and howls of the shanty town's debased population. Dust roiled through the air, momentarily obscuring the ruins around him. Oleander briefly considered putting his helmet back on, but discarded the idea after a moment. It was hard to sing, inside the helmet. 'Song of my soul, my voice is dead, die thou, unsung, as tears unshed...'

Abruptly, the cacophony rising from the shanty town

died away. The only sounds left were the phantom screams and Oleander's singing. But these too faded as the sound of heavy boots crunching stone and bone rose up. Oleander could barely make out the approaching figure through the dust and the wind. He reached for his bolt pistol.

'No need for that, I assure you.' The vox-link crackled with atmospheric distortion, but the voice was recognisable for all that. Oleander relaxed slightly, though not completely. The dust began to clear. A large shape stepped forward.

The warrior's power armour had been painted white and blue once, but now it was mostly scraped grey or stained brown with blood and other substances. Black mould crept across the battle-scarred ceramite plates, like oil across snow. A sextet of cracked skulls hung from the chest-plate, wreathed in chains. More chains crisscrossed the Space Marine's torso and arms, as if to keep something contained. Like Oleander, he also wore the accoutrements of an Apothecary, though his had seen far more use, under heavier fire. A curved falax blade was sheathed on either hip.

'Waiting for me?' Oleander said. He kept his hand on the grip of his bolt pistol.

'I heard the beasts howling,' the other said. He reached up and unlatched his helmet. Seals hissed and recycled air spurted as he pulled it off, revealing a familiar, scarred face. He'd been handsome, once, before the fighting pits. Now he resembled a statue that had been used for target practice. 'And here you are. Still singing that same dreadful dirge.'

'No mask, no mask,' Oleander said, finishing the song.

'Learn a new tune,' the other said.

'You were never a music lover were you, Arrian?' Arrian Zorzi had once served at Angron's pleasure, on the killing fields of the Great Crusade. Now he obeyed a new master. Oleander thought Arrian had traded up, if anything.

Angron had been a puling psychopath even before he'd taken his first steps towards daemonhood. Worse even than glorious Fulgrim, whose light was as that of the sun. A master you chose was better than one chosen for you. At least that way, you had no one to blame but yourself.

'Exile agrees with you, brother.' Arrian's voice was soft. Softer than it ought to have been. As if it came from the mouth of some inbred outer-rim aristocrat, rather than a savage draped in skulls and chains. A considered affectation. Another way of chaining the beast inside.

'I left of my own volition.'

'And now you're back.'

'Is that going to be a problem?' He would only have time for one shot, if that. Arrian was fiendishly quick, when he put his mind to it. Another memento of years spent wading in someone else's blood, for the entertainment of a screaming crowd.

'No.' Arrian's fingers tapped against the hilt of one of his swords. 'I bear you no particular malice today.' He reached up to stroke one of the skulls. The cortical implants dangling from it rattled softly.

'And them?' Oleander said, indicating the skulls. The skulls had belonged to the warriors of Arrian's former squad. All dead now, and by Arrian's hand. When a warhound decided to find a new master, bloodshed was inevitable.

'My brothers are dead, Oleander. And as such only concerned with the business of the dead. What about you?'

'I want to see him.'

Arrian glanced over his shoulder. He looked down at his skulls, and tapped one. 'You're right, brothers. He's watching,' he said, to the skull.

'Is he, then?' Oleander said. He turned, scanning the desolation. When he turned back, Arrian was leaning against the archway. He hadn't even heard the World Eater move.

'He's always watching, you know that. From inside as well as out,' Arrian said. 'Enter, and be welcome once more to the Grand Apothecarion, Oleander Koh. The Chief Apothecary is expecting you.'

CHAPTER TWO

The Grand Apothecarion

Their footsteps echoed hollowly in the cavernous spaces of the shattered palace. Oleander and Arrian walked side by side through the entry halls, past defensive hard points. Urum had come under attack more than once since Bile had established his laboratories there. The two moved in easy silence. They'd never had much to talk about, even in better times. Now, Oleander could feel Arrian surreptitiously studying him. Sizing him up for the chopping block, perhaps. Arrian had always been the most loyal of all of them to Bile's ideal, for reasons of his own. But then, what else could one expect of a warhound?

'New sword?' Arrian said.

'My last one broke.'

'You always were quite hard on them, as I recall. A Tuonela mortuary sword. A fine weapon for a fine warrior.' Arrian cocked his head. 'What are you doing with it?'

'Spoils of war,' Oleander said. 'I had to shoot its owner.'

'In the back?'

'Obviously.'

Arrian laughed. The sound put Oleander in mind of a dull blade scraping across wet flesh. The Consortium, as their master called it, had always been an uneasy alliance at best. Its members were not brothers, save in the most figurative sense – they were all Apothecaries, but from different Legions and warbands. Drawn together by a shared desire to learn more of the arts of flesh and bone, of gland and organ, from the acknowledged master. The human body was a mystery that they were all desperately trying to solve, and so they came to sit at the feet of its greatest student, and learn all that he had to teach them.

Some, like Arrian, had been here for centuries, even accounting for the way time moved in the Eye of Terror. Others stayed only for a few months, or even weeks. Some came to learn a specific lesson, others were sponges, absorbing all that their host knew. And some few learned nothing, and became a lesson themselves.

But of all of them, Arrian Zorzi had always been the most dangerous. He smiled too easily, thought too quickly, for what he was. Those pain-inducing cortical nodes had only honed him into an even deadlier predator. Oleander longed to wipe the smile off the other renegade's face, if only to find out what was hiding beneath it. Arrian was a monster who refused to admit it, and was somehow all the more monstrous because of it. Oleander restrained the desire, with some difficulty. Renewing old grudges wasn't why he'd returned.

He distracted himself by studying his surroundings. While the outer palace was all but empty, the inner was anything but. The diverse chambers here had once housed decadent feasts, bloody gladiatorial games and indulgent orgies. Now the labyrinthine warrens of unnatural construction were home to the various apothecaria and vivisectoria established by the members of the Consortium. The palace had become a bedlam of grotesquery, filled with the sounds, sights and smells of abomination. Screams, both human and otherwise, echoed through the vaulted corridors and along the rows of hermetically sealed operation chambers. As well as these, Oleander could hear the rattle of surgical tools, the hiss of pneumatic chem-pumps and the quiet murmur of voices engaged in debate and study.

Faces peered at him from shadowed archways, their gazes by turns curious and baleful. He had not left under the best of circumstances. Many of those who came to Urum did so seeking some form of sanctuary. A safe place to indulge in their own depravity, abetted by one whose utter corruption far outstripped their own. And some of those, like the half-men outside, even worshipped their benefactor in a way. A cult of genius had taken root here, and those who abandoned it were viewed with disdain, if not outright hostility.

Those laboratories closer to the outer palace were smaller, and the Apothecaries who had claimed them were the newest to join the Consortium. Oleander observed a cavalcade of horrors through the armourglass portholes set into the entryways. Crude surgeries and childish experiments filled these chambers. 'To do is to learn,' he said.

Arrian glanced at him. 'And to learn is to know,' he said, completing the old phrase. It was a joke, of sorts. A rationalisation for the irrational. 'You haven't forgotten everything you learned here.'

'I forget nothing.'

Arrian chuckled. 'For your sake, I hope so. You know how he likes his little tests.'

Stunted mutants hopped and crawled along the corridors, giving the two legionaries a wide berth. They wore ragged cloaks which obscured their twisted forms and hissing rebreathers. They carried equipment to the various laboratories, or else acted as surgical assistants when necessary. Oleander kicked lazily at one when it drew too close. 'Vat-born maggot,' he said. The creature shrank back, whining.

Arrian slid in front of him. 'Cease. They are not yours to play with.' His hands rested on the pommels of his falax blades.

'It almost touched me,' Oleander said. 'I cannot abide being touched by something so... so *utilitarian.*' He practically spat the word. The vat-born didn't even have the distinction of being uniquely hideous. They all looked alike, sounded alike, even smelled alike. As if they had been stamped from a mould. It grated on his senses. Such banality was anathema to him.

'And yet you frolic with the beasts outside,' Arrian said.

'At least they offer some variety.' Oleander made a face. 'I'm surprised there are any of them still left. Have you seen what they're building out there?'

Arrian shrugged. 'We leave them to their own devices. They've begun to cobble together a crude society of sorts. They have wars, sometimes. It's entertaining, in its way.'

'And what does the master think?' Oleander said. 'Is he entertained as easily as you?'

Arrian glanced at him. 'The Chief Apothecary doesn't think of them at all, Oleander. They're meat, and of little use for anything save as an early warning system. Why are you back?'

'I told you, I want to see him. And he obviously wishes to see me, else we would not be here. What about the others?' Like any group, the Consortium had its fair share of favoured individuals. Those who had proven their use beyond a shadow of a doubt, or who were so deeply indebted to Bile that they could not refuse him. Oleander still wasn't sure which of those described Arrian.

'Skalagrim is leading an expedition to Belial IV – Chief Apothecary Fabius wishes to establish a second facility there,' Arrian said. Oleander grunted in distaste. Skalagrim was a renegade twice over, and untrustworthy even at the best of times.

'What about Chort?' Chort took great delight in crafting new flesh-forms. Many was the warlord who had begged for a chance to hunt the inexplicable monstrosities Chort had devised. 'And old Malpertus?'

'Chort vanished a month ago, on some errand or other for the Chief Apothecary. Malpertus... died on Korazin,' Arrian said.

'Died?' Oleander said. Malpertus' face swam to the surface of his mind – hollow cheeks, filmy eyes and yellow teeth, worn to nubs. Malpertus hadn't been his real name, and his armour had been scoured of all insignia. That alone had been enough to betray his true allegiances, as far as Oleander was concerned.

'We were all very sad,' Arrian said, sounding anything but. 'Especially Saqqara.'

'Saqqara is still alive?' That was a surprise. Saqqara Thresh had led a Word Bearer kill-team to Urum. They'd been looking to deliver Bile's head to the Dark Council for some unspecified slight. They'd failed, of course. Urum ate daemons as easily as it ate men, and Saqqara's force had gone from impressive to pitiable in a few days. By the time the Consortium had struck, the Word Bearers had practically been begging for death.

Only Saqqara had remained sound of mind and body, thanks to his skill with daemonancy; one of the reasons Bile had decided to spare the diabolist. Daemons were a fact of life in Eyespace, and it was no more than prudent to employ the services of one skilled in the art of their summoning and banishment, however unwilling.

'You'd be surprised at how little a man like that wants to meet his gods.' Arrian scratched his chin. 'We caught him trying to cut the bomb out a few months ago. He'd got all the way to the meat by the time we stopped him.'

Oleander laughed. Saqqara had been attempting to remove the chem-bomb Bile had surgically implanted between his hearts for years. When the bomb went off – it wasn't a question of if – Saqqara's body would be reduced to bubbling protoplasm. It was the most obvious of the modifications Bile had made to the Word Bearer. The Chief Apothecary claimed to have implanted a thousand and one contingencies into his most reluctant servant. Saqqara occupied himself trying to discover them, when he wasn't attempting to stir up a rebellion amongst Bile's followers.

'What of Honourable Tzimiskes?' Oleander asked as they ducked beneath a cracked archway and entered what had once been a garden. Now the only thing that grew here was a peculiar species of red weed. Beside the crumbled remains of what had once been a fountain stood a sextet of towering shapes, their once vibrant purple colours dulled by grime and neglect to a muddy bruise. Castel-lax battle-automata, he realised, the shock-troops of the

Legio Cybernetica. Servo-skulls hovered about the war machines like flies, their auspex humming.

'Does that answer your question?' Arrian said. Oleander saw two familiar figures standing among the battle-automata. Both were legionaries, but one's power armour was an older mark, and heavy. It was daubed in drab colours, save for the gleaming stylised iron skull emblazoned on one shoulder-plate. Tzimiskes Flay was an exile from Medrengard, as far as Oleander knew, though there was some debate on that score, as well as a substantial amount of wagering. Nonetheless, the Consortium welcomed all practitioners of the arts of the flesh, whatever their origins.

As Oleander and Arrian drew close, one of the Castellax took a halting step forward and trained its bolt cannons on them. The barrels bobbed and rotated as internal targeting arrays calculated distance. Arrian slammed a forearm into Oleander's chest. 'Don't move. They're overeager. Endorphin pumps wired to their firing mechanisms, I think. Tzimiskes – brother – call your creature off.'

Tzimiskes stared at them for a moment, as if considering the possibility of a live-fire exercise. Then, with a shrug, he opened the chassis of the agitated war machine, revealing the worm-pale features of a semi-human face within. The face was nestled in a web of wires, and its mouth opened and closed soundlessly as Tzimiskes fiddled with the internal mechanisms. It squalled in protest. The robot sank down to one knee and lowered its guns as the thing inside moaned petulantly.

'Slave-brains,' Arrian said. 'He's been growing them in his laboratorium, in the eastern wing of the palace. Better reaction times than standard battle-automata, or so some of the others claim.'

'Ever the artisan, my brother,' Oleander said, loudly. Tzimiskes turned and cocked his head, perhaps in greeting. Maybe just in acknowledgement. If he was surprised to see Oleander, he gave no sign. Not that Oleander had expected any sort of welcome.

'You're back,' the other renegade said. 'I thought you were smarter than that, Oleander.' Saqqara Thresh looked much as Oleander remembered – pinch-faced and fang-mouthed. His crimson power armour had seen better centuries. There were few places on it not covered in lines of cramped, curling script, or adorned with blasphemous iconography. The lines of script were lifted from the ritual texts, hymns and cult doctrine that Saqqara and his brothers considered a suitable replacement for common sense. Suture scars marked his bare flesh, following the curve of his skull and the line of his jaw. Bile had surgically inserted numerous control implants, obedience nodes, and at least one miniaturised fragmentation detonator in the Word Bearer's brain matter and jaw muscles.

'And I thought you'd have blown yourself up by now, Saqqara. Looks like we were both mistaken. Still hectoring poor Tzimiskes, I see.'

Saqqara smiled. 'We were discussing the seventh and fifteenth tracts of Grand Apostle Ekodas, in his third address to the Dark Council. Tzimiskes is quite devout, for an Iron Warrior. Something you would know nothing about.'

Oleander looked at Tzimiskes. As ever, he did not reply. To the best of Oleander's knowledge, the Iron Warrior had never spoken.

'Our silent brother is polite, if nothing else,' Arrian said.

'Another thing you would know nothing about,' Saqqara said. Arrian smiled and stroked his skulls. Saqqara met his gaze and held it. There was no faulting the Word Bearer's courage.

'Come, brother. I have come a long way, and time is short,' Oleander said, breaking the tension. 'Is he still trying to provoke the others?' he asked, as Arrian led him out of the garden. Inciting treachery was Saqqara's sole avenue of resistance. Oleander suspected that Bile kept the Word Bearer around as much to weed out the foolishly disloyal as to summon the occasional daemon.

'He's been working on Tzimiskes for a while now. Like the proverbial bird and the mountain,' Arrian said.

'Probably hoping our silent brother will snap and unleash a horde of mechanical murder-machines on the rest of you,' Oleander said. The inner palace was much as he remembered. The broad corridor, with its titanic pillars reaching up into the shadowed reaches of the roof above; the scattered remains of ancient statues; the faded murals depicting scenes from the history of Urum's former rulers. There was a sense of sadness here, as much as one of horror. Broken grandeur was still grandeur.

Oleander stopped before one of the murals. He studied the entwined figures, trying to discern where one ended and the others began. There were stains on the wall. Some old, most new. Blood and other substances. Oleander spread his fingers. The walls of the palace spoke, sometimes. When the wind was high and sand scoured the city. If you listened, you could hear the songs, the moans, the screams of those forgotten revelries. But he heard nothing now.

'They've been quiet, since you left,' Arrian said.

'I was the only one who appreciated them,' Oleander said.

'We are here to learn the secrets of life, not listen to the complaints of the dead,' the World Eater said. 'You might have retreated into the past, but the rest of us have always moved ever forward.'

Oleander laughed. 'There is no "us" here. Only him. The rest of us are nothing more than raw materials yet to be rendered down.' He looked at Arrian. 'What has he taught you since I left, Arrian? What secrets have you learned?'

'None I'll share with you,' Arrian said. His hands fell to the hilts of his blades. 'Though I'd be happy to show you, if you wish.'

Oleander shook his head. 'Still loyal to a madman, after all these years.' He looked back at the mural. 'I wonder if that's why he keeps you around. For a surgeon, you make a wonderful butcher, and you have little interest in building monsters. And yet here you are, as in favour as ever. Always at his beck and call.'

Arrian said nothing. Trying to goad him was a fool's game, although Oleander couldn't help but try. It was like watching a tiger asleep in a cage, and knowing it dreamed red dreams. 'Oh the beast I could make of you, brother,' he said softly. 'What beautiful horrors you would wreak then.'

'No, brother. Never a beast. Never that,' Arrian said. His voice was tight, and his face might as well have been a slab of stone. His hands twitched slightly, where they rested on the hilts of the falax blades. The chains wrapped about him creaked slightly, as if they were on the verge of snapping.

The moment passed. Oleander inclined his head. 'As delightful as this has been, I am ready to see him. Take me to him, Arrian.'

'That is what I have been doing, brother. He is in his laboratorium, hard at work.'

'On what?'

'Himself,' Arrian said. He turned away. Oleander hesitated a moment, and then followed. As they drew closer to the heart of the palace, the temperature dropped substantially. Cooling units chugged loudly in out-of-the-way corners, filling the corridors with a chill, counterseptic mist. Vox-casters and pict-recorders hummed and whirred atop support pillars and along the walls. Nothing went unseen or unrecorded in the Grand Apothecarium. Monsters howled somewhere in the dark. Once, Arrian waved Oleander to silence as the way ahead was suddenly blocked by indistinct shapes. They padded forward through the mist, eyes gleaming gold. The World Eater raised his hand and let the assortment of medicae devices built into his vambrace skirl to life. The shapes scattered as silently as they had appeared.

'What were they?' Oleander asked.

'For now – test cases,' Arrian said. 'Later – who knows?'

'He's letting them run loose now? In my day, he used to seal things like that away, in one of the outer rings.' The true size of the palace had always been a matter of some debate. It was a labyrinth of concentric rings, both larger and smaller than it appeared from orbit. Whole squads of would-be explorers had vanished into its outer rings, never to be seen again.

'We still do. Sometimes they get out. They come back... changed,' Arrian said. 'He finds it interesting. So he lets them roam, and we study them, when we're lucky enough to capture one.' He cocked his head. 'That doesn't happen often, sadly.' He showed his teeth in a broken smile. 'They are getting smarter, out there in the dark.'

Oleander rested his hand on his bolt pistol, suddenly

alert. It was a welcome feeling. He had missed this place. The sense that a new horror lurked around every corner. One never quite grew used to it. Intoxicating in its way.

The rattle of weapons caught his attention. They had come to a reinforced doorway, where several men and women stood on guard. They were clad in grimy fatigues and battered carapace chest-plates. Equipment belts and ammunition bandoliers completed the image of a rag-tag planetary militia. But these were no normal humans. The muscles in their arms and necks bulged with almost Astartes-like thickness, and there were series codes tattooed on their cheeks. They stank of chemicals and other, less identifiable things.

Gland-hounds. The New Humanity, as designed by Fabius Bile. Stronger, faster, more aggressive than the brief sparks that sheltered in the shadow of the Imperium. The first generation had been born of partial gene-seed implantation. Those first few crude attempts had become more refined over time, as the master had devised his own, lesser form of gene-seed. One which was not so likely to kill its host out of hand.

They came alert instantly. There was a disconcerting intensity to their blank gazes – as if he were some large bovid who had wandered unknowing into the midst of a carnosaur pack. It had been a long time since anything had looked at him that way, and he shivered in delight. 'They say, in the lands of milk and sorrow, that those pale echoes of our brothers now gone know no fear,' he said to Arrian. 'It saddens me to think of it.'

As he spoke, one of hounds stepped forward, setting herself between them and the doorway beyond. She crossed her muscular arms, and gazed steadily at them. 'Igori,'

Arrian said. There was an odd sort of respect in his tone, Oleander thought. He bridled at it. Arrian was free to consider the creature his equal, but Oleander was under no such obligation.

'You're new,' Oleander said, looking down at the woman – Igori, Arrian had called her. He sniffed, and grimaced. 'But I can tell you're one of his. I can smell it from here.'

Igori said nothing. Her face was square. It might as well have been chiselled out of marble. Everything about her was perfect. Too perfect, too symmetrical. As if she were nothing more than a machine of meat and muscle.

'Where is he? Take me to him,' he said.

Most humans were frightened of his kind. Even the strongest of them were but fragile things compared to a Renegade Space Marine, especially one hardened by centuries of living in the Eye. But Bile's Gland-hounds had no fear. Or, rather, they didn't express it in the same way a normal human did. At his tone, her hand fell to the hilt of the blade sheathed on one hip. The other hounds tensed, ready to leap at the slightest provocation.

Oleander grinned. It had been an age since he'd carved the guts out of one of his old teacher's pets. They took a pleasingly long time to die. He reached for the hilt of his own sword. He stopped as something tapped his shoulder-plate. He turned, and saw the flat of one of Arrian's blades laying across the ceramite.

'I wouldn't, brother,' Arrian said, softly. 'She is his favourite, currently. Look at that necklace of baubles she wears. What do you see?'

'Teeth,' Oleander said.

'Whose?' Arrian's voice was a rasping purr.

'So long as they aren't mine, I don't particularly care,' Oleander said.

'You were never very observant.' Arrian leaned close. 'Space Marines, brother.'

The Gland-hounds were built to hunt Space Marines. Or, rather, their gene-seed. One on one, they were no match for their prey, but in a pack they could pull down even the most frenzied of Khorne's chosen. Bile doted on them. He even gave them as gifts, sometimes, when the mood struck him. They were prized by those for whom limited stocks of gene-seed were still an active concern, such as the Iron Warriors.

Oleander shrugged Arrian's blade away. 'I don't care where she got them. No human threatens me and lives. I'll make a fine robe from her flesh.'

'You will not,' Arrian said. 'She is not yours to kill.'

Oleander nodded obligingly. He could resist the pull of the moment no longer. 'No. I suppose not.' He spun, slapping Arrian's blade aside, and leapt on his fellow Apothecary. They crashed together and Arrian stumbled back. Oleander whipped his sword free of its sheath, just in time to parry a killing blow from the falax blade.

'Oh, how I have dreamed of this,' he said. The Gland-hounds had retreated, unwilling to get between the two. Oleander ignored them. Fierce as they were, they were outmatched and knew it. 'I've owed you a humbling for some time, World Eater.'

Arrian stepped back, arms spread. 'Well, come then, brother. Come and take your due.'

Oleander lunged. Their swords met, separated and met again. The hilt twisted in his hands as he spun, leapt, and lunged again. Though he fancied himself a swordsman, he knew that he was, at best, serviceable. It was an affectation, and one sadly common to the warriors of the Third. They all desired to be a Lucius, form and function combined in lethal harmony. Oleander's Apothecary training gave him an edge in most duels – he knew exactly where to strike to cripple, or to kill. Places most warriors never even thought of.

But Arrian knew those places as well. And he was a better swordsman. He'd drawn his second falax blade and he slapped them together. 'It's been some time since I've been able to practise on something other than mutants,' he said. 'I suppose I should thank you.'

Oleander bared his teeth and stepped forward, sword whistling out. Arrian caught the blow on his blades and forced the sword down. 'Do you remember how we used to spar for the privilege of assisting him, Apothecary Oleander? First blood only, for we knew our value. But these days, your value is greatly lessened.' He held Oleander's blade down, trapped against the floor. Before Oleander could wrench it free, Arrian lunged forward. Their heads connected, and Oleander lost his grip on his sword.

He stumbled back. Something struck the back of his legs. Already off balance, he fell to one knee. The tip of a blade pressed against his jugular. Igori looked down at him. He made to strike her, and she retreated, whipping her knife away from his throat. He forced himself to his feet, ready to leap on her. Before he could, Arrian kicked his sword towards him.

'Pick it up,' the World Eater said. 'Let us finish, before you find a new partner.'

Oleander hesitated, and then knelt to scoop up his sword. As he stood, the vox array mounted on the wall above crackled suddenly. *'Be at peace, all of you. Sheathe your blades, Arrian. Step aside Igori, there's my loyal child. I have been waiting on our guest for some time, and would delay our reunion no longer. Apothecary Arrian... assemble the others in the auditorium. I am sure that they will wish to hear what has compelled our prodigal brother to return.'*

The voice echoing from the vox was that of the former Chief Apothecary and Lieutenant Commander of the Emperor's Children. The being known variously as Primogenitor, Clonelord and Manflayer. The creature Oleander Koh had once called master...

Fabius Bile.

CHAPTER THREE

Master of the Apothecarion

The inner sanctum of Fabius Bile was a place of wonder and horror. It was the largest chamber in the palace, and filled with the machinery of life and death. The wide, high ceilings were packed with power conduits and sparking grids. Bunches of cables hung down like jungle vines, to stretch across the room or wind their way along the floor. Combat-servitors had been wired into the entry alcoves, their legs replaced by gyroscopic plinths. Their weapons cycled as he passed them, and dead eyes tracked him.

In places the ancient walls had been gouged through in order to allow for the free passage of power supply cables, blood pumps and tube-feeds. Dimly flickering lumens hung from the support pillars and brackets on the walls, illuminating nutrient tanks occupied by clusters of insensate tissue, waiting for harvesting. Milky eyes blinked mindlessly from within thickets of tangled optic nerve, and newborn hearts hung suspended like fruit from crooked branches composed of muscles and veins. The air stank of counterseptic and somewhere a vox was playing music. The jaunty melody echoed eerily through the chamber of horrors. A piece by Kynska, scratchy with age.

Powerful refrigeration units stacked along the walls belched a chill mist into the chamber, draining the air of all warmth and hiding indistinct shapes, which crawled noisily across the floor, babbling softly. Vox and pict-recorders were mounted throughout the room, recording everything that occurred within, and playing it back on scavenged viewscreens arranged haphazardly throughout the chamber. Oleander could see himself from a hundred different angles, but none of them were quite right. More of the stunted vat-born scurried to and fro through the chamber, grunting softly among themselves as they organised the immense collection of raw materials, which filled every available space.

Jars containing catalepsean nodes, occulobes and Betcher's glands rested alongside steel racks of fibre bundles and prosthetic limbs. Most of these appeared to have been procured from the bodies that hung from meat hooks attached to the ceiling. The carcasses had been stripped to the black carapace, and in some cases beyond. Oleander caught sight of a squirming cocoon of some sort implanted in the chest cavity of one, while another was obviously being used to cultivate fresh skin cells. Vat-born climbed the bodies with simian ease, slicing off parts or checking bio-readings.

Oleander threaded his way through the laboratorium, following the harsh rasp of Bile's voice. 'Begin with a standard Y-incision, first medial to lateral...' His words were punctuated by a mechanical whine as some unseen machine began its work. Oleander shivered. He knew that sound all too well. Bile's chirurgeon – a spider-like assembly of blades, saws and drills, shears and syringes that the former Chief Apothecary had designed himself.

'Damage to subcutaneous tissue evident upon initial incision.' There was a wet sound, like the peeling of a crustacean's shell. 'Extensive infection to rib-plate. Ossified growths spreading at impressive rate. Bone deformation noted.'

A rancid smell filled Oleander's nostrils. The stink of burning bone and meat. Bile's voice murmured. Oleander caught sight of him at last – lying on a medi-slab, angled sharply beneath a tangled web of lumens and pict-recorders.

The skin of his torso was peeled back, exposing the black carapace that resided beneath the epidermis and dermis, buried within the subcutaneous tissue. Transfusion points and neural sensors of varying sizes lay exposed to the air. A section of the black carapace had been removed, and sat on a tray balanced on the back of one of the quivering vat-born. The thin limbs of the chirurgeon bent over Bile's narrow body; flaps of his flesh were pinned back.

Fabius Bile looked much as Oleander remembered, despite the open wound in his torso. Hollow-cheeked and unkempt, with cold, empty eyes. He stank of at least a dozen comingled scents – embalming fluid, sour blood and the raw chemical odour of sterilising unguents among them. The stench of him was like a physical blow to the enhanced senses of a Space Marine. Oleander closed his eyes and inhaled slowly, trying to parse the corrupt bouquet. Bile's reek was as good as a status update.

Oleander's eyes popped open. 'Master, you smell...'

'I'm dying.' Bile gestured to himself. 'You can smell it

on me, can't you, Oleander? The tang of sour meat, the fug of preservatives. I reek of death, as is only appropriate for walking carrion.' He smiled. Oleander's hand fell to the hilt of his sword. It was that sort of smile. An expression more suited to a corpse than a man.

'You look remarkably healthy for a dying man, master.'

'Don't call me that, Oleander. I haven't been your master for some time. If you must address me so formally, use my rank – Chief Apothecary. Pass me those forceps, please.' Bile held out his hand. Oleander hesitated. The articulated limbs of the chirurgeon clicked and whirred in what might have been warning. It crouched above Bile like an over-protective scorpion. Bile clucked his tongue. 'Have you never seen a man operate on his own organs, Oleander? Physician, heal thyself. The forceps, if you please.'

Oleander picked the tool up and handed it over. Bile reached into his open abdomen and began to root around. He gave no hint as to the pain it must have caused him. Whether that was due more to fortitude or dead nerves, Oleander couldn't say. He'd seen worse, in his time. But somehow, Bile's lack of joy and the sickeningly sterile smell of the operating theatre combined to make Oleander uneasy. It was a delicious sensation, if distracting.

'I am dying,' Bile said, matter-of-factly. 'Slowly, but surely. I expect that I will be dead in a matter of centuries. This body, in mere decades. It is not my first, nor will it be my last.'

Oleander nodded. He'd aided in more than a few brain transplants during his time with Bile. Clone bodies didn't last long, especially given Bile's predilection for tinkering. 'The rate of degeneration is increasing then?' Early in their Founding, the Emperor's Children had suffered from a genetic blight. It had almost exterminated them. As far as Oleander knew, Bile was the last living sufferer of that malady.

'Steadily,' Bile said. 'So, you will forgive me if I come to the point – why have you returned, Oleander? What grand scheme festers in that garish lump you call a heart?'

'Perhaps I simply missed your guiding wisdom, master.' One of the chirurgeon's insectile limbs flashed. The blade mounted on the end pricked the hollow of Oleander's throat. He froze.

'And perhaps I am in no mood for the usual niceties,' Bile said. 'Speak. Or I will add your larynx to my collection.'

Oleander took a single, diplomatic, step back. Rubbing his throat, he said, 'I come bearing a proposition, master. An arrangement of equal benefit.'

'Oh? And what could you possibly offer me?'

'Eldar.' Bile didn't laugh. Oleander took it as a good sign. He pressed on. 'An eldar craftworld. Weak. Ripe for the picking.'

Bile continued with his operation. Oleander cleared his throat. There were things in the jars staring at him. He felt a delicious thrill of trepidation, considering the implications of that. Sometimes Bile didn't bother to dispatch his raw materials. They made the most hellacious racket, on occasion. Oleander reached into his belt and retrieved his pipe.

It had been a gift from a daemon of his acquaintance. She claimed to have carved it from the finger bone of Konrad Curze himself. It was long enough, and tipped with the splintered remnants of what might have been a talon. Abominable words had been delicately etched into it, and gilded apertures punched along its length. The tiny glass philtres that hung from his neck could be inserted into the apertures, allowing for the inhalation of a number of pleasurable stimulants. He slipped in a green one and stuck the pipe between his lips.

'Still suckling on that foul thing, I see,' Bile said.

Oleander inhaled. 'Foul is fair, fair is foul.' He coughed. An old bit of doggerel.

'Ever the poet. What is it this time? Fats culled from the soft bones of hrud broodlings? The blood and sputum of a Donorian fiend?'

'The tears of an angel,' Oleander said. 'I pried them from his head myself.' He coughed again and lowered the pipe. His eyes strayed to the wound in Bile's midsection. There were things in there that ought not to be. Pulsing lumps of meat that did not belong in a healthy body. Webs of cancerous tissue, glistening in the light. Bile sliced the strands with deft precision, and removed tumour-laced gobbets. He plopped them into nearby containers for later examination. Bile had been studying his ongoing deterioration since before Fulgrim had led their Legion into the dark. He seemed no closer to unravelling its mysteries now than he had the last time Oleander had seen him.

'Why would I be interested in a craftworld, Oleander?'

Oleander blinked, trying to focus. 'I can think of a dozen reasons, master.'

'I only asked for one. And stop calling me that. It is wearisome.'

'Raw materials.'

'A good reason. Though I do not lack for such, as you can see.' Bile motioned to the racks of jars and the horrors they contained. 'Did you know that the great crypts of Urum were untouched when the eldar abandoned this place? Thousands of mummified bodies, sealed down in the dark and the quiet.'

'Mummified is fine, but fresh is better,' Oleander said. The first lesson any aspirant to the apothecarion learned: fresh materials were always preferable to those of reduced quality, especially when it came to physiological study.

'Not just bodies,' Bile continued. 'Millions of those peculiar stones they place such value in, as well. Do you remember Iydris, and how our brothers cracked them open to taste the delights within?'

'I remember,' Oleander said. And he did. He could still taste the essence of the spirit stones, even now, after so long. He salivated, just thinking of it. He'd never known they were below. Then, Bile hoarded secrets like a miser. He could learn as much with a simple question as a lesser Apothecary could with a full laboratory. He kept what he learned to himself, to be used when the situation warranted, and not before.

'I'm sure that you do,' Bile said. 'The ones here are all shattered, unfortunately. I should like a few more, and intact. As well as... other things. Your offer has merit. Congratulations, Oleander, I suppose you get to live a little longer. Now, perhaps you'll tell me why you've brought this tantalising gift to me?'

Oleander hesitated. Now came the delicate part. 'The Radiant King, in His Joyful Repose,' he said. 'You have heard the name?'

'That's a description, not a name, but yes. His name was once Kasperos Telmar, I believe. One of Eidolon's pets. The captain of the Twelfth Company, when such things mattered.'

'They still matter to some,' Oleander said. 'Not me, obviously. But some. I have the privilege of serving as the Radiant's Chief Apothecary, and as one of his Joybound.'

'A dubious privilege, I'm sure,' Bile said. 'And what is a Joybound?'

'A lord commander, without the privileges or respect.'

'You always were ambitious.'

'One finds shelter where one can,' Oleander said. 'The Radiant seeks apotheosis. To join the Lord of Dark Delights in his infinite celebrations. He seeks a sacrifice worthy of the name – pure souls, in great quantity, offered up to Slaanesh.' He smiled. 'And we both know that the Prince of Pleasure values the souls of the detestable eldar above all others.'

'Do we? Or is that another of those quaint superstitions that warp-brained fools pass along as if it were scientific fact?' One of the chirurgeon's blades twitched. 'It is the height of folly to attribute motive to a random confluence of phenomena, Oleander. Slaanesh is not a who, it is a what, and thus can value nothing, least of all individuals.'

Oleander frowned. Bile held fast to his own peculiar faith, despite the things he'd seen. In him, the fires of the Great Crusade still flickered, however weakly. To Bile, gods were for the weak-minded and the foolish. He cleared his throat. 'As you say, master. And yet the Radiant believes his ascension is at hand.'

'And what do you believe?'

Oleander considered his next words carefully. 'I believe that there is opportunity for advancement. Specifically, my advancement.'

Bile leaned back on his table. 'A warband of your own. How your priorities have changed since last we spoke. I'm almost disappointed.'

'And what about your priorities, master? Have they changed?' Oleander said, stung. Bile had led warbands in his time, after all. But this was about more than manpower.

'My priorities are the same as they ever were, Oleander,' Bile said, as he began to suture the wound in his gut. 'My work. Mankind. Not as it currently stands, of course. But the soul of it – humanity as it should be, as it must be. Perfected by my hand, driven by my will. This new mankind shall flourish, and spread through the New Night, carrying the light of my wisdom to every corner of the cosmos.' He stepped down off the medi-slab. 'A light you turned away from. A light you abandoned.'

'I found it over-bright,' Oleander said.

Bile laughed. 'You are not the first. Few have the stomach for it. Then, a moment ago, neither did I.' He grunted as the chirurgeon pressed itself against him, and slid its anchoring blades into place, locking onto his spine and collarbone. Bile stooped slightly, bowing beneath its weight.

Oleander chuckled politely at his master's joke. Bile's sense of humour was a corkscrew of black whimsy, and it was best to acknowledge it, unless you wished to become its subject. The pleasant haze of the pipe was passing as quickly as it had come. He felt a twinge of craving, the urge to taste it again. That too had been a gift from the daemon. A love token such as only one of her kind could conceive, combining a little pleasure and a little pain in one.

'An interesting proposition. And how will I help you in this matter? Surely my old comrade, Kasperos, does not require my aid in attacking so ripe a target.' Vat-born clustered about him. Bile gestured, and the small mutants scuttled forward, clutching his armour. They clambered atop the benches and operating table, and began to dress their master, all the while whimpering to each other in their own shrill tongue.

'The eldar are wily.' Oleander tensed as he spoke, ready to move one way or the other. 'Their sensors are far in advance of anything we possess. There are ways around that, but they have means other than mechanical of detecting us. I theorise that we who are blessed of the attentions of the Prince of Pleasure give off a certain psychic spoor that the eldar find abhorrent.'

'They can smell you coming, like a prey-animal scenting a hunter on the wind,' Bile said. He sounded amused. 'And so? Does this not please your new master? The Kasperos Telmar I knew drank fear as if it were sweetest nectar.'

'It pleases him, but it does not solve the problem. The craftworld is swift. It will flee, and where it goes the war-fleet of the Radiant will not be able to follow. You know of what I speak.' The look on Bile's face said that he did. The eldar had sub-space capabilities far in advance of anything that mankind possessed. They could travel from one end of a system to the other in little more than the blink of an eye. Such travel was dangerous for them, but no more so than enduring a protracted assault.

'Get to the point, Oleander. I am growing bored.'

'I know that you possess a great quantity of psychically sensitive genetic matter,' Oleander pressed on. He knew, because he'd helped Bile cull much of it, at one time or another. Bile's nutrient tanks held raw material harvested from entire populations, including biological samples acquired from the witches and mutants that hid among them. 'Matter which could be put to use towards a common goal, should you so desire.'

Bile gestured, and the vat-born scattered, grunting and chirping. He stood, fully arrayed in his war-plate. Even armoured, he was skeletally thin, like some parasitic insect crouched inside the shrunken carapace of a previous victim. His power armour had not seen the careful attentions of a serf for some time. The deep amethyst had faded to a dull hue, and bare ceramite showed through in places. A vat-born brought a folded lump of tanned flesh forward, and Bile took it, sliding it on with an elegance bordering on the indulgent. The coat of shrieking faces had been culled from the dead and dying, and it was Bile's one sign of vanity.

Oleander watched the faces stretch and flex with Bile's every twitch and gesture. 'You know how to find this craftworld?' Bile asked, after a moment.

'I do. Finding it isn't difficult. It's getting close enough to engage it before being detected that's the problem. And one beyond the scope of my meagre abilities.' Oleander bowed. 'And so, I have come crawling back, throat bared, palms uplifted, to beg your aid, oh my master.'

'Again, that word. You are not my slave, Oleander. Have some self-respect. Still... an intriguing puzzle. And a heady prize, upon its solving.' Bile studied him for a moment. 'It has been many months since I left my facilities here. I fear my implements grow dull from disuse. But I find myself growing nostalgic for the grand military escapades of my youth... as well as the screams of chattels as they are harvested.'

'Does that mean you will help me, master?'

'It means that I will consider it, Oleander.'

* * *

Fabius Bile turned away from his old student, fighting
to hide the smile that threatened to split his sallow features. He leaned over his examination table, and made as
if to study the gobbets of cancerous matter he'd extracted
from his innards. It was, on the face of it, a simple enough
proposition. That alone was enough to make Bile suspi-
cious. Nothing was ever simple. His studies had taught
him that much, at least.

The problem Oleander had brought him was a curious
one. He could see no less than a dozen ways of solving
it. None of these solutions involved travelling to a crone
world, risking death or worse, all to merely lay it at the
feet of his old master. So, why had he come? An olive
branch, perhaps. An apology for past misdeeds. But this
was Oleander, and so Bile discarded the possibility.

Oleander had been one of the first to join him in his
work. One of the first to fully understand what Bile was
trying to accomplish. Many of the other Apothecaries
under his command had succumbed all too readily to the
most shallow of indulgences. They'd shattered under
the weight of possibility, and sought solace in perform-
ing unnecessary surgeries on themselves or others for the
pleasure of it. But not Oleander. Oleander had grasped
the full potential of their situation and joined Bile in his
efforts. Until, at last, he'd sought to bend those efforts to
his own ends and been banished for his hubris.

Bile's mind still functioned, whatever the state of his
body. Possibilities were conceived, analysed and discarded
in microseconds. A trap? Possibly. The remnants of the
Third Legion bore him no love, despite all that he had
done for them. Fulgrim himself had set a bounty on his
former Apothecary's head, though few had sought to claim

it in the years since the debacle at Korazin. Not to mention Canticle City.

He closed his eyes, remembering the shadow of the dying frigate as it had plunged prow first into the heart of the Third's stronghold. More than just a world had died that day. The Third Legion had ceased to exist as a singular entity the moment Ezekyle Abaddon had decided to punish Bile for trying to repair the mistakes of the past. His hands clenched. The Despoiler had truly lived up to his name that day. A century or more of work, erased by one overzealous thug, wearing his gene-father's hand-me-downs.

But his enemies were many and varied these days, and they wore all colours, not just black or purple. The Dark Council of Sicarus, the Lernaean Proxies, the Hive-Klutch of Thol... all wanted him dead, or worse, under their control. Past mistakes and missteps dogged his path. He'd never been one for brotherhood, and it was costing him now. He thought of the massive bio-vaults, hidden far below, and the thousands of gene-seed samples they contained. Whatever else he might have done, he was still widely acknowledged as a master of his craft. The services he provided, in keeping the Traitor Legions from withering into irrelevance, kept him safe for the moment.

But he suspected that soon it wouldn't be enough. He was not alone in his art, merely the greatest, and the time was coming when the desire for quantity would outweigh quality. A stab of pain, somewhere in the vicinity of his kidneys, made him blink. With a thought, he activated the chirurgeon. A syringe pierced his neck and flooded his system with a mild stimulant. He let out a short breath and the chirurgeon clicked softly, pleased to have been of help.

He had designed the complex harness himself. It clung to his shoulders and spine with a strength that surprised even him, at times, and its spidery limbs had a will of their own, on occasion. That the device had developed something akin to semi-sentience was not surprising, given what he knew of the Eye. The chirurgeon was programmed to learn, after all. Just what it was learning was perhaps up for debate.

Sometimes, when he allowed himself a rare moment of slumber, Bile dreamed that the harness detached itself from him and scurried about his apothecarion, conducting its own investigations and making improvements to its functions. And sometimes, in the lonely hours, he suspected the irregular pulses of pain that plagued him were the chirurgeon's doing, rather than a result of his own deteriorating physiology.

Bile pushed the thought aside. He looked down as something at his elbow grunted. One of the vat-born crouched beside him. The snuffling mutant hefted a casket of brass and bone. Inside it lay a skull-topped sceptre. Bile sighed and took it. Power thrummed through it, sinister and greedy. It yearned to be used.

Torment was a hell-forged artefact, older even than Urum. It had once belonged to the daemon prince Sh'lacqclak. Bile had taken it from the dissolving claw of the so-called Marquis of Mutilation himself, and had it reforged into a less ostentatious tool more suited to his own purposes. The sceptre was an amplifier; the slightest touch could elicit a raging torrent of agony in even the strongest subject.

It was a trifle blunt for his tastes, but had nonetheless proven useful in controlling unruly subjects as well as for self-defence. It also filled him with a strength that he would otherwise be sorely lacking. A distasteful symbiosis, but unfortunately necessary for the moment. Such were the compromises one made to ensure that the sun always rose, and that the future was not swallowed up by the present.

'Benefactor,' a soft voice said. Bile glanced around and saw Igori standing nearby, holding a holstered pistol-like weapon in her hands. It was her honour and her pleasure to help arm him, at times. Or so she claimed. Like Oleander... like all of his creations, she was ambitious to a fault. Without ambition, one might as well be a servitor. Perfection could only be attained by the ambitious, for only they had the drive to seek it out.

He turned towards her and lifted his arms. She smiled and stepped forward to belt the holster about his waist. She stroked his coat as she pulled it aside, and he restrained a laugh. She was a clever thing, and inquisitive as well. Curiosity had not been in her design, and yet she possessed it. An unforeseen thing, but not unfortunate. The unexpected was not unwanted, in his experience. He had long considered teaching some of what he knew to his creations, in case the worst should occur. The work must continue, even if the one who conceived of it should perish, due to mischance or murder.

When Igori had finished, he drew the Xyclos needler from its holster. He had designed the weapon himself. He often had a need to test new chemical concoctions under battlefield conditions. Even the smallest scratch from one of the thin darts it fired could induce madness or death, depending on the solution in question. He aimed it casually, testing his hand-eye coordination.

He swung it towards Oleander, who twitched, but otherwise remained still.

Bile studied his former student over the barrel of the needler, noting the few, scattered physiological changes since he'd last seen the other Apothecary – oil-black eyes, extended canines, a metallic sheen to his shaggy, unshorn hair. Like an angel gone to seed. Such minor adaptations were to be expected in the Eye of Terror. The unique nature of Eyespace caused something akin to a rapid evolution in those who experience extended exposure. Said evolution was unpredictable and often the next best thing to useless – one of the reasons that Bile limited his own exposure, when possible. He'd found that a combination of drugs, mental discipline and exploratory surgery was enough to keep him from sprouting any new limbs.

He felt another twinge of pain, from his chest this time, but ignored it. Pain was merely a sign that the body was still functioning. It was only when the pain stopped that he need worry. He glanced at the amniotic caskets stacked against the far wall. Indistinct yet achingly familiar shapes floated within the specially designed bio-mechanical wombs.

There they – he – rested in nutrient baths, ready to be awakened at a moment's notice. Similar caches were hidden throughout the galaxy, guarded by loyal servants whose identities were known only to him. His name was spoken on thousands of worlds, and he exploited his reputation for all it was worth. Foresight was the watchdog of genius.

The flesh he wore was not his original flesh. It was not even the third or fourth husk he'd been forced to reside in since he'd departed Terra for the last time. Nor would it be the last, unless his studies took a more positive turn in the near future. Already it was beginning to wear out. His reaction times were fractionally slower, his system struggled to repair minor damage, and his senses were frayed and dulled. Not to mention the tumours, which clung like barnacles to most of his major organs, stunting their functions. It was all the chirurgeon could do to keep him on his feet, at times.

He did not fear death, so much as he was frustrated by it. All living things died; such was the nature of the biological process. Without death, there could not be life. Immortality was a fool's errand at best and a curse at worst. At most, one could hope but to persist for as long as possible. 'Until my work is done,' he said, softly. The words might once have been a prayer, a plea to some higher power. Now, they were merely a statement of intent.

'Master?' Oleander said.

'I said nothing.' Bile holstered the needler. 'And do not call me that.' There were no gods. No higher powers. Divinity was born neither in an alembic nor in the madness of the cosmic maelstrom. The things men called gods were anything but. The sheer hubris of the concept staggered him at times.

Bile was not a god. Nor did he think so little of himself as to accept such a paltry title. Rather, he sought to be that from which all petty gods were descended. The highest universal principle, the formal and final cause of all existence. He had a duty to his own legacy, a responsibility to bring about the next steps in humanity's long journey towards its proper place in the universe. A place ordained by him. The galaxy would burn, and from its ashes would rise a new galaxy and a new people, made strong by his ministrations.

But for that, he needed time. More time than he had.

He glanced at Igori. Preeminent among his children, a pearl salvaged from the muck. Raised up from feral savagery to a height just shy of transhuman. He reached out and traced her jaw with gentle fingers. She leaned into his touch, eyes alight with what he took to be joy. 'You will be mother to a new race, my dear. One way or another. That I promise you.'

'I live to serve you, Benefactor,' she said.

He laughed. He almost believed her, when she spoke so prettily. 'I know. I made sure of it.' He looked at Oleander. 'Tell me more of this craftworld of yours, Oleander. What is it called?'

'Lugganath,' Oleander said. 'They call it Lugganath.'

CHAPTER FOUR

Brotherhood of Monsters

Bile swept through the corridors of the palace, followed by Oleander and the Gland-hounds. Oleander kept one eye on Igori and her packmates. If Bile gave the order, they would leap on him without hesitation. He didn't doubt he would survive the fight that followed, but it would take more time than he had to kill them. Igori met his glances with a stony expression. He wondered if she were thinking the same thing.

'Are you listening, Oleander?'

Oleander's attentions snapped back to his former master. 'Yes,' he said, automatically. Bile stopped and turned. A crooked smile contorted his features.

'No, you weren't. That has always been your problem. You never listened. Do not think that because I have spared you thus far, I will tolerate your flaws as I once did. Listen, or I will strip you to the bedrock and mine your bones for useful material.'

'I am listening, master. Your every word resonates upon

my consciousness like the voice of Fulgrim himself,' Oleander said. He bowed with florid grace, eliciting a chuckle from Bile. Amusing the Chief Apothecary was no easy task, but it was well worth it. It had kept him alive and whole, where better men had wound up on Bile's operating table, dissected and scattered.

'Good,' Bile said. He extended his sceptre and lifted Oleander's chin. 'I have considered your offer, and come to a decision. You will present your proposition to the Consortium as a whole. If some among them find merit in your proposal, then I shall take such action as I deem best.'

'And if they do not?'

'If none among the Consortium are interested in your proposal, I shall break you down into raw components and forget your name,' Bile said. 'You were exiled for a reason, Oleander. It is only just, then, that punishment be meted out accordingly.' Oleander stepped back, rubbing his chin. Bile followed him, leaning close. 'Without rules, we are barbarians. Don't you agree?'

'There's something to be said for barbarism.'

'Yes. Much of it unintelligible. He who dares, wins. You've risked much, coming back. It seems only fitting you push your luck a bit further, eh?' Bile looked at him. There was an unnatural gleam in the Chief Apothecary's eye.

Oleander frowned. A bit of theatre then, to see him squirm. No, more than that – a test. As Arrian had reminded him, Bile loved his tests. His little games were legendary. Few among the Consortium had not suffered in some way from the Chief Apothecary's twisted attentions, but that didn't make it any more bearable, when you were on the other end of the scalpel. Bile couldn't help but probe and test the minds and wills of those who followed him. It was as if he were looking for something in particular, though he'd never said what.

Well, if it were a test, Oleander intended to pass. He grinned. 'Why not? Let us see how far this particular ligament can stretch before it snaps, shall we?'

The auditorium was a cavernous chamber, carved out of the heart of the palace. It had been an arena once, and blood had been spilled on its floors. Massive pillars held up the cracked shell of the roof. Semicircular benches ascended from the floor to the uppermost reaches around the centre of the chamber. Sickly vegetation clung to the buckled flagstones and cracked walls, winding amongst the benches. The walls had once been covered in carvings both obscene and grisly, but were now chiselled bare, to make way for diagnostic screens and hololith overlays, allowing those in the middle of sensitive experiments to participate without having to leave their laboratories.

A great dais had been installed at the centre of the chamber. Heavy examination platforms lay crouched around the dais, their surfaces covered in old stains. It was from here that Bile often delivered his most pointed lessons. But it was also a gathering place for the Consortium as a whole, when matters of import reared their head – it was a war-room, cloaked in collegiate terms. In those matters that concerned them all, Bile was determined to appear as nothing less than egalitarian. This had less to do with magnanimity on the Chief Apothecary's part and more to do with a subtle demonstration of his authority. Those who publicly disagreed with him often ended up exiled, or worse.

Some of the benches were occupied. Renegade Apothecaries from a variety of Legions and warbands sat or stood, waiting for them. There were thirty of them, not counting their accompanying slaves, bodyguards and servitors. He saw some faces he recognised, fellow sons of the Third Legion. Others were new arrivals. The members of the Consortium came and went as it pleased them, unless Bile wished otherwise.

Whatever their origin, all bore some signs of their calling – coats of flayed flesh worn in overt mimicry of their leader, ornaments of bone, surgical dendrite harnesses and signs of self-experimentation abounded. These alterations often went beyond the cosmetic and into realms of wild fancy. Nartheciums whirred and clicked, as internal sensors tested the air and took surreptitious bio-readings. Brutally modified servitors and mutant scribes stood behind their masters, patiently noting muttered observations. The work could not be postponed, not even for a meeting such as this. Servo-skulls hovered about the chamber, recording all that occurred, for Bile's later examination. Those who failed to show the proper level of interest would be punished, or perhaps promoted, depending on his whims.

The stink of the Consortium hall was like a physical blow. It washed over Oleander as he followed Bile down to the dais. The air was thick with a fug of chemicals, spoiled meat and sour blood. It was not the smell of the slaughterhouse, but instead that of discovery. The reek of exploration. Here, as nowhere else, were the secrets of life and death studied and improved upon. Here, in these halls, new races of gods and monsters were raised up and dashed down. He'd almost missed the smell of it.

Igori and the other Gland-hounds took up positions near the doors, as was tradition, their weapons trained on the gathered Apothecaries. It was more a symbolic gesture than an actual threat, but few questioned it. At least not more than once. No one would be allowed to leave until a decision was reached. Those who tried often found themselves occupying several of Bile's nutrient tanks simultaneously.

Bile took his place on the dais and thumped the floor with his sceptre once, twice, three times, until every eye was on him. 'Brothers, attend me,' he said. 'We have a matter of some import to discuss. Step forward, Oleander Koh. Step forward and be recognised by the Consortium.'

Silence fell as Oleander stepped up onto the dais. He scanned the gathered faces, spotting Arrian and the others instantly. Saqqara looked as if he'd rather be anywhere else, uncomfortable among the ranks of those he considered heretics. Arrian lounged, murmuring to his skulls. And Tzimiskes... was Tzimiskes. As unreadable as a wall of iron.

'Speak, Oleander,' Bile said, gesturing him forward. 'Convince them, if you can.' Oleander cleared his throat. He let his hand rest on the pommel of his sword.

'Greetings, brothers. It has been some time,' he said. A murmur swept along the benches. Oleander waited until it grew quiet before continuing. 'We have come through dark times together, my brothers. From the killing fields of Terra to the seas of Gnosis, we have only ever sought illumination. When Canticle City burned, a century or more of knowledge was lost, and many of our brothers with it. Killed, by savages, by a Chthonian barbarian and his band of murderers. But we persevered. We rose from the ashes, borne aloft on wings of purpose.'

'Get on with it,' one of the Apothecaries said. He wore a cowl and robes made from stretched and sutured flesh over his battered war-plate, and the skins' still-functioning capillaries flushed as he gestured impatiently.

Others added their voices to this demand. The Consortium had never been what one could call serene. A band of lunatics, bound by deceit and malice, ever seeking their own perfection at the expense of their fellows. They had little patience for anything that took them from their experiments for even the briefest of moments. Another way in which the students emulated the master. He glanced at Bile, and wondered what the point of this particular test was. Bile gestured, and Oleander continued.

'And it is that purpose which brings me to you today. In the void, a treasure trove of raw material sits undefended – a craftworld of the perfidious eldar. I offer it up to you, if you will but aid me in taking it.'

A moment of silence followed. A craftworld was a prize worth a few seconds of consideration. Then suspicion reared its head. 'And what do you get out of it?' someone asked. The Apothecary was clad in red, his armour flexing like a second skin as the drug pumps affixed to his armour's power unit hissed. Weirdly coloured smoke spilled out of the vents of his helmet. A servitor, its bulky frame studded with chemical tanks, stood behind him. Its mouth had been replaced by a dispensing node, and a profusion of canisters bubbled there. It shuddered as its master extracted an empty canister from his pumps, and replaced it with a full one drawn from the servitor's maw.

'The joy of fighting alongside my brothers once more, Gorel,' Oleander said. A ripple of derisive laughter spread through the chamber.

'The joy of picking over our corpses, more like,' Gorel

said. He had always been a sour creature, concerned only
with the potency and effects of his chemical concoctions.

'Like he did with Scaripedes,' someone else added. The
Apothecary wore stained penitent's robes over his power
armour, concealing everything save the serpentine dendrites that coiled and thrashed about him. One of the
dendrites stiffened abruptly and slid its sharpened tip
into the scarified flesh of a bond-slave squatting nearby,
extracting what passed for blood. A second slave bent
close, waiting to be tattooed with whatever conclusion
her master had suddenly come to.

Oleander could almost feel the hostility radiating from
the gathered Apothecaries. None of them liked to be
reminded of what had happened to Scaripedes, however
necessary it had been. He had been a Lernaean agent, but
well liked for all that. No one blamed the sons of Alphar-
ius for doing what came naturally. And no one wanted
to be reminded that they were all ultimately expendable,
in the eyes of their leader.

An Apothecary in the dark armour of a Night Lord rose
to his feet. Decorations of bone rattled against ceramite
as he did so, and his bodyguards growled eagerly, goatish lips peeling back from broken fangs. The goat-headed
mutants quivered, hands on their skinning knives, ready
to attack on their master's order. 'You have no brothers
here, Oleander,' he said. 'Or if you did, you butchered
them. The way we should butcher you, and feed your
guts to the beasts that howl around our towers.' He activated the drill on his narthecium for emphasis, and his
beasts yelped hungrily.

'Strip his glands first, Duco,' Gorel said. 'I'd wager his
progenoids are still good.'

'If you get those, I get his Betcher's gland.' This from the one in the penitent's robes.

'Have what you want, but his Mucranoid implant is mine, Marag,' said another, a leprous monster with stained bandages on his bare arms, and syringes on his fingertips. He bared teeth gone black with rot in a too-wide smile. 'And maybe a dermal sample as well.'

'I'll have his brain, but I'm willing to share,' Duco, the Night Lord, growled. 'One bite apiece, what say?' He looked around. 'There must be something of value in that crooked mind of his, otherwise Fabius wouldn't have spared his life...'

Oleander tensed as voices rose from the benches, harvesting him where he stood. Drills whirred and blades clicked throughout the chamber. Bile smiled at him. 'You see how they've missed you, Oleander?' he said. 'Have no fear, I'll not let Duco have your brain, nor any of the others. I have such... interesting plans for it.'

Bile thumped the dais with his sceptre as the roar from the benches swelled. The gathered Apothecaries fell silent almost at once. 'My brothers – please attend carefully. You have heard Apothecary Oleander's proposal. It is now time for you to determine its merit. Who will step forward to join his fate to that of our prodigal brother?' Bile said.

Oleander felt the gaze of every Apothecary in the rotunda fix on him. He was no witch, but he could tell their thoughts well enough. For most, he was nothing more than a momentary distraction from their experiments. For the rest, he was a bundle of spare parts. The eyes of these fixed on him with greedy intensity, already parcelling him out according to their requirements. He began to wonder if this were not a test at all, but rather the prelude to an execution.

Silence held, for long moments. Oleander scanned the auditorium, wondering if he could fight his way out for the second time in a lifetime. Even if he could, there was little chance he would reach his ship. Not in one piece, anyway.

Tzimiskes stood, and silence fell. The Iron Warrior slowly made his way to Oleander's side. All eyes watched his progress. A gauntlet dropped heavily onto Oleander's shoulder. Iron fingers tightened, and a disgruntled sigh went up from the crowd. Oleander looked at the other Apothecary. 'Brother?' he said. Tzimiskes nodded and turned to face the crowd.

Arrian stood. 'Ah well. I can't let gentle Tzimiskes go alone. Who knows what might happen to him, without someone to watch his back?' He strode up to the dais, hands on the hilts of his blades. 'Besides, I haven't tasted eldar flesh in some time.'

Bile nodded approvingly. 'Excellent. Anyone else – Saqqara?' He gestured, and Saqqara stood. 'You will accompany us as well, I think. Do you have any objections?' The Word Bearer stopped before Bile and spat at his feet. Bile laughed. 'No, I suppose not.' The Chief Apothecary thumped the dais with the haft of his sceptre.

'The proposition is accepted. The rest of you are free to return to your experiments. Gorel, you shall be in command of the apothecarion until I return.' Gorel twitched in surprise. The auditorium began to empty. Baleful glances were tossed Gorel's way, but no one spoke out. Oleander wondered what he'd done to earn Bile's ire. The chances of him still being in one piece when they returned were slim.

'Very well, Oleander. You've managed to save your skin, for the moment,' Bile said, as the last of the Consortium

left the chamber. 'I know why you wished for my help.
But now, perhaps, you will share the first step of your
daring plan with your fellow Apothecaries?'

'Of course, master,' Oleander said. 'We require a guide
capable of leading us to where our quarry currently lurks,
or to wherever it might choose to flee.'

'You've come to the wrong place then,' Saqqara said. 'I
doubt any of us here know how to find your craftworld,
unless Tzimiskes is keeping secrets.' He glanced at the
Iron Warrior, who shrugged. The Word Bearer tapped one
of the icons that adorned his armour. 'I could seek aid
from the Neverborn...'

'That won't be necessary, will it, Oleander?' Bile said.

'I know where to find a guide,' Oleander said. 'But I
doubt that they will be willing.'

'When are they ever?' Arrian asked.

'Quite.' Bile pointed Torment at Oleander. 'Where will
we find this guide of yours?'

'Sublime,' Oleander said.

CHAPTER FIVE

Sublime

Sublime existed in spite of itself.

The world hung suspended in the darkness like a jewel, trapped on the edge of the Eye of Terror, where the raw stuff of unreality gave way to the hard fact of real space. It was caught between moments, on the cusp of obliteration. A frozen fractal of diverging rock and superheated gases, expanding away from a boiling core. This expansion was a thing of infinitesimal slowness, immeasurable by any applicable standard. No one knew when it had begun, or when it would end.

The world was dead and yet not. Eternally dying, trapped in its final instant. Its ruptured crust was pockmarked with thousands of oases of varying sizes, shapes and geometric intricacies – some were monumental bastions, studded with flak-cannons and defensive arrays, while others were seas of tall tents, clustered among once-graceful ruins beneath barely functioning atmospheric generators.

Each of these communities was independent of the

other; individual fiefdoms eking out what existence they could, as best they might. Alliances and wars between these city-states were not uncommon, and the long night was occasionally punctuated by nuclear fire. Ships and cruisers prowled the corona within, waging war on behalf of the blazing cities that clung to the underside of the broken world.

'All roads lead to Sublime,' Oleander said, gazing at the hololith. 'That is what the Phlogiston-Seers of the Fire-wild say.'

He and the others stood on the compact command deck of the *Vesalius*, around a hololith projector. The ancient Gladius-class frigate was Bile's personal vessel, claimed in some long-ago raid on an Imperial world. Every trace of its previous owners had been scoured from it over the intervening centuries, as had its former name. Now and forever, it was simply *Vesalius*, and whatever darkling spirit now haunted its core seemed happy enough with the name.

'This world is a den of thieves and scramblers after forbidden delights. Sybarites, decadents and fools,' Saqqara said, studying the holo-image. 'I once begged leave of my superiors to set it aflame from orbit, in the name of the dark gods. No world should be allowed to defy the judgement of the warp in such a fashion.'

'Perhaps. But it is beautiful in its own way,' Arrian said. He stood nearby, looming among the cadre of Gland-hounds who accompanied Bile everywhere. The augmented warriors stood at rest, not speaking or even looking at anything in particular, save their creator. As if Bile were the singular sun which they orbited. Oleander recalled that feeling well. Once, he'd shared similar sentiments. Now, he was adrift. Unfettered to anything save his own ambition. He couldn't say which feeling was better.

'It is not the world itself which concerns us,' Bile said. One of the chirurgeon's limbs extended and tapped the glowing image, bringing a section of the broken world into sharp relief. Data scrolled across the air. 'Rather one small part of it: Black Golan. The largest archaeomarket in this region of the Eye, stretching across the remains of two continents.' Metallic limbs clicked and whirred. More information spilled up and out. 'These markets are necessary – they are as near to neutral ground as the regions close to the Eye get, and useful. Even Abaddon abides by the ancient laws which protect their sanctity.' He smiled. 'Of course, we feel no such compunction. Necessity drives, brothers.'

'We will have to pay a toll to get past the orbital defences,' Oleander said. He reached out and tapped the hololith, causing the image to recede, revealing the porous membrane of space-fortresses and orbital weapons platforms that all but encased Sublime like a makeshift Dyson sphere. 'Castle Sublime, as they call it. I can think of better names, but then no one asked me.' Tzimiskes gestured, and Oleander nodded. 'They are archaic, yes. You have a good eye, brother. Not to mention cobbled together from half a dozen technologies, most of them of unknown origin. Eldar, hrud, it's all wired in there somewhere. All to keep the peace in the markets... or to keep the wars of Sublime from spilling out into the wider sector.' He gestured. 'If we had a bigger ship, I'd suggest shooting our way past. As it is... well, there's an open docking port we can use.'

'No. I have no wish to waste time bargaining for leave

to enter this place with its master,' Bile said. 'So we must effect an entrance with all due subtlety.' He looked at the hololith and tapped the image, bringing up a real-time pict-capture of the region. A pale haze stretched lazily across the black, towards Sublime. It bypassed the orbital defences entirely, and ships gave it a wide berth. 'There,' Bile said. 'We'll use that.'

'And what is that?' Arrian said, as he leaned forward.

'The Carrion Road,' Oleander said. A chill sliced through him, sharper even than the blades on Bile's chirurgeon. 'It is the route the Neverborn take into the inner-death of Sublime. A raw wound in reality opened by the warp storm which claimed Sublime so many millennia ago. It never closes, never heals...' He'd never seen it up close, and had never wanted to. Such eddies in the terrain of the imma-terium were incredibly dangerous, even to one well versed in the ways of the Neverborn. Which he was not. 'Those who study such things contend that Sublime is a Warp Star in the making. The more Neverborn who flock to it, the closer its chrysalis comes to its predetermined end.'

'It is full of daemons,' Saqqara said. 'I can feel them – hear them – from here. Laughing and screaming and whispering as they walk the Carrion Road into the world's dying core, to drink deep of its eternal agonies.' Olean-der glanced at the Word Bearer. Saqqara's face was tighter than normal and pale. His eyes flickered with a bloody light. The diabolist was no sorcerer. He couldn't draw fire from the air, or cast lightning from his eyes. But he could call daemons, and did so with skill.

'Yes,' Bile said. 'And we will do the same. It will ensure that our approach receives no unwelcome attention.' He looked at Saqqara. 'You know what to do.'

Saqqara grimaced. 'It will be dangerous.'

'As dangerous as that bomb I put in your chest?'

'Yes,' the Word Bearer said, without hesitation. 'If we try and take the Carrion Road, we will be walking a path of madness. Where daemons walk, worlds burn. Stars go cold. Minds splinter and souls fray.'

'How very poetic.' Bile turned back to the hololith. 'We will need to suspend the Geller field for the duration, otherwise we will almost certainly be detected. All other non-essential functions will be terminated, in order to limit potential damage to the ship's systems.'

'Without that field we'll be dead in moments,' Oleander said. 'The Neverborn will flood the ship.' He took a step towards Bile, but stopped as Arrian intercepted him. 'Arrian, surely even you can see the madness of this...'

'Think of it as a new experience,' Arrian said. 'That is what the sons of Fulgrim do, isn't it? Seek out new experiences, new pleasures?'

'I've experienced it. I did not particularly care for it,' Oleander said, hands clenching uselessly. 'And I would rather not repeat it, if there are other options. Like the docking bay.'

'I have made my decision,' Bile said. 'You may enter via the docking bay, if you like, Oleander. You might find it difficult without a ship, but you are nothing if not resourceful.' He looked at Saqqara. 'Begin.'

'No. You do not understand – none of you,' Saqqara said. 'That is not some mere cosmological phenomenon... it is a river of soul-stuff. It is a torrent of thoughts and emotions, waves of anguish and desire rolling along on a tide of pure hatred or despair. It is the will and thoughts of the gods themselves made manifest. There is no controlling such a thing. It is a blasphemy to even try. One can but ride it out, and hope to survive.'

Tzimiskes put a hand on his shoulder. Saqqara shook his head, and made to protest further, but a gesture from Bile silenced him. 'I have estimated the time it will take to enter the Carrion Road and traverse it to the first point past the orbital array. It will require only a few moments, no more than that. The Geller field will be restored as soon as we are close enough to escape detection,' Bile said. 'It is a calculated risk. The variables are within acceptable parameters.'

'It's a death sentence,' Oleander said. 'If not for us, then definitely for your mortal pets.' He gestured to the Gland-hounds. Igori glared at him, as if his words were a challenge.

Bile gestured to her, and she went to him. 'They will be protected.' Bile bent Igori's head to the side, displaying a glittering patch of circuitry just below her ear. 'Sub-dermal electoo. A hexagrammatic symbol of Saqqara's devising. The entirety of the crew has been marked so, for just this sort of eventuality. He assures me it will see them through this sort of thing, so long as they can defend themselves against physical attacks. And if it does not, I have my own methods.' He tapped the Xyclos needler in its holster. 'A special concoction I have been saving for an occasion of this kind.'

Oleander stared at him, wondering if perhaps this was simply another of Bile's games. Bile's behaviour could seem erratic, almost impulsive, at times, unless one was familiar with him. It wouldn't be out of character for him to have planned to enter the Carrion Road all along in order to field test whatever new serum he'd devised.

Perhaps that was why he'd insisted that Saqqara come along.

Or, possibly, there was a more mundane explanation. It didn't surprise him that Bile had visited Sublime before. War-torn worlds made excellent testing grounds, after all. And the fiefdoms of Sublime went to war so regularly that you could set a chronometer by it. Oleander had fought in one or two himself, on one side or another. Renegade Space Marines were a common enough sight on the battlefields of the sectors close to the Eye. But Bile had a tendency to wear out his welcome. His goals were rarely the same as those who invited him in, and the liberties he took tended to sour relations swiftly.

His enemies were Legion and Legions alike. Bile was useful to the renegade Legions, but he was a wildcard in the greater game of Eyespace. He served no one save himself, and knew too much to be safely ignored or left to roam free. Agents of the Lernaean Proxies had tried to murder him more than once, and had even succeeded, briefly, on Korazin. The Dark Council of Sicarus had set warband after warband on Bile's trail, hunting him from one end of the Eye to the other – Saqqara had merely been the latest. Angron himself had nearly collected Bile's skull on Gnosis. And Fulgrim's bounty still stood unclaimed.

But the Clonelord had more enemies than just his former brothers. Oleander tapped the pommel of his sword. Enemies who feared what Bile might yet do, rather than wishing vengeance for what he had already done. Enemies who would do anything to see him diverted from his chosen path... even sacrifice their own kin...

The *Vesalius* groaned in what might have been protest, or perhaps eagerness, as its engines carried it towards the daemonic haze. A ship in motion was never silent. Rivets squealed and bulkheads shifted. Consoles hummed and alerts pinged. The crew spoke in muted whispers, or at least those who had the tongues to do so. Oleander wondered if they understood enough about what was going on to be frightened.

There were whole tribes of mutants lurking in the deep places of the ship, venerating the engines and weapons batteries with a devotion equal to any Mechanicum acolyte, and waging wars in service to that devotion. They were the descendants of the old crew, led by those few officers whom Bile had found worthy of augmentation, like the strategium overseer, Wolver.

Oleander glanced at the creature, where it stood overlooking the servitor crew in their control-cradles, and the few ragged mutants allowed anywhere near the bridge. Wolver was a thing of hard metal and glass. An alembic, contorted into a vaguely human shape. A living brain glistened in the glass head, and eyes connected to it by optic nerves peered out through the sockets of a polished brass death-mask. Whether those eyes had once belonged to a man, or a woman, or something else entirely, Oleander could not say. For as long as the *Vesalius* had served the Consortium, Wolver had served the *Vesalius*.

The glass head turned. The miniature vox-grille set between brass lips crackled. '*Vesalius* is unhappy,' Wolver said. It placed a steel-framed hand on the bolt pistol holstered on its hip.

'Can a ship be unhappy? Or happy, for that matter?' Oleander said, somewhat surprised the creature had spoken directly to him. Bile fostered a cult of informality among his servants, likely because he found the rituals of servitude to be tedious. Oleander thought that was just asking for trouble. The lower orders got ideas, when they weren't reminded of their place. He glanced surreptitiously at Igori.

'*Vesalius* is unhappy,' Wolver repeated, in its crackling monotone.

'Well, what do you expect me to do about it?' The crew, those of them with eyes, were staring up at the command deck, watching him. They were nervous. He could smell their fear, and wished he had the luxury of stoking it to greater heights. He half reached for his pipe, but stopped himself. Now wasn't the time. The key to indulgence, he'd learned, was moderation.

A bell tolled somewhere deep in the belly of the frigate. It was a dull, black sound. It reverberated up through the deck and into Oleander's bones. 'What is that? I've never heard it before.'

'*Vesalius* is–' Wolver began.

'Unhappy, yes I know.'

'It is a warning,' Bile said, from behind him. '*Vesalius* is a predator, and it knows it is entering unfamiliar waters, so to speak. It is letting whatever lurks in that haze know that it is coming, and will brook no interference.'

'That won't work.'

'The ship doesn't know that.' Bile clasped his hands behind his back. 'In truth, I fear I have spoiled it... feeding it easy meat on raids, and bowing to its petulant demands. But a good ship is hard to find. One must take care of them, when one finds the right vessel.'

'I'd hardly call this taking care of it.'

'Needs must when necessity drives, Oleander. *Vesalius* understands.'

On the occulus viewscreen, the Carrion Road expanded

to encompass them. The haze became distinct, as did the shapes moving within it. There were colours there, such as no colour Oleander had ever seen, and lights which were not light. Cold fire flickered among the asteroids and gases which were Sublime's lifeblood. Things danced in the flames, or ran or waged war. A thousand wars across a thousand scattered moments. The shapes were a solid torrent, hurtling from parts unknown into the dying core of the ruptured world. They blended together, a mad cosmic riot of faces and limbs such as no living thing had ever possessed.

'There must be thousands of them,' Oleander said.

'Millions,' Saqqara croaked. 'Tens of millions. Come to feast on the agonies of the world's core. It is a sweet thing, when a world dies. The ghosts of all who ever lived and ever would live upon it are caught there with it, waiting to be plucked like fruit from the vine. I can hear them screaming... and laughing.' The Word Bearer pressed his knuckles to his head. 'They will see us as soon as we lower the Geller field. They will come, first to investigate and then to feed. We must be... we must be ready. I must be ready.'

Oleander's hand dropped to the hilt of his sword. He'd fought daemons before. You couldn't live long in the Eye without doing so. Most were weak things, all hunger and no brains. But others were more subtle, more deadly. Those were the ones he feared. He smiled, treasuring the tiny node of animal panic as it flickered in his belly.

'Drop the field,' Bile said, his voice serene. No fear there. If Bile had ever known such, it had long ago been seared from him, cast off with old skin and bone. Wolver transmitted the order. There was a protesting hum. The frigate's lighting flickered.

And then, the *Vesalius* plunged prow first into hell.

CHAPTER SIX

The Carrion Road

It began with voices, at first. Quiet murmurings, barely audible. Then came the deranged screams, and the lurid whispering. The hull echoed with dull thumps and thuds, as of something trying to smash its way in. The vox crackled as someone – something – on the other end began to sing, softly. Oleander didn't recognise the song. Bile ordered it switched off. A sea of screaming faces stretched across the viewscreen, some almost human, most not.

At Bile's order, the view shifted, separating into multiple angles. Daemons clung to the frigate like barnacles. Some were as vast as the ship itself, while others were no bigger than a man. Something like a great tiger prowled across the forest of sensor nodes which lined the hull, hunting its weaker cousins. Lithe, pale entities danced atop the weapons batteries.

Saqqara moaned. Oleander tore his eyes from the screen. The Word Bearer had one hand stretched out, fingers moving in a spidery fashion. He muttered words and phrases in the tongue of ancient Colchis – rituals of binding and protection, Oleander thought.

'Can he handle this?' he said, looking at Bile.

'If he can't, we'll know soon enough, won't we?' Bile turned to Wolver. 'How long?' Wolver rattled off a number. Bile nodded in satisfaction. 'Not long then. Good.'

The thumping was soon replaced by scratching, like vermin gnawing at the walls. The whirr of wings echoed from everywhere and nowhere. One by one, the servitors slaved to the bridge consoles began to scream and beat their reinforced craniums against the sides of their control-cradles. The drumming of their skulls took on a dolorous rhythm.

'We should shut them down,' Oleander said.

'And then who will fly the ship?' Bile said. 'No. Leave them. I reinforced their craniums for a reason. A bit of thumping will not injure them in any way that matters.' The nutrient fluid filling Wolver's body began to bubble, and it staggered. Bile hissed something, and one of the chirurgeon's limbs flashed out. It slid home into a feed-node set into the strategium overseer's neck-frame. The nutrient fluid turned a pale ochre, and Wolver steadied. It murmured in gratitude. Bile ignored it.

The hull creaked. Without the Geller field, the ship only had its armour and speed to protect it. The deck shifted beneath Oleander's feet as the ship's engines flared, propelling it forward swiftly. The *Vesalius* surged forward through the empyrean. Something vast and loathsome surged to meet it, planet-sized jaws wide. *Vesalius* tore through it like a scalpel. The deck yawed and pitched as the abominable immensity came apart like a cloud. Saqqara had begun to sing a damning hymnal, his voice high and surprisingly lovely.

Oleander watched the Word Bearer, fascinated despite himself. Saqqara's eyes were glazed over, and his lips were flecked with blood as his song rose to meet the daemonic noises. Strange, indistinct shapes shimmered and writhed about him.

A Gland-hound staggered suddenly, clutching his stomach. He vomited up a white sludge, which steamed where it struck the deck. Tiny shapes moved in the sludge, tittering in amusement. Arrian crushed the shapes with his boot, and injected a stim-agent into the suffering Gland-hound's neck. 'Master, the electoo doesn't seem to be working.'

'No. How disappointing. Still, make a note of the time. We shall factor that into our calculations for the future. For now, however...' Bile smoothly drew the needler and fired. The Gland-hounds staggered as he hit each in turn. One collapsed, clutching at his head and screaming. Another gave a wail and tore at her eyes, until Igori knocked her from her feet and pinned her to the deck. 'A solution derived from the genetic material of a psychic null. It doesn't last long, and sometimes has unfortunate side effects. But I think the risk is well worth it, in this case.' He holstered the needler.

'What about the crew on the lower decks?' Oleander asked.

'They shall have to see to themselves, as best they can. I did not breed sheep,' Bile said, dismissively. He spread his hands. 'This is nothing. A natural phenomenon given meaning by small minds. What you hear, what you see, it is all from within you. We impart shape and purpose on that which has neither, and suffer for it.' He turned, one hand raised, the other behind his back as if he were a lecturer at a scholarium. 'Purge your minds of all such thoughts, and this will cease. Control yourselves, and you will control this.'

Something like condensation began to stream down the inner curve of the bridge walls. Where it beaded, the metal stretched and thinned. Things pressed against it from the other side – hands, faces, mouths, and other, less identifiable shapes. A tar-like substance began to drip down between the seams of the walls, and bubbled up from between the deck plates. As it congealed, it transformed into flat facets of obsidian. In the dark of the facets, shapes swam towards the light.

Oleander stomped on one as the shapes within it drew too close, shattering it. He snatched his bolt pistol free and fired at the others. 'Don't let them reach us,' he said. Tzimiskes and the others followed suit. Oleander heard a rivet pop and turned to see a deck plate twist and burst from its housing. Metal buckled and ran like wax, as grey gave way to pink. The tendril snaked towards Saqqara, mouths blossoming along its length like tumours.

'No,' Arrian said, as if disciplining a pet. He chopped through the tendril with his blades. Something far out in the aether roared, and the deck heaved like a wounded animal. *Vesalius* was screaming, though whether in pain or rage, Oleander couldn't tell. He steadied himself against the hololith. The image of Sublime crackled and vanished as hands of holographic light caressed his face. He shoved himself away and whirled. The face that stared back at him was impossibly sensual. She – it – rose from the stream of data and pixels like a goddess rising from the sea. Hands reached towards him, beckoning.

Oleander, it crackled. *It has been so long, my love... come to me... come...*

He took a halting step forward, despite himself. Desire
surged up in him, rising wild. His limbs trembled with
need and his brain sparked with longing. A face swelled in
his mind's eye, inhuman and beautiful and terrible in that
beauty, teased into the open by the electric fingers stroking
his soul. He had danced to this rhythm before, however, and
he recognised a lie when he heard one. He forced himself to
stop, though his every instinct begged that he go forward.

'No,' he croaked. 'No, I know her febrile stink, and you
are not her,' Oleander said. 'She would not ask – she
would demand.' He tore his sword from its sheath and
slashed wildly at the holographic phantasm. The shape
exploded into shards of light with a frustrated shriek.
The light surged about him like a flock of startled birds,
scorching his armour and stinging his eyes. He stumbled
away from it, and nearly fell, but for Bile.

'I did not give you permission to fall, Oleander,' Bile
said.

'And I would not fall without your permission, master,' Oleander said, steadying himself. He caught sight of
Saqqara. The Word Bearer stood as if braced against a hurricane wind. His lips still moved, but no sound came from
them now. Blood streaked his cheeks, spilling from the
corners of his eyes and mouth. Ghostly maggots crawled
in and out of his eyes and spilled from his mouth. Claw
marks from invisible talons scored his armour and flesh.
'Can he hold them back for much longer?'

'You've asked that before. He can,' Bile said. 'It is one of
the reasons I keep him alive.'

Inhuman faces pressed against the bulkheads, as if struggling to free themselves from the metal. The sound of
wings was thunderous now, and strange shadows spread

across the bridge. A console sparked, and something began to haul itself into the world. Arrian stepped forward and removed its head with a quick sweep of his falax blade. The crew, those not slaved to command-cradles, were weeping and praying. Bile curled his lip in derision.

'Prayer. Last refuge of the damned. I really must investigate the neuropsychological benefits of selective surgery on the right parietal lobe, when this is all over,' he said. 'If we could but remove such foolishness from the outset, my task might be easier.'

The voices were clearer now, more distinct. The strongest of the interlopers were drawing closer. Saqqara groaned suddenly and sank to one knee. Shadows congealed in lightless corners. Something like a rat with a human face tittered and scurried between Oleander's boots. Bat-like creatures, with the faces of lost children and forgotten lovers, clumped and crawled across the ceiling far above, whispering amongst themselves. Bizarre silhouettes tugged at his eyes – iridescent globules which spun and burst, only to re-form giggling and speaking in a language he didn't recognise. Non-Euclidian shapes gambolled through the chill air, carving trails of light even as they warped and expanded past the limits of his understanding.

Oleander, a voice whispered in his ear. He turned, but there was nothing there, save the echoes of mad laughter. *Oleander, Oleander, Oleander...* from all around him now, filling his skull with the sound of his own name. He coughed, lungs suddenly full of something. Pearl-coloured smoke spewed from his mouth, as fingers tugged his jaws open from within. It rose and spread as he dropped his sword and clutched at his throat. Pain wracked him as things moved inside him. His bones were jostled and organs squeezed as he fell forward and something set a dainty hoof on the deck. He felt as if he'd been cored out and left open to the sun.

The Keeper of Secrets turned, surveying the bridge. 'Well, what have we here?' it said. Lupine fangs clicked in a bovine jaw. Massive horns, wrapped in golden chains and dripping with a king's ransom in precious jewels scraped the ceiling plates above. It was a long thing, and lean, at once loathsome and beguiling, with four arms, two ending in great snapping claws. Its two hands, meanwhile, held delicate blades forged from smoky glass and limned with the light of a dying sun. 'I am Kanathara, Whose Hooves Shatter Mountains and Whose Voice Lulls the Sun. You have called and I have come. Are you not pleased?'

'No one invited you,' Arrian said. His voice was steady, despite the thing's aura, and Oleander hated him a little more for it.

'I beg to differ, little vessel,' the daemon said as it bent towards the World Eater. 'You stink of thwarted potential. How delicious. Might I taste of you?' It extended one of its blades. 'Just a nip, I assure you. Kanathara's kisses are dainty things.' Arrian slapped its blade away with one of his own. The daemon reared back with a derisive snort. 'How disappointing. If you are not here to be eaten, why come?'

'You will eat no one on this ship,' Bile said. 'Your kind are not welcome here. Be off with you, back to whatever child's nightmare you crawled out of.'

Kanathara turned towards Bile. Its lips peeled back from too many fangs. 'Chief Apothecary Fabius. I'd know your unique stench anywhere. You reek of unbelief, of hubris and madness. You are almost too sweet a delicacy for even my senses to comprehend. Still, one must try, mustn't one? Else what is the point of life?' It took a step towards him. The deck beneath its hooves moaned like a dying animal. Oleander crawled towards his fallen sword as lesser daemons, things with flowing flesh and circular maws, seeped up through the deck plates in Kanathara's wake. They loped towards the others, gibbering eagerly.

'You think you frighten me? I have seen worse things while cutting away a tumour on my brainstem. Hallucinations, even audible ones, hold no terror for me,' Bile said. He spread his arms. 'Come then... test me, figment.'

The daemon sighed in pleasure and lunged. Oleander could only watch in horrified fascination as its swords sliced through the air towards Bile. The chirurgeon whirred and its limbs flickered, trapping the blades scant inches from Bile's skull. The device whined as the daemon strained against it. Bile gave it no opportunity to redouble its efforts. Torment licked out to crack against the daemon's knee.

Kanathara whipsawed in agony and stumbled back. Bile nodded approvingly. 'I have long wondered whether this device would work on one of your sort. It seems that it does. I shall note that in my lexicon. Further analysis is in order.'

The daemon hissed and thrust out a claw. Bile stepped to the side, and one of the chirurgeon's limbs darted down to pierce the daemon's flesh. A syringe depressed and Kanathara shrieked as cancerous black lines ran up its arm. Bile ducked under its thrashing blow and slammed Torment into its opalescent stomach. Still shrieking, the daemon brought the hilt of one of its blades down atop him, knocking him to one knee.

'Chief Apothecary,' Arrian said. It was as close to panic

as Oleander had ever heard him come. He and Tzimiskes broke free of the lesser daemons and hurled themselves at Kanathara. Power axe and falax blades bit deep into abominable flesh. Ichor spurted and the daemon's screams grew shriller as it spun to confront its attackers.

It backhanded Arrian, sending him flying out over the bridge to crash into the occulus screen. Daemons surged towards the fallen World Eater with cries of glee. Tzimiskes continued to chop at Kanathara with the single-minded tenacity that so characterised his Legion. Kanathara reversed its blades and raised them up. Oleander shoved himself to his feet and leapt, tackling the Iron Warrior out of the path of the descending swords. They pierced the deck in a welter of sparks and torn metal.

'Pain... such delicious pain,' the daemon burbled, stroking a wound with its claw. It tore its weapons free of the deck. 'Like the most delicate acid upon newly sprouted nerve clusters. I do so love the sensation. I've been alive since time began, and I never grow tired of it.' Kanathara pointed one of its swords at Bile. 'Come, Fabius, let me taste the fruits of thy bile.'

'*Vesalius* is unhappy.'

'What?' the daemon said, turning. Wolver shot it in the face. Kanathara reared back, more in surprise than pain. Wolver fired until the bolt pistol clicked dry. The strategium overseer ejected the spent clip and reached unhurriedly for a second. The daemon screeched and slashed out, cracking Wolver's glass body and knocking it from its feet. The bell deep in the ship's cavernous reaches sounded again, the echoes filling the bridge. The daemon staggered, clutching at its head. 'What is – stop yowling,' Kanathara snarled, stamping on the deck.

'You are not welcome here,' Bile said. 'This ship knows falsehood when it sees it.' Oleander scrambled to his feet, searching for his sword. He helped Tzimiskes up. The Iron Warrior made as if to go to Bile's aid, but Oleander held him back.

'I will help him, brother. See to Arrian,' he said. He darted towards his sword, hoping he could reach it before the daemon noticed him. The command deck heaved with battle. Igori and the Gland-hounds were protecting Saqqara as best they could, employing blade and gun against things that barely noticed either. Luckily, daemons were disinclined to attack when their prey had been dosed with extract of null. Saqqara's chanting seemed to have some effect, too; without it, Oleander had no doubt that the ship would have been overwhelmed and inundated in moments.

'You test me, sweet Fabius,' Kanathara said, pawing at the wounds in its face. 'You invite me in and then insult me – assault me – does hospitality mean nothing to you? Perhaps I shall not deliver my message after all.'

'And what does it mean to you? You are not even real,' Bile said. 'A bit of grit in the empyrean is what you are. Whatever message you have is worth less to me than the hiss of a lanced boil.'

'Wait. Stop. Let me gather myself,' Kanathara said, holding out a claw. 'I am all aflutter from that assertion.' It grinned, showing its fangs. 'I see you are still singing that same sad song, Fabius. Blind devotion to a creed you once spat on, when it suited you. Do you seek salvation, in your waning years?'

'What I seek is none of your affair, figment.'

'I have a name, Fabius. Why don't you use it?' Kanathara wheedled.

'Names are for the sentient,' Bile said.

The daemon stared at him. The leer slipped from its muzzle. Oleander felt his hearts seize in his chest, as his fingers found the hilt of his sword. 'Three times you have denied me,' Kanathara said, as if in wonder. 'Three times you have spat upon my existence. Even the basest mind aboard this hollow tube of metal knows of my glory, and yet you still deny me? Cruelty, thy name is Fabius.'

Bile shrugged. 'I have never been a great believer in glory.' He coughed. Oleander saw blood speckle his lips and chin. Bile touched his mouth and studied his fingers. 'Pleasure is an illusion. Only pain is real.'

'You think you have suffered, Fabius?' Kanathara growled. 'You think the pain you feel can compare to the ecstasy offered by the Lord of Dark Delights?' It crouched, readying itself to spring. Oleander tensed, wondering if he could intercept it in time. Wondering if he should. It wasn't his place to put himself between a man and the gods. But he needed Bile alive. 'The suffering you feel now is but a splinter compared to the agonies yet to come...' the daemon continued, in its sickly-sweet voice.

'You tell me nothing I do not already know,' Bile said.

'Oh but I do,' the daemon growled. 'I think I will leave a trail of fire across this universe, just to see that final realisation blossom in your eyes, Chief Apothecary Fabius.' It glanced knowingly towards Igori and the Gland-hounds, where they fought against its lesser kin. 'Just to see that moment when you at last understand that all of your desperate alchemy has come to naught. When you at last know the truth of me. Of all that you have denied, so spitefully.'

'What would you know of it?'

'Not me. But the Phoenix says hello, Fabius,' the daemon said, with a leer. 'He is a dear friend, and it was he
who sent me here, to deliver his greetings – and warnings – to you. The skeins of fate grow tight about you,
Fabius. Chains of moment and decision are being fitted
to you, to hold you tight to your course. Be wary, lest you
find yourself trapped in a prison of your own making.' It
extended a blade. 'Such a caring father.'

Bile stared at the thing, his face as still as a mask. Then
he drew his needler and fired, putting a needle into the
centre of the daemon's eye. 'Your message has been delivered,' he said. 'You can get off my ship now.'

The daemon screamed as the poison took effect. It was
another of the null darts, Oleander realised. The solution tore the entity apart from the inside, unbinding the
strange matter that made up its form. Kanathara dropped
its blades and tore at itself, ripping chunks from its dissolving flesh as if to dig out the infection. It stumbled on
melting hooves, almost dancing in its agonies. It wailed
unintelligibly, gabbling at Bile until at last its skull collapsed in on itself and the whole reeking mess sloughed
to the deck. What was left bubbled for a moment before
seeping between the deck plates and vanishing.

Wolver staggered to its feet, one hand pressed to its leak-
ing wound. '*Vesalius* is happy,' the strategium overseer said,
looking at Oleander.

'I am overjoyed to hear it,' Oleander said. He glared at
Bile. 'What was that about?' he asked. Bile looked at him,
and Oleander couldn't help but recoil from the expression on his face.

Bile holstered his weapon. A grisly smile crept across
his cadaverous features. 'A sign from the gods.'

Meat for the Beast

The *Vesalius* speared out of the Carrion Road and into the interior of Sublime, wreathed in smoke and fire and not a few daemons, too stubborn to know when they were beaten. Despite appearances, the frigate had sustained only cosmetic damage. The Geller field had been reactivated after Kanathara's dissipation, and the daemonic flood had slackened to a trickle before at last ceasing entirely.

There were still Neverborn aboard. Trapped by the Geller field and Saqqara's rites, they prowled the lower decks or fled before hunting parties of mutants. *Vesalius* tracked them with its internal sensors, and alerted the crew to their whereabouts with a brutal glee. Iron stakes and flamer-units were employed to pin down and burn the writhing masses of unnatural flesh wherever they were found. Samples were collected by chanting mutant priests, offerings to the Pater Mutatis for his flesh tanks.

The crew were not alone in this entertainment. The

Consortium moved through the ship in ones and twos, stalking their prey with the patience of surgeons; they also needed to spot-check the ship for any damage the sensor sweep might have missed. Daemons were subtle things, as well as malignant. They could infect systems and bulk-head controls as easily as they possessed flesh and bone. This was Tzimiskes' task, as Saqqara's was the binding of those daemons weak enough to be controlled. The rest were left for Oleander and Arrian.

Together, the two of them had begun cleaning the lower decks of infestation. More because it gave them some-thing to do as *Vesalius* completed its orbit of Sublime's core and came to the proper heading, than out of any concern for the crew.

Screams had drawn them to a smoke-filled junction near the main access shaft. A number of the crew had been drawn into the walls, their distorted bodies fused with the metal. That they still lived was testament to the hardiness instilled in them by Bile's modifications. Unfortunately, the two Apothecaries weren't the first to follow their shrieks of anguish. Daemons capered about the dying crewmembers, tormenting their trapped forms with bestial glee. Intestines and ligaments had been drawn like streamers across the width of the corridor. Loose skin flapped liked hoods about still-screaming skulls. One by one, these skulls fell silent as their tormentors turned to meet the Apothecaries.

'I'll take the two on the left. You can have the thing on the right,' Oleander said. Arrian inclined his head.

'As you say, brother.'

Oleander lunged forward and smoothly pinned a squealing shape, made from the bodies of two servitors, to a bulkhead with his blade. It was strong, and began to haul itself up the sword's length, twin jaws snapping. Oleander cursed and shoved his narthecium against the closest skull. He activated the carnifex, and an adamantine bolt punched through bone and into the warped brain within. He repeated his action on the other a moment later. The bodies slumped. He twisted the sword and jerked it free, letting the merged carcass fall.

'I wonder why they do that,' he said, looking down at the awkward conglomeration. It wasn't the first such monstrosity he'd dispatched in the last few hours. Daemons seemed to have a fascination for combining things into new and more grotesque shapes.

'Do what?' Arrian replied. His opponent, a thing with too many limbs and not enough bones, flung itself at the World Eater. He caught it on his blades and sent it tumbling to the deck. He slid smoothly from defensive stance to offensive, moving with a surety that Oleander couldn't help but envy. He whipped a falax blade out in a controlled arc to slice away a tendril, before reversing it with a twitch of his wrist, and bisecting a scrabbling talon.

Oleander stepped back to avoid the thing's thrashing. 'Build such unwieldy bodies.'

'Trial and error,' Arrian said. He stomped on the squirming daemon, and held it in place. 'They do not understand how our bodies work. Can't blame them for being creative, despite their ignorance.' He spun his blades about and drove them into his prisoner's gelatinous body. 'You, however, should know better.'

'What is that supposed to mean?'

'Sometimes, brother, you display a marked lack of caution. It will be your downfall, I suspect. Impulse is to be channelled, rather than followed.'

'At last, the secret to your success,' Oleander said. 'Why didn't I think of that? Perhaps I should take a scalpel to my cortex, and scrape the weakness away. Why the sudden concern for my well-being, Arrian?'

'Not concern,' Arrian said. 'Merely a warning. You should be careful. Unless you wish to end up like poor Haruk.' He tapped the side of his skull. 'One bolt-shell to the brain and you might as well be a vat-born.' He strode past Oleander, towards the dying men. Man, really. Only one still lived, in the wake of the daemons' ministrations.

Oleander frowned. 'Didn't Haruk receive that inadvertent lobotomy because he was hunting you? He chased us from Gnosis all the way to Tarngek, trying to deliver your skull to Angron. I don't see much similarity in our respective situations.'

'That aside, if the Chief Apothecary decides that you're more useful as drooling hulk, that's what you'll be. He only tolerates your antics because you amuse him. Keep at it, and he might yet forgive you.' Arrian thrust his blade up through the dying man's heart. One quick thrust, and the wretch's misery was at an end. 'Help me cut him out of the wall. We might be able to salvage most of the major organs from this one.'

The work went swiftly. A few slashes, and what was left of the mutant slid free of the bulkhead and plopped wetly to the deck. Arrian cut open the limp wrists and tied the wreckage together with its own ligaments. He slung it over his back, and Oleander fastened the dripping bundle to the World Eater's backpack.

'Your hands are still steady, at least,' Arrian said, as they continued on.

'I've had plenty of practice. The last ship I was on, the

crew drew lots to see who would serve as prey for the Radiant and his favourites. They would stalk the unlucky creature through the darkest reaches of the ship, where metal became flesh and the walls between worlds were thin. A jungle of the most perverse sort, full of unseen dangers. Quite exhilarating, really.'

'You were one of the favourites, I assume.'

'Obviously. Apothecaries are thin on the ground, brother. We are a dying breed, despite the best efforts of our esteemed master. But then, few enough of our brothers require our sort of help these days. And there are some among the Radiant's warband who might as well be legionaries, though they never fought in the Great Crusade.'

'We've bled ourselves white, and now we pass from history,' Arrian said.

'You sound almost pleased by that.'

'Such is life, brother. We are born, we struggle, we die. That is the way of it. There's an old saying I'm quite fond of... this too shall pass.' He glanced at Oleander. 'All we do here is not for ourselves, but for those who come after. That is our purpose. We are midwives to the future, Oleander. A great thing will be born from our efforts.'

'What? Like the vat-born? Or the Gland-hounds?'

'Perhaps. Perhaps it will be as different from those as they are from each other. Already, things change. Did you know that the vat-born haven't been born in vats for a decade or more? They breed like vermin, in the dark corners of the Grand Apothecarion. A surprise even to the Chief Apothecary, I suspect.'

Oleander blinked. A disconcerting thought, on several levels. Clones were sterile, normally. As were most things that spilled out of the artificial wombs that Bile used to develop his creations. If that were no longer the case... He hesitated. Something Bile had said in passing on Urum rose to the surface of his thoughts. He'd called Igori 'the mother to a new race.' He was about to mention it, when he heard a bray of excitement.

Something scuttled across the ceiling, moving in jittery fits and starts, at once too fast and too slow. A crowd of mutants and beasts pursued it. Autoguns chattered, projectiles ricocheting from the deck and ceiling. Crude pikes thrust at the daemon, trying to dislodge it. Oleander could smell the oily discharge of a flamer unit as well. 'Helmets,' he said.

He and Arrian slid their helmets into place as the daemon vaulted to the deck with a high-pitched laugh. It had decided to make a stand. It was a tall thing, slim and lithe. Milky white skin stretched across birdlike bones, and a harness of human flesh and bone provided a token modesty. The daemonette was a gossamer thing, too soft to be real. 'Hello, sweetlings,' it moaned, opening its arms as if to welcome the stumbling pack into its embrace. Its voice sent a warm thrill through Oleander. The courtiers of the Prince of Pleasure were deadly things, however fragile they looked.

It spun suddenly, claws snapping, honeyed voice raised in song. Mutants stopped and stared, caught up in the song. The delicate claws snapped shut on necks and limbs, severing heads and hands and feet. It whirled, dancing atop the growing pile of bodies, its song swelling. A mutant stumbled back, flamer dripping fire, promethium sloshing in the tanks on its back. A claw caught the fuel line and tore it loose. The explosion rocked the corridor.

Oleander hunched forward as the flames washed over him. The optic lenses of his helmet darkened to compensate for the sudden light. Sensors pinpointed the daemonette as it danced towards him through the flames.

Claws slammed into his shoulders, forcing him back. A face wreathed in a fiery halo pressed itself against the front of his helmet, black eyes wide and unblinking. A tongue pierced by numerous barbs of bone and turquoise slithered across rebreather hoses and the vox-grille. 'Oleander,' the daemonette crooned. 'They will appear in the north, Oleander. Beware.'

Oleander grabbed the creature's burning hair and jerked it back. 'My thanks, lady. But I do not think that message is meant for me.'

The daemonette shrieked and laughed. 'Not yet,' it said. 'But soon.' A hoof flashed, catching him in the midsection. He bent forward and the daemonette flipped backwards. Its hooves struck the far wall and it crouched there, head turning. It spotted Arrian and licked its cheek. 'Would you like to know what lies your teacher told you?'

'Not especially,' Arrian said. A falax blade snapped out, but a claw intercepted it. The daemonette bent at an impossible angle and drove its free claw into the World Eater's side. Ceramite cracked and Arrian stumbled. The daemonette wrapped itself about him like a snake.

'Won't you, oh won't you walk with me?' it sang. It caught his throat with its claws. Arrian fell backwards, his arms pinned to his sides by its legs.

Oleander hesitated, but only for a moment. He recovered his sword and raised it over his head. 'My lady, might I escort you from this harsh realm?'

The daemonette rotated its head on its swanlike neck.

It tittered and bowed its head. 'Make it hurt,' it purred. Oleander's sword fell, chopping through unnatural flesh and bone. The body began to dissolve as Arrian fought his way free.

'Do you normally ask permission before you kill something?'

'Good manners go a long way in the Eye,' Oleander said, helping the other Apothecary to stand. 'Especially when it comes to the servants of the Prince of Pleasure.'

'Still, a lucky blow, brother,' Arrian said.

'Hnh. I have this feeling that my luck is none too good,' Oleander said, thinking of what the daemonette had said. He was not surprised it knew him, but that it had decided to warn him was worrying. He ran a hand along the surface of the blade. Ichor clung to it, despite his best efforts. He dabbed his finger into it and brought it to his lips. 'My desire outstrips my skill, you see. It's been that way for as long as I can remember. I lust for all the things the gods promise... but I lack the skill to claim those things.' The daemon's blood was potent. His eyes fluttered as it hit his system. It was like fire and ice, and he hissed in pleasure.

'You and every other fool in the Eye,' Arrian said. 'The whispers you hear are not daemons or gods, but your own petty ambitions reflected back at you.' He paused and tapped one of his skulls with the pommel of a blade. 'Correct as always, brother. Say, rather, that the gods are us and we are the gods. Our masters are our slaves, and vice versa.' He kicked at the dissolving remains of the dae-monette. 'And such things as this are even less.'

'So you're saying I have no one but myself to blame?'

'It is my considered opinion that you should always blame yourself, Oleander. Even if it wasn't your fault,'

Arrian said. He paused, head cocked. 'Perhaps especially if it wasn't your fault. You could do with some perspective.'

'You don't like me very much, do you?'

Arrian clashed his blades together and turned. 'I do not think about you. That you think I do is your problem, not mine.' He tapped his head with the tip of a blade. 'I see things as they are, not as I might wish them to be.' He swatted the faded caduceus symbol on his shoulder-plate with the flat of a blade. 'It is the only way I can hold on to who I used to be.'

'I'm not sure that there's anything left of the man I used to be,' Oleander said.

'Don't worry. From where I stand, you're still the same petty, shallow deviant you always were,' Arrian said. He spun his blades and thrust them home into their sheaths.

'And you're still the same dismissive fool I remember,' Oleander said, peering down the length of his sword. 'It's nice that some things never change, isn't it?' He sheathed the blade with a flourish. He still felt the pleasant warmth of the daemon's blood on his lips. He would discover what its warning had meant when it was time and not before.

'Yes,' Arrian said. 'Especially in the Eye.' The vox crackled. 'Our master calls.'

'So he does,' Oleander said. 'Must be time to go planetside.'

They made their way back to the command deck. Bile was waiting on them, along with Tzimiskes and the Gland-hounds. The augmented humans had come through the daemonstorm in good order. Only one had died, her head twisted up into a tight spiral of flesh and bone by something that'd had a child's laugh and a wolf's face. The daemon's remains were now one of many crucified

against the wall of the deck, its ichor being drained off
into several ritually prepared flasks by a number of chittering vat-born.

'Tzimiskes and the adepts have seen to the necessary
repairs and system cleansings. We are approaching our
destination,' Bile said, his eyes on the viewscreen. 'You
are unhurt? *Vesalius* registered an explosion...'

'A flamer went up. Nothing serious,' Arrian said. 'Oleander had a conversation with a daemon.'

'And what did it say?' Bile said, still looking at the screen.

'Nonsense, mostly, and of no concern.' Oleander
shrugged. 'Not to me, at least.'

A smile quirked at the edges of Bile's mouth. 'How
fortunate.'

Saqqara joined them before Oleander could reply.
From the chill that accompanied him as he clomped up
onto the command deck, Oleander thought he'd been
successful in binding those lesser daemons he'd found.
A number of small crystalline flasks, etched with sigils
and banded in iron, now hung from his armour. Within
each of the daemon-flasks fanged maws gnashed silently
and impossible limbs flailed. 'I have the last of them,' he
said, without preamble.

'Some of them. We dispatched the rest,' Arrian said.
Saqqara glanced at him, and then away. His face was
pale, his expression strained. Oleander wondered how
much it had cost him to protect the ship from the full
force of the daemonstorm. There was always a price to
be paid for such things – a toll of mind, soul and body.
But then, Saqqara had likely bargained away at least one
of those long before he'd ever had the bad luck to cross
paths with Bile.

'Excellent,' Bile said. He tapped one of the flasks, disturbing the cloudy shape within. 'I can make use of these. Well done, Saqqara.'

'If I did not have this bomb in my chest, I would unleash them upon you, idolater,' Saqqara said. He didn't sound angry. More resigned, than anything. Oleander almost felt sorry for him. It was no easy thing, to be a man of the gods in godless company.

Bile nodded. 'I am certain you would.' He turned. 'A successful test, I feel. And perhaps a sign of greater things to come, if one puts stock in such things.' He looked at Wolver. 'Take us in.' The strategium overseer passed along the command and the *Vesalius* slid forward, following the trajectory Wolver had devised. The occulus split, showing what lay before them from multiple angles before settling on one.

'Well, there's something you don't see every day,' Oleander said.

The core of the world bled fire. It was like staring into the sun, only with fewer pleasant after-effects, Oleander decided. Continent-wide skeins of magma and superheated gas stretched out like a shimmering spider's web, connecting the disparate shards of Sublime to one another. Occasionally, minuscule motes of light flickered on these boiling strands.

'What are those?' Saqqara said.

'Gas-miners. Ore-sifters. There are pumping stations and listening posts as well,' Oleander said. 'I know of one fellow who collects vox-captures of Sublime's death-scream and sells them at the howl-markets on Barakshi.'

Saqqara looked at him, puzzled. Oleander gestured to the core. 'The planet is still dying, brother. Just very, very slowly. Some people like to hear that sort of thing. Music of the spheres, you might say... why, on Barakshi you can purchase a small moon for the price of the sound of a black hole devouring itself.' He smiled at the Word Bearer. 'Have you ever heard such a sound? It is... transcendent. Dare I say, even life changing?'

Saqqara turned away. 'I should like to hear it some time,' he said, peering at the screen. 'It looks as if there's a war brewing.'

Sprawling hive domes clustered against the underside of the planet's expanding crust. Lights flashed among them. Not the light of industry, but of war. Artillery, designed to hurl death across oceans, now sent it screaming through the void. 'Beautiful,' Arrian said, as a city vanished in nuclear flame.

'It is proof of the strength inherent in the base materials,' Bile said. 'Humanity adapts so that it might wage a more efficient form of war. They will endure any hardship, just for the chance to cave in a neighbour's skull. Look – see. This is the tenacity which conquered the stars, and which shall, in the end, conquer even the Eye itself.'

'With our help,' Arrian said.

'Yes. We were created to guide mankind into the future. To oversee the birth of a new race. One which will outstrip even our accomplishments. We do not set the fire so that we might rule the ashes, my brothers... no, we set it so that the old might give way before the new.' Bile clasped his hands behind his back. 'Take comfort, my brothers. It is a battle we cannot lose, for we have already won.'

Oleander suspected that last bit was directed not at them, but at Kanathara. It was plain to him that the daemon's words had disturbed Bile. There were cracks in his

armour of contempt. Thoughts of mortality creeping up
on him had weakened the foundations of Bile's faith in
himself, and the daemon had exploited them. Oleander
studied his former master. When he'd first joined the Consortium, Bile had seemed almost... godlike. A lunatic god,
to be sure, but divine nonetheless. Now, he looked older.
Almost... broken. Like a statue, weathered into featureless
ruin by time and neglect.

But not completely. There was a spark there. Bile spoke
of setting fires and Oleander intended to do just that
before this affair was over. Burn away the mistakes of the
past, so that the future might prosper.

'There it is,' Bile said. Oleander looked at the screen.
Black Golan rose wild before them. The archaeomarket
occupied the largest section of Sublime's broken crust,
spreading across both sides as well as within. A massive
corridor had been bored through the rock, large enough
for dozens, if not hundreds of ships to pass through, and
the market stretched along the inner curve as far as the
eye could see or sensors could capture.

As *Vesalius* passed through the borehole, the vox began
to crackle with traffic. Small personal craft and larger
escort vessels jostled each other for space, occasionally
breaking into open conflict. While Black Golan itself was
inviolate, its airspace was not. Oleander watched a small
craft spin out and streak into the void, trailing fire. 'I have
missed this place,' he said.

'I see no eldar craft,' Saqqara said. 'Are you certain they
are here?'

'The Corsairs come to sell their spoils here. Black Golan
is one of the few places near the Eye that they can do so
safely. They are here – or they will be,' Oleander said.

'But how do you know?' Saqqara said.

Oleander looked at him. 'You have your daemons, brother, even as I have my own.'

Saqqara made as if to press the point further, but Bile silenced him with a gesture. 'Oleander knows better than to drag us out here on a fool's errand. If he were not certain, we would not be here.' Bile scratched his chin. 'Nevertheless, I do not care for the thought of simply waiting for them to show up.'

'Nor do we have to.' Oleander smiled. 'I already have hounds on their trail. All we must do is find them, and they will send us on the right path.'

'Find a man to find a man to find a man,' Arrian said. 'It's like a game to you, isn't it?'

Oleander glanced at him. 'If you like.'

'And what happens when we find them?' Saqqara asked. 'Do we flush them out? Find where they congregate and attack?' He sounded eager.

'No,' Bile said. 'We are surgeons, not savages. The scalpel, not the sword.' He looked at Igori and the Gland-hounds. 'This is what you were built for, my dear. Ready to go hunting?'

Igori lit the narc-stick and sucked a lungful of acrid smoke into her lungs. All at once, she felt a wave of calm roll through her, soothing her anxieties. She did not feel fear, as she once had. But her experience on the command deck had come close. The daemons had whispered things to her. Nonsensical things. False things. She had tried her best not to listen. They were lies made flesh, as the Benefactor said.

But the Benefactor had made her curious, as well as

strong. Curious enough to listen, just a bit. To hear and consider the creature called Kanathara's parting words. She knew who the Phoenix was. Fulgrim, daemon-primarch of the Third. The thought of such a creature made her ill, and she forced it aside. She puffed on her narc-stick, enjoying the taste, letting it calm her. Vices were to be indulged, in moderation. That too was as the Benefactor had said. Moderation kept you sharp, hungry, and ready.

She stood in the deployment bay alongside her cadre, watching as a slave-crew of mutants saw to the preparation of the *Butcher-Bird* for deployment. The gunship was a hulking thing, all sharp angles, missile-pods and gun-muzzles, and its hull and thrusters were bound to the deck by heavy chains. It had been cobbled together from a diverse array of parts, including the remains of several Stormbirds, by Apothecary Tzimiskes, and its machine-spirit was a testy chimera. Its pilots had been hardwired servitors, but they were long since mummified by exposure to the vacuum. No one knew what piloted it now, and the Benefactor didn't appear to care, so long as it followed his orders.

More than once, *Butcher-Bird* had escaped its cage aboard *Vesalius* – or been released; the frigate had a nasty sense of humour – and strafed the ruins of Urum, killing anything it could. She admired such implacable dedication to murder, just not when it was aimed at her. Murder was how they served the Benefactor. Murder was how they repaid him for his kindness. They murdered, so that he might make miracles.

She glanced at her pack, studying them. They had performed admirably enough, when the daemons had spilled into the ship. Only one had died, and Sasha was no loss in the grand scheme of things. They'd showed no fear, no weakness. That was good. Weakness had to be excised from the body, so said the Benefactor. She could smell their eagerness for the hunt to come. It wasn't often that they were unleashed off the battlefield. This would be a good hunt. Exciting.

Idly, she played with her necklace of teeth. The Benefactor frowned on trophies, but he'd made an exception for her. He rarely denied her anything, though she was careful not to abuse his consideration. The Benefactor giveth and the Benefactor taketh away. As she inhaled another lungful of smoke, she noticed one of the gunship's autocannons tracking her every move. Luckily, *Butcher-Bird*'s ammunition hoppers were kept dry until just before take-off. Even so, she stepped back, putting more slaves between herself and the gunship. No reason to tempt the beast. In any event, it would glut itself before the hunt was done.

'Scared, First?'

Igori didn't turn. 'No. Just cautious, Second. What about you? Was that your piss I smelled on the bridge?'

Muted laughter swept the bay. Igori turned then, stubbing out her narc-stick on her palm. The pain was good, if too brief. She felt her adrenal glands tighten in expectation. She flicked the remains of the narc-stick at her Second. Ortiz grimaced and swiped the ashes from his chest. Ortiz was bigger than she was, but not by as much as he liked to think. He was a scar-faced slab of brute-muscle. A gripper, rather than a chaser or a stalker. Almost as strong as one of the Benefactor's brethren, thanks to the glandular augmentation he'd undergone.

'I piss acid, First. If it had been mine, it'd have burned a hole in the deck.'

'Or in your–' one of the others began. Ortiz whirled, fist plunging out like a piston. The joker fell back with a yelp, clutching his face. Igori sighed. She could smell the anger bleeding off her Second. The fear and the fury mixing into aggression. Her hand fell to the knife sheathed on the back of her belt. It was a special knife, that one. Her heart-picker. The blade was rounded and shaped to core through a Space Marine's reinforced breastbone with one good whack. It'd do for Ortiz just as well.

He turned back to her, grinning. His teeth were blackened spikes. He'd shaved and stained them himself. And he'd put them to good effect more than once. They could also deliver a potent venom, derived from some death-world insect the Benefactor cultivated in his apothecarium. His smile was a warning, as much as anything.

Ortiz had been testing her for months now. Prowling around her, waiting for her to hesitate. To show weakness. Igori didn't blame him. She'd done the same, in her time. She hadn't always been First, after all. But Ortiz was too eager, too hungry for it. It'd be a shame to lose him, but there it was.

'I think you were scared, First. I heard you scream,' he said. He flexed his fingers. He could rip up a deck plate with those fingers.

'Surprised you could hear anything, the way you were carrying on, Second,' she said. She didn't tense. If she tensed up, she'd give the game away. He'd know she was ready for him, and he'd back down. She was tired of having to back him down. It was time to be done with it. 'Crying like a baby, you were.'

The others watched them in silence, alert to the sights and smells their leaders were giving off. Whoever died, one of the others would be getting a promotion. Third would become Second, and so on. It was all very polite, until you got to the razor's edge. Then it all went red and wet. That was life for you. 'Weren't crying, neither,' Ortiz said. He licked his teeth. He was blinking too much. Something was running through his system. Probably several somethings. 'Growling, First. Showing my teeth.'

'And what big teeth they are,' Igori said. She wrapped her fingers around the hilt of the knife. 'Step close, and I'll break them for you.'

Ortiz snapped forward. His blow was precise, but too slow. She slapped it aside with the flat of her palm as she drew her knife with her other hand. His eyes widened a fraction as he heard the hiss of the blade leaving its sheath. She whipped around, driving the knife into the small of his back with every iota of strength she possessed. Ortiz was too strong to play with. She needed him down soonest. Bone crunched, and his legs lost their strength.

Igori stepped back as Ortiz sank to his knees. Whining, he clawed for the blade. She kicked the knife, severing his spinal column. There was no honour in a fair fight. Only in victory. That was the first lesson the Benefactor taught his dogs. She looked around. 'Well?' she asked quietly. Eyes flicked away from her. That was good. They knew their place. 'Darax... you're Second now.'

Darax nodded. He was a sallow-faced, hollow-cheeked thing. His skin was stretched tight over reinforced bones, and his limbs were dotted with implant-studs. He scratched at one and said, 'Ortiz?'

'Meat for the beast,' Igori said. She turned and set her foot to the back of Ortiz's neck. She shoved him over and retrieved her knife. He gave a short scream as she did so.

He glared up at her through tear-filled eyes and snapped his teeth. She kept her hands out of reach. He couldn't walk, but he could still bite. She caught the back of his leg and began to drag him towards the *Butcher-Bird*.

The gunship twitched in its chains when it caught sight of her. It rose slightly off the deck, thrusters humming in appreciation. Its weapons shuddered and thrashed eagerly. Even with its hoppers dry there were things it could do. Ortiz began to whine again when he realised what she intended. She heard a hiss of bubbling metal and glanced back. 'Hunh.'

He did piss acid, after all.

CHAPTER EIGHT

Black Golan

Black Golan spread across the shattered city like a fungal outbreak. Vast tents and temporary bunkers jostled for space with less coherent structures – crystalline towers that shone with all colours and none, mounds of heaving filth and vast, unnatural beasts, which plodded along carrying shops and stalls on their backs or in their gullets.

Everywhere voices were raised in a threnody of opportunism. Some were human, most were not. Humans were not the only sapient species to seek refuge in the roiling expanse of the Eye of Terror. Nor were they alone in their acquisitiveness, when it came to the detritus of long-dead empires. There were hrud Ssaak-merchants, wrapped in thick rags and proffering bottles of see-mist to passers-by and enigmatic Zygo bartering with eight-legged Rak'Gol pirates over the spoils of raids for bionic implants and weapons.

Oleander inhaled and sighed rapturously. 'I do so love going to market,' he said, stepping over a scuttling, reptilian creature clad in a hauberk made of copper scales. 'So much to see – to experience.' He wore a thick, shape- less cloak over his armour, and a heavy cowl over his head. While renegades of all sorts were a common sight on worlds like Sublime, it wouldn't do to draw unnec- essary attention. There were eyes and ears everywhere in the archaeomarkets and the right word in the wrong ear could complicate matters.

'We are not here to indulge your petty desires,' Saqqara said, pulling his hood tightly about his face as he side- stepped an undulating Sslyth. 'We are here to hunt.'

'Indeed,' Oleander said. 'And I think I see a trace of our quarry.' He pointed towards a group of spindly-limbed, vile-faced Cythors hunkered in the mouth of a cul-de-sac. 'There they are. Just past that knot of Cythors.'

'Where?' Saqqara said, looking around. 'I see no eldar.'

'Who said anything about eldar?' Oleander moved away from the main flow of traffic, heading towards the cul-de-sac. Towering edifices of alien origin rose together, and the cul-de-sac rested between them, nearly hidden by the buboes of rock and root that anchored the structures to the street. The Cythors scattered at Oleander's approaching, bobbing away on too-long legs. Oleander stepped into the cul-de-sac. Saqqara followed him, one hand on his bolt pistol.

'What is that stink?' the Word Bearer muttered. 'It smells like rancid milk and... and...'

'Mint,' Oleander said. 'It takes some getting used to, I admit, but I would say heady rather than nauseating. A true connoisseur of odours might describe it as... poign- ant, even.'

'It stinks,' Saqqara insisted. 'Worse than any servant of Nurgle.'

'Well now that's just hyperbole. I – ah. No sudden movements, brother. They're a twitchy lot,' Oleander said softly. Saqqara looked around. His eyes widened when he caught sight of the monstrous shape clinging to the wall. Yellow eyes stared at the two from the shadows. A second shape scuttled across the upper reaches of the opposite wall.

'Loxatl,' Saqqara said. His voice was thick with revulsion. The sons of Lorgar had many opinions on xenos, mostly revolving around the correct method of dispatch. The Word Bearers wished to share the blessings of the dark gods with no other race but humanity.

'Quietly now,' Oleander said. He extended his hands, showing that they were empty. It was all a formality, really. If the Loxatl had believed him to have bad intentions, they'd have killed both him and Saqqara the moment they set foot in the cul-de-sac. A shape padded forward, out of the dark. It gurgled in greeting.

'Hello, Phot,' Oleander said. 'Is that a new scar?' The Loxatl resembled a massive slimy, scaleless reptile. Its broad, toothy head bobbed on the end of a thick neck, and its purple tongue flickered in and out of its mouth with a disturbing rhythm. Though it crouched on all fours, the xenos was almost the size of a man. A vivid whitish scar marked the side of its grey skull.

Phot gave a gurgling bark. Oleander nodded genially. 'Well, that's what happens when you eat a brood-mate's eggs. Still, you came through intact and that's all anyone can ask. Now... tell me what you've seen.'

The Loxatl gurgled in reply. Oleander smiled when it had finished. 'Excellent. The usual payment will suffice? Good. Same place as last time.' The Loxatl growled, jaws snapping. Oleander glanced at Saqqara. 'Back out slowly.

Phot has a sense of humour and it doesn't translate very well.'

When they'd reached the street, Oleander said, 'Our prey have camped on the Street of Dreams, in the Yupik Quarter. It's not far. They're here to sell their latest spoils.'

'I've heard the Corsairs of the Sunblitz Brotherhood are deadly warriors,' Saqqara said.

'Not so deadly as to worry us.'

Saqqara grunted. 'You seemed on good terms with that... creature. How you can associate with such filth is beyond me. They do not even know the names of the gods, much less how to properly venerate them.'

'Beauty hides in the strangest places,' Oleander said. 'For a time, I was working on a way to replicate the iridescent patterning that flashes and moves across their skins. There are a great many among the Radiant's followers who would kill for such a thing. Unfortunately, Loxatl don't live very long once you remove their skin, and once they die – well.' He shook his head. 'Upon such disappointments are the foundations of knowledge built, they say.'

'Who says?'

'Does it matter?' Oleander looked at Saqqara.

'I was merely curious,' Saqqara said. He looked up, and murmured something. Oleander felt a chill.

'What did you just do?'

'We are being watched. I sent a spy of my own to watch the watcher.'

'You brought a daemon with you?' Oleander asked as he peered upwards, searching for any sign of Saqqara's spies. He suspected he knew who they were, but no sense in spoiling the surprise by sharing that information. They'd reveal themselves soon enough.

Saqqara looked at him and tapped one of the daemon-bottles hanging from his armour. It was now empty, Oleander noted. 'I bring daemons everywhere. They feed on spite, of which I possess an inordinate amount.'

It was Oleander's turn to stare. That had sounded suspiciously like self-awareness, a trait he did not associate with a fanatic like Saqqara. 'Do you?'

'Of course. One must have a bellyful of spite, to contend with the Neverborn,' Saqqara said, piously. 'A heart full of spite, a mind full of hatred and a will of iron. These are the three qualities outlined by Lord Erebus in his seminal treatise...'

Oleander held up a hand in surrender. 'That'll do, thank you.'

'You're afraid of them, aren't you?' the Word Bearer asked.

'I am cautious.'

Saqqara smiled. 'That's not what they say. They say you are worried.'

Oleander's hand fell to his sword. 'Do they say about what?'

Saqqara looked away. 'Not yet.'

'Let me know when they do. It is time to contact the others. We have a xenos to catch.' He activated the sub-dermal vox-link and said, 'If anyone is listening, we have the scent.'

'*Good. Butcher-Bird is en route. We will converge on your coordinates.*'

Oleander severed the link and looked at Saqqara. 'Let's go. The Yupik Quarter is that way.'

'What is this Street of Dreams you mentioned?' Saqqara said, as they forged a path through the crowded streets. 'It sounds decadent.'

'It can be,' Oleander said. 'Depends on the dream. The merchants there trade in them. Nightmares as well. And buy them, if you're of a mind to sell. I know of a warrior of the Third who bartered away his recollections of Fulgrim's apotheosis for the dream of a hrud migration. Another sold his last dream of the Corpse-Emperor for the price of a nightmare involving the fleshworks of the Dark City.'

Saqqara snorted. 'A bad bargain.'

'Actually, I thought I got the better end of the deal on that one. I intend to visit Commorragh one day. A man could learn and experience much there, if he's of a suitably strong stomach.' Oleander laughed at the look on Saqqara's face. 'Keep your daemons close – they might prove useful.'

The avenues of the city swelled or dwindled without rhyme or reason. Like Sublime, the city was dying. Collapsing over the course of centuries, rather than days or weeks. Phantoms wandered the streets, hollow wisps of soulfire that clustered about the stalls and tents. They scattered like frightened birds at the approach of the Chaos Space Marines.

'There,' Oleander said. He pointed towards a free-standing stone archway that loomed above the avenue. It was hung with broken swords and shattered pieces of armour. 'Welcome to the Street of Dreams,' he said, as they passed beneath it.

'It looks like every other street in this flea-pit,' Saqqara said. He lurched away from an iron gibbet-cage, as the Chaos spawn trapped within began to yowl and gibber. What might have been the remains of crimson power armour showed through the folds of iridescent,

FABIUS BILE: PRIMOGENITOR

suppurating flesh as it pounded on the frame, and shrieked nonsense syllables.

'Looks can be deceiving. They say the gods hold more sway here.'

'We are near the Eye, Oleander. Where do the gods *not* hold sway?' Saqqara said, still staring at the gibbering spawn.

'I'm merely passing along a bit of folk wisdom, Saqqara,' Oleander said. 'No need to make a debate of it.'

'Dogma is like tough meat. It is best well-chewed. So says Kor Phaeron, in his seventy-second epistle,' Saqqara said. 'I wonder who he was.'

Oleander glanced at the gibbering spawn. 'No one of any consequence,' he said. Only the weak or foolish allowed themselves to be ruined so. The gods were best kept at arm's length, unless you had the wit to deal with them.

'All are of consequence, in the eyes of the gods. In every man is the seed of a newborn glory, waiting to take root and flourish.'

'You sound like the Chief Apothecary.'

Saqqara turned. 'Even in him, the seed waits.'

'Is that why you haven't killed him yet?'

Saqqara touched his chest. 'My reasons are manifold, sybarite. But that is one, yes. When daemons speak, a wise man listens, so that he might sort truth from lie.'

'And what do the daemons say about our master?'

'That he has run free too long. And soon he will be brought to heel.' The Word Bearer's scarred features split in a crooked smile. 'I look forward to that day, and my part in it.' He stiffened. 'There. Look.' Oleander turned.

Ahead of them, lithe shapes in orange and gold armour cut through the crowd. It was easy to recognise eldar, even in a crowd as diverse as this. No other race moved with such casual, arrogant grace and implied disdain for their surroundings.

'Bargaining for dreams and narcotics, just as Phot said,' Oleander said, watching one of the creatures approach a stall.

'They will flee the moment they see us,' Saqqara said.

'Well, that is the plan,' Oleander said. He flipped back his hood, and parted his cloak, so that his armour showed through. The crowd parted around him. He could taste the fear, and found it good. The Legion Wars were over, but the inhabitants of the regions around the Eye had long memories. He drew his sword, and began to sing. The song had no words, so far as he knew. He'd learned it from a gladiatrix of Commorragh, one sweet evening. Her brain had tasted like pain and regret, and it made his soul shiver to recall it.

The Corsairs whirled as the first notes struck the air like metal striking crystal. Oleander smiled. 'Set the dogs on them, brother. Leave one alive. Butcher the rest.'

Saqqara unsealed several of his daemon-flasks, and spoke a single, deplorable word. The air grew cold and something unseen speared past Oleander as the fabric of reality tore like thin cloth. The daemons solidified as they neared their quarry, lumps of solid meat and bone growing from a flickering fog. There were three of them, and they resembled elongated, skinless dogs, trailing blue ichor in their wake. Shuriken catapults whined as the Corsairs scattered, seeking cover in the panicking crowd. The daemons overturned stalls and tore through hapless merchants as they bounded towards the eldar. One daemon burst like an overripe fruit, torn asunder by a burst from an eldar weapon.

A daemon sprang onto a Corsair, bearing it to the ground. The alien groped for a blade as the daemon snapped fuming jaws. A knife flashed, and the dog-thing's head spurted free of its neck. Saqqara cursed. Something flickered out of the corner of Oleander's eye and he spun, snatching his bolt pistol from its holster. His shot caught the Corsair in the chest, the explosive round nearly bisecting the alien. The Corsair's final shot went wild, striking the gibbet-cage behind them. The Chaos spawn surged out, free.

The monstrosity ploughed towards Saqqara. It tackled the Word Bearer and they slammed backwards into a poison stall, scattering vials and shattering vats of noisome concoctions. Oleander turned to help Saqqara as the last daemon gave a yelp and melted into sludge, its body shot to pieces. The remaining eldar fled, moving more quickly than his eye could follow. 'They're running,' he said, into the vox-link. 'I'll follow, as soon as I fish Saqqara out of this Chaos spawn's belly. Release the hounds.'

Igori ran. It was one of her great joys in life, to run. To chase. To hunt. She leapt across the gap between rooftops and platforms without slowing down. Every nerve, every sense was firing as she moved. The weight of her weapons was a comfort as she moved. She'd added a laspistol and an autogun to her gear. Both were sufficient for the hunt at hand. Eldar were fragile. Nothing like the Angels she normally hunted.

She leapt and caught hold of tent pole. Without slowing, she swung around it and sprang to a broken rampart. She scrambled up the incline, dislodging loose stones in her wake. She could smell the stink of her quarry's fear.

Eldar had a peculiar odour – brittle, yet distinctive. Like too-cold water, or melting ice. They were beneath her, racing for the safety of their encampment. Searching for strength in numbers.

A good plan. Too bad the Benefactor had thought of it. He wanted them scared and running, ready for a war that never came. Looking one way, while something else happened behind them. That was how the Benefactor fought – misdirection and shadows. Open battle was for fools, and a waste of good materials.

Igori kept her eyes on her quarry. The Benefactor only needed one. She'd chosen at random, relying on her instincts to gauge the weakest. This one was wounded, leaving a blood trail. It was always best to start with the weakest. She'd learned that as a child. Weak, and feeding on other weak things. Catching squealing rats, down in the dark and quiet.

Her memories of her life before the Benefactor were faded things, empty of all colour and meaning. She remembered being hungry. Being cold. Being afraid. Now she was none of those things. Now she was strong. In her veins flowed the blood of the gods themselves. But she still enjoyed feeding on weak things. She swung her autogun up on its strap and fired without slowing, stitching a wall ahead of her prey. The eldar darted aside, away from its kin.

'Run-run, little meat,' she growled. She heard the rattle of gunfire and the howls of her pack, as they widened the gap between her quarry and the other Corsairs. Cutting off all avenues of retreat and aid. She laughed, pleased. Darax was already proving more competent than Ortiz.

Her laughter turned into a yelp of surprise as a shuriken

pistol spat. She leapt from the roof and hit the street, rolling to her feet. She swung the autogun around, only to have it torn from her hand by another rapid shot from the xenos weapon. The alien crouched atop a fallen stall, smoking pistol extended. It had one delicate hand pressed to a gash in its side, where something had torn open its psycho-reactive armour.

It took aim, readying itself for another shot. Before it could pull the trigger an autogun roared, chewing the stall to flinders and sending the eldar ducking for cover. Hampered by its wound, it fell heavily. The shuriken pistol skidded from its grip. When it rolled to its feet, there was a thin-bladed knife in its hand.

Darax and the others began to fire, driving the creature back towards her. She considered going for her laspistol, but grabbed her knife instead. It was better with knives. Hunts ended in blood either way, but she wanted to see the pain in her prey's eyes up close. She drew her blade and charged, using the rubble that littered the avenue to launch herself at it.

The eldar moved with boneless speed, slicing at her even as she landed. Igori leapt back, not quite quick enough. Blood dappled her belly where the tip of the xenos' blade had kissed her flesh. She laughed. 'Close, meat.' Igori drew her knife. 'Now – try again,' she said. She made a come-hither gesture. 'Come on. Hurry, little meat.'

The eldar did. It whipped forward, snake-swift. Their knives connected with a screech and Igori staggered back, momentarily surprised by her quarry's strength. She shoved back and the eldar retreated, falling into a defensive stance. Even wounded, the creature still had some fight in it. The Corsair extended a hand and copied her earlier gesture.

Igori laughed. 'Your wish is my command,' she said. She lunged forward, blade held low. The eldar's weapon flashed down to meet hers as she'd hoped. Igori slid and rolled, driving her shoulder into her opponent's chest. They slammed back into the wall, cracking the ancient masonry. The Corsair's knife kissed her again, forcing her to drop her own blade. She drove her fingers into the wound in the creature's side and twisted. The eldar shrieked, and Igori smashed her reinforced skull against the front of its helmet. Alien metal buckled and cracked.

Igori staggered back, head aching. She raised her fingers to her mouth and tasted them. 'Like honey,' she said. The eldar spat something in its musical tongue and slashed at her with its knife. The blow was wild. Igori bent away from it and caught her opponent's arm at the wrist. She struck the eldar's elbow with the palm of her free hand. Bone cracked, and the Corsair cried out again. Igori smashed her elbow into the side of the swaying eldar's neck, and hooked its ankle with her foot.

It clawed at Igori as it fell, and she collapsed atop it, pinning it with her weight. Catching hold of its throat she raised her fist. She struck it with piston-like blows, hammering at the cracked helmet and the head within. Her knuckles were bleeding and her fingers ached by the time it sagged into unconsciousness. Shaking her injured hand, she clambered to her feet.

Darax and the others trotted towards her, grinning and laughing. It had been a good show. 'It's still twitching, First,' he said. 'Want me to gut it?'

'The Benefactor wants it alive, Second. So leave its guts where they are.' Igori reached over and tore the sleeve from his shirt. She wrapped it around her hand, knotting the makeshift bandage with her teeth. They healed quickly, thanks to the Benefactor's ministrations. The rag would do, until everything scabbed over.

'Look, it dropped its toy,' one of the others said. He held up the shuriken pistol.

'Give it,' Darax growled. 'I'm Second, it's mine.'

Igori let them snarl at each other for a moment, as she recovered her knife. When Darax yanked the weapon away, she tapped his shoulder with the flat of her blade. He handed it over, a sullen expression on his face. She thrust it through her belt. 'My kill. My toy,' she said. 'Arguments?'

No one met her gaze. Ortiz's fate was still too fresh in their minds. She smiled and activated the vox-link implanted in her jaw. 'We have it, Benefactor.'

CHAPTER NINE

Harlequinade

The gabbling hordes of the marketplace had dispersed by the time Bile arrived. The air trembled with the sound of transports and crawlers, as many sought safety elsewhere in the labyrinthine avenues of Black Golan. Others hunched in their stalls or crowded beneath their tents, watching the procession of renegade Apothecaries with fearful gazes. Eldar reavers, clad in spiked, chitinous armour, hissed amongst themselves as they made way for the renegades. Off-world mutants and warp-blessed human cultists knelt in silent devotion, murmuring prayers to the dark gods as the Space Marines passed by.

Bile ignored them all with studied indifference. He led the way, hands behind his back, as if he were strolling through his laboratorium on Urum. Oleander and the others followed, hands on their weapons. They were not undefended – Tzimiskes had decided that now would be a good time to test one of his Castellax. It lumbered in their wake, murmuring ponderously to Tzimiskes in static-laced binary.

'I envy you, brother,' Oleander said, looking at Saqqara. 'What an experience that must have been.' The Word Bearer's battered armour was covered in swiftly drying sputum and the marks of oscillating fangs marred its surface. 'What was it like, inside that spawn's belly?'

'I'm amazed it didn't regurgitate him as swiftly as it swallowed him,' Arrian said.

'It was... unpleasant,' Saqqara said, scraping at his armour. 'I'm going to have to re-etch all of this,' he added, morosely. He made a sign of blessing as mutants clutched at his legs, babbling unintelligibly.

Oleander restrained a laugh. Saqqara had been taken by surprise, more than anything. The Chaos spawn had nearly swallowed him whole, growing a new mouth, and inflating its gullet just for the occasion. Only the Word Bearer's quick thinking had allowed him to find the thing's shrivelled brainstem and rip it free from its malformed skull. The spawn had deflated like a punctured balloon, leaving Saqqara standing amidst the wreckage.

Neither of them had mentioned the shattered chunks of crimson power armour within that wreckage. Armour with a distinctive burning sigil, and words scratched across its surface. The Eye could kill you in a thousand different ways, and sometimes it did worse than that. Sometimes what survived wasn't you any more, or wished it wasn't.

His good humour faded. Some degradations were too far, even for a warrior of the Third. But unavoidable, if you trafficked in the stuff of the empyrean. The warp was like slow acid, eating away at you one drop at a time. First went oaths, then discipline, then brotherhood, and then, finally, your sense of self. The Emperor's Children were perhaps too far along that path to be salvaged. But while the body lived, there was hope.

That was what this was all about – hope. Hope for the future, hope for greater pleasures and meaningful pains. Something caught his eye, a spindly shadow-shape, crouched beneath a slumped tent. He could not see its face, but he recognised it nonetheless. He gave no sign that he had seen it. Let them play their game. He would play his.

The Gland-hounds were waiting for them, like the loyal curs they were. Igori sat on top of the unconscious eldar, playing with a curious crystalline knife. She slid the knife through her belt as she rose to her feet. Hand resting on the butt of a shuriken pistol, she said, 'It lives, Benefactor. As you commanded.'

'So I see, Igori. I am very pleased.' Bile caught up her bandaged hand. The Gland-hound winced as the blades of the chirurgeon sliced through the blood-soaked rag, revealing the bruised and torn flesh beneath. 'Oh, this won't do. You have weapons for a reason, my child.'

'Expedience was called for, Benefactor,' Igori said.

'Yes. Nothing too serious. A few shards of psycho-reactive metal in your knuckles. Your body will expel them in time. Until then, I shall close these cuts...' The chirurgeon hissed, as a bone-torch flared and passed over Igori's hand. Her face paled, and the smell of cauterised flesh filled the air. Oleander expected her to scream, but she had remarkable control. Bile released her hand and waved away the smoke. Igori cradled her hand, jaw tight.

Oleander stooped and rolled the eldar over. The Corsair was clad in orange and gold, with an ashy check pattern along one arm. The sigil of the Sunblitz Brotherhood decorated its tabard. Its helmet had been dented and cracked. Carefully, he eased it off. The face beneath was female, he thought, though it was hard to tell with eldar. Even harder, given the amount of blood and bruising that obscured its features. He checked its bio-signs with his narthecium. 'It still lives. Just.' He probed the wound in its side. A clear pus dappled the flesh there – daemon-sign. 'We'll need to see to its wounds, if it's to survive, however.'

'And so we will, when we are safe aboard the *Vesalius*,' Bile said, rubbing a spot of blood from Igori's cheek with his thumb. 'More than once I have questioned the Emperor's wisdom in bestowing his gifts upon but one half of the human race. For in man, as in all beasts, the female is the deadlier of the species. You are a thing of furious beauty, my dear, and never let anyone tell you different.'

'She nearly killed it,' Oleander said, rising to his feet. He heard a deep thudding overhead and looked up. Precipitation began to patter down from above. The rain was more like blood, or perhaps oil, than water. It left greasy streaks across his armour. Perhaps what was left of Sublime's atmosphere was weeping.

A moment later he staggered as a number of gleaming, monomolecular flechettes bit into his forearm as a shuriken catapult barked. He stepped back, cradling his arm. Arrian and Saqqara fired their bolt pistols in the direction the shot had come from. Orange-clad shapes streaked through the rain and sought cover among the tents and stalls. 'They've regrouped more quickly than I expected,' Oleander said.

'That's why we brought Tzimiskes' pet,' Arrian said. 'Brother.' Tzimiskes nodded brusquely, and the Castellax battle-automaton's weapons systems whirred to life.

At the Iron Warrior's gesture, the war-engine lurched into action, sweeping the marketplace with suppressing fire. The bolt cannons thundered with predatory precision, zeroing in on any movement, no matter how small. Eldar and merchants alike died, caught in the crossfire. Oleander laughed, watching the carnage.

His good humour faded as he caught a flash of chromatic light and motion out of the corner of his eye. His vox-link crackled, and he thought he heard laughter. There were more than just Corsairs out there. He cursed.

'What was that?' Saqqara said. Oleander wondered whether the Word Bearer had heard the laughter. He shook his head. He doubted it.

'Just calling down the curses of the Prince on them, brother,' he said.

'Good. Piety does you credit,' Saqqara said, satisfied.

As the Castellax drew the Corsairs' fire, Bile snapped a command. Igori stooped, and hauled their captive up across her shoulders. The Gland-hounds formed up around them, weapons barking. 'Time to depart, I think,' Oleander said, flexing his injured arm. The wound had already sealed, but the pain would last for hours. He wished he had the time to enjoy it. A flash of orange caught his attention. More Corsairs, racing to intercept them. Their jump packs carried them quickly through the twisting streets, more swiftly than any Renegade Astartes.

'They are all around us,' the Word Bearer said, calmly firing at the darting shapes.

'Did you think they were just going to let us leave with one of their own?' Oleander said. The Corsairs were trying to stall them, keep them pinned down. His vox-link crackled, and he heard something that might have been a chuckle. *Count Sunflame led the ragged king to-oh the city,* someone whispered through the static.

'Grenades,' Bile said, calmly. Oleander palmed a grenade from his belt. He primed it with a flick of his finger. Saqqara did the same. They hurled the grenades in opposite directions. The explosions shook the marketplace. Arrian and Tzimiskes joined them, until the air was throbbing with thunderous reverberations. Tents and stalls were torn asunder, or set on fire. Exotic concoctions and alien weapons overheated and exploded, adding to the confusion. Panicked traders ran in every direction.

A Corsair, clad in more ornate armour than the rest, raced forward out of the resulting smoke, propelled by its jump pack. It dropped down, sliding between the legs of the Castellax. It bounded to its feet without slowing and leapt over Tzimiskes, as he swiped at it. The Corsair pelted towards Bile, sword hissing as it swept down. Bile smiled, unconcerned. 'Arrian, if you please.' Arrian moved to intercept the xenos warrior.

Their blades connected with a crash. The Corsair twisted in mid-air and dropped down. It lunged and Arrian met it again. It was faster than the World Eater, but lacked his sheer strength. They swayed back and forth in the oily rain, blades clashing briefly and then springing apart. Wherever the eldar went, Arrian was there to meet it, if only just. They came together and broke apart, moving so quickly that Oleander had trouble following them. A few moments in, an almost casual blow from Arrian's fist sent the eldar skidding back a few paces.

The Corsair rose swiftly, but hesitated, obviously weighing its chances. The shooting had died down during the duel. It cocked its head, as if listening to something.

Oleander heard the laughter again, and he growled in annoyance. They were going to ruin everything.

'Stop flirting and kill the beast, Arrian,' he said. He drew his bolt pistol and took a bead on the Corsair. Before he could fire, the eldar was gone, vanished into the downpour.

Arrian glanced at him, but said nothing. He slid his hand along his blade, freeing it of water, before sheathing it. He turned, studying the smoky street. 'Why did they leave? They had us pinned.'

Oleander hesitated. 'Maybe we killed too many of them. Even Corsairs value their lives.' He holstered his pistol, and turned to find Bile watching him. There was a look of calculation in his old master's eye that he didn't like. 'We should leave while we can.'

Bile nodded. 'Yes.' He looked down at the unconscious body slung across Igori's shoulders and smiled cruelly. 'Besides, this one will serve us well enough.'

The *Butcher-Bird* was waiting for them in the next square, its guns howling as it cleared the area of any potential threat. The Corsairs seemed reluctant to get too close to the gunship, not that Oleander blamed them. Tzimiskes' Castellax was still hunting the market, shooting anything that moved.

When *Butcher-Bird* registered their presence, it cycled down its weapons with a final, petulant screech. 'Get our prize aboard,' Bile said to Igori. 'The rest of you – secure the landing zone. I want no more distractions.'

Even as he said it, a streak of light and fire erupted along the gunship's hull. *Butcher-Bird* squalled in anger and heaved itself back up, thrusters screeching. A second flash followed the first, and then a third, driving the gunship higher and higher. *Butcher-Bird* arced upwards through the rain, seeking to climb out of range. 'What now?' Bile said.

As he spoke, the ground erupted around them, filling the damp air with fire and boiling chemicals. Oleander heard a grisly chuckle emanate down from the rooftops above, and a smattering of polite applause.

'No,' Oleander hissed. 'Not now.' He saw Arrian watching him. 'Did you see where it's coming from?'

'Hard to tell with the rain. My armour's sensors can't get a fix on them. There's more than one, or they're repositioning after every shot,' the World Eater said. 'They've caught us in a crossfire either way. Clever.'

Green and black and gold flashed across the street, as lithe shapes burst into view, but only for a moment. Gland-hounds fired, but hit nothing. Occasionally, a high, whining shriek would sound and an unlucky Gland-hound would burst into flame, or else collapse as if disembowelled by an unseen blade. If the intent of such attacks was to cause panic, the augmented humans didn't oblige. They held their ground, clutching their weapons more tightly and snarling in growing frustration as they huddled in the rain.

Oleander's vox-link spat gibberish. *Prick his flesh, crack his bones, that's the way the story goes.* A moment later, the first of the Harlequins bled out of the rain.

The garishly clad eldar capered forward, blades gleaming. Saqqara turned, slowly, too slowly, but just fast enough to block a fatal blow. Oleander blocked a thrust that would have pierced one of his hearts. Out of the corner of his eye he saw a colourful shape sprint towards Bile. The troupe master's tall crest was gold and green, shot through with black, and its white mask was long nosed and wide eyed.

Bile twisted, but too late. A blade carved through his ceramite as easily as if it were flesh, and blood spurted. A second darted in, as the troupe master flipped away. Bile caught the second Harlequin a blow on the side of the head with his sceptre, obliterating its leering mask and the skull beneath. The body tumbled bonelessly to the ground.

The Harlequins' laughter slipped up and down the vox-frequency, an eerie wordless hum of insect noise. Blades licked out, scoring points off Oleander as he defended himself. The eldar sang as they fought, as if the ambush were nothing more than a performance. *Prick his flesh, crack his bones, that's the way the story goes. Urge him up, strike him down, call him out and pass him round.* Out of the corner of his eye, he saw them circling Bile like brilliantly hued birds, clawing at him and spinning away before he could land a blow.

Tzimiskes charged towards Bile, as the Chief Apothecary sank to one knee. The Iron Warrior's power axe traced blue lightning as it chopped down, shearing bristles from a Harlequin's crest. The eldar turned, and Tzimiskes drove the weighted haft of his axe into its belly, knocking it sprawling.

Oleander moved to help them, but something tangled his legs and he toppled forward. He twisted, and saw his attacker raise its staff in mocking salute. It wore a familiar mask. A mirror of silver, trailing diamond-motes of light. He scrambled to his feet, but the creature was gone a moment later, drifting back into the rain as swiftly as it had appeared. As if that had been a signal, the rest of the Harlequins, even the dead, vanished as if they had never been.

'That's why the Corsairs left,' Bile hissed. 'Harlequins.' He levered himself to his feet, eyeing the colourful shapes that stalked between the tents and stalls warily as he slapped a sealant patch on the hole in his armour. 'A trap, and one we must chew our way out of. Fall back and scatter. Rendezvous at the secondary landing zone. Saqqara, Tzimiskes – accompany Igori. Get our prize to safety, whatever the cost.' He caught hold of Saqqara's gorget and dragged him close. 'Guard our prize with your life, or I will make your last moments stretch for an eternity.' He gestured to one of the other Gland-hounds. 'Darax, you will come with me. We will lead away those we can. Arrian–?'

'Chief Apothecary?'

'Go kill something. You too, Oleander. Make yourself useful and buy us a few moments.' Bile was coughing as he spoke. His wound had already ceased bleeding, but he looked as if it still pained him. Veins stood out starkly in his pale face. Oleander thought of the crumbling statues in the palace on Urum and tried to calculate how much longer Bile's current body would last. It was no wonder he rarely left the crone world.

'Of course, master,' Oleander said. He lurched to his feet and started forward, bolt pistol bucking in his grip. He heard Arrian do the same. And then he heard nothing save laughter, and the skirl of unseen pipes. The Harlequins were all quicksilver and smoke, moving between eye-blinks. They fought with breathtaking synchronicity, barely pausing to strike at Oleander, or avoid his blows. He was forced to holster his pistol when it became obvious that shooting was simply a waste of ammo.

He'd fought their kind before – you had to interrupt the performance, throw off the rhythm, to have any hope of beating them. But that meant knowing which performance it was. He watched them, his armour's sensors recording the movements and trying to match it to older recordings. There was a puerile sort of beauty to be found there. It was as nothing next to the majesty of Slaanesh, obviously, but it had a raunchy sort of splendour.

A readout flashed red and he lunged, catching a handful of check-marked cloth. The Harlequin squawked in dismay. Oleander dragged it out of step and slung it into a stall. 'Someone's out of step,' he said. He twisted back, driving his forearm into the belly of another, as the eldar skittered towards him. The alien bent double and fell, organs ruptured and bones cracked, if not broken. The rest pulled back, changing the choreography.

He set his foot on the chest of the wounded Harlequin. 'Veilwalker,' he said, softly, trusting them to hear. An expectant hush fell over the market. The shadows cast by Sublime's flickering core thickened and lengthened. Hands clapped, not in applause but in accompaniment. A thin shape danced forward, whirling, stomping, clapping in a riotous display of joy. Shrill whistles slipped out of the dark. A new performance had begun.

Oleander felt himself twitch in response to the sight. Something about it drew him in, though he tried to resist. The light went soft and the air pulsed with more than just clapping and stamping. A staff swept out and crunched into the grille of his helmet, rocking him on his feet. He stepped back, and the wounded Harlequin scrambled away. More applause sounded.

'Veilwalker,' Oleander roared. His sword bit air, as the

slim shape whirled aside. 'I know you can hear me, witch. This was not part of our arrangement. Why do you seek to hinder us?'

'You know the way to Lugganath, Oleander Koh. Why do you steal our kin?' a breathy voice whispered almost into his ear. He twisted, but saw only fading motes of light.

'Sacrifice one to save millions,' he said. 'He would have suspected me otherwise.'

'Would he? I think the King of Feathers sees only his regrets. He looks back, not forward. Down, not up.'

'You do not know him.' He turned. The shape was there, but not. He could hear the sounds of gunfire, and the whine of power armour in motion. Arrian was close.

'Oh, but we do. We know all of you, and intimately. You are but brief scenes in a performance as old as time.' It surged forward in a burst of shadows and light. Oleander caught the staff on the length of his blade. The tableau held, impossibly. The Harlequin hung in the air above him, as if it were balancing on the edge of his sword. He could see it clearly now, clad in whirling rags of green and black and gold, and a mirrored mask beneath a cowl of yellow and purple diamonds.

'Shadowseer,' he said.

'Hello, Oleander. Don't be stubborn,' the Shadowseer whispered. 'You are the fulcrum upon which this performance hinges. Accept it, or don't. The play remains the same.'

'What? Why do you attack us? I am doing as we agreed...'

'Such was your part, and you could do no less. You played the role well, mon-keigh. And now we must play ours. He will be bent back into the role fate has decreed, however much he struggles... the King of Feathers must shed his rags, and take his throne.'

Oleander snarled and shoved the seemingly weightless shape back. It flipped gracefully through the air and dropped to the ground. It rose smoothly and contrived a small dance, ending in a deep bow. 'That is the outcome I am attempting to engineer,' Oleander said. 'And you are hindering me.'

'Not hindering, no. Helping. We are all actors on this stage. You are Count Sunflame, seeking to burn away the old king's rags and set him back upon his throne. And we are the ghosts that haunt him. The ones you will drive away.' Oleander took a step forward, feeling impossibly slow and awkward next to the eldar. It bobbed upright, fixing him with a silvery look. 'Are you afraid of the dark, Oleander?'

'I am the dark,' he said, raising his sword.

The Harlequin laughed. 'There is dark and then there is dark, dark, dark. Which are you? Not the one, but sadly, sweetly, the other.'

'What does that mean?' he asked. He swept his blade out, but the Harlequin eeled away from the blow, rolling and spinning over it. The colourful staff crunched against his helmet again, cracking one optic lens and knocking him from his feet. The Harlequin crouched over him, its thin hand sliding up his chest, leaving motes of searing colour dancing along the contours of his armour.

'It means that fate binds tightest those who struggle the fiercest. So relax,' Veilwalker purred. 'All of your arguments are but noise. And those of your master with you. The drama unfolds, and we must all play our parts.' Gravel crunched. The Harlequin sprang up and spun, shuriken pistol spitting. Arrian bulled forward, into the teeth of the fire. The Shadowseer deftly avoided his blades and sprang away, laughing.

Arrian looked down at Oleander. 'Now who's flirting?'

CHAPTER TEN

The Castellan of Castle Sublime

Fabius Bile stalked the market, swatting aside tents and bodies alike with Torment. Darax and the others kept pace, with great difficulty. The Gland-hounds howled and fired at fleeing merchants with seeming indiscretion, as the group made its way to the secondary rendezvous point in a roundabout fashion. In reality, they were drawing the enemy in. Letting them get close, for the final, fatal bite.

He much preferred fighting from a position of strength. Walls, turrets and enough cannon fodder to keep the noise to a dull roar. War was something to be avoided when possible and endured when necessary, in service to a greater cause. He winced and touched the wound in his side. It was healing, but more slowly than normal.

The chirurgeon murmured softly, its impulses flickering up through his thoughts like flashes of lightning. Readouts and displays overlaid his vision, warning him about the imminent failure of this organ or the faltering of that one. He blinked, scrolling through the chemicals that currently inundated his system. He'd overexerted himself. Sadly, an easy thing to do these days. He was running short of time.

But perhaps that wouldn't be a problem for much longer. If he could survive the next few minutes, the likelihood increased significantly. He'd recognised their attackers for what they were almost immediately. Harlequins were a particularly pernicious sub-faction of the species. Cunning and unpredictable, with a distressing tendency to show up when and where they were least wanted. He'd faced them before, much to his regret.

'Almost there, Benefactor,' Darax said, from ahead of him. 'We shall – uhk.' Darax stumbled, slipped and fell to pieces. Bile slid to a halt as all around him, his guards – his creations – died all at once, and silently. One moment they ran, and the next, they fell, and in wet chunks. Bile turned slowly, eyebrow raised in consternation.

Monofilament wires had been stretched across the plaza like the web of some great insect. They glimmered in the light of Sublime's core. Then, with a hiss of displaced air, they retracted. Bile ground his teeth in frustration. 'Rudely done,' he called out, flicking a bit of Darax off his shoulder. 'Those were costly to make.'

A whisper of alien laughter greeted his words. He turned slowly, studying the marketplace. In the light of the core, everything was tinged a dull ochre, even the rain. Shapes seemed to dance and sway just out of the corner of his eye. His armour registered multiple life signs converging on him from all directions. Another trap, then. He recalled the Kanathara's words, before he'd banished the daemon. Was this what it had been trying to tell him?

'Well?' he said. No reply was forthcoming. The only sound was the hiss of the rain. He grunted. 'Panic is the natural predator of strategy. I was blooded in the fires of one of the greatest military undertakings in human history. I will go no further.' He turned. His sensors pinged, their reach muted by the rain and background radiation from Sublime's core.

'You may as well come out. No sense in hiding from me,' Bile continued. 'Take your cue. Strut upon the stage, if you are so eager to perform for me.' More laughter. Light applause pattered down and out. He could perceive them now, but only dimly. Watching. Waiting... for what? It hit him a moment later. 'Ah. Enter the lead.' He turned.

Multi-coloured robes flared out, swirling about the lithe form. Bile stepped back as a blade licked out, nearly taking his head off. He snatched the Xyclos needler from its holster and fired. Thin capillary tubes shot through the air, but the Harlequin avoided them all with sinuous grace. The troupe master paused, bowed low enough that its great, multi-coloured crest of hair swept the muddy street and continued the dance as the rest applauded with gusto. Bile cursed and swept his sceptre up, parrying his attacker's blade as it darted for his throat.

'A weak start,' he said. The white mask, with its too-long nose and fixed grin gave him no indication as to whether the creature even understood him. The Harlequin circled him, moving with incredible speed. A blade drew sparks from his pauldron. He lashed out with Torment, but an almost leisurely backflip carried his opponent out of reach. More applause from the motley audience.

Grinding his teeth in frustration, Bile restrained himself from pursuing the creature. He'd done so earlier, and been wounded for his trouble. So, instead, he waited. It circled him slowly. The carved smile of its mask made it seem as if it were laughing at him.

Look at him, the King of Feathers, dressed in rags... blind to his throne...

Bile twitched, as the voices hissed through his vox-link. 'I suppose this is what passes for drama among your kind,' he said, trying to elicit a reaction. 'Pedestrian, at best. The conclusion is foregone, and with little in the way of true dramatic tension.' One touch with Torment would be enough to dispose of the creature. Pain flared anew in his side. He still hadn't fully recovered, and his exertions had taxed him to the limits of his deteriorating endurance.

He is old... old... old... and alone... alone... alone. Will he, won't he, take the throne?

'Gibberish,' Bile said. The xenos bowed mockingly. He wondered if it could tell he was injured. He slumped, hoping to lure it closer. 'Well?' He coughed. 'Bring this farce to a close.' Instead of darting in, however, the Harlequin backed away, lowering its blade. Bile heard the crunch of boots behind him. 'Master, are you injured?' Oleander said.

'Not as such. Shoot this thing for me, if you would.' Bile coughed into a clenched fist. Blood speckled his gauntlet. Something had torn inside him. The earlier wound had been deeper than he'd suspected.

Even as Oleander fired his bolt pistol, the Harlequin was pirouetting away. 'My apologies, master,' Oleander said, firing into the tangle of tents and shacks, as the others vanished as well. The performance was over. 'Like trying to shoot shadows.'

'Shadows don't fight back.' Bile forced himself to straighten. It wouldn't do to show weakness in front of Oleander. The Harlequin had been toying with him. He was certain of it. But for what purpose? He tightened his grip on Torment. If Oleander hadn't shown up, he might've found out. A fortuitous arrival, but for whom? 'You came at an opportune time.'

'You're welcome, master.'

'What of our prize?'

'Tzimiskes and Saqqara got it back to the lander. The Harlequins weren't interested in them. Arrian is heading back that way now.' Bile nodded. He looked down at the bodies scattered across the street. So much potential, cut short. They'd been too slow, too clumsy against the eldar. He would have to fix that, in the next generation. Strength was not enough. They needed speed as well.

The sound of galloping hooves filled the damp air. Bile grunted in annoyance. 'Damnation. It seems my efforts at concealing our presence have been for naught.'

'What? What is that?' Oleander turned, scanning the empty market.

'We have been discovered,' Bile said. The sound of hooves grew louder. 'I had hoped to avoid this, but two battles in a row... well, too much to hope for, I expect.' He pushed himself erect and levelled his needler. 'Such is life.'

'Master... we are not alone,' Oleander said. The market was no longer empty.

Bile turned, studying the newcomers as they took up positions in the tents and behind the abandoned stalls. They were a mix of races – human, xenos, even a few Renegade Astartes, their armour scrubbed clean of all Legion or Chapter insignia. All previous allegiances had been cast aside. They were loyal now only to Castle Sublime and its Castellan. Weapons of various makes and models were levelled at him and Oleander, but their wielders did not fire. They would not, until their master had had his say.

The sound of hooves grew louder. Bile kept the needler extended. 'It is truly the mark of a provincial backwater when the local lord employs such theatrics, don't you agree, Oleander?'

'Local lord?'

'Come, come, Oleander. Surely you recognise the sound of greatness when it approaches. We are about to be greeted by the Castellan of Castle Sublime in all his dubious glory.'

Oleander hissed in frustration. 'This is not going how I planned.'

'Life so rarely does.' Bile had hoped to avoid this moment. It was a distraction from the matter at hand, and one he could ill afford in his current state. He wiped blood from his lips. 'One must adapt,' he said, even as the rider at last burst into view.

The rider was clad in baroque armour which seemed to shift and warp by the moment. Sometimes it resembled the power armour of a Space Marine, other times the bulky war-plate of a medieval knight. Colours slid like water across its surface, and faces as well. Leering, screaming, weeping, laughing and constantly moving, as if they were jostling for space.

The rider's steed was equally monstrous. Its resemblance to a horse was only superficial – oily flesh clung to sub-dural cybernetics like tar, and its mane was a shaggy tangle of sparking wires and loose implant plugs. Pistons and pumps wheezed and shook as the great hooves tore at the ground. Its tail was a lashing whip of serrated steel blades, and its teeth were shards of hot metal. It squealed piercingly and reared, tearing at the air with its hooves.

The rider extended the spiked mace he carried. 'Fabius Bile. Manflayer. Fleshcrafter. Tumourking.' Then, simply,

'Butcher.' The street echoed with the hollow monotone of the rider. 'It has been a thousand years since last I saw your feverish rictus, Father-of-Monsters. Not enough. Never enough.'

'Mordrac,' Bile said, conversationally. 'Still referring to yourself as "count" or have you promoted yourself to "king"? A swift rise from sergeant.' He glanced at Oleander. 'It hasn't really been a thousand years. He likes to indulge in melodrama.'

'I am Castellan of Castle Sublime, Abominator. That is enough. You were warned. Why have you returned? Why have you broken the peace? The Sunblitz Brotherhood seeks recompense, in blood or water or both.'

'None of your affair, I assure you, Mordrac.' Bile snapped his fingers dismissively. 'And that for the Sunblitz Brotherhood. I have what I came for and now I am leaving. Feel free to turn around and pretend you never saw me.' He was taunting the creature, but he couldn't help himself. For all his power, Mordrac was a self-pitying fool. That such abilities had been gifted to one so unsuited to their use was proof enough that the universe was governed by nothing more than happenstance and circumstance.

The spiked mace slid through Mordrac's armoured grip. It crackled with a hellish energy. It was no natural weapon. Neither was the sword sheathed on Mordrac's hip. Though they took the form of outdated weapons, they were anything but. 'You flayed me to the bone, Fleshcrafter. Tore the meat from the soul, and still... I live. Still, the flesh endures. And so Castle Sublime is barred to you, as long as I persist. I told you that a century ago. You have broken the laws of Black Golan. Not once, but twice. Our people shriek for your head, Butcher.'

'No place is barred to me,' Bile said. 'And your persistence is purely a matter of spite. If you wish to die, then die. Toss yourself into the planet's core, if you like. But do not whine to me about your good fortune, Mordrac.'

'Is this why you made us take the Carrion Road?' Oleander hissed. 'To avoid this... individual? What in the name of the Maelstrom is he?'

'Annoying,' Bile said. 'Mordrac would never have let us in, had we come honestly. We would have had to fight our way through. Something I was trying to avoid. Never fight a battle you don't have to, Oleander.'

'Your history is nothing but mistakes,' Mordrac said, raising his voice. He didn't like being ignored. 'And this will be your last.' He urged his horse forward, mace raised. 'I will break your legs, spider. I will pluck out your eyes and set your mind to working on my behalf. That is your fate. That is your end.'

Oleander raised his bolt pistol. Bile considered telling him it would do no good, but decided not to waste his breath. It was almost touching, to see how quickly his prodigal student leapt to his defence. Almost as if he had some ulterior motive.

A proximity alarm beeped softly in his ear. Bile laughed and leaned on his sceptre. 'No man alive knows my fate, Mordrac. Especially not a provincial lout like you. Break my legs? I have more. Take my eyes? I will find new ones. And my mind is my own. It only works on behalf of me, myself and I.'

Mordrac snarled and his mount broke into a gallop. Oleander fired, but his shots did little to deter the engine of destruction barrelling towards them. Bile shoved him aside, and stepped back, grunting in annoyance as the mace cracked against his shoulder-plate. The chirurgeon hissed in alarm as Bile's collarbone fractured and his arm went numb. More stimulants flooded his system, swamping the pain before it could fully register. Bile fired his needler, hoping to slow Mordrac's steed. The beast wailed in pain as the needles sank into its flank. It reared, nearly hurling Mordrac from the saddle.

He felt the hot ping of a las-round as it caromed off his power armour. Mordrac's men had decided to join the fight. He heard the boom of Oleander's bolt pistol.

And then, a moment later, *Butcher-Bird* screeched down, strafing the market. Autocannons roared, and men and xenos died. Their bodies were blasted apart or hurled into the air. Mordrac was punched from his saddle by the gunship's first pass. His horse squealed and fell, legs kicking. Fist-sized holes had been punched into its flanks and skull. A foul-smelling ichor spilled onto the street.

Bile peered up as the gunship arced overhead, its thrusters boiling the air. It wasn't often the machine got to indulge itself, and still less often that he got to observe it doing so. There was a brutal simplicity to its assault.

Mordrac hauled himself to his feet, mace in hand. He shouted something that Bile couldn't make out, and raised his weapon as if in challenge. The gunship screamed back towards him, weapons spitting, chewing the ground to either side of the Castellan of Castle Sublime, drawing closer and closer. The gunship enjoyed it when its prey ran, but Mordrac didn't appear inclined to give it the satisfaction.

Butcher-Bird shrieked again, this time in frustration, as its guns finally locked on to Mordrac. High-velocity rounds punched into the Castellan, gouging wet chunks out of his archaic armour. Somehow Mordrac remained on his feet. When the hand gripping the mace was ripped from his wrist, he drew his sword with the remaining one. The blade came free with a dull groan, like the clangour of a mourning bell. It was limned with a weirdling light.

Mordrac slashed out, and the light flared. Bile's eyes adapted instantly, and his armour's sensors recorded the energy emission, cataloguing it for later study. A burning, wailing heat boiled from the sword and speared towards *Butcher-Bird*.

The gunship rolled through the air with almost avian grace. The wash of heat swept past, barely scorching its undercarriage. An instant later, every weapon at its disposal spat fire, and Mordrac ceased to exist. What was left of him tumbled smouldering through the air, dappling the ruined tents and splashing across the street.

Bile rose to his feet. 'Come, Oleander. Time to take our leave, before he manages to pull himself together and call for reinforcements.'

'There's nothing left but a crater,' Oleander protested. Bile snorted.

'And so? He's immortal. We could toss him into the corona of a star and he'd eventually tumble out, smelling of cooked meat and as self-pitying as ever. Give him enough time, and he'll be coming after us again. *Butcher-Bird* is only carrying so much ammunition, and I don't feel like wasting it or our time.'

The gunship lowered itself to the street with a grumble of its engines. Every so often, it let off another burst from its guns, causing the dead to jump and twitch. Something that might have been a giggle slithered from the vox as Bile and Oleander clambered aboard. 'What was he?'

Oleander said, as the gunship climbed back towards the inner atmosphere of Sublime.

'He was one of us, once. Now he is a monster, like the untold billions that inhabit the Eye,' Bile said. 'He can't die, you see. No matter what occurs, his body endures, beyond even the few limits of transhuman physiology. Lop off a limb, it sprouts anew. Burn out his eyes, he can see again in a few moments. Dissolve him in acid, he soon springs unharmed from the steaming froth. I took him apart piece by piece the last time I visited Sublime, just to see if there was a limit to his durability. There was not.'

'I can see why he hates you,' Oleander said.

Bile laughed. 'Oh, he doesn't hate me for that. No, he hates me because I failed to kill him.' His smile twisted into a grimace. 'Immortality is wasted on such creatures.' He leaned forward, trying to ignore the ache in his chest. 'Short-sighted, mewling worms. They do not see the potential in themselves, Oleander. They are blind to the light.'

'And would you be immortal, master?'

'I would live long enough to see my work completed,' Bile said. 'True immortality is a burden, and I scarcely have need of another of those. Upon my back rests the weight of the future. But all things must end, to have any purpose at all. True beauty is found in beauty's end. A saying our gene-father was fond of, once upon a time. Before he lost sight of things.'

'The Radiant would not agree with you, I fear.'

Bile chuckled. The chuckle turned into a cough, and he thumped his chest. Something filled his lungs. Blood, perhaps. Mordrac's parting gift. The chirurgeon plunged a syringe into him, and began to draw out the fluid. Bile braced himself against a bulkhead and spat to clear his mouth. When he looked up, he saw Oleander watching him. Though his expression was hidden beneath his helmet, Bile could guess what it was. He smiled. 'Kasperos Telmar and I agreed on very little, even before Fulgrim's apotheosis. I do not see why that should have changed. He was a fool then, and he is almost certainly a fool now.'

The gunship shuddered suddenly, and gave out a piercing whine. Bile heard the whirr of *Butcher-Bird*'s assault cannons. 'Mordrac must have pulled himself together and called for reinforcements,' he said. The hull pinged, echoing as something struck it.

'We're taking fire,' Saqqara said, as he and Tzimiskes staggered into the bay, their armour stabilisers attempting to compensate for the wildly pitching deck. The *Butcher-Bird* shrieked as its pursuers continued their attack. Its vox-system crackled with sulphurous, electronic curses in a dozen voices and different dialects.

'So we are,' Bile said. He looked at Tzimiskes. 'Can it take it?'

The Iron Warrior nodded and knocked on a bulkhead. Bile nodded. 'Good. Head up to the pilot's compartment and make sure it doesn't get any ideas about turning and fighting. We've wasted enough time and I have an old acquaintance to renew.'

PART TWO

THE RADIANT KING, IN HIS JOYFUL REPOSE

CHAPTER ELEVEN

The Radiant King

Fabius Bile studied the eldar. It had said nothing since its capture. It sat cross-legged in its containment cell aboard the *Vesalius*, attention turned inwards. Meditating, perhaps.

He reached down, caught the xenos by the throat and slammed it back against the wall. The force of it further damaged its cracked armour. The alien spat something and clutched at his wrist. It thrashed like an angry felinoid. 'Stop that,' Bile said, examining it.

It was female, he thought, given the bone structure and general body shape. Eldar possessed similar secondary gender signifiers to humans, despite diverse internal differences. Its fists hammered against his forearm, seeking to break his grip. Feet caught him in the gut. He barely twitched. It hadn't eaten in two days, and the wound in its side was festering, further sapping its strength. It was no threat.

Still, there was no reason to risk it injuring itself further. The chirurgeon whirred and jabbed a syringe through a crack in the armour into the pale flesh beneath. The Corsair stiffened as the tranquilliser took effect. It slumped in his grasp. It would feel no pain in the operation to come. Bile had considered the merits of sadism early in his awakening, and discarded them not long after Fulgrim had traded his legs for a snake's tail. Torture was a useless thing, in and of itself. It revealed more about the inflicting party than the subject.

He had devised more efficient means of stripping knowledge from prisoners. He whistled, and a vat-born waddled into the cell, grunting softly. The vat-born held a wide tray, containing an array of tools, nutrient jars and a singular apparatus, which resembled nothing so much as a centipede with a flat, segmented carapace of flexible metal and numerous fibrous antennae. The mind-worm.

Bile was quite pleased with the design. It had taken him a standard year to complete a working prototype, even with Arrian's help. He stroked its carapace. The mind-worm undulated at his touch, pincers clicking softly. Like all of his creations, it was equal parts grown and built. And it possessed a bit of him in its composition.

'Then, is that not the way of it? I am its creator, and there is always a dab of the creator in the created. A bit of blood, a drop of sweat. I have long theorised that this very thing was a factor in Horus' foolishness. The father's imperfections passed along to the sons – and magnified, even. I trust that you have more of my virtues than my vices.' He glanced down at the vat-born. 'But then, vice is what makes virtue bearable, is it not?' The vat-born gurgled in reply. Bile nodded. 'Even so, even so. I am allowing myself to be distracted.'

He turned back to his captive. The tranquilliser had

done its work. The eldar dangled insensate in his grip. He examined the wound in its side. The bladed limbs of the chirurgeon peeled back the ragged edges of the armour and the mesh weave beneath, exposing the infected flesh. The Neverborn carried a form of poison in their claws and teeth, though few of those they attacked lived to suffer its effects. He prodded the swollen, suppurating wound gently. He snapped his fingers, and the vat-born held up a specimen flask.

'There is much to learn from even the smallest elements. For instance, this venom is mostly hypothetical... it exists, in part, because of its victim's belief. Circular logic, of course. A vicious cycle. One I hope to break, sooner rather than later,' he said, as the chirurgeon lanced the wound open. Blood and oily poison spattered into the flask. He held it up and swirled the contents, frowning. He'd synthesised a number of potent compounds from such excretions – stimulants, mostly. In one case, a fairly potent poison. No two were ever the same. Once he had the secret of it, however, it would be quite useful.

He finished draining the wound and sprayed it with an antibacterial agent of his own manufacture. He had coaxed a fairly substantial medicinal garden to life in the *Vesalius'* hydroponics bay, with samples culled from a thousand worlds within the Eye. The plethora of healing unguents and salves he'd devised from its contents had made the effort well worth it. He ran a quick diagnostic scan, checking for any other signs of infection or malady. There was no telling what sort of parasites the creature was infested with.

Something flickered on the creature's chest. He glanced at the shimmering gem and plucked it free of its casing without a thought. A spirit stone. The eldar twitched, as if its dreams had suddenly become nightmares.

'What secrets do you contain, I wonder?' he said, rolling the spirit stone between his fingers. It felt warm to the touch, and more besides. He could almost feel the panic of the thing it contained. Though its body yet lived, part of it was already inside the stone – hidden. 'A most curious practice, and one that has long intrigued me. Do you still think, within the stone? Are you still you? Does your mind still exist? Pertinent questions, I feel. I suspect the answer is affirmative, given certain of your war machines that I have observed. No, the real question is... how? How do you accomplish this?'

He eyed the unconscious creature. He tilted its chin first one way and then the other with his thumb. 'It is rare I find myself in possession of a specimen in good working order. I shall learn much from you, in time.' He set the stone back into place. 'But first...'

Bile peeled back its eyelid with his free hand. The whites of its eye showed. 'Some capillary damage, but nothing serious,' he said. He glanced down at the vat-born. 'Note the time.' The chirurgeon hissed and a limb slid forward. The forceps slid into the eye, cradling it gently. Slowly, carefully, it plucked the eye from its socket, dragging the optic nerves into the open air. 'Slowly,' Bile said. 'We don't wish to snap them, do we?' He looked at the vat-born. 'Patience is the soul of the thing. A philosopher of some note said that, though I do not recall his name at the moment. It would do you well to remember it, though. Let it be your guiding dogma.'

The vat-born burbled in reply, and Bile smiled. 'Yes. I like it as well.' When he judged the optic nerves to be stretched to their limit, the chirurgeon deftly sliced them with a heated scalpel, cauterising the wound in the same moment. He took the eye and dropped it into the nutrient jar. He lifted the mind-worm and held it up to the eldar's empty socket.

The antennae began to flutter. Tiny segmented claws flexed, lifting the carapace. It crawled forward, swelling, whirring, twisting, until it filled the socket. Antennae slid beneath the skin, stretching across the curve of the eldar's skull. Others were already inserting themselves into the brain, via what remained of the optic nerve. The xenos moaned and began to twitch in Bile's grip. Blood dripped from its nose. The back of its skull thumped against the wall. The chirurgeon injected a second dose of tranquilliser, along with a muscle relaxant.

The mind-worm would copy the brain patterns of its host, and store them in its core. Thoughts, memories, dreams, would all be downloaded into the apparatus, for easy transfer to a data-spike. A more elegant way of consuming an enemy's knowledge than simply eating their brain matter. Also, this way wasted nothing. The route to Lugganath would be found and uploaded to the fleet's cogitators, and the eldar would survive for further testing. Bile eased the eldar down. 'Never let it be said that I am not merciful,' he murmured.

'*Master – we've arrived.*'

Bile straightened as Oleander's voice crackled through his vox-link. 'Good. I will meet you in the embarkation bay.' He looked down at the vat-born. 'Make sure that it doesn't harm itself or try to remove the mind-worm if it wakes,' he said. He paused, considering. 'Break its hands, if you like. That might take its mind off things.'

The vat-born chirruped in pleasure and bobbed its hooded skull. It took so little to please them, and they gave so much in return. Bile smiled and left the vat-born to its task.

Oleander and the others were waiting for him in the embarkation bay. The *Butcher-Bird* growled in its traces, ready to be off. 'Are you sure that you don't wish us to go with you?' Arrian asked. 'Oleander and Tzimiskes are hardly an honour guard.'

'Thank you, Arrian, but I am no petty lord. Pomp and ceremony are for lesser men. Besides, someone must tend to things here.' Bile looked at Oleander. 'They know that we are coming? I have little wish to be blown apart by some overenthusiastic gunner.'

'I've alerted them. The Radiant is... curious about your intentions.'

Bile sniffed. 'Better than the alternative, I suppose.' He looked at Tzimiskes. 'When we arrive, you will stay with the *Butcher-Bird*. I wish no impediments, if we should have to leave in a rush.' Tzimiskes nodded and thumped his chest-plate with a fist. Bile turned. 'Come. It has been too long since I have enjoyed the hospitality of the Third.'

The *Vesalius* hung stationary in the lee of a gas giant, hidden by its halo of debris. They were some distance outside the malign envelope of the Eye near Krendrax, in the greater wilderness of Segmentum Obscurus. The vox-caster caught snatches of signal from Cadia as well as Elysia, and once, briefly, even Fenris, as it scanned for any sign of enemy activity. Imperial fleets were as thick as fleas in these stars, especially after the pillaging of Helosian.

Butcher-Bird sped through the field of shattered asteroids and swirling vaporous clouds like its namesake, arrowing towards the small fleet that waited beyond the swirling planetoid. Bile watched their destination approach through the gunship's bay viewscreen. 'Five ships. Impressive. Most would-be warlords can barely keep one in working order outside Eyespace,' Bile said.

'The Radiant is more composed than most,' Oleander said. 'He has even been invited to attend Abaddon's councils, and swear fealty to him.'

Bile snorted. 'Oh yes. As have I. Ezekyle is very forgiving, when he wants something.' He studied the viewscreen. 'No sense in putting my neck in the noose. If Ezekyle wants me, he'll have to come and get me.'

Despite Bile's bravado, Abaddon was becoming more of a concern with every passing day. As his armies grew, so too did the Eye roil. Sides were being chosen, claims staked and wars declared, all of which disrupted Bile's studies. Ezekyle seemingly had greater designs than simply claiming the vacated thrones of the daemon-primarchs. Then, what else could you expect from one who'd taken the title 'Warmaster'?

The attack on Sublime had reminded him of why he'd fled to Urum in the first place. For years after the fall of Canticle City, his foes had hounded him. Not just rivals and renegades, but eldar and worse things. His chosen course had set him at odds with a thousand factions, and all of them wanted him in chains or dead.

Perhaps it was time to begin building an army. An army of Gland-hounds, and New Men, to protect his holdings, his experiments, his... no. No. That was a trap. A diversion from his chosen path. If he wasted his time squabbling with those who sought to chain him, he was only trading one cage for another. He would not play that game. He pushed the thought aside as proximity alerts sounded.

'There she is,' Oleander said. 'The Radiant's flagship... the *Quarzhazat*.'

Bile considered the ship as they made their final approach. The *Quarzhazat* was a ship unlike any other. It had been a ship of the line once, a Lunar-class cruiser with a different name, but in the years since the destruction of Canticle City, it had become something more. The scars of ancient lance-fire still marred its flanks. But now, immense wings of metal and void-flesh jutted from it, and writhing tendrils of iridescent matter, each one hundreds of leagues in length, sprouted from its hull and aft-decks. The docking bays resembled the fleshy jaws of mantrap plants or fang-studded beast-maws, and its gun batteries looked more akin to the stingers of some lethal species of insect. 'That is not a ship,' he said.

'Not any more,' Oleander said. 'Hence the name.'

'I was wondering about that,' Bile said. The Quarzhazat – the original Quarzhazat – had been a legend on Chemos. A great monster said to lurk high in the poison skies, and pluck whole cities and lone travellers alike from mountain tops. A child's tale, meant to frighten the gullible. 'How like us, to cloak ourselves in the glories of others.' He crossed his arms. 'A trait passed along from our gene-father. Fulgrim was always so greedy. That was his problem. He swallowed a serpent, and it devoured him from the inside out.'

'It devoured us all,' Oleander said.

Bile looked at him. 'So it did. But some of us were smart enough to cut our way free.' He looked away. The daemon-ship drew closer, filling the occulus. *Butcher-Bird*'s engines grumbled as it neared the docking port. The gun-ship's machine-spirit disliked docking with any vessel except *Vesalius*, and even then only when it had to.

'You could have stayed, you know,' Oleander said, as the

docking seals locked into place with a hiss. 'After Abaddon. You could have come back. The Third Legion would have rallied around you...'

Bile laughed. 'You think so, do you? Is my charisma so matchless, then, that I would be a shining beacon for my fallen brothers? No. It was only by cunning that I managed it once, and only due to necessity that I even contemplated it. I did what I had to, for the good of the patient.' Pain rippled through him. The dull, twisting sensation of tumour-laced organs struggling to function. He swallowed blood and closed his eyes. 'It would be even more difficult now. Our Legion is gone, Oleander. It was broken on the reefs of Fulgrim's desires.'

'Desires you helped fulfil.' It wasn't an accusation, so much as a statement of fact.

'I saw the world differently then,' Bile said. His voice was flat, even to his own ears. 'There was a glory amidst the madness. A sort of divine rebellion, Oleander. You experienced it as much as I did. Where our gene-father led, we followed. Blindly, devotedly, wholeheartedly. We lapped it up, like eager dogs. Gorged on it, until we were fit to burst – and until it consumed us in its turn.'

'Not all of us,' Oleander said.

'Most, then.' Bile's thin lips quirked. 'I was free, and in that freedom found only a new form of enslavement. Without rigour or direction, scientific exploration is ultimately nothing more than self-gratification. Just because one can, does not mean one should, and just because one should, does not mean one can.' The words were like ashes in his mouth, even now. Limits were anathema to him, and always had been. But they served a purpose. They kept one's intellect focused, and mind honed.

'Strange words coming from you, master.'

'As I said, I am different. On Terra, in those final days, I saw for the first time what we had become – what I had become – and I thought it such a waste. We could have been so much more, had we but tried. Instead, we succumbed to base instinct. We revelled in our squandered potential, like petulant children.'

Oleander was silent. Bile pressed on, though he was unsure as to whether he was trying to convince Oleander – or himself. 'We had our chance, and we wasted it. Our moment is done and all that remains is the slow passage into night. The Third Legion is dead, Oleander. Whatever it once was, it will never be that again.' Oleander looked at him, and made as if to speak, but a proximity alarm sounded. The bay doors descended, opening onto a phalanx of hostile faces and raised weapons. Their power armour was a riot of colour and modification, as were the bolters they held. Tall crests of white and turquoise rose over helmets scooped to unnatural points. Golden chains hung from shoulder-plates, jostling for space with scraps of obscenely decorated parchment and other grisly decorations.

A woman forced her way through the press of warriors. She was taller than the others, and slim, with long jointed legs ending in heavy black hooves. She wore a suit of a pale amethyst power armour, likely ripped from the body of a dying Space Marine and crudely modified to fit her unusual shape. White hair, bound into a profusion of whip-like braids, hung like a lion's mane from her narrow skull. Strange sigils and signs had been carved into her brow and cheeks, and one nostril was pierced with a trio of golden rings. A necklace of bolter shells, medallions and fangs clattered against her chest-plate as she set one hoof on the bottom of the ramp. She grinned up at Oleander. 'You're back, Apothecary,' she said. A forked tongue flickered among the thicket of her fangs. 'How sad. I'd hoped you'd died. Ever the disappointment.'

'You'll learn to live with it,' Oleander said. 'Unless, of course, you've decided now's the time to finish our game, Savona.' He spread his hands.

'Now is most certainly not the time,' Bile said. Savona's eyes widened at his sepulchral tones and she backed away. Her hand fell to the power maul dangling from her hip. Her attendants reacted with similar hostility. They all knew him. There wasn't a warrior of the Third who hadn't suffered Bile's ministrations at least once.

'The Clonelord,' she said, almost spitting the title.

'I prefer Primogenitor,' Bile said, as he stepped fully into the docking bay. He leaned on Torment. 'And you are...?'

'Master, may I introduce Savona of the Ruptured Skein, Lady of the Spinward Conflagration?' Oleander said. 'Third among the Joybound. Or have you dispatched Merix in the time I've been gone? If so, that'd make you second.'

'Merix lives,' Savona said. 'And so do you, for the moment.' She eyed Bile's lean figure with distaste. 'Why are you here, Manflayer? You are not welcome in the encampments of the Third Legion.'

'There is no Third Legion,' Bile said, as he stepped past her. 'It was dead and buried long before you were born, child. And unless you wish to join it, you will direct me to your commander. Where is Kasperos Telmar?'

'I do not answer to you,' she began.

'No? Then you will almost certainly answer to my old compatriot, Kasperos. It was he who invited me. I come here at his request, and you would deny me entry? Shall I leave then? How shall he react to that, I wonder...' His lips quirked. 'Perhaps he will give you to me. A suitable apology, I think. I should like to discover what secrets lurk within your altered flesh.' Savona stared at him. Bile leaned forward, smiling. 'Would you like that, my dear?' The chirurgeon clicked as if in eagerness, its articulated limbs spreading around Bile like wings.

She stepped back, black eyes wide. 'I am content in my shape,' she said, her voice harsh. She looked at Oleander. 'He's in his quarters. He asked to see you the moment you arrived.'

'Of course he did,' Oleander said, striding past her. Savona's warriors stood aside and he and Bile moved through them. The eyes of every living thing in the docking bay, from the most raggedy slave to the haughtiest warrior, followed the two Apothecaries as they departed.

The transit elevator growled like an angry dog as it rose through the ship. The shaft and the thousands of access tunnels lining its length whipped by at great speed. The platform juddered beneath their feet as if it might rip loose from its moorings at any moment.

Old cabling hung in serpentine bunches from the roof, looped incautiously around the gothic carvings that decorated the walls and cage. Someone had tried to paint something unpleasant on the deck, but only got halfway before they'd been interrupted.

'Who are these Joybound?' Bile said, suddenly.

'The Radiant's sub-commanders,' Oleander said. 'You've met Savona.' Savona was an oddity among the servants of the Radiant. A mortal warrior, risen to high rank among Renegade Adeptus Astartes on the strength of her savagery.

'What of the others?'

'Gulos Palatides, a praefector of the Seventh Company. Or he was. He is the first of the Joybound now. He fancies himself a swordsman. Like Lucius.'

'Don't they all,' Bile said. 'I've heard of him. He led the remnants of the Seventh, Thirty-First and Twenty-Third Companies off Quir, after that rather disastrous raid on the black mills of the Mechanicum.' He smirked. 'Lady Spohr, the Magos-Queen of Quir, was quite put out with them.'

Oleander nodded. 'That's what brought him to the Radiant's attention. He has all of the vices and precious few of the virtues, such as they were, of Fulgrim's champion.'

'Who else?'

'Nikola Varocar and Blessed Lidonius. The former is a sneak, the latter a brute. Both were sergeants. Both from Twelfth Company, late of nowhere in particular. Both have been with the Radiant since the beginning. Neither is particularly ambitious – Lidonius lacks the wit, and Nikola lacks the courage.' Oleander hesitated. 'Or maybe he's wiser than the rest of us.'

'And this Merix, you mentioned earlier?'

'He does a very good job of pretending to be an idiot. Equerry to Hellespon, though why he left his service I don't know.' Oleander looked away. 'As you've probably guessed, I do not get along with the other Joybound.'

'The more things change...' Bile said, with a thin smile. Oleander grunted. He couldn't deny that Bile had a point. But things were different now. He longed to light his pipe, but it was not the time to have anything other than a clear head.

'Now is probably not the right time, but I must admit

that I may have... misled you, somewhat,' Oleander said, carefully. The platform creaked around them. Sparks spewed through the cage and he stepped back.

Bile thumped the deck with the end of his sceptre. 'Oh?' His expression hadn't changed.

'I might have implied that I sought you out on the orders of the Radiant.'

'I gather from your tone that you did not,' Bile said. It wasn't a question.

'Better that I tell you now, than you find out when it's too late,' Oleander said.

'Oleander, there are times I regret not pulping your scheming skull when I had the chance.' Bile looked at him. 'Why am I to assume the burden of leadership in this endeavour?'

'The proposal will mean more coming from you than me.'

'I am not angry,' Bile said. 'Indeed, I applaud your initiative. You have ensured success, without risking failure. But tell me... why should I not kill you now and simply leave?' He lifted his sceptre, as if to tap Oleander with it. Oleander twitched back, just out of reach. He'd felt the touch of Torment before, and had no intention of getting a second taste in this lifetime. Some agonies were too intense even for him.

'All that I said before still holds true, Master. The opportunity is here, and we must seize it. A craftworld of living specimens, waiting to be harvested. Will you deny yourself that, merely because I obscured the truth?'

Bile lowered his sceptre. 'Pragmatism must be balanced by sentiment, ruthlessness by mercy. But mercy has its limits. Is there anything else you are not telling me?'

Oleander shook his head. 'Nothing, Master.'

'For your sake, I hope you are right.'

The transit elevator juddered to a halt, and a long corridor opened out before them. Unnatural flesh clung to the walls, veins pulsing with oil and electricity. Bundles of cables squirmed like drowsy snakes in the flow of rancid air from the vents. Ragged shapes sat slumped against the walls and deck, their bare skin one with the soft tissue that hugged the walls.

Bile stopped before one, and knelt. The huddled shape moaned softly as the chirurgeon took a tissue sample. Bile studied the sample. 'Intriguing. The ship is actually adding to its mass. A most efficient means of refuelling.'

Oleander decided to refrain from stating the obvious, as the warning grunts of the Radiant's personal guard filled the corridor. The guards had been human, once. Now they were obese monstrosities. Their tiny heads were hidden beneath featureless helms of armaplas, etched with ruinous sigils. The helms were riveted to fanged gorgets, which protected their necks. They wore nothing over their swollen arms and torsos except oil and scar tissue. Their bowed legs were hidden beneath scavenged fatigues. Each carried a massive chain-glaive, and they activated these as Oleander and Bile drew near. Bile looked at him. 'Your work?'

'An early attempt to replicate your work with muscle-building enzymes on Pilgrim's Rest,' Oleander said. 'A bit crude, but they survived. Mostly.'

'Their heads are quite small.'

'Only in comparison,' Oleander said.

'As you say. Perhaps you should announce us.'

'He already knows we're here. If nothing else, the ship probably told him.'

'Indeed I do, brothers. Enter and be welcome.'

The voice echoed out of vox-units welded to the masks of the guards. The guards sank onto their haunches and deactivated their glaives. Oleander led Bile past them, and into the inner sanctum of the being once known as Kasperos Telmar.

The Radiant's private quarters were larger than Oleander remembered. Then, given that they were more a part of the warp than the ship, perhaps that was only to be expected. They expanded or shrank according to his whims. At the moment, they resembled nothing so much as the throne room of a barbaric potentate. Tattered banners from companies across the width and breadth of the Nine Legions hung from the ceiling, undulating in the fan-stirred air. The carpet was sumptuous, made from the flayed hides of a now-extinct species of carnivore. Great bones lined the walls. Shattered skulls leered and fanged jaws laughed silently as they strode past. Bells, chimes and chains clinked arrhythmically. Slaves, tattooed and branded with the company markings of the 12th lined the deck, proffering up platters of spoiled meat and other unpleasant consumables.

The Radiant King in His Joyful Repose lived up to his title. He lounged at the far end of the chamber, on a wide throne made from the fused flesh and bone of still-living slaves – siblings, in fact, Oleander recalled. They were fused at the joints, arm to arm and leg to leg, facing one another. Their eyelids had been removed and their heads fixed in place, so that they were unable to look away from each other, and the horrors their kinsmen had become. Their agonised screams were muted by internal vox-dampers, which could be turned off to allow for enjoyment of their howls. The Radiant thought it a lively tune.

That the slaves were still alive after so long was a point of pride for Oleander. He had designed and constructed the throne himself, and enjoyed every moment. Granted, he'd never considered such applications for his skills before joining the Radiant's coterie, but one learned to adapt. Better a glorified carpenter than a corpse.

The Radiant was beautiful. Not handsome, but beautiful. Perfection had rendered his features almost androgynous. His throne room was a hall of mirrors, each one reflecting the glory that was him from a thousand improbable angles. Braziers spewed narcotic incense into the already thick air. Half-formed daemons capered about, slinking and dancing through the surfaces of the mirrors like fish through water. They had the faces of beautiful women and handsome men, and the claws of insects and crustaceans. There was a disconcerting rhythm to their movements, and Oleander realised that they were putting on a performance.

'That explains why he's clapping, I suppose,' Bile said, when Oleander shared his realisation. 'Can you make him stop? I find this tiresome.'

'As I have always found you, Master of the Apothecarion,' the Radiant said, breathily. 'Why Fulgrim tolerated your sagging corpse I will never know.' He turned towards them, his eyes burning like miniature suns. He leaned forward, setting his boots on the deck. He wore what had once been a suit of Crusade-pattern power armour. Shaggy white fur was wrapped about his greaves and the vambraces of his gauntlets. His chest-plate had been decorated with a grotesque mural depicting Fulgrim's moment of apotheosis. One of his shoulder-plates had become fused and twisted into the shape of a leering feminine face. The face whispered softly as the Radiant rose to his feet.

A daemon slid past him, tittering. He took the claw it proffered and they spun in a brief, courtly dance. The daemon clicked its fangs in disappointment as he brought its claw to his lips for a kiss of polite dismissal. 'What do you think of my courtiers, Fabius?' he asked, as he stalked towards them. 'Beautiful and terrible, even as we are.'

'Beauty is in the eye of the beholder,' Bile said sourly. Oleander cast a wary eye over the daemons as they continued to dance. He thought they might be drawing closer with every sinuous motion. His hand fell to the hilt of his sword, but he refrained from drawing it. It wouldn't do to insult the Radiant in his own throne room.

'Why are you here, Fabius?' the Radiant said, circling them, glancing at himself in the mirrors from time to time. Bile didn't do him the courtesy of turning with him. Instead, he looked at Oleander. His expression was inscrutable. Oleander tilted his head. Bile snorted.

'To help you, Kasperos. *Captain* Kasperos,' he corrected. The Radiant stopped. 'I wish that you would not call me that, Fabius. I am not him, and he was not me. To hear his name is no longer a pleasure, even a guilty one.'

Bile laughed. 'Forgive me, but I refuse to indulge you in your childish fetish for descriptive titles. Kasperos you were, and Kasperos you are.'

The Radiant frowned. As one, the daemons hissed in rage. They were dancing no longer. Instead, they crouched like angry cats, ready to pounce. Oleander made ready to defend himself. The Radiant's eyes slid towards him. 'Oleander. I was wondering where you'd gone. I do not like it when my Joybound leave without telling me.' There was a hideous strength in that gaze. It pulled you in, and crushed you at the same time.

'I...' Oleander began. Bile waved him to silence.

'Leave him, Kasperos. He is mine. He was mine before he was yours, even before the walls of Terra fell. You do remember the walls, don't you, Kasperos?'

The Radiant laughed. 'I remember many walls. Some big, some small. Reality is a wall, and I chip at it, every day in every way, seeking my perfection.' He reached towards Bile's face. 'You smell strange, Fabius. Like a corpse pickled in chemicals.'

Bile gently, but firmly, pushed the Radiant's hand aside with the head of his sceptre. A spark of energy leapt from the skull-head to the Radiant's hand. 'And you smell like incense and ashes. I've come to help you with your wall, Kasperos.'

The Radiant stepped back, rubbing his hand. The daemons clustered about him, cooing abominably. He smiled boyishly. 'Have you then? How delightful. It is a very strong wall, Fabius. But I have almost cracked it.'

'Persistence was always one of your few virtues,' Bile said. The Radiant laughed.

'We all seek perfection in our own way. Oh, I've missed you, Fabius. Come, tell me, how will you help me?'

'With infinite and varied skill, Kasperos,' Bile said. 'All I have is at your disposal, if you wish. My mind, my skill, bent to your purpose.'

'And what purpose might that be?'

'I am given to understand that you pursue a most elusive quarry, Kasperos. One that has drawn you out of the safety of the Eye, and into the fringes of real space.'

The Radiant nodded. 'The craftworld,' he said.

'The very same.'

'You know how to find it?'

'Indeed. This contains the location of our quarry,' Bile said, extending a portable data-spike from his gauntlet. It contained a copy of everything his mind-worm had rooted out of the Corsair's brain. 'As well as rough schematics for the upper levels of the craftworld. Enough to devise a plan of attack, if such a thing is still of interest to you.'

'How did you get this?' the Radiant said, staring at the data-spike.

'Simple. I took it. We have a prisoner. Its every memory and observance, conscious or otherwise, concerning this craftworld you pursue has been copied onto this data-spike.'

'A... prisoner. An eldar?' Oleander could hear the greed in the Radiant's voice.

So could Bile. He smiled. 'A prisoner. Leave it at that.' He waggled the data-spike. 'Take it, Kasperos. As a sign of good faith in our joint endeavour.'

The Radiant took it. He tapped it against his lip, eyes narrowed. 'Why didn't you mention that you had taken a prisoner sooner?'

Bile shrugged. 'Because I still have use for it. It's called Lugganath, by the way.'

'I know what it's called,' the Radiant said.

'But do you know what it means?' Bile laughed. 'Light of the Fallen Suns or some such. An evocative title, don't you think? Their insignia is a black sun, which is a reference in itself to lost glories. Fitting, no?'

The Radiant smiled. 'Yes, quite. A fallen sun... well, I will become a new sun, and cast my light over them all.'

He looked at Oleander. 'Do you think they will welcome me, Oleander?'

'No,' Oleander said. 'But then I expect that most of them will be dead by then, so it doesn't matter.'

The Radiant laughed. 'How do I know that this isn't a trick?'

'It is a bargain,' Bile said. 'That, for this.'

'And what is this?'

'Of no consequence, until you agree,' Bile said.

The Radiant's smile had returned, wider than before. 'And I cannot agree, until all debts are paid. Isn't that so, Oleander?'

As if by a prearranged signal, the doors cycled open behind them. The Joybound entered, one by one, weapons in their hands. Oleander sighed. 'I was hoping to avoid this.'

'Avoid what?' Bile said, glaring at the approaching warriors.

'His just punishment,' one of them said. His arms were bare of armour, exposing corded muscle and scarred flesh. Amulets, icons and finger bones clattered against his chest-plate, and his matted hair was bound back in a single, tendril-like braid.

Behind him came the hulking monstrosity known as Lidonius, his warp-touched features twisted in glee. Nikola, a lithe, colourfully clad killer, with a tri-part crest rising over a helmet wrought in the shape of a beast's skull, strode, as ever, at his side. And then, finally, Merix, in his antiquated suit of power armour, daubed in soft, garish hues. All of them bore the markings of the 12th somewhere on them. Whatever loyalties they might once have had, they were the Radiant's warriors now.

'You should have stayed away, fleshcrafter,' Savona said.

'Why… it's the gauntlet, brother, surely you remember?' the Radiant said, laying his arm across Bile's narrow shoulders. 'The punishment due all deserters from the Third Legion. He must seek his forgiveness in the test of steel.'

Bile's eyes narrowed. He shrugged the Radiant's arm away. 'The Third is dead. He has returned. Do not be ridiculous, Kasperos.'

'Oh, Fabius, if it were up to me, I would forgive him.' He looked at Oleander. 'I would forgive you anything, my Apothecary. A fleshcrafter of your skill should be shown some lenience, but… ah. There is the morale of the company to consider. The forms must be observed. There are rules, even in indulgence. You left me, dear Oleander. Abandoned your post. Punishment is due. So you will run the gauntlet.'

The Radiant sank to his haunches and ran his fingers through the filth that clung to the deck. He grinned up at Bile and said, 'Savona, my sweet – the honour of first blood is yours. Make him scream.'

Savona hissed in pleasure, and swept her power maul out. Oleander staggered as the blow connected with his side. Bile glanced at the Radiant. 'If you damage him, he is of no use to me.'

'Do you need him?'

'I do not know yet.'

'Let us hope that you do not. Gulos – strike, strike true,' the Radiant said, as he rose to his feet. The one called Gulos howled and his swords sprang from their sheaths. A spray of sparks rose from Oleander's forearm as he threw up his arm to protect himself. He stumbled back. Gulos and Savona circled him from opposite sides.

'Nikola, Merix, Blessed Lidonius – have your say, my brothers.' With each name the Radiant called out, one of the Joybound lunged forward to join the attack. Blades, hammers and flails thudded heavily into Oleander, driving him to one knee. He snatched his sword free of its sheath with desperate ferocity, and momentarily drove his attackers back.

The Radiant applauded. 'He has some skill at the cut and thrust,' he said. He looked at Bile. 'Don't you agree, Fabius?'

'I am no judge of such things.'

The Radiant frowned mockingly. 'Perfection was once your art, Fabius. And you were a master of it. You were always so proud of your work, and so paranoid of failure.' He lifted his hands. 'Eidolon's words, not mine. Still, one has to ask – when did you give up?'

'I did not,' Bile said, watching the fight. Oleander was holding his own. Impressive, given how badly he was outnumbered.

'And yet here you are. All but forgotten in your exile. We discuss you sometimes, when we gather in our solitude.'

'Who is we?'

The Radiant leaned close. 'The Phoenix Conclave,' he whispered.

'And what is that?'

The Radiant tapped his lips. 'It's a secret.'

'Of course, how foolish of me. This is a waste of time, Kasperos.'

'I asked you not to call me that, brother,' the Radiant said, his voice deceptively mild. 'I am more than I was. Would you call a moth a worm?'

Bile looked at him. 'Forgive me. This is a waste of time, oh Radiant King.'

The Radiant smiled. 'Then bring it to an end, my brother, by all means.' He licked his lips. 'If you can. As I recall, you were never one for undue exertion.'

'The key word is undue,' Bile said. He hefted his sceptre and started forward, skin-coat swirling about his legs. As he walked, he silently activated the stim-pumps in his armour. A flush of cold filled him, billowing outward, leaving strength in its wake. The cocktail of drugs was tailored specifically to his physiology. It made him faster and stronger, though there was a price to pay for it. There was always a price. Every unnecessary exertion brought his body one step closer to complete failure.

One of the Joybound, Merix, turned as he drew close, crackling electro-flail whirring about his head. His power armour was of an older mark, and decorated with wide swathes of harsh colour. The pelts of beasts flapped about him as he swung the electro-flail down. Bile sidestepped the blow and rammed Torment into his opponent's chest. The Chaos Space Marine's pastel-daubed armour offered precious little protection from the sceptre's deadly energies. It cut through ceramite like a scalpel through flesh.

Merix arched his back and screamed shrilly. The flail fell from his nerveless fingers. Bile caught him by the throat and wrenched him from his feet. Merix didn't resist as the Chief Apothecary hurled him aside. 'Fight, Oleander. Fight, if you would survive,' Bile said, joining the other Apothecary. Back to back, they faced the remainder of the Joybound. 'I have no use for one who surrenders at the first sign of difficulty.'

Oleander didn't reply. His sword crashed against Gulos' twin blades. The Apothecary twisted around and drove his shoulder into Gulos' chest, knocking him back a step.

Bile lost sight of them as the hulking Joybound called Blessed Lidonius attacked him with a humming thunder hammer. Lidonius was warp-touched; his power armour had cracked and ruptured at some point, exposing swollen, mutated flesh. His skin swam with iridescent colours, and it bubbled and steamed like hot mud.

Bile ducked under the warrior's first blow, and twisted aside from the second. He could feel his bones pop with every undulation, and the wound he'd taken on Sublime had begun to ache, but he ignored it. He lashed out with his sceptre, but the brute was quicker than he looked. A rugose paw enveloped Torment, and Lidonius giggled as Bile activated it. 'Pretty pain,' the Joybound said. 'I like it.'

'Oh? Have a taste of this then,' Bile said. He snatched the Xyclos needler from its holster and fired, blistering Lidonius' malformed face. Lidonius released his grip on the sceptre and staggered back with a screech. He dropped his power maul and clawed gobbets of waxy meat from his face as the toxins burned through him. Bile lowered his aim and fired again. Lidonius' screech rose an octave. He clutched at himself and sank to one knee.

Bile drove his sceptre into the side of the Joybound's head hard enough to buckle mutated bone. Lidonius slumped with a last, plaintive gurgle. Bile didn't waste time engaging the others. Nikola stumbled as the Xyclos needler spat again. The vulpine champion sank to the deck with a low moan, steam spewing from his pores, his tri-part crest sagging. Gulos whirled at the sound and his sword hissed out, slicing through the needle meant for him.

'You are skilful,' Bile said.

'Why do you seek to protect him?' Gulos said. He left

Oleander to Savona and lunged for Bile. His blades flashed. Bile avoided the first and caught the second on the haft of his sceptre. 'I know the stories, lieutenant commander. Aye, and spit on them. You led us to death, at Canticle City. I was there. I saw you flee with your prizes when all was lost. What are you but a scuttling parasite, hiding in a midden-pit of spoiled meat?'

'And what does that make you?' Bile said.

'Better,' Gulos said.

'Perhaps,' Bile said. He swept Torment out and the Joy-bound spasmed as it thumped into his chest. The sceptre shrieked in joy and Gulos staggered, dropping his swords. He clutched at the sceptre, but could not pull it away.

He screeched in agony as Bile forced him to his knees. 'Then, perhaps not,' Bile said. 'You are spoiled ingredients, nothing more. A thing meant to die for your betters. Do you see? Do you understand? If I am a parasite, then you are even less than that.'

Gulos screamed again, wailing like a flayed cat. Bile's face twisted into a leer. 'At times like this, I feel as if I fully understand why the Phoenician took the path he did.' Then, with a snarl, he tore the sceptre away, releasing the Joybound from its agonising grip.

He looked around, his gimlet gaze sweeping across the others. Savona had stepped back from Oleander. Merix was on his feet, but only just. Both Nikola and Lidonius were still writhing on the deck.

'We are all damned,' Bile said. 'But do not think that makes us equal. I saw Chemos at the height of its glory, and was with the Phoenician in his moment of apotheo-sis. I walked through the fires of Isstvan and made a coat from the skins of my brothers. I am father to a new age of gods and monsters.' He let the sceptre slide through his grip until he was leaning on it. 'I have seen and accomplished more than any warrior in this pitiful excuse for a fleet. The weight of my destiny would crush the strongest of you.'

The Joybound were silent, save for Gulos' moans. They didn't look particularly cowed, but Bile hadn't expected them to be. Yet they were chastened, and that was enough for the moment. The Radiant applauded. 'Excellent. Excellent.'

Bile looked at him. 'I trust honour is satisfied?'

The Radiant spread his hands. 'Honour is never satisfied, Fabius. You know that. But it will do, for now.'

'And my offer?'

'You have not yet said what you wish in return,' the Radiant said.

Bile reached into his coat and removed a miniature hololith projector. He activated it. 'This is your prey. Beautiful, is it not?' The craftworld rotated slowly. The Radiant leaned close.

'How did you get this?'

'How does one get anything? I paid for it. There are those who make a habit of collating such things. To you and I, one den of xenos is much like another. But there are differences. I will make my modifications accordingly.' Bile looked at the Radiant. 'This is what I want.' Bile tapped the hololith, enhancing a portion of the craftworld. 'There is a chamber here, or close by, which is said to contain the crystallised forms of xenos psykers.' He grinned. 'A peculiarity of their species. I want them.'

The Radiant frowned. 'Why? What use could you have for such things?'

'That is my concern, not yours.'

The Radiant laughed. 'Fine.' Bile made to deactivate the hololith, but the Radiant stopped him. 'Give it to me. It will be a gift, from one brother to another.'

Bile tossed it to him. The Radiant ran his fingers through the image and smiled. 'I will amuse myself with this mirage, until I have the real thing.' He made a dismissive gesture. 'You may leave. I will consider your offer.'

CHAPTER TWELVE

Entropy in Action

'Five ships will not be enough,' Arrian said. The World Eater was examining a hololithic representation of the Radiant's fleet. 'A craftworld is no mere vessel. It is a world unto itself, and armed to the teeth.'

Oleander leaned over the hololith, studying the *Quarzhazat's* schematics. 'So are we. Besides the *Quarzhazat*, there are two frigates, the *Sly Tongue* and the *Orchalius Unbound*. The others are the battle barge, *Feather of Zamhperyos*, and a strike cruiser...'

'The *Sixth Eye*,' Saqqara said. 'I recognise it. I saw it in action over Beauty's Fall. The crew are all eunuchs, their minds lost to realms of pleasure beyond the physical.'

Oleander looked at him. 'I didn't know you were at Beauty's Fall.' As bad a battle as any in the Legion Wars, with no clear sides to define it. Just ships ripping chunks out of one another, as they spun silently in the void. Oleander had been left clinging to a shattered spar of metal, his armour frosted over, until the Radiant's ship had retrieved him.

'There's a lot you don't know, sybarite.' Something in
the way he said it caught Oleander's attention. The Word
Bearer traced the sigils carved into his chest-plate as if in
silent prayer. Or perhaps he was simply listening to the
hum of the device implanted between his hearts. It was
hard to tell, with Saqqara.

'Quiet, both of you,' Bile said. 'A pretty fleet, if small, as
Arrian said.' He stood with his back to them, staring out
over the command deck. A sad, strange melody echoed
through the vox. A song from Old Terra, unintelligible
now with thousands of years of linguistic drift. One of
Bile's favourites, he recalled. He collected music with the
same determination he showed in acquiring raw materials. Orchestral compositions from across the width and
breadth of the galaxy sometimes echoed through the great
palace of Urum, when Bile was in a contemplative mood.
He hummed softly under his breath as his mind worked.

Oleander looked at Arrian, who shrugged. 'Powerful,
though,' Oleander said, arms crossed. 'The Radiant is no
fool. These are tested ships, with veteran crews. They've
fought their way past Imperial defences, and through the
asteroid-bastions of the Fourth Legion. Any one of them
would be a prize worth having.'

'But will they survive attacking a craftworld?' Saqqara
said.

'Some of them will, and that is all that matters for our
purposes,' Bile said, not looking at them. His eyes were
closed, and his knotted fingers twitched in time to the
music. Oleander wondered what he was thinking.

He was still somewhat surprised that Bile had moved to
aid him in his fight with the Joybound. That wasn't like
the Chief Apothecary he remembered. He wondered if

his words had sparked some ember of brotherhood that yet smouldered in Bile's heart. Or perhaps Bile had simply been returning the favour from Sublime.

'There will be the usual detritus as well – chaff before the scythe. Renegades, pirates, and those warbands seeking to curry favour with the Radiant,' Oleander said. 'As soon as word spreads of what we're attempting – it already has, like as not – others will come looking for a taste of the spoils. They're already arriving, in fact, if the vox-chatter is to be believed. The fleet will double in size before we reach Lugganath... or triple.' He looked at Bile. 'Are we taking the *Vesalius* in?'

'No,' Bile said. He glanced at Wolver, who stood silently beside him. 'The *Vesalius* will wait on the fringes, in case we need to escape. We'll take *Butcher-Bird* in. The gunship should be enough to get us where we're going, and out again.'

'And why are we going in at all?' Saqqara said. 'Why not simply let the Radiant do the work, and then reap the spoils after?'

'What joy is there to be had in that?' Arrian said. 'Besides, lions do not trust jackals.'

'Arrian is right,' Bile said. 'Kasperos will not let us hold back. He will want us there. It is the showman in him. He does not trust us.'

'He does not trust *you*,' Saqqara said. 'They will attempt to betray you. The Third has ever been full of traitors and fools. The Radiant wants you in a cage.'

'And you know this how?' Oleander said. Saqqara smiled.

'There are daemons aplenty clinging to the skin of this vessel, and they have whispered to me of perfidy and ruin.'

The Word Bearer passed his hand through the hololithic projection. 'You have set your hand in the wolf's mouth, degenerate. You should take care lest you lose it.'

For a moment, Oleander wondered who the Word Bearer was talking to. In the light of the hololith, Saqqara's face was monstrous. 'Kanathara howls in the void. I hear it, and more. I understand its words.'

'And what does it say?' Bile asked. 'More warnings from the lips of the Phoenician for his favoured son?' There was a distinct bite to his words. Oleander understood, and suspected the others did as well. The warriors of the Legions had been all but abandoned by their gene-fathers long before they'd fled Terra in disgrace. The Primarchs had ascended, become something other, and left their sons to fend for themselves as best they could.

'The ways of the Reborn and the Neverborn are not for mortal minds to understand. We can but follow the pattern they lay out before us.'

Bile laughed. 'And that, Saqqara, is the reason you are where you are. With a bomb in your chest, and your life in my hands.'

'Who's to say I am alone in that?' Saqqara said. 'The skeins of fate–'

'Fate is for fools. It is what the weak blame for their failures. I have ever forged my own path. Now, be silent before I forget how useful a tool you can be.' Saqqara fell silent. Bile looked at Oleander. 'How long will Kasperos wait to give his answer?'

'A few hours. Until he's certain you're telling the truth,' Oleander said. 'He'll run the data you gave him through the cogitators, just to be sure. He's eager, but not a fool.' And in the meantime, the rest of the Joybound would be scurrying about, trying to decide how to take advantage of the situation. When the Radiant ascended, the leadership of the 12th would fall to the strongest. He wondered which one would try and kill him first. Savona possibly. Gulos, almost certainly. It didn't matter. They would all have to be dealt with, eventually.

Bile turned. 'I am going to my laboratorium. I do not wish to be disturbed, unless the situation warrants. Whether he agrees or not, certain preparations must be undertaken without delay, if we are to accomplish what we came to do.'

Oleander watched him depart. He thought again of what the Shadowseer had said to him on Sublime. When he'd made his bargain with the xenos, he'd thought it fairly straightforward. Now it seemed to be anything but. Why had they attacked on Sublime?

He shook his head, annoyed. Too many questions. He pulled out his pipe and lit it, inhaling coloured smoke. Daemon shapes danced in the query marks of vapour, and his head began to clear of conundrums. None of it mattered, really. Fate was an avalanche. There was no avoiding it. All you could do was ride it out and hope for the best.

Perhaps he should have known better than to barter with such creatures. A Kabalite warrior of his acquaintance had once shared an old saying with him: Harlequins bearing gifts weren't to be trusted. But he needed them, and they needed him. They all wanted the same thing. The attack on Lugganath stymied. The Radiant gone.

And a new commander for the 12th Company of the Emperor's Children.

* * *

In his laboratorium, Bile let events replay themselves on the underside of his mind. An old trick, one he'd learned as a novice. The subconscious could easily sort through myriad lesser problems, while the conscious focused on more immediate tasks. Hololithic screens fuzzed as he slammed a fist against a console. Sometimes it took a bit of convincing to get everything to work properly. 'Then, we knew that, didn't we?' he said to the vat-born that scurried about his feet.

As he waited for his armour to establish a neural-link with the apothecarium equipment he looked around, making sure everything was where he'd left it. The vat-born had a tendency to move things about. Magnetised trays of surgical tools occupied the walls, alongside diverse charts documenting his experiments and observations. Enhanced pict-captures of in-progress dissections jostled for space with chemical readouts and scraps of poetry, culled from a dozen worlds. Beauty amidst the wreckage.

He strode over to a bio-vault containing a collection of progenoid glands, and traced the identi-sigils that marked each. Much of it had been harvested from battlefields within Eyespace, and displayed signs of mutation. Some had been collected on more mundane battlefields or stolen in raids, however, and were relatively pure. Samples had been culled from each, regardless of purity, and new organs were being artificially cultured from them in his nutrient tanks, including the lesser gene-seed he implanted in his Gland-hounds.

Many of the warbands he dealt with wanted stable gene-seed for their recruits, but most weren't choosy. Instability was simply a fact of life within the Eye – unavoidable and inexorable. Nonetheless, he maintained a certain professional pride in the sturdiness of his cultivations. Indeed, many in the Consortium had first come to the Grand Apothecarion seeking his secrets in that regard. He fancied he was responsible for the survival of more than one Legion, whether they'd admit it or not. And most wouldn't. His name was a curse.

The lab's equipment began to synch with his vox-node. He winced as a squeal of feedback scratched across his eardrums. For a moment, it almost sounded like laughter. It was getting worse all the time. Tzimiskes kept things in working order, but he was a tinkerer, rather than a proper adept. He activated his armour's vox-recorder. It was an old habit, and one he saw no reason to break. Even the most mundane of his musings might be of some use in the future.

'Entropy in action,' Bile said, running his fingers along the row of greasy specimen jars that occupied one wall. The jars were mag-locked to prevent the contents from being disturbed – or getting loose. 'The centre cannot hold. Some poet or other said that,' he said, glancing at one of the vat-born. 'Everything falls apart.' He tapped a jar, causing the disembodied head within to champ its jaws spasmodically. 'Everything changes. But not all change is beneficial, or necessary. Take the world of Fenris, for instance. The alteration of otherwise viable genetic sequences on a massive scale, resulting in a specific series of evolutionary adaptations, none of which are remotely beneficial outside one specific environment. Those born of Fenris will die with Fenris, when and if such a cataclysm occurs. Speculation? Possibly. A theory, at least.'

A theory, he has a theory, a voice crackled in his ear. He paused. Feedback, perhaps. He heard something that might have been a chuckle, and wondered whether they'd scoured all of the daemons from the *Vesalius* after all.

One of the vat-born patted his arm, and he absently stroked its sloped skull. 'It all comes down to entropy. A fire raging out of control, devouring all in its path. The universe winds down, and we wind down with it. The Eye is a wound that grows ever larger. What will be left in its wake, I wonder?' he said. The vat-born didn't reply, save in gurgles.

The King of Feathers wonders, oh he wanders-wonders-wishes-woes...

More feedback. Bile cleared his throat and continued. 'It all comes down to time, in the end. Never enough time. It speeds up as we draw closer to the terminus point, until it goes off the rails entirely and becomes meaningless. That's why time is so... diffuse in the Eye, of course. Again, entropy. It cannot be halted, but perhaps it can be controlled. Adapted to.'

The rest of the vat-born stopped what they were doing. Their wet, black eyes stared at him unblinkingly, attentively. They always listened when he spoke. He gestured and they snapped back to work. He turned and studied the pict-feed from the containment cells. The eldar lay where he'd left it, twitching as if in the throes of a dream. The containment cells contained sensory apparatus of his own design, capable of monitoring the biological state of its inhabitant down to the molecular level. He brought up a scan of the Corsair and peeled back the layers of digital flesh one after the next – epidermal, dermal, sub-dural, organ function, circulatory system, genetic structure.

'Subject's wound is healing nicely. No sign of infection, physical or otherwise. The mind-worm functioned as designed, with no sign of rejection. It will have completed its final mapping of the central nervous system in fourteen t-standard hours, allowing for the harvest of the necessary cells without fear of information loss.' Already, the mind-worm was transmitting a rough 'map' of the Corsair's full memories to the *Vesalius'* databanks. Once it was complete, he would know everything the Corsair knew – every secret, every hidden base.

Such information might prove useful, should the Sunblitz Brotherhood decide to make a nuisance of itself in the future. Bile had no doubt that they would seek recompense from Mordrac. And Mordrac would be more than happy to put them on the *Vesalius'* trail, but not soon enough to do any good. They had seen no pursuers since leaving Sublime. Even Mordrac's servants had given up, once *Vesalius* had unlimbered its batteries and scoured the void clean of attack-craft. By the time the Corsairs realised where they had gone, it would be too late.

Unless, of course, the affair on Sublime was all part of some esoteric scheme on the part of the Harlequins. That might explain why the Corsairs had yet to make an appearance. Bile grimaced, unsettled by the thought. The Harlequins would have to be added to the list of those who sought to interfere in his destiny. The creatures were abstract concepts, illogical and unpredictable.

And, for a moment, he thought they were in the cell with his prisoner. He froze, unable to process what he was seeing. Lithe figures, dancing about the unconscious Corsair, as if they knew someone were watching. The movements were hypnotic – unquantifiable – and then, they were gone, as if they had never been. He blinked, and summoned up multiple angles of feed.

There was nothing there. A dull ache hammered at the underside of his skull, and he rubbed his face. A hallucination. He wasn't unfamiliar with those, and they grew more frequent as his body broke down. Also, he hadn't slept in... he couldn't remember when. He needed rest – *his body* needed rest. And perhaps his mind as well.

But after. After. He cut the feed to the containment cell and turned away. 'Get me Subject P-12,' he said, more harshly than he'd intended. The vat-born hurried to obey, scrambling over the material storage cylinders arranged along the far end of the laboratorium.

The cylinders had been built to his specifications by an adept of his acquaintance – the Lady Spohr of Quir. The Dark Mechanicus had their uses, especially when it came to replacing his failing Crusade-era medicae equipment. He smiled, thinking of warm evenings spent on the Lady Spohr's brass veranda, far above the smog-sea which hid the black flesh-mills of Quir. They'd had a number of fascinating discussions on the arts of material preservation, in his time there. 'A rare creature,' he said.

The muttering vat-born dragged the body he'd requested from its storage unit. It was covered in preservative fluids, and had dozens of intravenous nodes implanted. The hardest part of his task was keeping the supplies fresh. That was what the cylinders were for. There was much that could be done with carrion, but for his work to proceed, he required fresh materials. Living bodies provided more opportunities for research than dead ones.

'Get him on the table,' Bile said, as he studied the diagnostic readouts. Bile had acquired the psyker after an attack on one of the Black Ships of the Imperium. He snorted at the thought. If there was a greater example of wasted potential in the galaxy he had yet to find it. The Loyalists fed a million souls to the Corpse-Emperor, all in an effort to stave off the inevitable.

'They and Abaddon deserve one another,' he said to the vat-born. The stunted creature looked up at him blankly. He was never entirely sure how much his creations understood, but he saw no reason to limit their education. Someday soon, they would have to make their own way in the universe. They needed to know what awaited them.

'Adaptation and evolution, not stagnation. Controlled adaptation, I should clarify. Uncontrolled mutations are worse than stagnation, frankly. Random elements will be the death of us all.' He turned to the body, examining it for any signs of damage. Finding none, he began his work. The subject was a powerful psyker. He'd displayed multifarious abilities, including low level sensory manipulation. Bile had deadened most of his major nerve clusters as a precaution, and slowed his brain functions to a crawl. Just enough to keep things ticking along, but not enough to be dangerous. The psyker might still be useful as a weapon at some unknown time. Until then, a sample of his brain matter would serve. His abilities could be grafted onto another and amplified, creating a sort of psychic fog that might prevent the fleet from detection. Combined with grafts taken from their prisoner, Bile was certain he could create the necessary sensory organs to both lead them to their prey, and hide them from its gaze. The chirurgeon stirred excitedly, ready to begin. 'Start incision on the left temple,' he said.

The doors to the laboratorium hissed open. Bile didn't look up. He knew who it was. Only one member of the Consortium was allowed to enter unannounced. 'Arrian...

come to observe my technique?' The chirurgeon's blades flickered. 'If I recall correctly, it has been some time since you last practised a cranial exhumation.'

'It seems a shame to waste such potential on behalf of something so rudimentary as an invasion,' Arrian said. 'And after all the effort we expended to acquire him.' The World Eater watched the chirurgeon work, arms crossed.

'Let us not forget the samples we acquired from the other prisoners,' Bile said, as the chirurgeon separated flesh from bone. 'One must always seize opportunity, Arrian. This subject's abilities make him invaluable for the task ahead. We will sacrifice a little to gain a lot.'

'Why are we doing this?' Arrian asked. 'Oleander is untrustworthy. This Radiant as well. They are not our allies.'

'No, they are not. And yet here we are. Does this worry you?'

'I am not worried. I am simply inquisitive, Chief Apothecary,' Arrian said.

'So I see.' Bile looked up from his work. 'You are an ongoing project, Arrian. Who knows what you'll become, when you've finally finished slicing away all that you were.' Sometimes he forgot how clever the World Eater was. He stepped back from the examination table. 'Why, you ask... the answer should be obvious, if you are half as observant as I believe you to be. What do the eldar possess that we do not?' Bile didn't wait for an answer. 'Longevity. And more besides... eternity. Continuity of thought and memory, across eons. A form of self-defence, in their case. But for me, freedom. Freedom from a broken, crumbling shell. Freedom from arduous and dangerous surgical procedures. Imagine, Arrian, a mind capable of passing from one body to the next instantaneously.'

Arrian nodded slowly. 'You need the spirit stones.'

'More than that. The stones themselves are useless. I need uncorrupted wraithbone. I need the mechanism of transference. I need knowledge, Arrian. So I intend to procure it.'

'Their seers,' Arrian said.

'At last, you display some modicum of understanding. Yes, their seers. Not the living ones, of course. But the dead... well. The dead can be made to talk more easily than the living.' He gestured to Arrian's collection of skulls. The World Eater touched them instinctively.

'That is why,' Bile said. 'You see now, why I risk the inevitable treachery of our allies? Entropy. My body is rotting on the bone. I must find a way of managing my disease, lest it impair the foundations of tomorrow.' He turned back to the table. 'So, it is worth wagering a bit of hard-won material in this gamble.'

Arrian was silent. Then, 'As you say, Chief Apothecary.'

CHAPTER THIRTEEN

Treachery

'Watching the stars burn out?' Oleander said, looking down at his fellow Joybound. Merix ignored him, the way he'd been ignoring him since they'd arrived. He sat on the edge of one of *Quarzhazat*'s massive vista-ports, watching the void. Its scute-shielding was raised, exposing the vast, cluttered emptiness beyond. The great tacticum-vaults of the Lunar-class cruiser were somewhere directly below them, and the immense, weirdly veined barrels of a gun battery extended out from somewhere just below the bottom lip of the vista-port.

True to Oleander's assertion, it had only taken a few hours for the Radiant to request Bile's presence. They had returned to the *Quarzhazat*, unaccompanied save for a motley gaggle of vat-born, brought to tend Bile's creation. The Joybound had been waiting for them, as he'd expected. The champions had escorted Bile to the Radiant's quarters without speaking. Their glares had spoken volumes, however.

The discipline of the Third had once been without equal. Now it had collapsed entirely, leaving only ambitious barbarism in its wake. Overeager savages, scrabbling for influence among the ashes. Grudgingly, he included himself among their number.

Bile had wished to speak with the Radiant alone. Oleander had taken the opportunity to renew his familiarity with the ship, and its crew. 'You aren't still upset about the gauntlet, I hope,' Oleander said. 'I only did what I had to do.' He looked around.

The observation deck had become a place of contemplation and experimentation for the masters of the *Quarzhazat*. A place to indulge in pleasures of body and mind. Slaves bearing immense narcotic generators staggered to and fro, filling the air with a pleasant fug. Emperor's Children sat on marble benches looted from Imperial temples and eldar crone worlds, or lounged on cushions made from the flayed hides of prisoners, speaking softly to one another of past debaucheries and future ecstasies. They wagered on gladiatorial bouts, watching as unlucky crewmembers gutted each other with rusty blades or, in some cases, hands and teeth.

Elsewhere, the crude gutter-poetry of lost Nostromo warred with ear-splitting songs culled from the manufactorums of Chemos and Cthonia. The more artistically inclined among them painted obscene murals on the wall and deck. Armour was peeled away from flesh, so that brands could be applied, or the bite of a tattooist's needle. In the shadows, more intimate entertainments were being enjoyed, to judge by the screams of slave and Space Marines alike. The smell of blood and worse was strong on the air.

Part of the deck had been converted into an auditorium. Curtains made from swathes of stitched flesh hung over makeshift walls made from melted and cut bone. Great benches, made from scrap metal, fossilised bone and other, less identifiable substances, rose up and away from the immense stage that dominated its centre. The benches around it were sparsely filled, and audience members came and went as the mood took them.

The stage, like the auditorium, had been made from flesh and bone. Unlike the walls and benches, however, it still lived. Bodies had been linked with heat and surgery, forced to grow into one another. Pruned, shaped and reinforced by careful attention. Oleander was quite pleased by the result. It had taken him a long time to get it right. The rear struts had kept dying.

The stage sighed, screamed and sagged in exhaustion as Kakophoni strutted and preened across its surface. Backs blistered and bled as taloned boots tore waxy flesh. Bones creaked with the weight of the Noise Marines as they unleashed an atonal caterwaul. The few visible faces hung from the edge of the stage like decorative gargoyles, moaning in pleasurable pain. The screams rose to a crescendo, matching the screech of the Noise Marines, and a bevy of dancers whirled wildly onto the stage from between the benches.

The dancers wielded knives, or else had blades lashed to festering stumps, and they slashed at one another as they moved in time to the music. Emperor's Children stood in the wings, lashing the slower slaves with barbed whips, urging them to greater heights of frenzy. Gulos moved among the slaves like lightning, leaping, twisting, stabbing. Slaves stumbled on their own spilling intestines, or else slumped, clutching at ruined throats. The crowd applauded.

Merix, however, seemed to be enjoying none of it. His indulgences had always been more philosophical than physical. He turned away from the display. 'What do you want, Apothecary?'

'Merely enquiring as to your well-being, brother.' Oleander snatched up a goblet from the tray of a passing slave. He gulped it down, feeling the delightful burn of Neverborn venom, spiked with something decidedly acidic.

'Not my brother. I have no brothers,' Merix said. His voice was a wheezing rasp, slithering out from behind a respirator grille. His flesh was an angry red where it touched the respirator – a sign of possible infection. Oleander studied the Joybound, noting the way he favoured one arm over the other, the way he twitched – bones badly set, possible nerve damage, exacerbated by the touch of Torment. One of his hands whined as it flexed – the prosthesis was badly in need of an upgrade. Merix was worn down to a nub. There were many like him, among those who'd fled into the Eye. Walking wounded, unable to heal, and unable to die. But still useful, despite that.

'No. I suppose none of us do, these days. Lean forward.'

'Why?'

'Your neck hasn't healed correctly from the last time you tangled with Savona. I can tell it hurts. I want to look at it.' The Joybound kept themselves entertained by trying to murder one another. Whole wars had been fought across the lower decks of the *Quarzhazat*, as the Joybound led tribes of slaves and mutants against each other in open battle. The Radiant seemed to enjoy these occasional slaughters, and openly encouraged them, when he wasn't leading a hunt or consorting with his Never-born courtesans.

'Get away from me, fleshcrafter,' Merix said, hauling himself to his feet. 'Pain is good. Better than pleasure, even, for it is ever sharp.' He flexed his prosthesis in Oleander's face. It vented dust and sparks. 'It helps me focus.'

'So people say. I think it just slows you down, myself. And you are no use to me slow.' He met Merix's bleary-eyed glare and held it. 'Sit.'

Merix sat back down with a grunt, and leaned forward. Oleander probed his neck, feeling the subtle wrongness of the bones there. There would be no fixing those. 'I thought you were gone for good,' Merix said, hissing in pain.

'No. I merely went to get help.' As he worked, he watched Gulos fight, scrutinising the way the Joybound's muscles tensed and flexed, the way his joints extended and retracted. He noted the way Gulos favoured his left for overhand strikes, and his right for slashes. The way his knees bent, the way his ankles turned. The human body was a roadmap of potential pain, each one with its own unique route. You simply had to observe it, to find the most efficient means of destroying it.

'For who? You... or us?'

'One and the same. What do Nikola and Lidonius say? Are they with us?' Oleander said, as he injected a cortical steroid into Merix's neck.

'Nikola is. He grows tired of Gulos' highhanded ways. Lidonius... is Lidonius. There's no way of telling whose side he's on. I doubt even he knows. Nikola believes he'll follow our lead, however.' Merix twisted his head. 'That feels better.'

'It won't last long. We can reroute the nerves there, or

replace them entirely. Your bones have changed – are changing.'

'I know. I am blessed by the gods. My pain is as good as prayer,' Merix said. He held up his prosthetic hand. 'Look – see what grows.' Strands of muscle tissue and feathery nerves coiled like creeper vines about the pistons and cables of the limb. 'Perhaps they'll be calling me Blessed Merix soon, eh?'

'Perhaps,' Oleander said. 'When the time comes...'

'When the time comes, we will do as the gods will.' Merix peered up at him. 'And you have no desire to lead, yourself?'

'No,' Oleander said.

Merix laughed. It came out as a mechanical croak. 'What of the Manflayer?' His eyes narrowed. 'Is he with us?'

'Oh yes. He knows all about it. He will help, in return for a bit of flesh and bone. And my brothers in the Consortium as well. Gulos will never know what hit him. And you will control the fleet.'

'We will control the fleet... brother,' Merix said. He clasped Oleander's forearm with his living hand. 'And we will do great things, when this foolishness is behind us. We shall return our Legion to glory.'

'So we will,' Oleander said. He studied Merix's face, searching for any hint of guile or deception. There was none. Cunning aplenty, but not deception. Merix was a fool, clinging to nostalgia and hope. The Legion Wars had broken him in more ways than one. And now the gods had their claws in the cracks, and were pulling him apart, bit by bit. Like Lidonius. Like the Radiant. 'Is that Savona I see, in the crowd down there?'

'Yes. She's watching Gulos, as always. We will have to deal with her as well.'

'Perhaps not.'

'She is not one of us, Oleander. She is not a warrior of the Third.'

'No,' he said. 'She is not.'

He left Merix sitting, and made his way towards the crude stage. 'Whose composition is this?' he asked Savona, when he found her.

'One of Nikola's, I believe,' Savona said, watching as Gulos beheaded a slave wrapped in barbed wires and chains. 'He has hidden depths. Unlike Gulos.' The noise rose and fell with savage intensity, ripped from the aether and hurled into the air. The Kakophoni shrieked in unison, causing the bone walls of the auditorium to buckle and splinter, and nearby slaves to drop dead in ecstasy. Savona closed her eyes. 'A fair tune.'

'Indeed,' Oleander said. He looked at her. 'Were you planning to interfere?'

'In what?' she replied, lazily.

He looked at Gulos. She laughed. 'No, fleshcrafter. Kill him if you can. It saves me the trouble.' She traced a claw along his vambrace. 'We will settle our own affairs afterwards.'

'And to the winner the spoils,' Oleander said. Savona laughed. The sound grated across his ears like the screech of metal on metal. Part of him longed to end her here and now. But no – one enemy at a time. He moved towards the stage.

Gulos swept the head from the last slave and turned, as Oleander drew close. 'I was wondering when you would slink over here, fleshcrafter. I'm surprised you're not clinging to Bile's coat. After all, he's the only reason you survived the gauntlet.'

Oleander studied the first of the Joybound. Gulos Palatides had been handsome once. And he still was, until
you got too close. Like a statue, weathered by time and
suffused with innumerable cracks and flaws. His face was
a thing by turns beautiful and grotesque, depending on
where you stood. 'I merely come to pay homage to you,
as is my duty as fourth of the Joybound,' he said, extending his palms in a gesture of ritual supplication.

Gulos laughed. 'Who said you were fourth?'

'Process of elimination. Savona is second. Merix is third,
Nikola isn't ambitious enough to be fourth, and Lidonius
is barely aware of where he is at any given moment.' Oleander rested his hands on the hilt of his sword. 'Don't
worry, I am not so foolish to seek the position of first.'

'No. You'd have to fight Savona and Merix both for
that,' Gulos said, stepping off the twitching stage. Bits of
slave slid from his armour as he moved, but he didn't
seem concerned. 'How is Merix, by the way? I saw you
talking to him.'

'Wearing down.'

Gulos snorted. 'He's weak.'

Oleander looked away. 'If you're planning to kill him,
do it quickly. He deserves that much at least.'

'Is that pity I detect in your voice?'

'Not pity, but consideration. He is our brother.'

'A brother is an equal, Oleander. I have no brothers,'
Gulos said. 'Those I did have, I killed. I am unique in the
galaxy, and I will make myself more unique still before
this affair is over.' He glanced at Oleander. 'My only concern is you.'

'Me?' Oleander said. He lunged, blade springing into
his hand. The crowd surged back, making room. Gulos

bent backwards with boneless grace, avoiding the blow. He bounded up, blades out, and crossed them against Oleander's throat.

'You missed,' Gulos said. 'You're too slow, Apothecary. Stick to your poisons and purgatives, and leave blade-work to the true warriors.'

'As you say, brother,' Oleander said. He'd known Gulos wouldn't kill him yet. But this close, he could get a better look at the minute stress fractures in the armour around Gulos' throat. A century's worth of repair and gilding had weakened the bonding of the ceramite. A weak point. A hole could be made in one blow there, and death would follow soon after, if it was done correctly, with precision.

Gulos shoved him back and sheathed his blades. He smirked. 'You are nothing more than an irritant to me, Oleander. Never forget that.'

'I think on it every day, I assure you,' Oleander said, still pondering the weak point. He'd spent years letting Gulos prove his superiority. The first of the Joybound knew, beyond a shadow of a doubt, that he was the superior warrior. That he had no weaknesses. And Oleander wanted him to keep believing that, until the moment to dispatch the first of the Joybound had arrived.

Gulos laughed and patted him on the shoulder. 'See that you do.' Oleander watched him leave. Slaves scattered about him, like minnows before a shark. Even other warriors of the Emperor's Children stepped aside, not out of deference for his rank, but to stay out of reach of his blades. Gulos was arrogant and deadly, in the way that Merix was foolish and broken. Both were weak, but in different ways. Of the two, Oleander preferred Merix.

Gulos, and the Radiant as well, were part of the cancer

that afflicted the Third. While they, and those like them, ruled, the Emperor's Children would remain a shattered Legion. He'd learned that the hard way, in his years in the wilderness. The Eye was mad and it made those who sheltered within it mad. But madness could be shaped. Even controlled. All it required was the right mind to guide it. And that the cancers afflicting the body politic be excised.

Something flickered, just out of the corner of his eye. A silvery mask, hovering in the crowd. Something chuckled at the edge of his hearing. Nearby slaves scattered like quail. The Emperor's Children took no notice, still intent on the Noise Marines' squalling performance. Slaves were fragile things, and took fright so easily. Oleander heard a snatch of song in a sudden squeal of feedback echoing through his vox.

He turned, studying the crowd. They were on the ship, here in the very heart of their enemy. Once, he would have thought such a thing impossible, though he had heard the stories of guerrilla raids on daemon worlds, and ambushes in the deep black motes of the Eye, where only the Neverborn dared to tread. But not now. Now he knew better.

This was how it had started. Whispers in the crowd. A voice in the dark. Shadows in the belly of the beast. 'Careful now. I know you are here, Veilwalker,' he said, softly.

Maybe. Maybe we are daemons, Apothecary.

The vox-frequency was isolated, meant for him alone. They were clever creatures, and cruel, but took no chances. 'Or maybe I'm simply mad. One more mad Apothecary, collecting voices along with the blood and flesh.' He sank down beside the remains of one of the slaves Gulos had killed, and took a blood sample.

It was turgid muck, as was to be expected. While fresh supplies of slaves were added to the mix regularly, the bulk of them came from the lower decks. They bred down in the dark like rats, leading short, brutal lives often punctuated by sudden violence. Most were mutants, their stock grown thin thanks to centuries of interbreeding and exposure to the Eye. But, occasionally, something more could be made of them. He had been hunting slaves for his experiments when he'd found the Harlequins. Or they'd found him. Deep in the dark, secret places.

Mad-ad-ad. No, Oleander. You are not mad. You are the hero, the Count Sunflame, striving to awaken the King of Feathers in his rags and regrets, to bring him to war, and his throne, once more. And you play your part beautifully...

'How did you even get on this ship?' he asked, trying to tease out answers.

Silence. Then, laughter. Still on one knee, he bent forward, clutching at his head. The riotous merriment cut through his skull like a blade, driving out all thought. He gritted his teeth, enduring it, relishing the pain. All at once, and too soon, it was over. He looked around. No one appeared to have noticed.

Come-come-come and see if you wish...

Oleander heaved himself upright, with a growl. 'I will. For we have much to discuss.'

'You have come to a decision then?'

Bile ignored the daemons as they twisted and gyrated in a wretched parody of lust. They pouted at him as they spun away, out of reach of his chirurgeon. They were inconsequential things. A random confluence of raw emotion, given shape by the Radiant's diseased psyche. If they spoke, it was only with the voice of the subconscious. He cleared his throat and repeated his question.

The Radiant turned, his fingers trailing through the gorgon tresses of one of his creations. 'Yes. Where is Oleander?'

'Renewing old acquaintances.' Bile smiled. It was the truth, in a sense. Oleander was scheming, no doubt. Seeking some advantage, in order to better position himself for the inevitable. Bile was content to leave him to it, so long as it did not interfere with the greater plan.

'You surprised me,' the Radiant said. 'The Fabius I knew of old would have left faithless Oleander to die a well-deserved death.'

'That only proves you never knew me at all. I despise needless waste, Kasperos. It offends me. Every scrap of flesh has its use, however small and unremarkable.'

'So Oleander has said. I suppose he took your lessons to heart. How are you planning to help me with my wall, Fabius?' The Radiant held up the hololith Bile had left with him. 'How will you help me take Lugganath?'

'The eldar can sense you coming. So we shall dull their senses.' Bile gestured and the pack of grunting vat-born he'd brought with him carefully wheeled forward a heavy nutrient tank. The ochre liquid within burbled softly, as the magni-filters set on the sides of the glass tank kept up a steady hum. Floating suspended in the liquid was the result of several long hours of diligent labour on the part of both man and machine – an intricate web of neural matter, spliced from the brains of over a hundred psykers culled from his collection.

'What is it?' the Radiant asked, half reaching towards the containment tank. Bile caught his wrist in a grip of iron.

'Fragile,' he said. He released the Radiant, as the daemons hissed at him in agitation. 'Mind the glass. It is older than this ship and I cannot easily replace it.'

'It looks like a bundle of nerves.'

'It is. Or part of one. Newly grown and spliced with parts from others. Samples taken from our captive were added at each stage, in order to accommodate differences in human and xenos central nervous systems. They have fully joined together, and the threat of cellular rejection has declined to acceptable levels. They can now be implanted, and activated.'

'It is very pretty, Fabius, but it does not look like a weapon.' The Radiant peered down at the fronds of nerve tissue and ran a finger over the curve of the glass. Bile frowned, but said nothing. 'What does it do?'

'It will emit a psychic miasma... a fog of the mind. Keyed specifically to the brain patterns of our prey, thus allowing for an uncontested approach.' He smiled. 'A work of subtle genius.'

'And how does it work?'

'Implantation, as I said. It will be layered over existing neural tissue. Then hardwired into the *Quarzhazat*'s central cogitator core. The effect will be akin to a Geller field. Ensuring that while the eldar might see us, they will not *perceive* us. Not until it is too late.'

'Oh, excellent. Excellent, Fabius,' the Radiant said. 'What do you require to complete this work of artistry?'

'Time,' Bile said. 'And flesh. You have psykers in this fleet of yours. Witches. Select me a few dozen. The strongest of those not put to better use elsewhere.'

'Why?'

'I intend to cut their skulls open and put something inside.' He laid his hand on the tank.

The Radiant blinked. 'Very well,' the Radiant said. 'What do you think of my collection?' He gestured to the wall. Hundreds of weapons hung there, draped in folds of silk and golden chains. Bile recognised the crude blades of orks and the elegant glass-glaives of the Racathian Hegemony. There were diamond-toothed eldar chainswords and Mars-pattern power swords. 'I built it myself, one enemy at a time.'

'Impressive.'

'You do not sound impressed. Tell me, Fabius, why did you leave Terra? The battle had yet to be won or lost, but you set your facilities to the torch and fled. We could've used your skills, during the retreat. Fulgrim was livid.' The Radiant stroked the edge of a friction axe.

'I had an epiphany,' Bile said. 'I saw the uselessness of what we were trying to accomplish and had no wish to further waste my time.'

'And was your loyalty worth so little then?'

'What was there to be loyal to?' Bile said. 'Even afterwards, when Fulgrim had departed to sulk in solitude, and I tried to bring some order to the madness, I was undermined at every turn. It was almost a relief when Canticle City burned.'

'It is still there, you know. Canticle City. Ruined, of course, but it still exists, spread out in the shadow of Abaddon's spear. We meet there, when the tides of the empyrean allow, and discuss our future. It has become a place of reflection for us.'

'And who is us? This Phoenix Conclave you mentioned earlier?' Bile said, curious despite himself. The Phoenix Guard had been an elite cadre serving as Fulgrim's personal retinue, but so far as he was aware, Kasperos had never been inducted into their ranks. But this sounded like something else. More like one of those blasted warrior-lodges than anything else.

'We are the elite,' the Radiant said, studying his trophies. 'And our numbers grow, in the silences. Eidolon, Lucius, dear Julius... the captains and commanders of the Legion, who yet remember what it means to bow before something greater. Fulgrim, our Illuminator, slumbers like the phoenix of legend. But when he awakens, the Third will be ready to serve.'

Bile snorted. 'So, a pack of fools, up to foolish things.' He heard a whimper and turned towards a curtained alcove behind the Radiant's throne. The Radiant smiled.

'Ah. They are awake. They were asleep when last you visited. Would you like to see them?' he said, gesturing to the curtain.

'What is it?'

'This is one of Oleander's great works – the Choir of Pain,' the Radiant said as he jerked the curtains aside. Six slaves stood in a row. They trembled, though whether in fear or excitement Bile could not say. Both, perhaps. Each one had undergone extensive bio-modification – jaws distorted, larynxes widened or narrowed, palates cleft, soldered and stretched. Throats and torsos bulged with cybernetic enhancements, all geared towards a singular purpose. Serpentine lengths of bundled cable connected one to the next, binding them irrevocably together.

The Radiant reached out and dug his clawed fingers into the pale flesh of one. A single note of sound burst from the slave's malformed jaws. As it quivered on the air, the others followed suit, one after the next, each emitting a further note, the cables pulsing in time.

Bile laughed. 'Clever.' Each of the slaves had been modified to produce but a single sound, an individual note in whatever melody the Radiant conceived. 'Simple, but with the possibility for infinite variation.'

'You see now why I wished to have my own Apothecary.'

Bile nodded, still studying the choir. Apothecaries as a species were nearly extinct in the Eye. The sundering of the Legions and their slow, inevitable decline had seen to that. Specialists required discipline and focus to hone their craft. To acquire the services of one was a point of pride for many warlords, former officers in the Legions or otherwise. He turned as he felt the Radiant touch his shoulder.

'It was a sad day when you left us, Fabius. We had none capable of carrying on your work. We were awash in aspiring artistes, with no master to wring greatness from them.'

'One would think you might have considered that, before you hounded me into the depths of the Eye.' Bile looked at the Radiant. 'You were there, Kasperos. You were there the day my brothers turned on me, baying for my blood. As if I had not risked all for them – gambled my very soul for their benefit.'

'Can you blame them? You nearly destroyed us, Fabius.'

'You destroyed yourselves. I gave you a chance to be a Legion again. To seize hold of greatness, of perfection, and take what was yours. And once again, you failed. Horus was your scapegoat the first time. And I, the second. Who will it be next, I wonder? Abaddon, perhaps. He seems ripe for a fall. Or perhaps it will be this Conclave of yours...'

'Bitterness has its place, Fabius. But I find it wearying. When this is done, when I have taken my rightful place, I wish you to stay,' the Radiant said.

'You will remain here?' Bile said. 'I assumed you would ascend, find new fields of plunder, new ecstasies.'

The Radiant laughed. 'I know. My Joybound assume

much the same. Isn't it delicious? Already, they fracture. Bonds of loyalty break and re-form, oaths of moment are tested, and schemes are teased to fruition. And those beneath them are much the same.'

'You're playing with them.'

'Of course. What else is there to do?' The Radiant turned away. He stroked one of the slaves across the cheek, eliciting a trilling whimper. 'They've grown complacent, I fear. We are mighty, but that might has not truly been tested in some time. The skeins of the immaterium draw tight, Fabius. Something has begun, in the depths of the universe. I have seen it in my dreams... a hunger unlike any other stretches towards us out of black seas of infinity, and the dead stir on a thousand thousand worlds.' There was a naked longing in the Radiant's voice.

'And you wish to see it all,' Bile said.

The Radiant turned towards him. 'Don't you?'

'Not especially. But then, the travails of the wider universe are of little interest to me.' Bile tightened his grip on Torment. 'What do you want, Kasperos? Really?'

'What do I want, Fabius? I want everything. I want to snuff the stars, and strangle the fates for all that they promised. I want to feel the heat of a dying sun on my face, and to write my story across the skin of a newborn world. I want you to be there, when I reach into the dark and find perfection. And I want you to join me in all that is to come. That is what I want,' the Radiant said. 'What about you? What do you want, Chief Apothecary Fabius? What can I give you, to make you stay?'

Bile looked away. 'There is nothing I want that you can give me.'

'There must be something. Some scrap of flesh, some

twisted genome ripped from the body of an enemy. Remember when we took Canticle City for our own? Or when we laid siege to the Monument, and rained down fire on Lupercalios? How we fought and bled to gain that which you desired?'

Bile did. It had been a last, masterful gambit. One last campaign for the Third and its allies, after the ruination of Skalathrax. One last chance to hold together that which was determined to fly apart. All for nothing. 'I will need one other thing from you,' he said.

'And what is that?'

'I will need a living body to act as the central node,' Bile said.

'What sort of body, Fabius?'

'An augmented one. Psychically or otherwise. Void-hardened. Capable of enduring stressors beyond the norm... as well as inflicting them.' Bile tapped his throat. 'Preferably in the vocal, as well as the aural.' He smiled. 'I am given to understand that you have a number of such subjects aboard.'

'*Kakophoni*,' the Radiant said, breathing the word. The daemonettes ceased their capering and fell silent. 'Oleander told you?'

'He did,' Bile said. 'A Noise Marine's altered physiology can withstand internal pressures that would burst any normal transhuman from the inside out. Pressures such as the one this neural web will create in its host. A normal psyker would burn out and die in moments. Even one of Magnus' sons would be unable to endure the raw psychic feedback. But the Kakophoni can.'

The Radiant nodded slowly. The gathered daemonettes hissed at Bile, but without any real malice. He turned back to his weapons. 'You will make your request at the House of Noise in person. I will not force one of Slaanesh's chosen to forego their due on your whim.'

Bile inclined his head. 'And what is this House of Noise, Kasperos?'

'I have asked you not to call me that, Fabius.' The Radiant took an eldar blade off the wall and ran his fingers along its edge. 'They've made a nest in one of the outer observation decks. You'll have to cross the hull to get to it. We sealed off all internal corridors long ago, due to an incursion of Neverborn. The Kakophoni wiped them out and claimed that area for their own. It is their citadel now. The House of Noise.'

'Then I shall visit them.' Bile studied the weapons. 'Why do you want me to stay, Kasperos? Most wish to be rid of me.'

'Why do you not wish to stay?' the Radiant countered. 'Am I so pitiful a beast that even Chief Apothecary Fabius is repulsed? Have I not made something beautiful here?'

'You are not the disease. You are but the symptom.' Bile shook his head. 'Mankind was on the cusp of greatness, Kasperos. And we yanked it away, on the advice of a shared delusion.'

'You sound as if you regret what we have done,' the Radiant said. He set the eldar blade back on the wall.

'Regret?' Bile said. 'No. But it is my nature to question, and our brothers have become ensnared by a dogma no less flawed than that of the Loyalists. We traded one form of servitude for another, and for what? The chance to become nothing more than the basest of slaves. Is your collar heavy, Kasperos? Have you noticed the weight yet? I would not share it with you for anything.'

The Radiant was silent for a time. Then, with a chuckle, he said, 'It is no wonder that you are so hated, Fabius. You did this to us, you know. You and Fulgrim and Lucius and Eidolon and all the rest... you led us into the daemon's maw. We followed, but you led the way. You showed us new ways to shout and revel and kill, and now you complain because – what? – we do not choose a life of austerity, as you have?'

'And what have you chosen, Kasperos? What ineffable glory awaits you, when you shed this mortal coil?'

'I will be a thing impossible to conceive, without limit or weakness. I will be as one with our patron god, and with our primarch.' He leaned close, his hand resting on Bile's shoulder. 'There are glories beyond your ken, Fabius. And I will experience them all, for an eternity.'

Bile shrugged the Radiant off and turned. 'And that is where we are different. For I do not do this for myself. I do it for all mankind. A better mankind, one able to easily weather the storm of madness which even now batters down the walls of reality. I may not live to see it flourish, but I will build its foundations on all of our bones if I must.'

The Radiant stepped back. 'Lucius was right about you,' he said. 'You are wholly mad.'

'No. I am simply terminally frustrated. Now, if you will excuse me, I must pay a visit to your Kakophoni.' He made to step past the Radiant, but a hand on his chest stopped him.

'They laughed at me, when I suggested offering you a place in our Conclave. They said you would not slither out of your hole for anything. But I know you will come to see the necessity.' The Radiant smiled. 'After all, here you are.'

'For now,' Bile said.

The Radiant's smile faded. 'Do not play me false, Fabius. I know deceit when I smell it, and the odour grows thick here. If you attempt to cheat me of my destiny, I will rip your ossified spine from your reeking carcass and beat you to death with it.'

Bile smiled. 'It is a pleasure to hear you sounding more like your old self, Kasperos.'

'I am pleased that you are pleased, brother.' The Radiant crushed the hololith between his fingers. 'Do remember what I said, Fabius. Keep it foremost in your mind.'

'Oh I will. Never fear,' Bile said, as he watched the pieces of the hololith fall to the deck. He thought he heard something in the shadows chuckle, but dismissed it as the work of daemons.

Oleander had descended quickly into the lowest holds of the *Quarzhazat*. The laughter of the Harlequins had teased and taunted him the entire way, pricking the edges of his hearing, drawing him deeper into the most unstable sections of the ship. As with the Radiant's throne room, these were places where the hard edge of reality grew soft and thin, allowing the warp to bleed through, changing whatever it touched.

There were dangers aplenty in these depths. Roving bands of mutants and the occasional semi-manifested Neverborn, trapped in a husk of borrowed flesh, stalked the lowest decks freely. Their cries echoed through the cavernous hold, as they waged their primitive battles for control of the ever-shifting terrain. At these depths, the ship was more environment than engine – bulkheads of meat, pulsing with veins and vestigial organs, blocked off passageways that resembled more the intestinal track of some great beast than the corridors of a ship of the line.

Fitting, then, that its guts were so full of detritus. These lower holds were full of plunder acquired over the course of centuries – loot taken in the retreat from Terra, and the Legion Wars, technologies acquired in raids since, all discarded down in the dark when it ceased to be of interest. The 12th Company had the ability to salvage it, but lacked the inclination to do so. Whatever wasn't of immediate use was discarded. He passed the remains of looted gunships and once, the slowly crumbling husk of some form of eldar fighter-craft.

The lumen-tracks set along the deck flickered weakly, barely illuminating the path ahead. Oleander activated the light-globe built into his backpack. Cold, pale light spilled out, revealing tangled hummocks of machinery, collapsed pyramids of bone and other grisly oddities, which filled the vast hold. He stopped before a skeleton crucified against a bent section of deck plating, and studied it. A servitor, he thought. Or it had been. Now it was a primitive signpost, nailed to an improvised wall of rusted metal.

He looked around. Entropy, the Chief Apothecary called it. The gradual slide of the complex into the simple. The breakdown of the machinery that made the galaxy work. That was the purpose of Chaos, as Bile saw it. The warp was an ocean, eroding the rock of reality.

Something clattered behind him. He spun, servos whining, his sword whipping out even as his light-globe caught a dozen pairs of beast-eyes. A goat-headed mutant slumped, crude hatchet clattering from its spasming paw. He retrieved its head and held it up by a crooked horn, displaying it to the rest of the pack. There were at least thirty of them. Twice that number would have been no threat.

He tossed the head to the largest of them and waited. One by one, they backed away, whining. Soon the last of them had vanished back into the jungle of wreckage, as silently as they had come. Oleander knelt to retrieve a sample from the body. Mutants were vermin, but hardy. And fierce. Their feral genetics made for durable materials.

Something caught his eye and he stood. Sweeping aside the carpet of wreckage, he found the burnt-out remains of a Domitar-class battle-automaton. Its chassis was burnt open, and it had been plundered for spare parts, but it was mostly intact. Whatever machine-spirit had once inhabited it had either fled or was dormant, leaving it nothing more than a rusting hulk. He ran a hand through the cobwebs and dust, exposing unit markings. He traced the scars that marked its hull, wondering how it had come to be here, forgotten in the belly of a beast.

'A proud warrior, reduced to ruin,' he murmured. The saga of the Third, writ in junk. Appropriate, perhaps. They'd shed everything else of use, everything that mattered, and waded into the roaring sea of Chaos without hesitation, seeking perfection in the simplicity of madness. All of their old glories, old loyalties, and old strengths were left to rot, like the battle-automaton. But without those things, what was left?

There was satisfaction in simplicity. But perfection was found in complexity. In the multifarious facets of the thing. A thrust from a sword could kill, but only in the perfect thrust, artfully done, was the perfect kill achieved.

'We have let greed blind us to our true purpose,' he said,

out loud. Even Fulgrim. But not the Master of the Apothecarion. Fabius still sought perfection, for reasons few understood. But Oleander knew.

Thus spake Count Sunflame, to the ghosts in the courts of ruin...

Laughter filled the vox. He caught up his sword and rose, his armour's sensors sweeping out. An eerie light glimmered in the depths of the hold, slipping through the tangles of wreckage to tease his eyes. He padded forward, as silently as possible. The light grew stronger, and it sparked with unrecognisable colours. His sensors registered the shapes before he saw them, and he looked up.

Improvised stakes of rusted metal rose from the deck, each one heavy with the bodies of several of the hold's feral inhabitants. Their blood dripped steadily to the deck, where it vanished in the pearlescent mist issuing from a pale edifice jutting from a clump of wreckage. Gaily attired shapes slipped and slid down the incline, dancing beneath the encumbered stakes, as if the dead mutants were an attentive audience. Or perhaps it was for his benefit.

'A webway gate,' Veilwalker said softly, from behind him. He turned, his sword stopping just at the edge of the Shadowseer's throat. The xenos didn't flinch.

'Left over from some vessel the Radiant King drew in and ripped apart, forgotten down here in the belly of his flagship. Like a bit of poison,' Veilwalker continued. 'It still functions, and has for centuries. The Veiled Path alone know of it, and much use have we got out of it.'

'Why are you letting me see this?' His sword didn't waver. If they'd brought him down here to kill him, he intended to see that the Shadowseer joined him in death.

'It will be destroyed soon.'

'And me?'

The eldar stretched out a finger and etched a curious rune on the air. It flickered briefly and faded. 'The inverse enigma. Riddles within riddles. A sign of ill-omened demise, I am told. But for who?'

'Enough riddles. Why do you continue to interfere?'

'You call it interference. We call it a performance.' Veilwalker's staff spun up, swatting his sword away. It retreated. 'It is a good saga. An old one. A king – the King of Feathers – gives up his throne, artfully won, after a great defeat. He retreats into the dark, wearing rags and gnawing over old regrets. But one of his courtiers – Count Sunflame – seeks him out, hoping to restore him to his throne, so that he might once again unite his fractured kingdom.'

Oleander stared at the creature. 'Does he succeed?'

Veilwalker nodded. 'Not without cost.'

He hesitated. 'Why do you care?' He'd asked the question before, but never got an answer. But Veilwalker seemed in a talkative mood. Perhaps this time would be different.

'Why do you?' Veilwalker asked. 'What matters our intent, so long as you fulfil your goal? The King of Feathers on his throne, and the first steps taken towards uniting the old kingdom. The king must shed the rags of the Apothecary, and take up the cloak of the commander. That is the way the story goes.'

Oleander turned as a rustle of fabric caught his ear. Harlequins surrounded him, watching. White masks and black, staring at him from the shadows and light. 'Why attack us on Sublime?' he said. 'What was the purpose there?'

'To stir him. To prick him, push him, press him...'

Veilwalker leaned low, letting its staff slide across its shoulder and along its arm. 'To force him onto the path. To remind him of what awaits a lone man, in the dark. He clings to his rags. We must remind him that he was once a king.'

'You're trying to frighten him,' Oleander said. He laughed. 'That will not work.'

'No. Not frighten. Remind.' Veilwalker sank into a crouch and leaned against its staff. 'The Light of the Fading Sun awaits. It hangs blind in the void, seeing nothing, hearing nothing, but waiting all the same.'

'Waiting for the Radiant,' Oleander said. As one, the Harlequins sighed.

False king, foul king, blazing king burns bright...

'Then our bargain still holds. I deliver the Radiant to you, and you deliver up a renewed Lieutenant Commander Fabius to me. We will retreat, and rebuild. From the ashes of the Twelfth, the Third Legion will be reborn.'

'And with the wounding of Lugganath, shall greater injuries be prevented,' Veilwalker said, head tilted. Its silvery mask seemed to shift and stretch, and he fancied that he could see something in its depths. Before he could look more closely, his vox-link crackled.

'*Oleander.*'

Bile. He straightened. 'I am here, master.'

'*Extricate yourself from whatever sybaritic indulgence you are currently occupied with and return to the Butcher-Bird. We have work to do.*'

'I am coming,' Oleander said. He turned to find the Harlequins gone. The only sign that they had ever been there at all was the ghost of a laugh, riding the static of his vox-link.

CHAPTER FOURTEEN

The House of Noise

They call it the House of Noise,' Oleander said. He looked around. Bile and the others stood waiting in the corridor before the hatch leading to the *Quarzhazat*'s hull. Arrian twitched and murmured to his skulls, eager for some sort of action. Saqqara stood silently at Bile's elbow, saying nothing. And Tzimiskes was Tzimiskes. He might as well have been part of the corridor.

'There are over a hundred of them nesting in there,' Oleander continued. 'Possibly more. They show up every so often, in groups or alone, and the Radiant has decreed that they be allowed to go where they wish. He thinks they are a sign of Slaanesh's favour.'

'And where they wish to go is this House of Noise,' Bile said.

Oleander nodded. 'There used to be an army of Neverborn in that section. Wild ones, picked up during a warp storm. The Noise Marines wiped them out. Sometimes you can still hear the echoes of the daemons' screams, through the bones of the ship. Even the Joybound aren't allowed inside.' He knocked on the bulkhead. 'It's been sealed from within. The only way to reach it involves walking across the hull. Slaanesh alone knows how they stand doing that on a regular basis.'

'I designed the prototype with a certain sturdiness in mind,' Bile said, as he slipped on his helmet. The others followed suit as the bulkhead hissed open, and the cold of space breathed out to envelop them. Led by Oleander, they stepped out into the dark.

The void spread out above and around them like a shroud, silent and stifling, as they began the long trek across the spine of the ship, towards the distant encrustation that was the House of Noise. The black was pierced through with winking starlight and dim, multifarious clouds of gas and celestial debris. They navigated a forest of sensor nodes and satellite arrays slowly, fighting the pull of the void.

Oleander glanced upwards as a diminutive cruiser drifted past, running lights winking like stars. Almost a dozen ships just like it had joined the Radiant's small fleet in the past few hours, drawn by the scent of war and plunder. Renegades, pirates and worse. A slim cruiser of unknown design drifted lazily off the port side of the *Quarzhazat*, jostling for space with a battered, amethyst-hued frigate that had seen too many wars and not enough repair docks.

'Are those eyes painted on its prow?' Saqqara asked over his helmet vox, studying the distant vessel.

Oleander glanced at the ship, and his armour's auspex translated the signal-glyphs etched into its hull. 'The *Fulgrim's Song*. Pirates and daemon-worshippers, mostly. Led by Golman Colos, formerly of the Seventy-First Company.'

'A high-ranking officer?'

'No.' Oleander laughed. 'He took the ship from its former owner in the wake of Canticle City.' Smaller ships clustered around the docking bays of the *Quarzhazat*, as their captains and commanders came to pay homage to the Radiant, and beg his leave to join the hunt. Some wouldn't bother to ask, of course. They would simply wait on the fringes, and follow, until the opportune moment to strike. They would likely be the first to be detected and destroyed by the eldar.

The Radiant had offered them a squad of his finest warriors to accompany them on their journey across the void-jungles of the ship's hull, but Bile had turned him down. The Consortium worked best alone. They had fallen into familiar patterns quickly, all of them orbiting Bile like planets around a sun. Oleander couldn't help but smile. How many dead, drifting ships had they explored in similar fashion, in better days? How many frozen cargoes had they stripped clean, how many mummified bodies had they collected, before they'd found a sanctuary in Urum?

Better days, before the weight of the galaxy had settled on them. Before he'd come to realise what such freedom truly meant. In the end, that realisation was why he'd sought out the Radiant. He'd been looking for brotherhood, true brotherhood, and the comforts of a legionary amongst his Legion. But he hadn't found it. Not in the way he'd hoped. It was broken. All of it, stretched out of joint and reduced to something unrecognisable. But it could be fixed. It had to be. Something shadowy and impossibly thin scuttled past, startling him. He froze and turned, hand on the grip of his bolt pistol.

The hull of the *Quarzhazat* was both forest and fortress

in one. Spinal battlements and jutting sensor arrays rose above tangled roots of unnatural flesh and warped circuitry. A veldt of fleshy cilia sprang up across the empty stretches like a fungus. Massive insect-shapes scuttled smoothly through the coiling roots, their carapaces glittering with frost particles. Great webs of tissue and power cable were strung between antennae and battlements, to catch gods alone knew what sort of prey.

'I have long considered the merits of composing a treatise on void life, and its many forms,' Bile said, studying one of the creatures as it watched them from the shattered cupola of what had once been a defence turret. 'Such hardiness is worth studying, I feel. Tzimiskes – compare these to the strange fleshy mites we discovered aboard that dead hulk in the Mengel Cluster – what was it called? – *Clutch of Heaven's Fist*?' Tzimiskes gestured and Bile chuckled. 'Yes. A shame we had to destroy it.'

'Might I suggest we discuss this later?' Oleander said. He kicked aside a thrashing cilia, lined with what appeared to be thousands of human teeth, as it snapped at his leg. 'And somewhere safer? There are things clinging to the skin of this ship which can bite a warrior in two.'

Safe-afe-afe, something whispered. A ghost of a sound, sliding along the frequency. *No safety, Oleander. Not for thee, not for free...*

'Where is your sense of adventure, brother?' Arrian said.

'I must have left it in my quarters.' Oleander swept the area with his auspex, trying to get a reading. The House of Noise was off limits to all but a select few. The Kakophoni were erratic at the best of times. There was no telling how they'd react to uninvited guests, and what traps they might have set.

'Quiet,' Bile said, suddenly. He'd stopped. 'What was that?'

'What was what?' Oleander said.

The King of Feathers stirs in his melancholy, Count Sunflame, a voice murmured, somewhere out in the black. The vox-link crackled in his ear. Oleander twitched, and wondered if any of the others had heard it.

'Did anyone hear that?' Arrian said. 'Or is it just my brothers talking too loudly again?' He touched one of the skulls dangling from his chest-plate. 'It sounded like... laughter.'

'I heard nothing,' Oleander said.

'Perhaps a star is going supernova, somewhere,' Saqqara said. 'Or maybe the daemons that infest this hulk are gathering.' The Word Bearer turned, scanning the way they'd come. 'I sense something watching us. Something familiar...'

Tzimiskes' vox-link let out a blurt of static.

'Tzimiskes is right. Keep moving,' Bile said. Oleander could hear the strain in his voice, however slight, and could see the syringe-pumps mounted on his armour working. More stimulants, more chemicals to compensate for his body's faltering systems. It was like looking at a staggering work of unparalleled genius, reduced to a few watered-down quotations. He had other bodies, and at least one was hidden somewhere aboard the *Vesalius*, but that didn't make it any easier to witness. A great man, brought low by cruel fate.

He is stubborn, this king. Content with ancient melancholies and false dreams...

The Harlequins were there, whatever the auspex said. They waited, in the jungle of cilia and circuitry, watching.

Oleander occasionally caught sight of them, brief flashes of light and colour amongst the shadows. Pale porcelain faces leering out of a fall of tangled cables or from behind a satellite array.

'I see them as well,' Saqqara said, softly, switching the vox-link to a private channel. Oleander looked at the Word Bearer.

'Why have you not said anything?'

The Word Bearer looked at him. 'Why haven't you?'

Oleander said nothing. The lights of a passing cruiser played across Saqqara's crimson helmet, illuminating the sigils carved into its surface. 'In the temples I worship in, there is only a knife and a stone,' the Word Bearer said. 'If you do not wield the one, you must lie upon the other.'

'How philosophical. What does that mean?'

'I know full well why the Dark Council wants our enslaver in chains. Like a daemon, he requires binding, so that he might be put to better use.' He tapped one of the daemon-flasks dangling from his armour. The amorphous thing within grew frenzied.

'Your enslaver. Not mine.'

'There are many types of slavery.' Saqqara looked up, playing idly with his icons and sigils. 'The Neverborn whisper that this affair might prove to be both knife and stone.'

'Careful, Saqqara. He hears you talking like that, he might just decide to set off that bomb a bit early.' Oleander tapped the Word Bearer on the chest.

'No. He will not. He finds me amusing. I am a living example of his power, a testament to his skill.' Saqqara looked at him. 'And unlike you, I have my uses. But why has he spared you, I wonder?'

The hull shuddered beneath them. The crawling circuit-veins that marked the hull plates had become flushed with a dark, oily colour. Nearby patches of cilia thrashed more violently than the others, as if the omnipresent vibration were agitating them. Oleander switched back to the open channel. 'We're here,' he said.

The House of Noise was a jutting edifice, wrought from steel, gilded in a system tribute's worth of gold. It extended outward in a curving wedge of burst metal and the semi-organic matter that marked *Quarzhazat*'s hull. Silently screaming faces pockmarked the gilding, their eyes rolling blindly. Oleander had heard them called soul-barnacles – the detritus of devoured spirits, digested and expelled by daemons, clinging to whatever passed through them.

A massive hatch rose at a steep angle from the line of the hull. It was decorated with the frost-encrusted bodies of servitors, their organic components mummified by exposure to the void. Lights still flickered in their optic sensors, and the broken skulls turned to watch as the Apothecaries drew close. Bile looked at Oleander. 'Well, Oleander? How do we gain admittance?'

'We could knock,' Oleander said.

'Very well.' Bile stepped forward, Torment in hand. He raised the sceptre, and felt its darkling energies surge through him. But, before he could strike the hatch, its locks disengaged and its seals crumpled. The hatch retracted, revealing steps covered in frost and throbbing cilia. Their vox-link crackled with distortion as they descended. The wall-plates of the shaft shuddered in their housings as the hatch slid shut. A jungle canopy of rerouted power cables and cogitator conduits hung above them, and shrunken, hairless shapes clambered through them, or else swung from the loose plates and burst housings of the walls.

'The people of the House of Noise,' Oleander said, as one of the pale creatures darted across their path, knuckling along the steps with a harsh squeal. It was smaller than a man, but barrel-chested and covered in strange, blister-like metal nodes. The creatures kept pace with them as they descended, clambering through the canopy or along the walls. Their screeches echoed like static.

'Enlarged lung capacity and thickened dermis,' Arrian said. 'Void-modified?'

'Void-adapted,' Bile corrected, absently. 'These things were born, not modified.' He glanced at Oleander. 'Isn't that right, Oleander?'

'The Kakophoni brought slaves with them, when they set out to make this place their own,' Oleander said. 'These are their descendants. I'm told they're everywhere on this deck. Strange things happen in the warp.' His hand snapped out, catching one of the pale beasts. He dragged it from the wall. It thrashed wildly in his grip, snapping oversized jaws. He took a sample from it, before slamming its skull against the floor. He tossed the body behind them, and the other creatures converged on the twitching corpse hungrily, forgetting all about the interlopers into their territory.

The internal bulkhead stretched out before them at the bottom of the stairs. It was open, its frame marred by blast marks and wide gouges. A monstrous cacophony blistered the air from within, causing the aural sensors built into their helmets to rustle painfully.

Past the bulkhead stretched the interior of the House of Noise. The deck had been all but gutted, and turned into a concave expanse, pierced through by gantries. The walls had been modified to reflect and enhance the sounds being emitted within, turning the space into an enormous resonator. Strange energies crackled along exposed power cells, and more of the atavistic slave-creatures loped or squatted along the upper reaches of the support frame, adding their howls to those of their masters.

Daemonic shapes twisted through the open air in a dance of agony, their partially materialised forms hammered into writhing fragments by the raw current of sound which echoed and re-echoed through the House of Noise.

'Fascinating,' Bile said.

'What now, master?' Oleander said. The seals of his armour creaked alarmingly. Power armour was built to withstand almost anything, but what was going on past the bulkhead threatened to shatter the ceramite of his war-plate.

'Now we go inside,' Bile said. 'The masters of the House of Noise await.'

The sound was a beast in a cage. It savaged the air and pounded on the walls which held it trapped. It rose and fell in snarling waves, pulsing first one way and then another. There were hundreds of Kakophoni, standing or sprawled on the wide gantries that crisscrossed the cavernous space, singing, playing, screaming. Twisting the atmosphere into new and unusual shapes with the strength of their sound. The largest knot of them stood together directly ahead, shrieking in unison. Psychosonic weapons rattled what remained of an observation port's frame.

Bile studied them as he led Oleander and the others

forward, intrigued despite himself. He had been easily inspired, in the early days of the Heresy. His head had been swollen with a plethora of ideas, and there had been no limit to the indulgence of his superiors. He had wrought masterpieces of flesh and bone then, though on the whole they'd lacked a certain subtlety of craft. Sometimes, he missed that time of heady experimentation, before he'd found his true purpose. He'd fancied himself an artist, when really he was a craftsman.

It had been some time since he had seen one of the original Kakophoni – these were a newer breed. He'd had no hand in their modifications, but he recognised the elements of his earlier work easily enough. All Noise Marines were, in some sense, descended from those first, crude surgeries he'd performed at Fulgrim's behest. It pleased him to think that his works would live on in this manner, passed between warbands and isolated practitioners like some secret knowledge from the days of Old Night.

Screaming slave-creatures shuffled across the gantry, fleeing at their approach. They clung to everything, even some of the Noise Marines. They screeched and fought one another around the feet of their heedless masters, seemingly driven to frenzy by the cacophony.

Bile stepped forward. The chill of the dark bit at him, even through his armour, and he relished it. There was nothing quite so bracing as the cold, utter emptiness of the dark between the stars. It gave one a sense of perspective. He activated his vox-link, scanning the frequencies until he found one not drowned in distortion. 'Brothers. The melody is different, but I recognise it all the same.'

As one, the closest Noise Marines fell silent and turned. They were a garish sight, clad in gaudily daubed power

armour. Only the most extravagant shades and patterns
registered with their inflamed senses – a regrettable
side effect of the sensory augmentation. Power cables,
pneumatic hoses and vox-relays hung like tabards from
their baroque gear. One had hundreds of golden coins
hammered into his armour, while another was covered
in a shroud of stitched flesh.

A squall of feedback slithered over the channel, causing
Bile to wince. One of the Kakophoni stepped forward, broken, frozen metal splitting beneath his tread. Slave-creatures
scattered at his approach, fleeing in all directions. The amplifiers of a doom siren rose over his shoulders, and his helmet
was wrought in the shape of a screaming face. He spoke,
but all Bile heard was a discordant squeal. He understood
its meaning, however. There could be no mistaking that.

'Indeed. My apologies for disturbing your performance.'

Another gust of feedback. There were words there now,
but just barely. Words and sentences ran together beneath
the discordance, becoming a wave of pure noise. It took
a practised ear to pick out the lyrics.

'Ch-ief Apo-thecary.' The voice was equal parts feedback,
distortion and animal growl. It was not a human voice,
not anymore. But it was still familiar.

Bile straightened. He heard hope there. Gratitude. He
stepped forward and brushed a handful of filth from a
twisted shoulder-plate, revealing a faded rank-insignia.
'Elian Pakretes,' Bile said. 'One of mine, weren't you? A sergeant of the Ninth Company, once upon a time. I thought
you long since perished, on the killing fields of Luna.'

'Th-e So-ng ne-eds a vo-ice,' Pakretes growled. He
twitched, and the amplifiers of his doom siren hummed.
The static in his voice thinned and smoothed over.

'The Song?' Only a Noise Marine would think such shrieking was a song.

'The Song. The only song. Slaanesh's song. The birth-song, the death-song. We seek its notes, in the black. The perfect note.'

Bile nodded. 'I have come to ask a favour, Elian.'

'You gave me a voice, Chief Apothecary. For that I thank you.'

'You can do more than thank me,' Bile said.

The malformed helmet dipped, the eye lenses flickering. Bile recognised his work, at least the roots of it. But things had changed in the intervening centuries, as they were wont to do. Crude augmentations, made by unskilled and overly enthusiastic hands, marked Elian – wheezing pneumatics, for forcing air through tortured lungs, rasped against rough bladders full of air. Power cables emerged from the cracks in untended power armour, and wound like sputtering serpents through the gaping structural pistons of prosthetic limbs.

'How much of you is left under there? Where does the machine leave off and the man begin?' Bile said. In a way, he admired Elian and his brothers. They were at once the pinnacle of his work, and a warning of what was to come, should humanity be allowed to brave the dangers of the galaxy without his guiding hand.

'Not enough. Too much.' The growl crumbled into dust, and Bile could hear the yearning there. Even these bodies, warped as they were, had limits. The other Noise Marines raised their instruments and loosed a melancholy wail. 'The Song of Slaanesh calls to us, and we to it, but we cannot reach it.'

'Not as you are, no,' Bile said.

Elian stared at him. Then, 'Do you hear the Song, Chief Apothecary? It is so beautiful. It shakes the roots of all that is and makes gods weep in desperation. It is a birth-song and a death-song. It is the song whose melody lulls suns to eternal slumber and whose reverberations crack the crust of a thousand moons. We can perceive it but dimly, and it hurts us so.'

'I can end your hurt, if you wish.'

The auspex in Bile's armour chimed. He glanced around, and saw hulking shapes appear out of the dark. They strode forward, stirring clouds of ice and dust. A dozen, two, and then more, many more. A dim cacophony rose along the vox-link. The sound of an orchestra of the lost, a choir of the damned. How many Kakophoni did the Radiant have under his aegis? Oleander was right. Captain Kasperos had quite the army.

He raised his hands in greeting as the Noise Marines approached. 'My brothers. It does my hearts good to see you prosper so. How many of you felt my knife? How many of you were wrought by my hand? Not many, I think. And yet, even so, you are mine. My art, my discoveries, my teachings.'

The vox pulsed, once. A single, atonal sound, made by many voices. A sign of recognition, perhaps. Or perhaps... pleading? Elian sighed. The sound made Bile's teeth itch to their rotten roots. 'The Song calls, Chief Apothecary. Will you help us join it?'

'I will, brother. You will join your voice to the warp itself, and your brothers will sing amid the ruins of a dying race. This I promise you,' Bile said. 'What do you say, brother... will you allow me to ply my trade upon you once more?'

PART THREE

THE SHATTERING

CHAPTER FIFTEEN

The Killing Cut

Quarzhazat's core hummed with malign awareness. Strands of muscle tissue stretched across the chamber, and ridged veins of metal and meat ran along the deck and walls. The ship's machine-spirit was a stunted, predatory thing. It was all hunger and rage, and the machine-priests who attended it were scarred and tribal. Ragged robes, stained dark with oily unguents, cloaked the spindly metallic shapes that clustered around the core-chamber, watching Bile and his Consortium warily.

Bile ignored the priests and studied the throbbing edifice of tissue and circuitry that made up the central core of the ship. He took note of the serpentine power cables which coiled in a heap beneath it, and the bone-like growths which held it anchored in place. It resembled nothing so much as a massive, crude heart, constructed by someone with only the most rudimentary understanding of how such an organ functioned. Couplings sparked eerily within the arched convolutions of twisted meat, causing the entire thing to twitch and pulse with thunderous rhythm. In a few centuries, *Quarzhazat* might become something unique in the universe. A true bio-organic organism, self-guided and motivated by the impulses of life, rather than programming.

'Master, we are ready to begin the operation,' Oleander said. Bile turned. His Consortium encircled the bulky shape of the Noise Marine, Elian. Half a dozen strands of fleshy cable had been torn loose from the deck and inserted into the power couplings that linked Elian to his doom siren. The doom siren's own power cables had been spliced into the access panels of the core. His legs and spine had been braced with sections of bone and metal torn from the walls, and mag-clamped into place. Sparks of energy pattered down from the crude couplings and spilled across the deck.

Elian shuddered and hunched forward, fists crossed over his chest. A sensor array exploded. Then another and another. The machine-priests chittered in dismay. They scuttled about, attempting to stabilise the systems and prevent further overloading. Bile checked the Kakophoni's bio-readings. Satisfied, he said, 'Excellent. Saqqara, remove his helmet.'

The Word Bearer carefully unlatched the modified helm, revealing Elian's mutilated features. The Word Bearer stepped back, one hand on his bolt pistol, his eyes on the circling priests. 'Watch them,' Bile said. Though the Radiant had ordered them to surrender control of the core-chamber for the duration of the operation, the machine-priests were loyal only to their own corrupted programming. If they thought *Quarzhazat* was in danger, they would attack.

The operation was a variation of an old experiment he had conducted in the Coronid Deeps, involving a reluctant Navigator and a void-hardened bio-sarcophagus. Wiring a living organism into a vessel's existing network was not unheard of, even outside Eyespace. It wasn't even particularly inventive. But it was difficult to do correctly. He tapped a discreet sigil on his vambrace, and a sweeping melody burst onto the vox-link. He always carried a selection with him. Music helped him work, when conditions were less than ideal.

The melody was old, and had been recorded some time during the early months of the Great Crusade. A piece dedicated to a great victory won by the Third Legion – some inconsequential skirmish likely long scrubbed from the historical records of the Imperium. It was based on an older song, some forgotten tune from the days of Old Night. The new was always built on the bones of the old. So it was for all great art, and even some not so great. So it was for all things, he thought. The past was the clay from which the bricks of the future were shaped.

For Bile, the tune brought back memories of better days, when the razor's edge was not so close. When his body had not been a seething mass of incipient tumours, held at bay by increasingly desperate measures. He began to hum, and tried to ignore the retinal readouts that flashed across his eyes, elaborating on his ongoing dissolution. The chirurgeon hissed, and a warning chimed. A moment later, a stab of pain twisted in his gut like the vulpid from the fable, trying to chew its way free. He thought, and the chirurgeon acted. A syringe rose above him and jabbed a vein. Cold fire filled him, burning away the pain.

He flexed his hands. 'Now. Let us begin.'

A few moments later, Elian groaned in pleasure as Bile cut open what was left of his brain. The deck plates rattled in their frames as the sound echoed out, and caused the lights of the core-chamber to flicker. Bile winced. 'Brother, while I understand your anticipation, please control yourself. I'm sure Kasperos would prefer that the ship's core remains intact.'

'He longs to sit at the side of the Prince of Pleasure,' Elian said. Even without the distance of frequency, his voice was a harsh crackle. At some point his larynx had been replaced with a miniature vox-caster, and it squealed and popped with his every exhalation. 'As do we all. Slaanesh sings, and there is not a one of us who does not wish to listen.'

'Not all of us, Elian. Not even most of us. The descent of the Third was less a plunge than a sidle in most cases. Oleander, for instance. A sybarite, a decadent, but he's hardly on the level of some of those haunting this vessel.'

'Oleander,' Elian breathed, touching the modifications to his throat. 'He did this. My song grew stronger by five decibels. I have never thanked him.' His eyes rolled towards the Apothecary. 'Thank you, brother.'

Bile ignored them. The neural centres of the Noise Marine's brain were abnormal in shape and thickness. Elian's mind more resembled the cogitator of a vox-station than anything organic. Amplifying nodes had been inserted into the meat, alongside relays and rerouting coils. The chirurgeon's blades plucked several of them free, slicing the strands of tissue that held them in place. Elian shuddered with every cut.

Bile paused, a relay between his fingers. It sparked, and his vox-link spluttered. *We see you, Apothecary,* a voice whispered. *You cannot escape us.* His fingers tightened convulsively, crushing the relay. His eyes flickered to the side, where the shadows thickened and congealed. He could see faces in the stains there – leering, laughing faces. Not daemons, but something just as fiendish. 'What do you want?' he said, softly.

'The neural webbing is ready, Chief Apothecary,' Arrian said, from across the chamber, startling him. Bile turned, composing himself.

'Bring it over – quickly.' Bile stepped back. His hand was trembling. He could not feel fear; not really. Fear had been burned out of him the day the Legion's Apothecaries had torn who he had been asunder and rebuilt him into the being he was. But he could feel frustration. Oh yes, that he could feel. Frustration was like a slow-burning fire, eating away at him.

He had made many enemies over the course of his life. A sign of greatness, in some circles. A man was measured in the worth of his foes, and Fabius Bile had many worthy foes indeed. The least of them commanded armies, and the greatest – well, he'd never got along very well with the concept of gods, let alone their self-proclaimed envoys.

If his enemies were gathering, even just a few of them, all he'd worked for would be in danger. He thought of Igori and the others, even the wretched vat-born. The history of the coming millennium would be written by his children, in all their fierce glory. He would not allow it to be otherwise.

He and the others worked swiftly, placing the neural webbing he'd grown from the fragments cultivated from psyker and eldar onto the surface of Elian's malformed brain. The Noise Marine's warped physiology would

ensure that no rejection occurred, and that the modifications took as expected. 'When we are done here, Elian,
your voice will pierce the heart of the void itself,' Bile said.

'Slaanesh will hear me,' Elian hissed.

Bile couldn't tell if it was a question or a statement, and
chose not to reply. Either way, Elian wouldn't hear him.
The Noise Marine began to twitch, froth spilling from his
ragged mouth. His eyes bulged, and he clutched at his larynx. A squall of noise erupted from their vox-links. Arrian
cursed, blood streaming from his nose and eyes. Tzimiskes
staggered back, clutching at his head. Oleander turned,
gagging. Bile kept working. It was to be expected.

The sound grew in volume as he made the connections, replacing the nodes and relays he'd removed with
new ones. Stronger ones. Elian's augmented lungs swelled
with new power, and his brain-meats bulged with potency
stripped from the flesh of a hundred lesser psykers. The
eldar tissue permeated his skull like a fast-moving cancer,
making connections where none had ever been. It would
soon blossom and fill the Noise Marine's cranium like
some lethal weed. His scream could kill before. But now,
it would become something greater than any weapon.

The Noise Marine jerked upright, his ravaged brain
sloshing in his reinforced head. He groaned, and Bile felt
his pulse spike. The chirurgeon reacted smoothly, injecting
a calming agent. Bile caught Elian by the shoulder. 'Calm
yourself,' he shouted, over the rising noise. A vox-caster
burst, ripping itself free of the wall. The machine-priests
chattered panicky bursts of code at one another. 'Control
it, brother – or it will burn you to a cinder before you
reach the crescendo.'

Elian's groan stretched into a moan, agonised and

strangled. The noise spiralled upwards, and then ceased.
The Noise Marine sagged. Bile took a breath and leaned
forward. Quickly, he replaced the sections of skull he'd
removed, searing them into place. Blood spilled down
Elian's face and neck, dripping through the bunches of
cable and wiring. He straightened before Bile could stitch
his tattered flesh. 'It is good enough. It is time, Chief
Apothecary. I can feel the song building anew. I cannot
resist its call, not for much longer.' He snatched his helmet
from Saqqara's grip and set it over his head with a squelch.

Arrian looked at Bile. 'Infection will set in, if that's not
fixed.'

'I doubt there'll be time,' Bile said. 'Come. Let us finish
this. I grow tired of the Radiant's hospitality.' He rubbed
his chest, tracing bloody fingerprints across the crinkled
surface of his coat. 'Elian... begin.'

The core-meat began to shudder in its housing of bone
and metal. Sparks poured down its quivering flesh as the
rerouted systems stabilised. Elian convulsed as power
flooded his armour, and coursed through it. He arched
his back and began to groan. The sound slithered through
every vox in the chamber, and the lights flickered.

Bile felt the air thicken and grow cold. A Noise Marine's
abilities were as much psychic as they were physical, disturbing the very environment. 'Report,' he said, into
the vox. The link crackled as information came in from the
other ships in the fleet. The witches and psykers he and
his Consortium had performed similar operations on over
the last ten hours were beginning to react to the resonance
the Kakophoni was emitting. Elian was the aleph – the
central node of a network of minds – and as he drew on
the *Quarzhazat*'s power, so too did they.

'Is it working?' Oleander asked.

'Of course it's working,' Bile said. The air twisted in on itself, and strange shapes moved insubstantially through the frosty air. In his mind's eye, he could see the wave of miasmic force expanding outward, ahead of the fleet. Like silt stirred from the ocean floor, it would mask their approach. But intricate as the system was, it wouldn't last long. The psykers were fragile, and the forces pulsing through them would burn them out in time. Elian would perish as well, though not until the end. And not until they'd reached their destination. 'Come. We'd best let Kasperos know that it's time to get under way.'

The groan of the transit elevator was omnipresent as it carried them to the command deck.

This one was decorated in stretched skins, flayed from the backs of half a dozen xenos species. The skins had been marked with abominable brands and vulgarities, and they continued to bleed, even now. Another example of waste, to Bile's mind. Why squander such perfectly good dermal coverings as decorations? Then, perhaps it wasn't his place to criticise such things. He smoothed the ragged folds of his coat.

He looked up to find Tzimiskes watching him. The Iron Warrior's expression was unreadable beneath the rictus of his mask, but Bile had grown adept at reading the silent Apothecary's body language. Tzimiskes was worried.

He recalled that it had been Tzimiskes who'd stood with Oleander, the day of his expulsion from the Consortium. Tzimiskes who'd convinced him to spare the other Apothecary. And Tzimiskes who'd stood first upon the prodigal's return. Despite everything he'd endured, or perhaps because of it, the Iron Warrior took the bonds of brotherhood they shared seriously. And it was that unnatural compassion that would see him dead one day.

Bile felt something that might have been sadness as he considered it. Tzimiskes had been of great help to him, for as long as he could remember. 'Do not fear, brother... the path ahead is thorny, but we will persevere as always,' he said. Tzimiskes nodded and tapped his chest. Bile laughed. 'Of course, brother. I'm sure Kasperos won't mind having your battle-automatons rampaging about.'

The transit elevator shuddered to a halt. The doors hissed open, revealing the hulking form of a massive Noise Marine. Heavy hoses and sonic relays hung from the Kakophoni's armour, which had been crudely reinforced by additional layers, gleaned from many marks. His helmet was covered in clusters of broadcast amplifiers, and the grille resembled the bared teeth of a wild beast. Bloodshot eyes glared at them through the shattered remains of a visor.

'Brother-Sergeant Elian,' the Noise Marine pulsed. 'We can hear him.'

'Can you?' Bile said, intrigued despite himself. He hadn't expected that the Kakophoni would be able to hear the dampening effect. He peered at the Kakophoni. 'And you are... Ramos. The Bull of the Eighth. I remember installing those sonic-ports. You cracked the Medean Gate, on Luna.'

'I... cracked the gate,' Ramos replied, as if uncertain. 'Sergeant Elian sings. We can hear him.' He stepped back, revealing a dozen Noise Marines standing behind him. Bile stepped out of the elevator.

'Is that why you came?'

'No. The Radiant sent us. To escort you. But we can hear the Song.' Ramos' big hands flexed, and the amplifiers built into his gauntlets whined like eager hounds. 'We can hear him.'

'I'm sure you can,' Bile said, smoothly. 'But this song is Elian's alone. Only he can sing it. Your time will come after. Then, you will sing in his name, perhaps.'

Ramos stared at him. 'We will sing for him, Chief Apothecary. We will shake the foe to their roots with our song.' He turned and ambled down the corridor. Bile and the others followed, the Noise Marines falling in around them as they made their way to the command deck. The Kakophoni whined to each other like eager hounds, and the air twitched with the racket that accompanied them.

When they reached the command deck, they found it occupied. Those warband leaders that the Radiant had deemed worthy enough to join the attack were with the Joybound on the bridge. There were a pitiful few mortal pirates as well, looking tiny and fragile next to the hulking Traitor Marines.

Bile recognised some of the new faces. To a man, all of the newly arrived Renegade Astartes wore the colours of the Emperor's Children. They were, like Kasperos Telmar, forgotten and ambitious remnants of the once mighty Third Legion, now merely looking to take whatever they could get. How the mighty had fallen. As he studied them, he wondered which were members of this so-called 'Phoenix Conclave', if any.

The gathered warriors fell silent as Bile and his Consortium stepped out of the access corridor and strode towards them. A fearful whisper spread through the mortal ranks, and a dull growl through that of the Renegade Astartes. Bile stopped a safe distance away and leaned on his sceptre. Torment shivered in his grip, eager to strike.

The *Quarzhazat*'s command deck overlooked a sea of
tiered control thrones, facing a massive occulus viewscreen. The thrones were occupied by a slave-crew of
servitors, each painted in garish colours and bound to
their restraint cradles by flesh and metal. A flickering
hololith occupied the centre of the deck, as it did on
the *Vesalius*. It fuzzed and crackled arhythmically, causing the grotesquely shaped vox-casters set at its corners
to emit squeals of mechanical protest.

Tattered banners hung far above, rustling in the recycled
air – the saga of the 12th, written in tapestries and trophies. Bile studied them, noting the progressive barbarity
as woven cloth gave way to tangled scalps and softly clattering braids of bone. 'Entropy,' he murmured. He looked
around. Once, two hundred or more soldiers might have
stood upon this deck, awaiting their orders. Now, barely
a hundred warriors lazed about its cavernous expanse,
talking and scheming amongst themselves. Petty rivals
and spiteful cliques circled one another with murder in
their hearts, waiting for their lord commander to arrive.

It was all depressingly familiar. Oleander spoke of
brotherhood, and the way things had once been, but it
all looked much the same now as it had then. The virtues which made for good soldiers were in actuality vices
and their vices, virtues. Bile had observed such then, and
saw no reason to change his opinion now. He tightened
his grip on his sceptre.

'The shadows lengthen,' Oleander said.

'What?'

'An old song. Or a poem. A bit of free verse, at any rate.'
Oleander frowned. 'Look at them. Beasts and fools. Grub-
bing in the mud for a kernel of perfection.'

'One works with the tools one has,' Bile said.

A bell sounded, tinny and fragile. He turned. The sound of duelling verse and songs fell away as the captain of the 12th Company made his way onto the command deck, accompanied by his harem of slinking devil-women.

The Radiant wore a cloak of woven scalps over his shoulders, and carried a sheathed power sword in the crook of his arm. His monstrous guards followed him at a discreet distance, grunting softly to one another. Slaves cavorted ahead of him, scattering handfuls of blood-soaked flower petals in his path, or else shaking great fuming censers about him. The Neverborn stalked in his train, singing and hissing as they clapped their claws or stamped their hooves. At a gesture from the Radiant, they fell silent.

'Is it ready then, Fabius? Are you ready to lead me to my destiny?' the Radiant said, loudly. 'I do hope so. Else I might have to feed you to the crew, piece by piece.'

'Spare me your theatrics, Kasperos,' Bile said. 'I have completed my operations.'

'Excellent.' The Radiant touched his chest. 'The spirit of the Third yet lives, in us. Were I of a more sensitive disposition, I might weep for the beauty of this moment.' He looked around, his smile stretching impossibly wide. 'My sons, my brothers, we stand on the cusp of glory. Do not let me deter you from your entertainments – please, carry on, as you were. Sing, laugh, dance... go, my sweets, dance for my warriors.'

The daemonettes pranced and swayed towards the Emperor's Children, who crowded forward eagerly. It was a rare treat to see the dance of the Neverborn, and more than one member of the audience would pay the price for it. Sometimes, when the creatures got too excited, they roamed the decks of the *Quarzhazat* in killing packs, leaving ruin in their wake. Oleander hoped the Radiant had better control of them this time.

'It is done, then,' the Radiant said. It wasn't a question. The engines throbbed, setting the whole of the *Quarzhazat* to trembling. The banners hanging above the command deck flapped, as if caught in a hurricane wind.

'It is done. As I promised. Are we under way?'

'The coordinates you provided were fed into the cogitators the moment you began. We are well under way, Fabius. Indeed, I feel we will be there soon. The auspex readings are quite stirring, if you'd care to examine them.' The Radiant gestured to a nearby console. 'Thirty-four hours away,' he said. 'Elian's sacrifice will be honoured. Perhaps I shall have his doom siren mounted on the back of my throne, when I have met my destiny.' He clasped his hands together. 'My hunger grows. I intend to claim in full everything we are owed. The Twelfth Company sails to war.'

He turned, surveying the assembled captains, pirates and renegades. 'Not a raid, this,' he said, more loudly. 'Not for simple piracy or slave-taking. This is true war, my friends. True battle, at last. After so long, we have an enemy worthy of us, worthy of the honour of the 12th. We, who burned the Geist-nests of Walpurgis, and seared the remains of the Sunset City from the flesh of Terra itself, shall turn our blades upon an enemy worthy of the name.'

He spread his arms. 'Do you hear it, reverberating through the hull? Brother Elian, blessed of the Lord of Pleasure, sings us to war. He sings the song of Slaanesh, and it is in her name that we do this thing. Hold that thought uppermost in your minds, and let it bring you

comfort in impatient hours ahead.' A ragged cheer went
up from the gathered renegades, some more enthusiastic than others.

The Radiant gestured to the hololith at the centre of the
deck. 'But enough speeches. Speeches are for victories. For
now, we must settle for plans. Gather around, my sons,
my friends. For it is no small thing we attempt.'

A hololithic estimation of the craftworld flickered to life.
Bile recognised the data he'd provided and smiled. It was
bare bones, lacking even the most basic of auspex-data,
but the crowd seemed suitably impressed. 'Look upon it,
friends – Lugganath, the Light of Fallen Suns. A monument to faded glories. Glories it will see anew, once we
have taken it for ourselves.'

The Radiant turned, studying his followers. 'I will not
pretend to command your loyalty in this. Some of you
will be eager to wet your blades and must do as the gods
or your desires will. I will not seek to prevent you. Serve
your desires in all things, and you will find your reward.
Thus spake glorious Fulgrim, upon the fields of Terra.' He
gestured. 'But, for those of you who are under my direct
command, well... my desires take precedence.'

He turned back to the hololith. 'Our main thrust will be
thus – the initial wave of boarding parties will form a trident formation. A bit archaic, but elegant in its simplicity.
The outer prongs will establish secure beachheads forward
and aft, while the centre will deliver our teleport homer
into the very heart of the craftworld.' As he spoke, his voice
lost some of the lazy purr that had characterised it until
now. He sounded less the daemonic aspirant, and more
like the warrior Bile had once known. 'I am sure most of
us here remember the *Maru Skara*? The Killing Cut.'

Bile nodded to himself. The stratagem was named after one of the most difficult strikes of the ancient Pan-Europic duelling-cults. It called for a precisely timed, rapid feint, designed to draw the opponent's eye and allow for a second, ultimately fatal blow. 'And which of us is the open blade, and which the hidden?' he said.

The Radiant smiled. 'Isn't it obvious?' He gestured. 'The trident is the open blade, designed to draw the eye. To pull the enemy in. Once they are caught on the tines, we will cut them with the hidden blade.'

'The teleporter,' Bile said, in understanding. Like many vessels with a large enough power supply, the *Quarzhazat* possessed a teleportarium, along with a choir of slave-psykers to guide those who dared risk its use. The ancient technology was prone to shorting out after use, or worse, depositing those who used it within solid matter, even with the benefit of a teleport homer. 'A risky gambit.'

'What is life without a bit of risk?' the Radiant said. He tapped the image, expanding a section of the craftworld. 'We are at a decided disadvantage when it comes to heavy weaponry and vehicles... but we still possess some. It can be put to good use in these wide avenues and obligingly open streets.' He looked up, seeking out one of his captains. 'Thalopsis, are your metal steeds well rested? Your bikes will take to these streets.'

A garishly armoured Space Marine stepped forward, his unbound crimson hair framing a snarling leonine death-mask of gleaming silver. A tabard of crudely stitched flesh was stretched across his torso, and a sharp spur of metallic bone jutted from the congealed mass of one shoulder-plate. 'Rested and ready, oh most radiant one. We shall ride them down, and grind them squealing beneath our tyres.'

'Excellent.' The Radiant turned his attentions to a hulking renegade. 'Pulchrates, you and your Havocs shall support him.' The brute inclined his head. His mismatched armour showed the endless cracks of resealing and battle-field repairs, and was festooned with bandoliers of heavy bolter ammunition. The grille of his crater-marked helmet was decorated with spent casings.

'Our guns shall roar until every tower has tumbled down, Shining One,' he growled.

'Indeed. Cause as much destruction as you wish – slay and burn until the air itself collapses beneath the weight of their screaming. You will be the leftmost prong of the trident. As for the rightmost... Merix. My Joybound. You will hold the flank. Sweep back towards the centre, once you have established your beachhead.' The Radiant gestured, indicating the craftworld. 'I have decided that you and your warriors will have the honour of escorting Ancient Diomat and his brethren into battle.'

Merix made a strangled noise. Then, 'I am... unworthy of such an honour, my lord. I shall gladly step aside...' He looked around as those nearest him stepped back.

'Oh, but I insist,' the Radiant said, smiling broadly. 'We would be cruel indeed to keep them from the fray. Already they stir in their amniotic sarcophagi, pulled from red dreams by the prayers of our adepts. Their weapons are being prepared and loaded, and their fists will soon be daubed in fresh blood. You would not wish to disappoint them, would you?'

'No, my lord.'

'I thought not. Your loyalty does you credit, Merix.' He laughed. 'Just stay out of their way and you should be fine.' He looked towards the hulking Lidonius. 'Blessed

Lidonius, you and clever Nikola shall support the centre prong. Ramos and the Kakophoni shall march with you.' He glanced at the Noise Marine, who inclined his head. 'Together, I expect you can make quite the joyful noise, to herald my coming.' He gestured to Gulos. 'Gulos, my brother, you shall have the honour of leading the vanguard in this effort. You will command the central tine of my trident. First in, and first blood to you. Are you not pleased?'

'I am, Most Radiant King,' Gulos said. He smiled unpleasantly at Oleander. 'Shall my brother join me, or is he to remain here, in the rear?'

'I shall be there,' Oleander said. 'And I won't be coming alone, will I, Tzimiskes?' The Iron Warrior nodded and patted the haft of the power axe resting in the crook of his arm.

'I hardly think one warrior more or less will matter,' the Radiant said bemusedly. 'Even one so doughty as this. There will be no time for wall building, brother. Or are you the type to knock them down instead?'

'Tzimiskes has a maniple of battle-automata at his command. These can be used to bolster the initial assault, and spare your men the burden of dying unfulfilled,' Bile said. 'They will also ensure that placement of the teleport homer is not hampered.'

'And you do not wish these machines to support your own efforts, Chief Apothecary?'

'I sacrifice them on the altar of necessity,' Bile said.

Merix flexed his prosthetic hand. 'The xenos have war machines of their own.'

'Which they will need time to deploy, time we will not give them,' the Radiant said, studying the hololithic image.

'Speed is our ally in this endeavour. Support elements will be launched around the main arteries of the craftworld. I do not hope for a coordinated assault, but some attempt at cooperation would be appreciated, my brothers.' More laughter. Bile frowned. The Radiant was making light of it, but a lack of coordination could prove disastrous. The element of surprise was a finite resource. Once the eldar regrouped they would counterattack and any gains the Radiant's forces had made might well be lost.

But then, perhaps the warriors of the Third no longer cared about such things. Bile looked around, seeing only gloating anticipation in the faces of those leading the assault. Where once they would have debated well into the final hour, seeking the perfect stratagem to triumph, now they seemed content with the mere promise of slaughter. The discord of battle had become the goal, rather than victory. He caught Oleander looking at him, and the other Apothecary nodded knowingly. Bile looked away.

The Radiant turned to Gulos. 'I trust that you fully understand your purpose?'

'We are the distraction,' Gulos said.

'Indeed,' the Radiant said. 'You are the open blade. You will hold their eyes on you, until the time is right for the killing stroke. Do not fail me in this, Gulos. If I cannot have the souls of the eldar, I will settle for yours.'

'You will be accompanying the second wave, then?' Bile asked. 'Or will you grace us with your presence from the outset?'

'I will play the hidden blade,' the Radiant said. 'Once the full weight of the craftworld's defenders has been drawn onto the central tine of the trident, the teleport homer will be activated, and I will make a suitably impressive entrance.'

Bile grunted. 'I thought as much.'

'And what of me?' Savona said. The Joybound pushed through the throng, her bifurcated tongue flicking in agitation. 'Where am I to be? Shall I have the honour of fighting by your side, oh most Radiant one?'

'Oh, if only, dearest child,' the Radiant said, stroking her cheek. 'But I have a more important task for you, my best beloved. You will accompany the Chief Apothecary on his own mission.' She opened her mouth to protest, and he caught her by the jaw. 'Quiet. It is my will. The floor, dear Fabius, is yours.' The Radiant stepped back, hand extended. He released Savona and she stumbled back, rubbing her mouth. Bile ignored them both.

He had expected the Radiant to send one of his curs along. It didn't matter which of them it was. The end result would be the same. If they interfered, they would be disposed of. Nothing could be allowed to stand in his way. Not the eldar, not the warriors of his own Legion. Not even Slaanesh itself would stop him.

'Arrian and Saqqara, you will both accompany me. Our target is the docking tower – here.' He tapped the image, bringing it into stark focus. 'Close to our destination, and sufficiently isolated. *Butcher-Bird* can defend itself, if it must, and a small squad should be sufficient to hold the arrival bay against any attempt to retake it from inside. Similar measures should be employed against other docking towers, if possible. Even then, most of the enemy's attention will be focused here, on the central entry point.'

Savona growled. 'Am I to miss any chance for glory, then?'

'There will be plenty of opportunities for glory, should you so desire,' Bile said. 'I intend to attack the eldar where it will do the most damage, and where resistance will likely be the heaviest. Feel free to die in Slaanesh's name at any point after our arrival, so long as it doesn't interfere with my objective.' Savona hissed and reached for her maul. Bile drew his needler and aimed it at her without looking. 'Or die now. Your preference.'

The moment stretched. The Radiant chuckled. 'Cede the point, dear Savona. Fabius has ever been a master of debate.' Savona stepped back, eyes narrowed. Bile grunted in satisfaction and holstered his weapon. He looked at Saqqara. 'After we make our initial breach, Saqqara will open a path for the Neverborn. They will flood the upper levels of the craftworld, and drown them in carnage. Clearing a path for us, and alleviating the pressure on the tines of the trident.'

'You have spoken to them? To the Neverborn?' the Radiant asked. He looked at Saqqara.

The Word Bearer smiled. 'I have. They say that they look forward to the delights to come.' He was surrounded by several of the Radiant's daemonettes. They hissed and stroked the sigils on his armour. Several warriors glared at him enviously. 'A great host of the Lord of Pleasure's finest warriors march beside us, across the endless stars. I hear the thunder of their drums in my soul.' He bowed to the Radiant. 'They are drawn by your dreams, my lord, and would witness your apotheosis first hand.'

'Yes,' the Radiant said. 'Yes, of course they are. And soon, I shall march with them across infinite fields of massacre and pleasure.' He closed his eyes and smiled. 'As the sun of Lugganath fades, I shall blaze bright, and rise into the heavens in its place.' He opened his eyes and sought out Bile. 'And I have you to thank for it, brother.'

Bile looked at the Radiant. 'Enjoy your moment of apotheosis, Kasperos. I will be attending to more important matters.'

CHAPTER SIXTEEN

Shackles and Chains

The time passed more swiftly than Oleander expected. But then, there was plenty to be done. Weapons to be distributed, leadership to be determined. The upper decks echoed with raucous conflict, as unit champions confronted one another, fighting for the right of first blood. Savage entertainments took over the corridors and transit shafts as the crew celebrated the coming bloodshed with a variety of debaucheries. Strange music and shrill screams echoed through the *Quarzhazat*, as fumes of cloying incense seeped up through the vents.

Oleander avoided it all. He descended into the launch bays, to watch as the ship's few Dreadclaws were prepared for launch. The bulky vehicles, as well as the larger Kharybdis variety, had been culled from the hulks of dead ships during the Legion Wars. Unlike the more common boarding torpedoes, Dreadclaws could take off after chewing through an enemy hull with their spiked maws. They became mobile bastions in addition, employing a wide assortment of defensive weaponry. The honour of riding in the Dreadclaws was given only to those who won the vicious duels that were occurring throughout the ship.

Besides the Dreadclaws, there were a number of semi-functioning Caestus Assault Rams being made ready in the launch bays, and at least one Skylance gunship. But most of the 12th would make worldfall on the dwindling supply of boarding torpedoes also being readied for launch. The torpedoes were bulky drill-mounts, all armour and engines, and as badly neglected as everything else on the ship that wasn't a blade or a gun. Each one could hold a squad, and would carry the majority of those who failed to win a seat on one of the Dreadclaws. Most of the torpedoes would be fired too early, or too late, if he knew his brothers. Those who survived such failed launches might find their way to the battle, or not, as the gods willed.

'As the gods will,' he said, to himself. It was less a statement than a prayer. If they were truly lucky, the gods would pay little to no attention until the end. But then, perhaps that was too much to ask, where Fabius Bile was concerned. He stood for a moment, watching as bestial mutants clad in piecemeal carapace armour and garish rags fought over the honour of accompanying their uncaring masters into battle. The beasts brayed obscene challenges and their horned skulls slammed together with a sound like a boltgun firing.

Past the duel, he caught sight of Tzimiskes' maniple of battle-automata. Tzimiskes crouched beside one, giving it a last-minute inspection. The machines were mag-locked in place at the centre of a drop pod, ready to be deployed the moment they landed. They would join the first wave, to help anchor the breach point. The quintet of automata would massacre everything in the drop zone with brutal efficiency, and clear the way for the Emperor's Children to take and hold the area.

Oleander brushed his fingers across the joints of a hulking Castellax as he stepped onto the drop pod. Something growled softly within the metal chassis. Tzimiskes looked up as he drew close. 'The hour draws near, brother.'

Tzimiskes stared at him blankly. Oleander suddenly realised that he'd never seen the other Apothecary's face. In all the years he'd known the Iron Warrior, Tzimiskes had never once removed his helmet. He wondered what was under that steel rictus, if anything.

'Why?' Oleander said, suddenly. 'Why did you join me on the auditorium floor, on Urum?' Tzimiskes said nothing. He might as well have been a statue.

The silence stretched. Tzimiskes turned back to his work, leaving Oleander standing frustrated. It gnawed at him, not knowing. He wanted to shake the Iron Warrior, to rip his helmet from him, to scream. But somehow he knew that even then, no answer would be forthcoming.

'Wasted breath, brother.'

Oleander turned. Arrian stood behind him. He held a refurbished bolt cannon in his hands. 'You're more like Saqqara than you'd admit, you know,' the World Eater said. 'Bird and mountain. Chip, chip, chipping away. Seeking something you cannot have.' He looked past Oleander. 'Brother, Igori has finished her repairs. It'll fire, now.' Tzimiskes waved him forward.

Oleander frowned and set his hand against Arrian's chest, stopping him before he could step past. 'What do you mean?'

Arrian looked down at his hand, and then up. 'Do you

remember when you asked me how I could remain loyal, after all this time?'

'You never answered me,' Oleander said, dropping his hand.

'No. I didn't. Because you wouldn't understand if I did.' Arrian patted Oleander on the shoulder with mocking familiarity. 'Brotherhood isn't solely determined by blood. A lesson I learned on Skalathrax.'

Oleander swatted his hand away. 'We all learned lessons on Skalathrax.'

'Not the same ones, I think.' Arrian leaned forward, scarred features twisting into a leer. 'If we had, you would not have left us.'

'I came back.'

'Would you like a parade?' Arrian set the bolt cannon down. 'You left because you wanted something. You came back because you want something. What will you do this time, if you do not get it?' Oleander's hand fell to his sword. Arrian smiled. 'I thought so.'

'I hope I am not interrupting.'

Oleander turned. The Radiant stood watching them. He was accompanied by a coterie of mutants and malformed machine-priests, who clustered about him seeing to the ritual sanctification of his power armour. Slaves clad in robes of deepest purple and masks made from razor-wire and rusty metal knelt behind him, softly reading passages from the *Chemosian Cantos*, the holy scripture written in the final hours of Chemos.

'Oleander. A word.' The Radiant gestured lazily.

'Your master calls,' Arrian said. Oleander hesitated, hand still on his sword. Then he turned away and went to join the Radiant. He still held his sword resting in the crook of his arm, but he'd dispensed with his cape and his daemonettes. Sigils dedicated to Slaanesh were being plasma-etched into the plates of his armour by the chittering machine-priests, but they ceased at his command. Mutants and priests scattered, leaving them alone.

'Tension in the ranks,' the Radiant said.

'Merely a difference of opinion, my lord,' Oleander said.

'Ah. I recall those. A waste of time, differing opinions.' The Radiant laughed. 'It is why I dispensed with the services of so many of my sub-commanders, in the days after the Battle of Canticle City.'

'A bold decision, my lord.'

The Radiant nodded. 'Even so. Do you know the name of this sword, Oleander?' He held up the sheathed power sword. 'Kobeleski. It is named after its first wielder, one of the tyrants of Old Night. Fulgrim himself gifted it to me, after the Pacification of 57-15. Were you there, then?'

'No, my lord. Before my time, by just a hairsbreadth under a century.'

'You would have enjoyed it. Quite a bloody affair, in its way. Kobeleski is a good sword. It has seen me safely through wars without end. A useful tool. Like you. And like you, I will happily sacrifice it on the altar of necessity, despite the affection I have for it.'

'I understand,' Oleander said.

'Do you? Nothing occurs without my notice, Oleander,' the Radiant said. 'I see all and hear all. A king must know how his court plots, after all.' He smiled, and, for a moment, something awful seemed to surface from beneath the shroud of his beauty. 'Poor Merix. So certain he has a friend in you. Or a dupe. And Gulos thinks you as weak as Merix. But then, he was never very bright.

One too many blows to the head, I suspect. Can that impinge on one's judgement? What say you, Apothecary?'

'It can, my lord.'

'You are wise in your generation, Oleander. Wiser than the others. Wise enough to know when you're beaten,' the Radiant said. 'And yet you continue to play. Why is that?'

Oleander kept his eyes averted. 'Because it pleases you, oh most Radiant King.'

The Radiant caught the back of his skull, but only gently. 'And that is why you are my favourite, Oleander. I do so hope you survive the coming conflagration. I will still need a fleshcrafter, even when I have shed my flesh.'

'I am overjoyed to hear it, my lord.'

'I thought that you would be. I would prefer two, of course. It would be quite a coup to bring Chief Apothecary Fabius to heel once and for all. Eidolon would gnaw his vitals in envy.' The Radiant frowned. 'Your pet Word Bearer isn't the only one that the Neverborn speak to. The handmaidens of Slaanesh whisper to me, Oleander. They say that this is fate, rather than coincidence. They show me things, sometimes, in their dances. Brief memories of things yet to occur. They show me the path your once and future master treads, and it does not best please the Lord of Dark Delights.'

'Chief Apothecary Fabius has never been one inclined to please others.' Unbidden, the thought of their encounter with the daemon Kanathara came into Oleander's mind. Had the warning from Fulgrim been real, then, rather than a daemon's lie? Was that what Saqqara had meant, with his talk of knives and stones?

'Oh, I know that, all too well. But he must be taught the value of a bowed head and a bent knee. His fate and ours must be as one, else all is... murky. Uncertain.'

'There is pleasure in the uncertain,' Oleander said.

'There is more in certainty, Oleander.'

'Is that why you sent Savona with him?' Oleander said. 'Certainty?'

'Of course. She will see him back to me in one piece, or mostly so.'

'And if he resists?'

'He must be shown that brotherhood is his path forward. Or he must be made to see it. I care not either way. I will have my armies of monsters, Oleander. I will have my craft-world and my apotheosis, as Slaanesh has promised. And Fabius Bile will learn his place. Else I will break open his skull and force-feed you his mind. One way or another, his genius will serve the Third again.' His grip on Oleander's head tightened convulsively, painfully. 'Do you understand?'

'I... yes, my lord,' Oleander said, wincing against the pain. The Harlequins, Fulgrim, Slaanesh itself, all of them wanted Bile bound in some fashion. Chained to his old Legion, shackled by duty. But why? He pushed the thought aside. It didn't matter. He had set his course. Perhaps with Bile seated at the head of the 12th, they might find answers to those questions.

The Radiant released him. 'Good. Now... go and find your other master and bid him come to me. I wish to speak to him once more, before we plunge into the mael-strom of sweet war.'

'What does not live can never truly die,' Bile said. 'Some ancient scrivener said that, I believe. Simplistic, yes, but accurate. I do not live, in any recognised sense of the word, and thus cannot die. I persist, I maintain, I exist... but live? No. No more than you do, my mindless friend.'

The servitor didn't answer. It moved slowly, if efficiently. Pneumatic pistons clicked and hissed as the thrall-machine went about its duties. Obscenities had been etched into its few remaining patches of flesh, and the metal of its limbs had been painted garish hues. It was not aware of these cosmetic alterations, nor of its missing mechadendrites. Bile watched the corroded stumps thrash uselessly at its side, vainly attempting to fulfil their function. He could still see the traces of the ancient craftsmanship that had gone into its construction, despite the damage that had been done to it.

Pain bubbled up from within him. One of the chirurgeon's arms darted forward, plunging a syringe into his neck. He grunted, more from the touch of the cold metal than any pain. He'd become feverish without realising it. A leftover infection from the wound in his side, perhaps. It had healed, finally. He chided himself for becoming distracted. Routine was the rock of discipline, and discipline the rampart separating the living from the dead.

He laughed. 'You'll forgive this momentary lapse. I dose myself with a variety of tinctures, all meant to keep my carcass tottering along in as efficient a manner as possible,' Bile said, as the chirurgeon's syringe depressed with a hiss of escaping air. 'Stimulants, mostly. The rest are a mix of purgatives, filtering solutions, thinners, thickeners, and reagents.' He held up a hand. His fingers trembled imperceptibly. As he watched, the trembling faded. He made a fist and nodded in satisfaction.

'I am living on my last breath. My bodies are blighted. They rot, as do all subsequent bodies culled from them. The duration of vitality lessens, the system breaks down, the centre cannot hold.' He stood and strode to the edge of the gantry. 'I am Chaos at its most basic – entropy made flesh. That is what your masters will never understand.'

Hands behind his back, Bile watched slaves ready the *Butcher-Bird* for flight far below. The gunship was old – a survivor from a more glorious age, much like himself. And, like himself, it had far to go before it could rest. Behind him, the servitor continued on its way, mechadendrites writhing. 'We are much the same, you and I... built for purpose, unable to cease until that purpose is fulfilled,' he said to it, as it clumped past. 'No matter how much we might wish otherwise.' He shook his head, annoyed with himself. 'Melancholia is the first sign of mental degradation,' he said, out loud.

'Is talking to yourself the second?'

Bile turned. Oleander stood nearby, one hand on his sword. His face had a strained expression. 'What do you want, Oleander?'

'Lugganath is within sight. The Radiant wishes to see you on the bridge, before we begin the attack. I'll see to things here, if you like.'

'Igori and the others are perfectly capable.' Bile made to stride past him, but Oleander stopped him. He jerked his hand away as Bile glanced at it. 'What is it, Oleander? Stop twitching and speak. I am past all patience with your antics.'

'I think you have more patience than you let on.'

Bile laughed. 'Lucky for you.'

'Was it? You decided to help me before that charade in the auditorium on Urum, didn't you?' Oleander said.

Bile looked at his former student. 'And so?'

'Why the game?'

'Why lie to me about acting on the Radiant's behalf?' Bile countered. Oleander looked away. Bile chuckled. 'I see through you, Oleander. You have never been the ambitious sort, and it ill-suits you now. Terrestrial ambition in an Apothecary is a wasted thing. Knowledge should be your only desire.'

'And to acquire that knowledge, one needs warm bodies. Assistants, orderlies, soldiers.' Oleander gestured. 'You taught me that. What else is the Consortium but your personal army?'

'They – you – are my students.'

'When you choose. And we are your dogsbodies, when you demand. We are nothing more than tools to you, Chief Apothecary Fabius. Raw materials. Just like your precious Gland-hounds.' He made to say more, when a bellicose, mechanical roar shook the hold. Bile turned, his hand dropping to his needler.

'What was that?'

'It's just Ancient Diomat and friends,' Oleander said, as the roaring hulks of metal and flesh were dragged along by gangs of slaves. The ornate sarcophagi of the Dreadnoughts thumped and thudded against the decks as the frenzied maniacs within struggled against the very systems that kept them alive. They were kept separate from their armoured shells until launch, to prevent the occasional untimely rampage. 'The Radiant has been collecting Dreadnoughts for decades. Adding them to his menagerie. Like the fleet, they are symbols of his power.'

'How many?'

'A dozen, in various states of malfunction.' Oleander looked at Bile. 'Do you remember Diomat? He was with us at Walpurgis.'

'I remember Diomat,' Bile said, softly. 'He spoke against joining Horus. We left him chained in the hold at Isstvan. Fulgrim's little joke.'

Oleander nodded. 'There's not much of him left. The Radiant won't let him die. I've worked on him myself. He weeps, sometimes. Begs for death, like a child.'

Bile watched as the sarcophagi were dragged aboard the boarding torpedo. 'Heroism is easily crushed by the weight of eternity,' he said.

'Some would say that he deserves better.'

'It is none of my concern,' Bile said.

'So you've said.'

'I sense that you are upset.' Bile studied him. 'What would you have of me, Oleander? An apology for how things have turned out? The state of the galaxy is hardly my fault.'

Oleander shook his head. 'I want things to be as they once were. We were a Legion once, brothers in arms as well as blood. We could be that way again. You led us, before Canticle City. You could lead us now. The other captains would flock to you, if you showed them that you were willing. You are the last...'

'The last what? The last sane man? The last true heir to Fulgrim?' Bile laughed. He laughed until his chest ached. 'Are you truly that foolish, Oleander?' He swept out a hand. 'What about Eidolon? Or Lucius? They were as close to Fulgrim as I was.'

'They are broken things. Them and Fulgrim all,' Oleander said. 'They are lost to their own desires, but you still see past yourself, master. I thought, once, that you were no better than they but I know differently now. You still seek perfection... with you leading it, the Twelfth can return to its former glory.'

Bile stared at him. 'And what then?' he said, softly. He'd thought the same himself, more than once. In those moments when the pain receded and he could see clearly past the next step, he wondered what would happen if he but reached out and took control. He could attempt to heal the Legion as a whole, as he once had individual warriors. But it was a fool's dream. A distraction from his work.

'And then we take back the Third. One company, one warband at a time. We break them, so that they might be rebuilt.'

Bile laughed sourly. 'You make it sound easy. You think Abaddon will allow a renewed Third to challenge him? And what of Fulgrim? No. I cannot allow myself to become distracted.' He looked at Oleander. 'A man should never reacquaint himself with past mistakes. Look forward, Oleander, not backward. The past is done. Leave it to the dust.'

Oleander said nothing for a moment. Then, 'The Radiant wishes to see you. On the bridge. Lugganath draws near.'

CHAPTER SEVENTEEN

Lugganath

The occulus viewscreen showed a dozen external, magnified views of the *Quarzhazat*'s hull. Each was from a unique angle, and each showed only a part of the marvel that was Lugganath. The craftworld was immense.

It was a kilometres-long leviathan of the cosmic depths, easily visible even at so great a distance. The colossal vessel of living wraithbone spread in all directions, and thousands of smaller vessels gathered in its wake, or clustered about its docking spires. A vast, interstellar fortress, the likes of which Bile had never seen.

Even in the Legion's heyday, he doubted that they could have mustered the strength to conquer such a thing. Now, it seemed the next best thing to impossible. He was careful to keep his thoughts to himself, however. Conquest was not his objective, after all.

'Lovely,' the Radiant said. 'That such a thing exists gives me hope for my own perfection.' He lazed in his command chair, one leg thrown over the armrest, chin balanced on his knuckles. He rolled his face towards Bile.

'Hope is the salve of the weak,' Bile said, still looking at the viewscreen.

'If your tongue were a lash, brother, I could inflict such exquisite agonies,' the Radiant said. 'Your... creation appears to be working. This is as close as we have ever got, in our hunts. They would be running by now, normally.'

'You're welcome.'

'I don't intend to thank you until this is over. Until the Twelfth raises its banner upon a hill of eldar dead.' The Radiant gestured lazily. 'It will make a fine flagship, don't you think? I will dedicate its every delicate arch and sweeping tower to Slaanesh. A radiant world for a radiant king. I will make it a pleasure-planet, and our brothers shall come... oh yes. They shall come to us, and my ranks will swell. Perhaps I shall name myself Emperor, then. Do you think the old corpse, on his golden throne, would mind?'

'I think Ezekyle would.' Bile crossed his arms. 'I think Abaddon will come looking to cast your banner into the fire, and your ambitions with it. What will you do then, I wonder?'

'What is Abaddon to me? I am beloved by a god. And he is hated by all.' The Radiant sat up. 'Perhaps I will take Horus' talon for myself, hmm? Would that delight you, Fabius? Why, with the blood that stains those claws, you might make a Legion of abominations for me – an army, fit for an Emperor.' He leaned forward, finger tapping at his lips. 'Would you stay then, brother? Would you stay, if I promised you that you could finish what you started in Canticle City? I am sure our brothers would thank you, when they understood.'

Bile said nothing. His mind whirred along half-forgotten tracks, thinking of old failures. He'd come close, in Canticle City. Closer than ever before. Close enough to understand, to see how things must be. But in the end, he'd failed. He'd wasted his efforts trying to fix what had been broken, rather than constructing something new. Something better. He composed himself and said, 'Is this why you demanded to see me? To make more promises you cannot possibly keep? And just as I was beginning to think better of you.'

'No. I just thought you would like to see this, brother,' the Radiant said, sitting back. He was frowning. 'The culmination of all your efforts in my name. We will wreak such incandescent horrors on them, and all thanks to you.'

'You can thank me by ensuring I have time enough to acquire what I came for.'

'Oh, have no fears on that score, Fabius. I intend to feast on this world for ages to come. It will make a fine flagship, as I said.' He smacked the side of his throne. 'Perhaps I shall give you this one, when I am done with it. Yours is so small. And this one ever so interesting. A fitting vessel for the Master Fleshcrafter of my armies. You see? I am kind as well as fair. My name is well earned, is it not?'

Bile laughed. 'I have a ship. It suits me well enough.'

'Be careful, Fabius. You can only spit upon my generosity so many times before it grows wearisome. Oleander is a fickle, untrustworthy creature, but perhaps he will be more amenable to my offer. And if I am forced to do that, you can be certain I will give him your brilliant mind to feast upon, so that your genius is not lost.'

Bile looked at him. 'You are free to do as you please, Kasperos.'

'And what does that mean?'

'Make of it what you will.'

The Radiant chuckled and pushed himself to his feet. 'Open a vox-channel,' he commanded one of the nearby machine-priests. He raised his helmet in his hands. For a moment, he studied its face, running his fingers along its contours. 'Sing, O sons and daughters of pleasure – sing us into the storm,' he said, loudly. 'Sing me a song of joy and death, my children, my brothers, my lovers. Sing, so that Slaanesh herself might take note of the glorious havoc we wreak in her name.' He pulled his helmet on. His voice echoed suddenly from every vox on deck. 'Sing us to our doom. Sing us the last hymn of Canticle City, in honour of him who has made this moment possible.'

And they did. Throughout the ship, Emperor's Children raised their voices in hideous rhapsody. A babble of sound flooded the vox, crackling across all channels. Slaves, too, joined their masters in the ecstatic dirge. The Radiant spread his arms and began to twist and gesture, like some macabre orchestral conductor.

'Do you hear them, Fabius? Do you see how they love me? Even as we loved Fulgrim, my Joybound love me,' the Radiant said. 'Truly, my moment is here. I shall strut upon the stage and make my final bows. A greater performance awaits me. Awaits us.'

'Whatever it might be for you, this is just the next step in my march to the sea, Kasperos,' Bile said.

'What sea? Is this another of your classical references, Fabius?' he said. 'How dull.'

'Once, we prided ourselves on our knowledge of rhetoric and quotation,' Bile said. 'Do you remember those great debates, Kasperos? Long into the night, we would

hunt meaning across the plains of thought. The Phoenician himself joined us, and we would bandy references
until the suns rose and it was time again for war, rather
than words.' On the viewscreen, ships surged forward like
hounds off the leash. Motes of fierce light flared in the
black, and *Quarzhazat* shuddered as its crew sought to drag
every available erg of speed from the engines.

'You sound terribly sad, brother,' the Radiant said. 'It is...
not as exquisite as one would hope. You could have been
the greatest of us, I think. But now you are broken and
imperfect. A dull sadness for a dull creature.' He turned
to shout last orders to the bridge crew. A harsh mechanical voice echoed across the deck.

Contact in ten... nine... eight...

'Dull? Maybe. But it is mine, and I hold fast to it,' Bile
said, softly, so that the other would not hear. The search
for perfection was what had led him here. Better sadness
than that. He watched the crew man their stations, and
listened to their excited babbling. The fleet would come
under attack the moment the eldar realised they were
there. But by then, it would be too late. Bile idly calculated how much time Elian had left. It wasn't much, but
Elian wouldn't care. He wondered what it must be like,
to find such fulfilment.

The Radiant turned back. 'Well? Why are you still here,
Chief Apothecary?' He leaned forward. 'Shouldn't you be
preparing to wage glorious war in my name? Rest assured,
Savona shall keep you safe. I would not have you miss
my moment of triumph.'

Bile bowed low and turned on his heel. The Radiant called out to him as he left. 'Remember, Fabius... if
you disappoint me in this, I shall ensure that whatever

black knowledge you hold in that sour brain of yours is scattered to the four cosmic winds, or else passed on to more fertile minds. I grow weary of this world and would soon see another.

'Even if I must do so over your twisted corpse.'

In the *Quarzhazat*'s core-chamber, Elian Pakretes, once a sergeant of the Ninth Company, felt the weight of the moment, and knew it was his undoing. His every cell was ablaze with primal fire as the song of Slaanesh echoed within him, fighting to be free of his husk. Cables popped loose of the hull and flapped about him as he twitched and thrashed, unable to control himself. Discordant noise slithered from the remaining vox-casters in the chamber. The twitching bodies of machine-priests lay scattered about him, their brains boiled to mush by the force of his voice. He had seared his own insides to smouldering wreckage. And yet still, the song hammered at his mind, his heart, his soul. And still, his body refused to yield. It would not, while he had anything left to offer up.

He gave himself to the song willingly, even gladly. To be one with the song was all that he had ever desired since the first moment he'd heard it, on some long-forgotten battlefield. Had it been Isstvan? He could not recall. His memory was a loose thing, all sharp gleaming shards rattling about in a sack of emotion. Whenever he reached back into it, he found only scattered moments of beauty and terror. Nothing mattered, save the song.

Elian had never felt so alone, standing braced beneath the stars. Daemonic shapes danced about him, graceful and alluring, but he barely saw them. The handmaidens of Slaanesh were doing as their nature dictated, drawn to his singing like moths to a flame, and hundreds of them swayed wraithlike in the chamber, adding their voices to his. The air was all colours and none to his perceptions, and it blazed like a sun, stretching before him like a beach of golden teeth, and a sea of dark wine. Every mote of light glowed so as to burn his eyes, and every sound swirled with a hypnotic rhythm, pulsing in time to his voice. The wall before him was a gaping maw, mouthing words his fractured eardrums could not catch, marred only by a flickering speck. The speck was a world. The world his song had blinded. He could see it clearly through the wavering solidity of the hull. The *Quarzhazat*'s sensors were his eyes, and its vox his voice.

A fitting death. He was nothing more than sound and fury now, trapped in a crumbling edifice. He stared straight ahead, willing himself to hold together just a while longer. He wanted the eldar to hear him in all his glory, and hear his part of the song, before it was ripped away by the cosmic winds. The speck grew larger and larger, spreading like a blight across the perfect discordance of the immaterium.

The craftworld was so immense that it could move only at sub-light speeds. It was surrounded by fleets of smaller ships, clinging like shoals of fish to the leviathan's shadow. It was home to millions, and soon, those millions would hear Slaanesh's call. His brothers would stride forth, their instruments raised, and carry the song into the very heart of the enemy. They would make the very wraithbone weep for the beauty of it, and they would teach the faithless eldar new ways to shout, and revel and kill.

They would free them from their chains, and show them how to live in wonder and glory forever more. He ignored the spasms of pain in his back and legs, and stretched up.

Arms spread, he mustered his remaining strength. His part in the song was coming to an end. But it would never die. He would go out like a light, but the song would roll on, gaining in strength. It would envelop the galaxy and all would know the divine joys of Slaanesh's favour.

The craftworld grew closer yet. He could feel the vox-frequencies of the fleet pulse within him, and the eager-ness of the *Quarzhazat* as it sighted its prey. The vessel shuddered like a canid on the hunt, and its engines panted thunderously. Ships edged forward, breaking ranks. Smaller raiders and hunter-killer craft hurtled out of for-mation, flinging themselves beyond the reach of his song, beyond the reach of the remaining tiny minds linked to his. They would die first, selfishly taking the deaths meant for grander warriors. But he could not fault them their exuberance. Once, he might even have done the same.

He reached out, as if to clutch the distant vessel to him, as his joints popped and the void-seals on his armour rup-tured at last. Every sound was like thunder, amplified in his cracking skull. The Chief Apothecary had built him strong, and made him stronger yet. His brain bubbled in his skull, perforated by spikes of non-human matter. He could hear the voices of those minds, as they were caught inside him, and their screams, as their strength was fed into his song. Psyker and witch alike, their souls were ashes caught in the wind of the song. He bent them to his will, and added their voices to his own.

His song split the void, bent it back and folded it over, opening a path for the *Quarzhazat* to lead the rest of the fleet through. He felt a rumble in the hull as the guns were rolled out. He could hear the klaxons clamouring, the excited shouts of the crew at their stations.

He could hear singing.

A kernel of pain flared within him, growing stronger. His singing began to falter. He was truly alone now, and beyond all redemption and recrimination. Armour plates peeled away from his disintegrating limbs, his cracking torso, his deflating skull. The daemonettes faded away, trailing their claws across his armour in bittersweet farewell. Or perhaps in acknowledgement of a life well lived and a song well sung.

Elian Pakretes, once a sergeant of the Ninth Company, crumbled away as the war began. But the song of destruction rolled on, only growing stronger.

'Do you remember Chemos, Oleander?' Gulos said, as proximity alarms began to scream and warriors rushed eagerly to their boarding pods, ready to be hurled to war. The monotonous rumble of weapons fire hammering uselessly against the *Quarzhazat*'s shields echoed throughout the boarding port. Useless for now. They were moving into the craftworld's orbit, and then the fleet would be beset on all sides, surrounded by thousands of darting enemy ships and one very large one. Void-shields would start to crumple quickly beneath a storm of plasma. Oleander was almost glad to be in the first wave.

'I was Terran-born,' Oleander said, instinctively checking the readiness of his equipment. Everything seemed in working order, more was the pity. He could have used the distraction. He'd never liked assaults. Too much could go wrong. Too little control.

'Chemos was a sick world, before Fulgrim,' Gulos said. 'He cured it. But it sickened again, soon enough. Like the Twelfth has sickened. But I shall cure it.' He gestured.

'In the drop pod, Apothecary. We have scalps to collect.' A squad of Emperor's Children were already in place, hunched in their restraint thrones, talking eagerly of the butchery to come. One sang softly, while another amused himself by carving strange designs in the bare flesh of his arm with a primitive-looking knife. The excitement was palpable.

Boarding actions were always savage affairs. But this would be more akin to making planetfall. The craft-world was simply too immense to overwhelm in the same way one might take a ship, even if the 12th had been a proper army, rather than a semi-organised rabble. But it was possible... just barely. If they could activate the tele-port homer at the right time; if Saqqara was able to do as he'd promised; if the other captains did as the Radi-ant had commanded, rather than as they willed. If, if, if. A slim hope, but a hope nonetheless.

Of course, none of that mattered if they were simply blown apart before they reached their target. 'It has been too long since we have gone to war together, brother,' Ole-ander said, as he tested the straps of his restraint throne. 'Have you missed it?'

Tzimiskes shrugged. He tapped his chest-plate and Ole-ander laughed. Gulos glared at them from across the aisle. 'What did he say?' the Joybound asked.

'It loses something in translation.'

'I'm sure it does,' Gulos said, his perfect features twisted in suspicion. 'Tell me anyway.'

'He said it was nice to go to war with brothers once more.' Oleander leaned back. 'I cannot say I disagree with him. To fight alongside those who share your blood and soul is a heady thing.'

'I'm touched. Do you consider us brothers, then?'

'Yes.' Gulos stared at him. Oleander leaned back. 'We are brothers, Gulos. Even now. Even after all that has happened... we are brothers.' He gestured. 'Canticle City was a death knell. We'd been dying the death of a thousand cuts before then... Skalathrax, Gnosis, a hundred other battlefields scattered throughout Eyespace. But Canticle City... Abaddon's spear... that was the moment we ceased to be a power and instead became a memory. Those few bonds that remained unbroken frayed loose and we were left horribly, terribly free.'

The others were silent now. Eyes that had for too long stared inwards at abysses of desire were now fixed on him. Oleander cleared his throat. 'Freedom is a grand thing, in measured doses. But too much of it chokes you. It drives you mad. And madness without purpose is a waste. We have no purpose save pleasure, and that too is a waste.'

'Then why are you here?' Gulos said, softly. For once, there was no challenge in his voice, no arrogance. Only curiosity.

'To save what is left of us. The Radiant has held the Twelfth together through fire and blood, and I would not see it shattered now, on the shoals of desire. I would save it, if I can. And the Third Legion with it. If that means I must set a new king on the throne, so be it.'

Gulos slumped in his harness, eyes glittering. 'You have hidden depths, Apothecary. I did not figure you for an idealist.'

'To be an Apothecary, one must see beyond one's own desires and find the best route for those in one's care. Sometimes extraordinary measures are called for. I do not plan to give up so easily.'

Tzimiskes dropped a fist against his shoulder-plate. It might have been a caution, or merely a gesture of agreement. Warning klaxons sounded. The interior of the torpedo was bathed in a bloody red light. 'And not without a fight,' he said, finally, as they were launched into the maelstrom.

CHAPTER EIGHTEEN

First Cut

The battle began with light and fury, but no sound. Prow-lances spat blazing javelins, and unwary vessels were ripped open, to be left floating and burning as the Radiant's fleet plunged towards their prey without formation or order.

Lugganath stirred with Elian's passing, aware now of the threat. The craftworld's defences activated, though sluggishly, due to the lingering effects of the psychic miasma. The ships which sought safety in its shadow suddenly turned and arrowed towards the approaching fleet, weapons batteries flickering. Doubtless, some only sought to escape. Others engaged the enemy willingly. In the end, the result was the same.

Fighters met in the no-man's-land between larger vessels, and engaged in slow, stately duels amidst a sea of searing death. The silence reverberated with the clash of frigates and the death-screams of cruisers as engines overloaded and void-shields collapsed. New suns were born, as reactors went critical, consuming smaller vessels in their birth pangs. Wounded ships slid down impossible inclines, drifting outwards, downwards and away.

Through it all, the *Quarzhazat* led the way, undulating like some immense cosmic serpent through the star fields. Every weapon the Lunar-class cruiser possessed was aflame with activity. Its crew did little to distinguish between friend and foe as it slithered towards its prey, mile-wide jaws agape, leaving a trail of floating wreckage in its wake.

Armoured bastions along Lugganath's flank awoke, and defence turrets spoke eloquently. *Quarzhazat* slammed into a wall of plasma and barrelled through, its void-shields pockmarked and ragged, a city's worth of guns roaring out a hymn of destruction.

Butcher-Bird dived through the firestorm, using the cruiser as cover. The transport bay shuddered as the gunship rode the currents of war, avoiding the worst for the moment. Bile braced himself against a bulkhead, studying the vid-screens. They showed flickering images of the battle raging outside. A confusing mess, as most such conflicts were. Ships rose and fell at odd angles, following intercept trajectories or pursuit formulas. Escorts and fighters spun in tight embrace, their duels personal and swift compared to the clash of their larger kin.

A flash stung his eyes, and identification runes climbed a screen. 'The *Sly Tongue*,' he said, though no one had asked. 'Not so sly, then.'

'We should've taken a boarding pod,' Savona snarled. She looked paler than normal. Her warriors shifted uncomfortably in their restraint thrones, bestowing glares on Igori and her pack, who occupied the other side of the bay. For their part, the Gland-hounds studied the Emperor's Children with wary malice, like cats eyeing unusually large rats.

There were thirty of the Renegade Astartes, each one an army unto himself. Their helmets were marked with a black hoofprint, signalling their devotion to the Lady of the Spinward Conflagration. They carried a variety of close-combat weapons – swords, friction-axes, power-axes and blades made from the sharpened bones of some sort of xenos. They were her champions – the strongest of her warriors. He recognised some of them. Oscada, a sergeant of the 45th. Bellephus, of the 67th. Others, all of whom had fought under his aegis at Lupercalios and a hundred other battles, before Canticle City.

Bile wondered what Savona had been, before she had become one of Kasperos' pets, and how she had come to lead a warband of the Third Legion. It was a rare thing, to see a mortal champion leading transhuman warriors. Especially ones as hardened as these.

He glanced at Igori. The Gland-hound met his gaze calmly. Twenty of her brothers and sisters sat with her, their veins full of combat-stims and battle-drugs of his own devising. They were armed and armoured with the best equipment he could provide, and more than capable of holding their own against a lesser opponent.

In addition to their ranks, he'd brought a trio of heavily modified combat-servitors. The lobotomised husks were clad in heavy armour, and each was armed with a spinal harness based on the design of his chirurgeon. Their multiple, segmented limbs were tipped with a variety of weapons – flamers, plasma torches, bone saws and the like – and each had a bulky combi-bolter built into the front of their armoured chassis. They crouched in their crash-alcoves like spiders, waiting for his command.

The gunship shuddered and Bile grimaced, placing a hand to his side. The wound still ached. A reminder to be faster, next time. He checked his vitals with dissatisfaction, noting several secondary organs on the edge of failure. Nothing which would impede him anytime soon, but another indicator that this body was wearing thin. It would be time to replace it soon. To strip his consciousness from one skull and seal it into another, so that the all too short dance could begin again. Unless he succeeded here. Victory here would assure his ultimate triumph over the enemy called time. 'Perhaps I shall inveigle a spirit stone of my very own, eh?' he said.

'Chief Apothecary?' Arrian asked.

'Merely thinking out loud, Arrian.' More flashes on the viewscreens. The eldar had been surprised, as he'd expected. But they were fighting back in earnest now. Soon, a strategy would emerge. Unless the Radiant delivered the killing blow, and soon, his assault would crumble, and his fleet would scatter. Discipline was in short supply in these fallen times.

'There was no reason for you to accompany us. You could have waited aboard the *Vesalius*,' Arrian said. He sounded as close to concerned as he could come. 'Your body...'

'My body is functioning. That is enough.' Bile looked at the screens, watching the battle. Another flare, another thousand souls tumbled screaming into silent death. 'There is a certain poetry to it, if one isn't in the middle of it,' he said.

Savona looked at him. 'What are you blathering about

now, Manflayer?' Her warriors stirred in their seats, ready to act at her order. Bile studied her through slitted eyes. Perhaps it was best to deal with the obvious threat sooner, rather than later. Unlike Oleander, he had no patience for games of threat and counter-threat.

'Hold your tongue,' he said. He kept his voice mild, but raised his sceptre meaningfully. Savona smiled, display-ing her fangs. She made to rise, but her restraint cradle resisted her efforts to open it. Her warriors were simi-larly trapped. One made to raise his weapon, but Arrian was on him in a moment, falax blade pressed tight to his throat. At Bile's command, the combat-servitors twisted in their alcoves, training their weapons on the trapped Emperor's Children.

'Settle, brothers, peace,' the World Eater said. 'Or death. It makes little difference to me.'

Igori slipped from her cradle and pressed the barrel of the shuriken pistol she'd acquired on Sublime to Savona's head. 'What is the meaning of this?' Savona snarled.

'Did you think I haven't had uninvited guests on this ship before?' Bile gestured meaningfully to their cradles. 'No gene-seed in you, I expect,' he said. 'But there might something worth harvesting.' He looked down at her. 'The Radiant has set you as my guard dog. But I will not be guarded, harried, or hurried.'

'What is that to me?' she said, through clenched teeth. 'Perhaps he cares more for you than you know. I know not, and care even less.'

'No?'

'No.' She glared at him.

'Then you will not interfere with me?'

'No.'

Bile nodded. 'Well, I'm glad that's settled. Now I don't have to crack open your skull, and claim the eldar did it. I do so hate wasted effort.' He gestured, and his followers fell back into their seats. 'I want what I've come for, and nothing else.'

'And then?'

'And then I leave, my dear. What you do after that is no concern of mine.' A proximity alarm sounded, and the bay was washed in emergency lighting. The gunship convulsed as its engines roared louder, hotter. They were rising above the *Quarzhazat* now, away from the main flow of battle. Their ascent was perilous. As they rose, boarding pods flashed past, spiralling down towards the domes and towers of the craftworld. Many were consumed in fire as they fell, but still more got through.

The *Butcher-Bird* flew towards one of the thousands of docking towers that dotted the upper reaches of the craftworld. Up close, the true enormity of the world-ship was impossible to deny. It filled every screen, and its gravity well pulled at the gunship. Hundreds of blister-like domes pockmarked its graceful surface, each one containing what might have been a city, or an artful ecosystem designed to resemble the environment of those worlds the eldar had once called home. Everything was being recorded, every pict-capture, every auspex reading, all of it, for future study. One never knew when having detailed information about such a thing would come in handy. Waste not, want not.

The gunship was not alone in its ascent. Other vessels followed suit. Some larger, some smaller, crewed by pirates, renegades and warbands not willing to bow to the Radiant's whims. They would be after plunder, rather than conquest, but would serve to distract and divide the defenders, if they made it inside. A green lumen flickered above Bile's head. 'We're approaching now. Arrian...?'

'Yes, Chief Apothecary. Preparing for incision,' Arrian said, thumbing the activation rune on a grenade as the bay doors cycled, and the gunship's assault cannons thundered, blowing itself an entrance to the docking platform. *Butcher-Bird* shrieked in joy as it clamped onto the tower and thrust itself into the wound it had blasted open. As the bay shook the restraint thrones unlatched, allowing free movement.

Savona snarled like a leopardess and shoved herself to her hooves, activating her power maul as she did so. Her warriors rose from their seats, hefting bolters and blades. 'Hurry, warhound. I've eldar to kill and souls to swallow.'

Arrian whipped the grenade through the bay doors as they opened. The resulting explosion sent a gout of smoke spewing back up into the bay. In the sudden dark, armoured bodies jostled one another as they poured down the ramp and onto the docking platform. Boltguns thundered, firing at shadows. Eerily shrill alarms whined, and a vox rattled somewhere with alien outrage. Nothing was there to greet them, save corpses.

Savona barked orders, gesturing with her maul. Her warriors took up defensive positions. Arrian pushed forward, pulling a second grenade as he did so. A smooth portal, more resembling wood or bone than metal, separated the docking platform from the transit tubes beyond. 'It's sealed,' he called out, over his shoulder.

'Then I shall unseal it,' Bile said, standing on the gunship's ramp. He patted his needler in its holster, and tightened his hold on Torment as he descended, followed by the combat-servitors. The Gland-hounds took up position around him, tense with eagerness. He took a two-handed grip on the sceptre as he approached the door. Power thrummed through it, sinister and greedy. It yearned to be used. To be smashed down again and again on bare flesh and fragile bone. At a thought, battle-stims flooded his system, adding their own unique clamour to the noise in his head.

While the sceptre was mostly a pain amplifier, it could also shatter metal as if it were glass. He braced himself and swung. The bulkhead crumpled inwards with an almost human scream, and sections of it pinwheeled down the sloped corridor beyond. He stepped through, drawing his needler as the chirurgeon's limbs forced the remains of the bulkhead up and back. Shuriken blasts hissed around him, singeing the side of his helm.

His helmet's targeting array crackled to life as the first of the eldar appeared, firing as they moved forward. Their armour was a fiery orange, save for their pointed helms which were a deep, lustrous black. One had a multi-hued diamond pattern marking one arm, startlingly reminiscent of the Harlequins, and Bile hesitated, wondering what it meant. Shuriken bolts crackled around him as they advanced. A calculated risk – a sudden rush to force the enemy back and isolate them on the platform until reinforcements could arrive. They were disciplined. Highly motivated. And the joints of their armour were obligingly vulnerable. Targeting glyphs flickered and the needler hummed in his grip. Bile smiled as tinny screams echoed through the transit tube. He stepped over the closest of the thrashing bodies and moved aside, so that Arrian could move past him. 'There's a junction ahead,' Bile said.

Arrian slung the grenade, and immediately reached for another. A dull crump sounded and the docking tower shuddered. He rolled two more along the corridor. When the smoke cleared, he strode forward. 'Clear. Two more bulkheads, both sealed. Five enemy casualties.'

'Good. Take samples. Eldar blood has an infinite variety of uses.' Bile turned to see Savona raising her maul over one of the twitching eldar – the one with the harlequin-ade arm. He blocked the blow with his sceptre. 'Those are not for you.'

'There will be plenty of prisoners later,' she said.

'Who said anything about prisoners? Saqqara... do as you will with these.' Bile gestured with the needler. The Word Bearer pushed between them, drawing a curvy blade from his belt. The knife glimmered with an oily sheen, as if the light could not quite catch it. The air became cold and sullen as he slashed it out in a complicated gesture.

'Stand back – all of you. They will be hungry, and in no mood to waste time discerning who is friend and who is foe,' Saqqara said as he dragged the dying eldar to its feet, and set his blade against its belly. 'Know that this gives me great pleasure, vermin,' he said. 'Rest assured that you are at last fulfilling your ultimate purpose, and aiding me in mine.' The jagged blade cut through psycho-reactive metal, mesh and meat with ease. Blood arced out as the eldar screamed in agony. Saqqara spun his blade, stabbing it through each of the creature's wrists in turn. He stepped back, studying his handiwork.

The eldar remained standing, held aloft by the growing skeins of blood. They stretched across the wall, spreading and darkening until it resembled a mirror of polished obsidian rather than any vital fluid. The eldar twitched

and moaned as more blood seeped from it, to be added
to the shimmering black. Saqqara thrust his free hand into
the wound he'd made in the xenos' belly. He twisted his
fingers, as if trying to open a latch. The eldar screamed
once more, and then fell silent. It dangled, held by the
blood. Saqqara withdrew his hand and stepped back a
pace, then two. A ribbon of blood and meat followed his
hand, and he sent droplets splattering against the ceiling
and floor in curious patterns.

'From the fires of betrayal, unto the blood of revenge, we
bring the name of Lorgar,' Saqqara said, as the air took on
a noisome disposition. Wisps of sound became audible,
like the howling of distant beasts. Gripping his athame in
his bloody hand, Saqqara dropped to his knees and began
to carve ruinous sigils into the still-twitching bodies of the
remaining eldar. As he did so, he chanted, lathering the
air with guttural invocations. The howling grew louder, as
if whatever he'd roused were coming closer. Frost crawled
across the armour and flesh of those assembled.

Bile couldn't help but admire Saqqara's technique as he
deftly plucked out each spirit stone. The dangling eldar
thrashed abruptly, and then crumbled inwards with a hideous sound, as if something were drawing it through a
pinhole. It left behind a pulsing, wet redness that gaped
like a grinning maw. Saqqara flung the spirit stones into
that wound, and it devoured them greedily before springing wide and disgorging a terrible light, a light which was
every colour and none. Bells sounded, and cymbals, and
other, less recognisable instruments. Inhuman laughter
flooded the corridor, followed by a skirling tune, at once
jaunty and horrid.

Coloured smoke spewed from the wound in reality, and

as it filled the corridor it shattered into solidity. Shapes danced into view, too many to count. Honeyed voices rose in song as beautiful faces fixed revolting eyes on Bile and the others. Hooves clicked against the wraithbone deck, and claws snapped eagerly as the daemonettes swayed forward, stopping at the line of blood Saqqara had dripped across the corridor. Some crouched atop serpentine beasts with flickering probosces, and Bile could hear the creaking of unseen wheels and the hiss-crack of whips. There was an army there, in the mist, though he couldn't see it.

A shape, larger than the rest, rose above the riot, chains hung with silver bells stretched between its coiling horns. Goatish jaws snapped together, and a deep, sensuous voice said, 'Faaabius.' The Keeper of Secrets stepped forward, diaphanous robes swirling about its twisted shape. 'Kanathara sends his greetings, alchemist. His rage is exquisite. Such a trick you pulled, inviting him in and then... well. Fulgrim warned him, as did we. But he did not listen. Such are the whims of youth.' An obsidian blade, longer than a man, was extended. 'Why have you opened our door?'

'Can't you tell? Are you not the shard of a god?' Bile said, meeting the creature's gaze steadily. He felt nothing, though he knew the others were not so lucky. The Emperor's Children abased themselves before the creature, and Savona knelt, leaning on the handle of her maul like a knight in prayer. Saqqara muttered prayers, and Arrian hung back, hands on his blades. Igori and the others had been dosed with his null-extract, but even they were nervous. He spread his arms. 'Can't you smell it?'

The daemon lifted its muzzle. Its nostrils flared, and a long tongue slid from between its fangs and rasped across its muzzle. 'Ahhh. Is this a... a *sacrifice*, alchemist?' Black eyes fixed on him. 'Do you at last admit our superiority, mortal? I am almost disappointed.'

'I admit nothing,' Bile said. 'Ravage, plunder, pillage to your liking, Neverborn. Rise wild and fill these domes with blood and bodies.'

'And why should we obey you?' the daemon said, leaning close. The blood on the floor abruptly flared and burned to ash. Saqqara grunted, as if he'd been struck. 'You are no friend to us, alchemist. Why should I not take my blade to your wormy soul, in recompense for the hurt you inflicted on laughing Kanathara, above the world-wound of Sublime?'

'Because there are better delights to be had here,' Bile said. His hand dropped to his needler. 'But have at it, if you would.'

The daemon stepped back, showing its fangs in a smile. 'Prince Fulgrim was right about you, Fabius. It is no wonder he worries about you so.'

'Fulgrim's worries are his own,' Bile said. 'My only concern is for my own path.'

'Shall I tell him you said that?' the daemon said, looking down at him. 'Such disdain from one of his own will wound him most delightfully.'

'I shall make a gift of my disdain, if you like.'

'Done!' The daemon turned away and slapped its swords together. 'We have an accord, alchemist.' The daemon-ettes let out a communal howl and surged away at their master's gesture, down the transit tunnels. The Keeper of Secrets stalked after them, shaking the corridor with its tread. A wave of daemonic flesh erupted from the wound and spiralled after, filling the tunnel.

Bile heard unseen bulkheads splinter like wood, and screams. The eldar reinforcements, too late to do anything but die. Savona led her warriors forward with a shriek of joy, and the Emperor's Children thudded after the horde of daemons, shouting hymns to the Lord of Excess. Saqqara and Arrian waited for him.

He turned and caught Igori by the shoulder as she and the Gland-hounds made to follow. She winced at the weight of his grip. 'Benefactor,' she said, eyes fever-bright with eagerness. 'We have collected many samples for the databanks already. Armour and weapons as well. We can learn much from them.'

'Ah, my Igori... when I built you, I broke the mould. You will wait here.' She frowned. He went on before she could protest. 'You will wait here for us until you are otherwise signalled. Hold this bay with all the ferocity at your disposal. Should that signal come, you will fall back to the *Butcher-Bird* and retreat to the *Vesalius* at all due speed. Do you understand?'

'What about you, Benefactor?'

'We shall find other means of egress, my child. Likely loud ones, punctuated by seas of blood. In that event, you shall take your pack and flee. We shall join you soon enough.'

'And if you don't?' she said, softly.

He hesitated, then leaned close. 'Then you know what you must do. Do not return to Urum. Retreat to one of the secondary facilities, and enact the appropriate protocols.' She flinched as he said it, and he smiled sadly. 'The work must continue, my child. Whatever else, we must always go forward.

'The future comes, whether we are ready or not.'

CHAPTER NINETEEN

The Open Blade

Tzimiskes Flay watched the maniple of Castellax battle-automata stomp into battle with something approaching pride. They unleashed a punishing barrage of firepower as they advanced on the orange-clad eldar taking shelter behind one of the crumbled walls marking the boundaries of the great plaza. He could hear the organic minds sealed inside the robots screaming in joy and hate as they smashed aside delicate statuary and wraithbone archways in their assault, and he felt a moment of satisfaction that he could give them such joy.

Shuriken bolts seared the air about him, as he turned back to the components scattered across the ground before him. The teleport homer had been shattered upon arrival. A lucky shot, or a very precise one; the end result was the same.

'Can you fix it?' Oleander asked. He crouched behind a toppled statue, hastily reloading his bolt pistol. Blast marks scorched his armour. He sounded impatient.

Oleander was always impatient. Tzimiskes suspected a chemical imbalance, due to impurities in the gene-seed of the Third. He made a note to take a blood sample from Oleander when the current situation had achieved stability. He considered replying, but decided it was unnecessary. He simply nodded and sank to one knee before the device.

He began to reassemble the homer with practised precision, rerouting torn circuits and stripping out burnt relays from the mostly intact brain matter. The sheer number of redundancies built into these early models made battlefield repairs easy enough to accomplish, if a trifle tedious. It was easier than setting a bone, or sealing a torn artery. Sparks pattered across his mask and cerebral fluid splashed his hands.

As he worked, the sensors of his servo-skulls, filtered through his armour's internal auspex, kept him appraised moment by moment of the flow of battle. He'd unleashed the drones to go wherever the wind took them. They could defend themselves well enough, thanks to his modifications. He couldn't resist the opportunity to develop a working map of the craftworld – such a chance came along only once in a lifetime.

The air was thick with smoke and heat. Their boarding pod had crashed through one of the central domes, obliterating transit tubes, towers and walkways in its descent into the shimmering sea of crystalline waters that occupied the heart of the plaza. The impact had shattered a ring of nearby structures, and the trees surrounding the waters were on fire now. The whole biome quaked as if in agony.

The Emperor's Children were taking up defensive positions throughout the plaza, occupying the newly made ruins that dotted the shoreline of the crystal sea, mostly around the three great Dreadclaws that had followed the boarding torpedoes down. Stragglers from other nearby breach points fought on walkways above and in the transit tubes below, moving steadily towards the plaza, seeking to consolidate their forces. The vox crackled with laughter, off-key singing and requests for aid from warriors throughout the craftworld. To the east rose a screeching dissonance, as Blessed Lidonius and the Noise Marines engaged azure-armoured Aspect Warriors in a duel among the burning wraithbone trees that lined the avenues there.

The Radiant's strategy was so far progressing as planned, but the eldar were reacting more quickly than they'd estimated. Towards the prow of the world-ship, the bikers and Havocs of the 12th duelled with eldar jetbikes amongst the tall towers and glittering avenues. Farther aft, eldar guardians retreated before the onslaught of a dozen monstrous Dreadnoughts. The roars of the ancient machines echoed through the tunnels and corridors connecting the domes.

Far above, through the shattered domes now sealed by wraithbone extrusions, Tzimiskes could just make out the shapes of the fleet as it duelled the eldar vessels. Every so often, a flare of light would envelop the dome and blaze down like a sun, as a ship ceased to exist. The craftworld shuddered from multiple impacts, as boarding pods and Dreadclaws continued to rain down across its titanic surface. Once he saw an assault ram skid by, pinwheeling through the air, its thrusters damaged and its hull wreathed in flame. The boarding action was a scattered, haphazard affair, but that worked in their favour – the eldar would not be able to keep the invaders contained to a single area.

One of his servo-skulls sent a signal-pulse. An image appeared on his retinal lens display – heavy weapons platforms were gliding into position around the outer avenues of the plaza. The eldar were coming in force. Tzimiskes gestured sharply. Oleander nodded and said, 'Gulos – the eldar appear to be mustering a cannonade. Go and disabuse them of any notions they might have as to their fire superiority, would you?'

'Are you giving me orders, Apothecary?' Gulos said, as he ejected the clip of his boltgun. As soon as a new one had clicked into place he began to fire. The Joybound stood behind a nearby fallen column. 'A bad habit, that. A good way to find your black guts in a tangle around your ankles.'

'Merely a suggestion, brother. My apologies, I assumed that you wished to survive this affray,' Oleander said. Gulos glared at him for a moment, before barking orders at his squad. 'Olios, Culkates... come with me. We've red work to do.' He tossed his boltgun to Oleander. 'I assume you remember how to use one of these, yes?'

'Oh yes,' Oleander said, holstering his pistol. 'You do me great honour, brother.'

'Try not to shoot me in the back.'

'Rest assured that if I ever shoot you, it will be in the front.' Oleander took aim at an eldar as it climbed towards a higher position, and plucked the life from it with a single shot. Gulos laughed and loped away, loosening his swords in their sheaths as he went. Tzimiskes saw Oleander turn, tracking the Joybound with the barrel of his weapon. He gave his brother a warning tap on the shoulder.

'You're right, brother. There'll be plenty of time for that

later, I suppose.' Oleander turned his attentions back to the eldar. Satisfied, Tzimiskes turned back to his task. He activated a flashing holo-link, and was treated to the sight of one of his Castellax crushing an eldar beneath its iron tread. The battle-automaton pivoted, bolt cannons roaring as it stitched craters across the swooping wraithbone architecture. Tzimiskes sent a command pulsing along the link, and the maniple began to consolidate their firepower on a nearby knot of guardians trying to guide a weapons platform into range.

Something green flashed across his line of vision, and the war machine spun as an emerald-clad Aspect Warrior attacked it with a whirring chainsword. The eldar skidded away, deftly avoiding the barrage of shots that pursued it along the boulevard.

Tzimiskes realised a moment later that the blow had not been meant to damage the machine, so much as draw its attentions. The Castellax's sensors redlined as a wash of incandescent heat enveloped it. Red-armoured Aspect Warriors crept forward, fusion guns dripping liquid heat. The damaged battle-automaton stumbled forward, screeching imprecations as the organic mind within went mad from the pain. Tzimiskes left it to its fate, and sent a single command to the others, ordering them to fall back towards the shore.

The ground shook as the maniple fell back, filling the air with barrage after barrage. 'Any time now, brother. Your automata are impressive, but they have a world's worth of their own to call on,' Oleander said, his voice tense. Tzimiskes glanced at Oleander, scanning him for injuries. Seeing none, he returned to his work. 'Your words fill me with confidence, Tzimiskes,' Oleander added sourly.

Tzimiskes smiled bitterly beneath his helmet, with what was left of his face. His brothers did not remember what it meant to be a part of a unit, to be a cog in a smoothly functioning mechanism. There was a rot at the heart of things, a cancer spreading ever outwards and the lack of unity was one of its symptoms. Even the Chief Apothecary suffered from it.

'Where is Merix? He should've joined us by now,' Oleander complained. 'We're being overrun, one chunk of stone at a time.' Shuriken blasts sent him ducking, and he thrust the boltgun over his head, firing blindly. 'I'm really starting to hate eldar.'

A Chaos Space Marine staggered, craters appearing across his vibrantly hued armour. As he fell, Tzimiskes noted his position for later progenoid recovery. He had few visible mutations, which implied potentially stable glands. Perfect for harvesting. Whatever else happened here, they were reaping quite a return of viable materials.

His armour registered a flurry of hits. None of them penetrated. He'd reinforced his armour and augmented its defences. Instinctively, he checked his own biological functions. Readouts scrolled across his internal display, charting spikes in adrenalin and blood pressure. He activated dampers, smoothing the chemical imbalance. No need to get excited, not yet. Patience was his art, and his practice.

Tzimiskes built ramparts out of considered conclusions and practical decisions. Moment upon moment, he crafted unassailable fortresses of possibility with mathematical precision. Minds and actions were as programmable as any engine, even in the midst of battle. Perhaps especially then. Thus, a response was called for.

He lifted his boltgun from the ground and turned, allowing his internal targeting array to guide his hand. He fired three times. Judging that to be satisfactory, he set the weapon down and turned back to his labours. It had been a long time since he'd had to rig a teleport homer in a battlefield situation. He was enjoying it immensely.

The teleport homer began to hum and he stepped back. 'Is it working?' Oleander said. Tzimiskes slapped him on the chest in an amiable fashion. 'My apologies, brother. I should know better than to question your skill with the inanimate.' An explosion caused them to turn. Tzimiskes caught sight of Gulos as he beheaded an eldar and kicked the twitching body aside. The Joybound was forced to seek cover, however, as a shuriken cannon opened up, chewing both the wraithbone and an unlucky renegade to pieces.

'Hostiles incoming,' Oleander said. Tzimiskes turned, his targeting array homing in on the orange-clad shapes darting along the eastern shore. They were accompanied by more shapes in blue and green. There was a pattern to their manoeuvres, a sense of coordination that had heretofore been mostly lacking. Someone was organising the defence.

An explosion ripped through the far wall of the dome, momentarily obscuring the eldar. Smoke billowed outwards, choking the twisting avenues. As it cleared, a number of familiar auspex-signatures became visible. 'Merix has arrived,' Oleander said, dropping his fist onto Tzimiskes' shoulder-plate.

Merix advanced at the head of a ten-strong squad of renegade Space Marines, their bolters hammering. Their armour was scorched and many were wounded. They'd had a hard fight of it, wherever they'd been. Merix shouted an order and they went to ground quickly, giving way before the monstrosities that stomped in their wake.

A Contemptor Dreadnought stalked forward through the smoke, clawed hands flexing. 'Weep, aliens. Weep for I am upon you, and death is sure to follow,' the vox-grille pulsed. One piston-like arm swept out and the inbuilt storm bolter roared a deadly hymn. Blue-clad eldar danced a fatal jig and were swept aside as it strode forward. 'Weep for Diomat, xenos. Scream for me, and die as I cannot. Die and be damned.' A massive fist stretched out, and wide fingers closed about a white helm, crushing it and the alien skull beneath.

The other Dreadnoughts followed Ancient Diomat's example, and spread throughout the plaza, weapons blazing. All of them bore signs of damage and heavy fighting. Some were missing limbs. One wept smoke from its cratered chassis. But they advanced regardless, rabid and unstoppable. The eldar began to fall back, their advance broken. The Dreadnoughts scattered, fighting and hunting as individuals rather than a unit. It wouldn't take long for the eldar to regroup. Tzimiskes sent a command to his remaining Castellax and the maniple lurched towards the eastern shore, guns thudding.

Behind him, the teleport homer gave a hum. He turned, as motes of light began to dance across the plaza. The air grew thick with the smell of burnt meat and charred stone. A proximity alarm pinged in his ear, and he twisted about. A power sword sliced down, nearly taking his arm off. He rolled aside, catching sight of an orange and black crest as he did so. Blue-armoured Aspect Warriors vaulted over the rubble in pursuit. Oleander cursed and turned his boltgun on one, before a stray blast snatched it from his grip. He staggered back as shots caromed off his armour. Tzimiskes scrabbled for his axe as the swordsman closed in on him.

The light swelled until it filled the dome, and the air screamed as if in torment. Indistinct shapes wavered and solidified, revealing gaudy ceramite. The Aspect Warrior pursuing Tzimiskes hesitated, caught off guard by the sudden squall of discordant noise that accompanied the light. A bolt-shell took the alien in the chest, and it toppled backwards.

Tzimiskes turned, as a tall, elegant figure stalked through the fading light of the teleportation flare, accompanied by a monstrous army. Emperor's Children rushed past, howling as they fell on the nearest eldar with savage joy. The Radiant King in His Joyful Repose had arrived.

He strode past Tzimiskes, unsheathing his sword as he went. His monstrous guards gambolled in his wake, grunting and shrieking as they hewed at the eldar with their shrieking chain-glaives. 'I am come, finally. The final curtain and the last song,' the Radiant roared, as he swept his sword out, cleaving an eldar warrior in two. 'And I will burn this half-world and clothe myself in its ashes before I am done.' He raised his blade, his face split in a mad smile. 'Children of the Emperor! Death to his foes!'

The daemontide had proved to have a purgative effect on the path ahead. A trail of mangled bodies and shattered bulkheads marked their route down through the docking tower. The cacodemonical horde spilled through transit tubes and across walkways, killing everything that dared attempt to stop them. The eldar fell back further, retreating, and the daemons pursued. The air pulsated with the sound of their passing and where they trod, wraithbone twisted and bulged with monstrous growths that spewed choking mists. Sighing grasses sprouted along flat surfaces and tortured trees of flesh and bone, crafted from the living flesh of unlucky eldar, pierced walls and steps.

Interesting as it was, none of it would last very long. The ritual Saqqara had enacted would only bind the daemons to the material world for a few hours at best. Just long enough to divert the attentions of the craftworld's defenders. When they reached the lower walkways leading into the great domes of the aft-section, Savona and her warriors formed the vanguard and spread out, advancing purposefully through the smouldering carnage, weapons ready. Several of them sang softly, harmonising instinctively with the anguished moans that pierced the air.

Stragglers from the daemontide danced and swayed everywhere, indulging their cruel lusts upon the dying. The daemonettes called out to Bile and the others, offering them glistening sweetmeats and handfuls of marrow in return for a kiss or a dance.

Bile ignored them, more concerned for his own well-being. He'd caught sight of strange shadows several times since their descent into the craftworld proper. They were being followed. Saqqara had sensed it as well. 'Something close on our heels,' the Word Bearer sub-vocalised. A number of new wispy daemon shapes filled his flasks, chained tight by his will and held in check for later use. These Neverborn were weak things, scavenger-spirits following the hunting packs of the Prince of Pleasure, and malleable.

'Ignore it,' Bile said.

'Should we not stop? Confront them?' He gestured with

the flask in his hand, and a daemon lunged forward, malformed jaws snapping in frustration as it reached the
end of its tether. Its shape roiled like a cloud, constantly
extruding a plethora of talons, tendrils and spines.

'And why would we do that? Especially when we are so
close to our goal?'

'Your goal, you mean,' Saqqara said, drawing the daemon back into its flask with a sharp, ritual gesture. The
flask glowed in his hand, the sigils etched into it pulsing
with an unnatural heat.

'My goal is our goal,' Bile said. He stepped aside as
a chunk of wraithbone came loose from overhead and
fell, snapping off a section of the walkway. The debris
tumbled into the sea of towers beneath. He paused, studying the tangled skein of structures which spread out below.
Immense walkways twisted about the trunks of great towers, or else turned upon themselves like the roots of trees.
Domed enclaves nestled in the curves of these turnings,
or else capped the towers. These enclaves contained cities, forests and other, less identifiable biomes.

Many of them were now cracked open and aflame. The
orange curve of the great central dome overhead was punctured by ragged wounds of black, through which the vast
shapes of the fleet could be glimpsed. Graceful fighters
screamed through the air, duelling amongst the towers
with those few Legion gunships which had managed to
make it inside. Thanks to the damage the craftworld had
already sustained, the artificial gravity fluctuated, making
these clashes even more deadly, as the craft were tossed
about as if caught in a tempest.

He could hear the distant bellow of heavy weapons
and the thud of artillery. Wherever a boarding pod had

successfully pierced the outer skin of the craftworld, the warriors of the 12th now fought. Most of these disparate bands were isolated, and would be easy pickings, once the eldar regrouped. But until then, they merrily slaughtered any who crossed their path, warrior or civilian alike, fighting for no other purpose than the simple joy of it. In the unseen streets below, untold hundreds were dying or else wishing for death, and their screams filled the air, rising up to mingle in a vast roar of suffering.

'The spider is curtain-bearer in the Palace of Chasrus and the night-bird sounds relief in the castle of Afresyab,' said Bile.

'What?' Saqqara said.

'A quote. From Terra, and ages long past. When the empire of the Parsi was obliterated by the desert-dwellers with whom they'd warred.' He turned away from the sight. 'It seemed appropriate.' Lugganath was dying a death of a thousand cuts. Even if it survived, it would never forget the agonies inflicted on it. For a creature like the Radiant, that was probably enough. So long as he got what he wanted, the conditions of victory were fluid.

It was all such a waste. He'd forgotten what slaughter sounded like. Any joy he might once have felt at the opportunities such carnage could provide had long since been burned out of him. Now he wanted only to acquire what he'd come for, and leave as swiftly as possible.

They passed into a long gallery, away from the confusion. Tiered and dim, it extended for some distance along the upper spine of the craftworld, branching out into silent nooks and crannies. Bubbles of wraithbone, concealing sentry posts or meditation cells, dotted its length, as well as thin boulevards, stretching towards nearby domes.

All was ruin. The daemontide had splintered and spread through the crooked gallery and along the boulevards, hunting whatever prey drew their fancy. Screams echoed from gaping portals of contemplation chambers, as the Neverborn ravened among those unlucky enough to seek shelter there. Alarm klaxons shrilled from unseen corners, and the sound of weapons fire came from a nearby archway. The Emperor's Children moved carelessly, without caution or concern. They stopped to pilfer from corpses, or sample the spilled wares from a drinking den recessed into the voidward wall of the gallery.

'They're not dying easily,' Arrian said, as he stabbed a body with the probe of his narthecium, collecting a sample.

'They are vermin,' Savona said, jostling a corpse with her maul. It dangled from a crack in the roof in the gallery, strung up by its own ligaments. Something had carved crude pictograms in its flesh. 'Fit only to be entertainment.'

'Silence,' Bile said. 'We are here.'

A pair of great curved doors occupied the far end of the gallery, marking the entrance to the dome around which it had been constructed. The doors had been decorated with an intricate design of gold and silver, dotted with teardrops of amber in the shape of an eldar rune. The Dome of Crystal Seers.

Ordering the combat-servitors to guard their rear, Bile approached the doors. He smashed them asunder with a blow from Torment. As he stepped through the splintered portal, he saw a dome of ochre vegetation, caught in a permanent sunset by the reflected light of the scintillating forest. 'At last,' he said.

There were no sentries – or if there had been, they were

otherwise occupied. 'I'm surprised the Neverborn didn't pour into this place,' Arrian said, as he stepped through the shattered doors, followed by Savona and her warriors.

'They couldn't, not until someone opened the doors for them,' Saqqara said. 'This place is warded against their kind. But they'll smell it now.' He looked at Bile. 'We must hurry. I will not be able to control them.'

'I am well aware of your limitations, Saqqara,' Bile said. The vitrified bodies of alien seers rose from the soil, stretching up and out into mighty trees of crystal whose canopy framed the stars above. All form and feature was subsumed in gleaming foliage, but some trace of what they had once been yet remained. Just enough to whisper their origins. Spirit stones were set into the curving walls of the dome, and each one shimmered with a sharp light.

Bile felt as if a thousand eyes were upon him. How many souls congregated here, trapped at the moment of death, preserved for eternity? The air was heavy with promise. Entire generations of xenos witches were rooted to this place, hiding within them lore older than mankind, older even than Terra itself.

He closed his eyes and tilted his head, inhaling the scent of secrets. The eldar hoarded knowledge the way vermin hoarded food, content to leave the wisdom of ages mouldering in the dark. There was much to be learned from this place. He would extract every mote of information from it, and put it to better use than its curators had ever dreamed of.

The glittering grasses crunched beneath his feet. He raised Torment and felt it quiver with excitement. He stepped towards a tree, ready to smash it to flinders and gather the pieces. The trees would provide him with the answers to his questions, he was certain of it. Before he could do so, however, a sudden wash of white-hot flame drove him back. Curses and cries of alarm rose from the others as more flames rose up on all sides, herding them back. A peal of laughter followed.

'Two birds, one stone,' a voice sang.

Bile lifted his sceptre. The voice was familiar. He'd heard it before, a whisper over the vox. 'What was that? Speak up,' he said, loudly. The flames died away, leaving no sign of their passing. An illusion of some sort.

'Two birds. One stone. That is a mon-keigh saying, is it not? And apt. Where is Kasperos Telmar, King of Feathers?' The voice sidled from every direction at once. 'Do you know his fate? Do you care?'

'His fate is hardly my concern,' Bile said, motioning Savona to silence before she could interrupt. 'It's not yours either, if you're here.' Glowing swirls of blinding mist crept from beneath the trees, stretching out towards them.

'Two performances in one night. One intimate, one distant. One quiet, one loud.'

'Two birds, one stone,' Bile said. More laughter. The ache in his side flared up. Syringes depressed and pumps hissed, dulling the pain. He could not afford the distraction, not now. This was not like the other times. No teasing rush, over before it had begun. No, this was the final act of the performance.

'Even so, even so,' it said, applauding.

'Name yourself, creature. I would see the face of my tormentor,' Bile said.

'No face, no face, but a name, certainly... Sylandri Veilwalker, at your service, Chief Apothecary,' the voice said. 'Or is it lieutenant commander?'

'Veilwalker – an assumed name, if there ever was one,' Bile said. His targeting sensors couldn't get a bead on the shadowy shape as it slipped from branch to shimmering branch. 'And I prefer Primogenitor.'

'Say, rather, a role. The role of a lifetime. I am she and she is me, and you are a mon-keigh.' Laughter echoed through the grove, not from one set of lips now but many. Too many. 'Primogenitor indeed. You are a naughty mon-keigh, Clonelord. Always reaching for what you cannot have and do not deserve. Like a greedy child, groping for a sweet.'

'If I am a child, then educate me. Or placate me, I do not care which. Give me what I want and I will go away,' he said, still scanning the crystalline canopy. He gestured, and Arrian sidled away, blades drawn. Savona and her warriors began to spread out. The Joybound looked wary, but eager as well. Practically salivating at the sight of the millions of spirit stones studding the walls of the great garden. Saqqara stayed where he was, murmuring a prayer to calm the daemons in his flasks. They screeched in desire, swiping at the glass and causing the sigils to flicker weirdly. They smelled the souls trapped here, and hungered for them.

'Educate, placate, insinuate, retaliate... what do you think we are doing here, Manflayer? Why do you think we let you get this far, Pater Mutatis?'

'In all honesty, I did not think of it, or you, at all,' Bile said. 'I have weightier concerns than the schemes of aliens.'

'A lie, a lie,' it sang. He saw it then, crouched on a branch above him, clothed in rags of jade and black and gold, with a mirrored mask beneath a hood of yellow and violet diamonds. It clutched a long staff in its thin hands.

He whipped the Xyclos needler around and fired. The Harlequin was gone in a flash, even as the needles thudded into the crystal tree. A soft groan filled the air. He turned. 'Lie, truth, none of it matters now. Stand against me, and you'll know the true meaning of pain.' He was angry now, though he didn't know why. Things were clicking into place. *Why do you think we let you get this far?*

Bile froze. 'Why?' he murmured. Had this been a trap, then? If so, when had it been set? Sublime – or earlier?

'Why ask why?' the Harlequin laughed, as it sprang from branch to branch, always just out of sight. 'Are you afraid of the dark, Chief Apothecary Fabius? What do you see, deep in the shadows?'

'Nothing that need concern you, witch,' Bile said, not bothering to track the creature. 'If you are not here to hinder us, then depart. If you are...'

'We are, and the dance has already begun.'

The lithe shape dropped down before him, staff spinning in its hands. He heard the roar of boltguns and Arrian shouting. Chromatic phantoms burst from the trees and raced to battle, tumbling, leaping, sliding like a flood of shimmering water.

He blocked the staff as it swept out towards his skull, but the eldar twisted away from the needler's bite. His targeting array couldn't keep up, and his own stim-enhanced reflexes were barely adequate to meet and counter its blows. The long shadows of the crystalline trees stretched and surrounded him, as if they were boles of silk, scattered by the movements of the Shadowseer. And in those shadows, he caught glimpses of movement. They hemmed him in on all sides, isolating him. The sounds of battle grew dim, and soon the only sound he heard was the creaking of crystal branches and the whispering of long-dead alien seers.

Bile turned, searching for his foe. Everywhere he looked, a different face was reflected in the bark of a crystalline tree. All of them his, but different. Some younger, some older. Some as perfect as he recalled once being, others as hideously malformed as he feared he might one day become. All standing in the crystal forest, all caught in the same moment. And they spoke as one. His voice, doubled and redoubled, folded over itself in a droning hum that pierced his brain. Bile clutched at his head, lost in the roar.

Moments spattered his consciousness like blood. Successes and failures, births and deaths, a quaquaversal dissonance of possibilities. He saw himself hurled from a high place by an angel in red, and felt his neck break in Melusine's delicate grip, as he hung in chains. He heard his own screams as the jaws of his abused creations seized upon him in the butcher-yards of Terra, and smelled the stink of his own, final corruption as the disease that permeated his cells caught up to him at last, reducing him to delirious obsolescence.

More images came and faster. He saw himself in purple and gold once more, leading the remnants of the Third in battle against their foes as Lieutenant Commander Fabius. The Eye wept fire as the Emperor's Children marched to war as a united Legion – proud. Perfect. Victorious. But he also saw himself die on Abaddon's claw, his hearts pulped, his cloned bodies destroyed, his apothecarion in ruins. He felt Fulgrim's coils tighten about his splintering bones, and heard his gene-father's whispered recriminations. He endured the gibbering of daemon voices as they tore his soul to flinders, and the screams of the gods themselves as they burned on a pyre of his making. A hundred thousand possible paths, a hundred thousand futures.

But all of them had one thing in common. If he took up the regalia of command, his survival was assured. But if he held fast to his course, he would perish. By the hands of his foes, that of his creations, or even his own – death was a certainty.

Through it all, the voices of his other selves continued to speak, urging him to become them, to avoid their fate at all costs, to kill himself, to flee, to take command. A thousand conflicting desires pulled him in a thousand directions – who was he? Which Fabius Bile stood here now? He sank to one knee. He could taste blood on his lips. The chirurgeon was hissing, its limbs twitching in agitation as his vitals went into freefall. His hearts shuddered in their cage of bone. Pain filled him, swelling up through him incandescent and purifying. Only pain was real. Pain was the thread that would show him the way through the labyrinth.

With a scream, Bile arched back, swinging Torment up. He slammed the sceptre down hard enough to crack the wraithbone floor of the grove, revealing the glowing infinity circuits beneath. A red glow blazed from the eye sockets of the sceptre, banishing the shadows and scattered fragments. All about him, the trees were screaming, and he was glad.

He wrenched the weapon free and stood, trembling. Bits of infinity circuit smouldered on its head, and he absently collected it. 'Did you think to overwhelm me with possibilities,' he said. 'With might-haves and could-bes?'

'A broken purpose for a broken soul,' a mournful voice said. 'You cling to your rags, afraid to meet your fate.' The

Harlequin circled him slowly, spinning its staff. 'We let you come this far, so that you might see that the throne before you is the only path...'

'His path is not yours to determine.'

The Shadowseer froze as the voice echoed through the grove. The screams of the trees rose in pitch as something monstrous shattered one with a blow from an obsidian blade. The Keeper of Secrets stalked out of the gloom, shards of crystal crunching beneath its hooves. Bile heard the laughter of daemons, and the shrieks of dying eldar, and realised why the trees were screaming.

The greater daemon peered down at him, its muzzle twisted up in amusement. 'The skeins of fate have been torn and cast askew about you, Fabius.'

'What are you talking about?' Bile demanded. Questions rose up within him. The Harlequins wanted him to take command of the Third, but why? And why would they risk their own people, just to convince him to do so? 'My fate is my own – it has ever been so!'

'Has it?' The daemon gave a braying laugh. 'But not even the Lord of Dark Delights knows what will come of your efforts here... and he dearly wishes to see what you will do next.' It turned towards the Harlequin and licked its lips. 'A delicacy, dark and unrivalled. I shall swallow your soul, little creature.'

The Harlequin stumbled as the daemon turned the full force of its attentions upon it. But it did not surrender. Instead, it leapt backwards, seeking safety in the shadows. The Keeper of Secrets snorted in derision. 'A hunt, then. How tedious.' It glanced at Bile. 'You may continue your work, Fabius.' Without waiting for a reply it loped into the trees, obsidian blades lopping off branches and gouging trunks as it passed.

Bile, head still ringing with the crash of possibilities, sank to one knee and began to gather what he'd come for.

Whatever else happened, he did not intend to leave empty-handed.

CHAPTER TWENTY

The Hidden Blade

The Radiant King in His Joyful Repose howled as he plucked the spirit stone from the eldar's armour and popped it into his mouth. Perfect teeth crushed the stone, even as shards of it gashed his gums. He swallowed blood and stone and shrieking soul. It was the twentieth such he'd devoured, and his stomach roiled with the remnants of stolen life. He felt bloated, but strong. The song of Slaanesh pounded in his skull, echoing down through the marrow of him, into the very roots, where the last flickers of Kasperos Telmar crouched, trembling. The man he had been screamed and shook the bars of his cage, as his soul burned black. The Radiant ignored him, as he had done since Isstvan.

The Prince of Pleasure was pleased. The Radiant laughed as shuriken blasts seared the fur from his armour and killed one of his guards. The obese mutant died giggling, as it clutched at its flensed intestines. The eldar were retreating, falling back from the plaza. 'Run, run little birds. There is nowhere the snake cannot find you,' the Radiant crooned as he stalked in pursuit. 'I will pull down your trees and dance upon the roots.'

This was the moment he had been born for. Born to be reborn. Reshaped and made whole at last. He snatched up another flimsy body and gouged out the spirit stone with the tip of his sword. He could feel fear flickering in its swirling depths. The panic of the trapped soul, desperately seeking some way of escape from the prison it had thought inviolate.

'Stupid little birds with your stupid little nests. Now I shall eat your eggs, one after the next.' He leaned his head back, and distended his too-perfect jaw, ripping skin and muscle from bone. He dropped the spirit stone into his gullet and sucked it clean of all that it contained. Smoke boiled from between his jaws, and every hair stood on end. He could feel the presence of the Neverborn, as they ravaged the craftworld elsewhere. More daemons pressed against the skin of reality, waiting for him to invite them. He was the key and the gate, all in one.

Pain shot through him. A good pain, a telling pain. He staggered, the world swimming about him as his senses went haywire. Kobeleski shivered in his grip. The sword knew what was coming, and its murderous spirit quailed in horror. 'Your namesake would've understood, I think,' the Radiant said, thrusting the blade point-first into the ground. 'All those Old Night tyrants. There was a poetry in them that even the False Emperor could not stamp out. They knew what it was to barter soul for soul I have no doubt.' He grimaced as things moved inside him, shifting and blistering as a great heat built in the heart of him. The fires of apotheosis had been kindled, and there was no going back now. No retreat, no fear, no pain, only pleasure.

He wished Fabius were here to witness his rebirth. He wished, oh he wished that the Chief Apothecary were not so stubborn. He wished that his old friend, Lieutenant Commander Fabius, still inhabited the broken shell of Fabius Bile. What was wonder and glory worth, if one had no friends to share it with? Was the story of the Third to be written in cast-aside meat and bone as, one by one, they shed the past and stepped into the future?

His memories spun like leaves in a firestorm. He was once more aboard the *Sunstone*, one step behind Decanus Grythan Thorn. The equerry fell into his arms, choking on his own blood as the heavy cruiser shuddered in its death throes. He again felt the blow of Luastus' fist, and bore the strike-leader's growling insults. Horror warred with respect as he watched the leaders of the abhuman Katara fall on their own blades, ending the war for the Kenuit system. The memories came faster and faster and were consumed in the heat of his change. All that he had been was coming to an end, and some part of him began to weep in sorrow.

That sorrow was not new. It had sent him into the arms of Eidolon and his Conclave, seeking to repair the imperfect thing he had become. In the shadow of Abaddon's spear, they had sworn an oath to rebuild the Legion. To gather its scattered strands and draw them tight, to raise new citadels and prepare for the end of all days. To prepare for the moment that they, as a Legion, would find Fulgrim in his isolation and demand that the Phoenix rise from the ashes, and lead his sons to war once again. If only Fabius could be made to see – to understand...

As the pain expanded, igniting nerve clusters, his regrets crisped and crumbled away, leaving only the joy of possibility. Even as the others had promised. 'Will I have wings, like the Broken Angel?' he said. 'Or great coils, like the Phoenician in all his majesty? Oh, the possibilities. I shall be magnificent.'

A blade caught him in the back, drawing ichor. He spun, and his fist connected with a white helm. The eldar hurtled away, limp and broken. The joints of his armour creaked as the flesh within swelled and thickened. He had grown too large to be contained by such frail artifice. Even the world was too small for him.

Eldar clustered about him like stinging gnats, seeking his death. But he was far beyond death now. And beyond life. He was a song without end, and a consequence given voice. He caught up one of the lithe shapes and laughed in its face, before he bit off its head. He spat the broken skull at one of its fellows, knocking the alien warrior sprawling. His muscles tore as the body slid from his trembling grip.

The Radiant threw back his head and howled for joy.

'Draw your sword, Apothecary,' Gulos said, as he spitted an eldar on his blade with a smooth thrust. 'Fight in Slaanesh's name, so that he might know of your joy. Sing to him, fool.' He and his warriors held a small square, offset from the main drag of the plaza. The eldar had tried to take it by force three times now, and failed every time.

'I'm sure he's well aware of my joy at participating in this celebration, Gulos. No need to bother him with my singing.' Oleander leaned over the fallen pillar he was sheltering behind and took a bead on a retreating eldar.

He fired, and the orange shape tumbled head over heels to lie still with its fellows.

He could hear Ancient Diomat howling for death and the thum-thum-thum of twin lascannons as the maddened Dreadnoughts wrought death in the thick of things somewhere close by. Despite the momentary shock of Diomat's arrival, the eldar were on the offensive. The xenos were trying to keep the Emperor's Children contained to the plaza, and doing a better job of it than he cared to admit. Weapons platforms occupied the avenues leading from the dome, and kept up a steady rain of fire. Everything was either on fire, or about to be. Orange-armoured warriors advanced with grim determination, striking at weak points, of which there were many, in the battle line of the 12th. 'It's been too long,' he said.

'What?' Merix growled. The other Joybound was hunched nearby, behind a cracked pillar, reloading his boltgun. His armour was cracked and cratered, and blood streaked the visor of his helmet. Barely a third of his men had survived the assault on the plaza's outer avenues. Of those, only a pitiful few still had the presence of mind to seek cover. The rest were roaming the battlefield like wild beasts, looking for scalps or else singing the praises of Slaanesh.

'It's been too long since we've fought an actual battle, against equals,' Oleander said. He fired again, cursing as his targeting array lost its lock. The smoke was playing merry hell with his sensors. He hoped the eldar were having the same problem.

'We have no equals,' Merix said. 'Though I must admit they're doing a good impression of it.' A shuriken blast chewed the stone next to his head and he ducked with a curse.

Oleander ejected a spent clip. Ammunition was going to be in short supply, if they survived this. He groped for another. Finding none, he leaned forward with a sigh, resting his head against the fallen pillar. He looked up. 'Any sign of Thalopsis, or Pulchrates?'

'The xenos have them pinned two avenues over,' Gulos said. 'They know these crooked paths better than we. It'll make hunting them most entertaining, when this half-world is ours.' He looked as if he had been doused in blood. Oleander doubted much of it was his.

'What about Nikola?' Merix said, as he twisted about and fired.

Gulos grinned and scraped his blades together. 'He went to pieces. Got caught by one of the xenos weapons platforms. Lidonius is beside himself. Can't you hear him?'

Oleander could. The hulking Joybound's bellows echoed across the plaza as he led another assault. A squeal of sound made him wince and he turned, gazing back down the avenue. The surviving Kakophoni were gathering in the ruins there, drawn together from across the battlefield by some inhuman instinct. The sounds they were making weren't their usual destructive dissonance. He wondered what they were planning. Bile might've been able to explain, but Bile wasn't here.

A crescent-winged xenos fighter swooped overhead, its engines wailing eerily. The flickering craft swept past his position with terrifying speed and grace. The underwing weapon-pods emitted lances of crackling energy which tore the life from anything unlucky enough to be caught in their path. He saw an ornately armoured Space Marine stagger back, clawing at himself. The warrior crumpled to the ground, a lifeless husk. More of the fighters streaked across the plaza, leaving a trail of limp bodies in their wake.

'Those are new,' Gulos said, unimpressed.

'Not for much longer. The Kakophoni have seen them,' Merix said. A blaring screech of sound pierced the din, and one of the fighters came apart. Burning debris pelted their position as the remaining craft abruptly changed direction and began to climb higher. A ragged cheer went up from the warriors stationed in the square. Oleander didn't join in.

He'd lost sight of Tzimiskes in the confusion. The Iron Warrior had vanished not long after the Radiant's arrival, likely going to join his beloved machines. He hoped his brother still lived. He hoped they all still lived. If Bile perished now, all he'd worked towards was for nothing.

A scream rocked the battlefield. Not the mechanical shriek of the Kakophoni or the crackling roar of a Dreadnought, but something more elemental. Oleander turned, his senses prickling. He felt as if he'd swallowed something cold and sharp. The light stung his eyes as he caught sight of the Radiant. He felt like screaming himself, as he watched the transformation begin.

The Radiant stood at the battle's heart, occupying a buckled slope of wraithbone, surrounded by dying enemies. His body expanded, swelling within the foul corona of light. Ceramite buckled and split as the body within became at once both more and less than mortal flesh. He screamed in pleasure as all that was within him boiled away to feed the fire burning within him. To feed the heat of his apotheosis. Flickering, half-seen daemon shapes spun about him, in a frenzied dance of welcome.

His screams echoed through the plaza, and the wraithbone walls of the dome groaned in agony. The Radiant twisted, convulsing. Shapes that might have been wings twisted in the light, gathering mass, becoming darker, more real. Bubbling flesh sloughed away from newborn scale as old, mortal bones cracked and re-formed into something stronger.

'It is done,' Gulos said. 'Look at it – look at him. It is beauty incarnate. He rises, Oleander... and you descend.' The swordsman spun on his heel and thrust his blade at Oleander's side. Oleander reacted on instinct, parrying the blow and stepping back. He glanced at Merix, who turned away. No help there. Not that he'd expected any. Then, neither had he expected Gulos to make his move so soon.

'You never did have any patience, did you?' Oleander said.

'Why wait for the end of the battle?' Gulos said. 'Killing you now means less trouble later. Unlike Merix here, you never knew your place. And the Radiant favours you overmuch for my liking.'

'I was thinking the same thing of you.'

Gulos snarled and lunged. Oleander swatted the blow aside, but did not riposte. Instead, he continued to retreat, drawing his foe in. 'He doesn't intend to leave, you know. He is not a generous captain, our Radiant King. A selfish child, spoiled and petty.'

Gulos lunged again. Again, Oleander parried, but did not reply in kind, saving his strength. 'Fight back, coward,' Gulos said. He slid forward, leaping over bodies, blades stabbing out. Oleander avoided one, but the other carved a notch in his shoulder-plate. The force of the blow nearly knocked him from his feet. He whirled, sword licking out to drive Gulos back. Gulos circled him, panting eagerly.

'Nowhere to run, Apothecary.'

'Just as well. We'll have a good view from here.'

Gulos paused. 'View of what?'

Oleander gestured. 'Of the Radiant's destruction, of course. I've been wondering what that daemonette meant. They will appear in the north, she said,' Oleander said. 'And there it is, and there they are.'. He pointed. Gulos turned and froze, caught by the performance beginning across the plaza.

Oleander could see the purpose of the eldar tactics now – to split the Radiant's forces, and open a path right to him. They'd used their own people as enticement, drawing off the Emperor's Children with the promise of easy meat, and then formed a killing corridor to hold back any who didn't take the bait. Now the fatal thrust slid home, in a riot of colour and crackling sorcery.

The Harlequin troupe danced and leapt, sliding, stamping, spinning forward in streamers of green and yellow coloured light. They stepped gracefully through the air, or scuttled eerily across the rubble. The troupe master led them, gesticulating grandly and cutting obscure symbols in the air with its sword, as if conducting a symphony. A Death Jester swaggered on the fringes, shooting down any who sought to bar the troupe's way. And amid the confusion of colour and noise came the orange-robed witches of Lugganath – a conclave of eldar warlocks, their silent dignity at odds with the clowns who escorted them to their prey.

The troupe master strutted towards the Radiant and bowed deeply to the convulsing figure. 'Greetings and salutations, diminished one. Long has your story been, but it draws now to a close. Your throne rises, precarious, and the seas of fate heave wild,' it said, in a voice as loud as thunder, but as soft as a whisper. 'We have seen this moment from a thousand angles and pruned away all but the most fortuitous. The threads of your story draw tight, binding you to this instant in time. She Who Thirsts calls to you. Will you deny her?' The narrow shape bowed again, even more deeply than before.

The Radiant staggered forward, and made as if to reply. Before he could speak, the troupe surged forward with breathtaking synchronicity, several leapfrogging the still-bent form of their troupe master. The Radiant shrieked and sought to defend himself, with limbs that no longer functioned as he remembered and a body that was rapidly sloughing into dissolution. He was a clumsy chrysalis, soon to be shed. But not soon enough.

The Harlequins spun about him, slashing and hacking. They leapt gracefully over his blows, and chopped chunks from his quivering flesh. The eldar psykers had formed a circle about the duel, and the air turned sour and electric as they swept their blades and spears in graceful arcs, carving strange, coruscating patterns on the thickening air. Occasionally, one would turn, orange robes flaring, and thrust his spear or blade into a Renegade Space Marine who'd got too close. But always they turned back to the circle.

The Radiant's mutating form began to steam. Strange motes of light whirled beneath his elastic flesh and his screams changed. No frustration there now, but something else... fear. A terror as pure as any Oleander had ever had the pleasure of hearing. Slowly at first, and then with quickening pace, the Harlequins slipped away, leaving the Radiant alone in his circle.

The warlocks raised their weapons as one, and simultaneously thrust them into the Radiant. He screamed and, as he did so, his body began to come apart. As he twisted about, pinned by the xenos blades, the substance of him dripped upwards, as if drawn to the stars that shone so coldly far above. Twisted bone splintered and spiralled upwards, caught by a sorcerous wind as daemonic flesh became as smoke. And then, with a crack of displaced air, the Radiant King in His Joyful Repose was gone.

Gulos snarled, whirling on Oleander. Oleander stumbled back. Gulos was faster than him, and he was angry. Oleander tried to drive him back as he had before, but Gulos caught his sword and forced it down. The Joybound stamped on the blade, shattering it, leaving Oleander with only a stump of metal. 'You were never very good with it anyway,' Gulos said.

Oleander retreated, nearly falling over himself to get out of reach of his opponent's swords. Gulos roared in triumph and swung. Oleander ducked and drove the stump of his blade up into Gulos' throat, through the weakened armour. The Joybound's eyes bulged out in shock. Oleander forced the jagged stump deeper into the soft tissue. When he felt it grate against bone, he snapped off the hilt. Gulos dropped his swords and stumbled back, clawing uselessly at the wedge of metal in his throat. 'A little Apothecary trick. It holds open the wound, you see. Your Larraman's organ would ordinarily prevent you from bleeding to death, but the metal fragment keeps scar tissue from forming correctly.'

Gulos sank to one knee. Blood-slick fingers caught at the sliver of steel, trying to pull it out. He glared at Oleander, but the fire in his eyes was dimming. Oleander set the carnifex of his narthecium to the Joybound's temple. 'Here's another trick – rest in pleasure, Gulos.' The piston of adamantine hissed and the fire went out. Gulos toppled over. Oleander shivered in pleasure. 'That was delightful. Better than I could have imagined.'

He tossed aside the hilt of his broken blade and scooped up one of Gulos' swords. The ancient relic-weapon quivered in his grip, and he felt its power thrum through his bones. He took an experimental swing. 'That was Gulos',' Merix said. He hadn't moved a muscle during the fight, proving that he wasn't as much of an idiot as everyone thought.

'I'm sure he doesn't mind,' Oleander said. 'Besides, I only intend to use it until I find something more suitable.' He rested the tip against Merix's throat. 'What about you?'

Merix hesitated. 'I have a blade,' he said.

'That's what I thought.' Oleander scanned the plaza. 'Grab who you can. It's time to fall back. The eldar are regrouping. I can hear their engines whining on whatever passes for wind here. We need to find somewhere more convivial for a last stand.'

'We're cut off from the docking tower. Back along the gallery,' Bile said, fighting to be heard over the whine of engines, the bellicose roar of boltguns and the wailing song of shuriken catapults. He lashed out with his boot, and sent an eldar tumbling from the walkway. The orange figure fell away, vanishing into the smoke rising from below. He turned, sceptre raised. Shuriken blasts pattered against his chest like a stinging rain and he staggered. His coat absorbed most of the impact, and fleshy rags flapped around the blades that jutted from his chest-plate.

Off balance, he fired his needler. An eldar jerked and stumbled, its weapon slipping from its grasp. Bile hissed and brought Torment down on its head, crushing both helmet and the fragile skull within. Another sound rose through the din of battle – barely audible at first, but growing louder with every passing second. It scrawled along every vox-frequency, increasing in strength. As if the sound were a sword being honed to a killing edge.

He knew that sound. The war-song of the Kakophoni, but amplified and layered, one source over the next. He wondered if this was what Ramos had meant, when they'd spoken aboard the *Quarzhazat*. A song, he'd said, to shake the pillars of heaven. Whatever the Noise Marines were planning, he suspected that it would be best to be gone by the time it happened.

Eldar guardians advanced swiftly through the smoke that flooded the gallery, firing as they came. Bile and the others had come under attack almost the moment they'd left the dome. And not just by guardians. Jetbikes swooped past the gallery, spitting shuriken fire at the retreating renegades. Their speed was such that retaliation was impossible, even for his combat-servitors. The hulking mechanoids were so much smouldering wreckage now.

One of Savona's warriors, caught in the open by the jetbikes, staggered and fell, bleeding from a thousand wounds. He laughed as he died, twitching in delight. The surviving Emperor's Children had charged as soon as they'd seen the newcomers. They'd met the advancing eldar in the heart of the gallery, and fallen upon them like wild dogs.

Savona pirouetted at the centre of the fray, her power maul snapping out to splinter bone and crumple armour.

The Emperor's Children were outnumbered almost six to one, but they took little notice. Knives and blades reaped a gruesome toll.

Above, the jetbikes banked at breakneck speed, coming about for another pass; Saqqara, face set, stepped into the open. Bound daemons, newly freed from their flasks, writhed about him like a monstrous halo, ghostly jaws champing at the air. He spread his arms and spat a single word. The temperature dropped and the air took on an oily tang as he released his hold on the Neverborn. Shrieking in joy, the half-formed shapes rocketed towards the approaching jetbikes.

As a jetbike exploded, Bile turned, glancing back at the grove of crystal seers. Despite the confusion, he'd managed to acquire samples from the trees as well as a precious few of the spirit stones, which had studded the walls of the dome. But not enough. He hesitated. Perhaps...

'Chief Apothecary, we must go,' Arrian said.

'Yes, of course,' Bile said. The eldar were retreating back down the gallery, leaving behind a number of their dead. The Emperor's Children did not pursue, content to amuse themselves with the dead. Savona was wrenching a spirit stone free of its housing when Bile said, 'We are leaving, woman.'

She dropped the weakly flickering stone into a pouch on her belt and rose. 'I think not. There are eldar to hunt, and souls to gather, for the Lord of Dark Delights.'

'The eldar are regrouping as we speak. There is safety in numbers.'

'Safety,' she said, derisively. 'There is no safety. You heard that scream as clearly as I did. The Radiant has perished, and all that remains is to indulge our desires in what time remains. The eldar will hound us to our doom.'

The scream had echoed through the craftworld, shaking it from pillar to post, cracking the wraithbone and causing the very air to burst into flames. Bile had been at Iydris, and knew the sound of apotheosis well enough. It was a thing that began in the deepest hollows of the soul and expanded outwards, until the whole body reverberated with an awful anticipation of the event. But what he'd felt hadn't been it.

Instead, it had been something akin to a blade being broken off in his brain. A sharp stab of pain, followed by a sudden bone-deep wrench. In the wake of the scream, the craftworld had fallen momentarily silent, as if all sound and fury had been drawn from the air and cast into the void. Now sound had returned, and the eldar had redoubled their efforts to dislodge the invaders.

Whatever had gone wrong with the Radiant's ascension, Bile suspected the Harlequins were behind it. The Shadowseer had as good as confirmed that this whole affair had been nothing more than a trap for him and perhaps the 12th as well, in its sing-song rantings. 'Even so, we must go forward,' he said. 'You can kill eldar there as easily as here.'

'Where?'

He tapped his ear. 'Follow the noise.' Savona blinked and looked up. The tempest of sound was louder now, surging beneath the clamour of war. It reverberated through the wraithbone, cracking pillars and buckling the delicate statuary.

'What is that?' she asked, turning. The eldar were massing on the curving walkways out beyond the gallery. Each walkway was a wide avenue lined with delicate columns, empty of any real cover save for chunks of debris strewn here and there – a killing ground. The xenos had obviously grown tired of trying to assault the gallery. Now they intended to wait the Emperor's Children out.

'The music of war,' Bile said, inspecting the eldar on the closest walkway. They were strung out in a staggered formation of fire-teams, supported by bipedal war-walkers. A gauntlet of death that only the mad or the foolish would risk running. 'That is the sound of the Kakophoni. I know it well. They will be with the main assault group. If we reach the central breach point, we can begin to organise a fighting withdrawal.'

'Who put you in command?' Savona said. She half raised her maul.

'The Radiant is dead. And I am still Lieutenant Commander of the Emperor's Children.' He checked his needler. Savona tensed. She glanced at her warriors, but they were looking at him. 'I know some of you,' he said, still examining his weapon. 'Oscada – I repaired your heart during the assault on Moon 65-78. Bellephus – I gave you new eyes, when your old ones proved imperfect. You were both among those who followed me as I tried to drag our Legion out of the mire Fulgrim left it to wallow in. Will you follow me again?' He looked up. 'What about you, Deucalius? Or you, Argimedes?'

'She is our commander,' Bellephus said. His armour was inscribed with lines upon lines of obscene Chemosian poetry. 'We swore to follow her.' He sounded uncertain.

'As you swore to follow me,' Bile said. He looked at Savona. 'You have done well, to come this far. But if you wish to go further, you must follow me.'

'Or you will kill me?' Savona said.

'No. But they will.'

Savona glanced around. Her warriors looked away, unwilling to meet her gaze. She looked back at Bile. 'I will follow you... lieutenant commander.'

Bile held her gaze for a moment. Then he turned his attentions back to the eldar. He pointed with Torment, indicating the closest walkway. 'There. We shall have to punch through them. Do not stop. Do not slow.'

'I know how to wage war, old man,' she said, glaring at her warriors. Oscada chuckled as he cleaned his knife with a dripping scalp. Argimedes whistled a jaunty tune as he hung a makeshift necklace of newly severed ears around his neck. The others checked their weapons or readied grenades. Twenty of them still stood. It wasn't much of an army, but it would do.

'I was waging war before you were a gleam in your ancestor's eye, child,' Bile said. He straightened and exhaled slowly. It had been centuries since he'd advanced across open ground. He hadn't liked it then, either. 'They will seek to draw us in and pick us off, once we're in the open. Make every shot count.' Bile lifted Torment. 'Let us see how these sophisticated degenerates handle a display of brute violence. Let us show them what it means to play at war with the Emperor's Children.'

The Emperor's Children opened fire as they stalked towards the line of orange-armoured figures. The eldar began to retreat slowly and purposefully, shooting as they did so. Those stationed on the other walkways began to converge, moving to support their kin. The Renegade Astartes fanned out in loose formation, moving with the drilled precision that had carried them through a thousand wars. Each of them was an army unto himself, and they fought with inhuman synchronicity, falling into the ancient rhythms of battle.

Frag grenades bounced across the wraithbone walkways and exploded, hurling eldar from their feet. Chainswords and axes whirred and bit into alien armour and flesh as the Emperor's Children overran the eldar forward positions, drenching the pale columns that rose alongside the boulevard with the blood of its defenders.

The chirurgeon trilled a warning in Bile's ear as he walked. He was burning through his stimulants and battle-drugs almost as quickly as they entered his veins. The medicae device was working to keep him standing, but it was running out of options. He banished the warning as the targeting overlay in his helmet flickered and spun across the curve of his eye.

His armour's sensors chose targets with mechanical precision. He fired his needler without thought and without hesitation, letting the sensors guide him. Twitching bodies attested to the accuracy of his aim.

His retinal lens display showed him Arrian at the vanguard, with Savona and the swiftest of her warriors, his blades splitting skulls and removing limbs with ease. Saqqara paced to Bile's left, choosing targets with cool disdain. The Word Bearer fired his bolt pistol with a prayer on his lips, calling down curses on the xenos who dared bar their way.

One of Savona's warriors stumbled and fell, his armour pockmarked with bloody craters. Bile stepped over him without slowing. Eldar drew close. Bile raised his sceptre, calling on its darkling energies, preparing himself for the fight to come. But as he drew close, he heard the tell-tale whirr of bolt cannons. A quartet of massive shapes stomped into view behind the eldar, striding through the smoke like avenging gods of war.

'Down,' he said, as he dropped to one knee. At his cry, the others did the same. The weapons of the Castellax battle-automata scythed the walkway clean of xenos. Cries of alarm went up from the xenos warriors. One of the great war machines advanced past Bile, its footsteps shaking the walkway. Its weapons thundered, chewing chunks out of the eldar moving up from the other walkways. It set itself, vox-grille spitting blood-mad gibberish, and raked its surroundings in a slow, deliberate arc, filling the air with death and debris.

Bile looked up, as Tzimiskes extended his hand. The Iron Warrior hauled him to his feet. 'Where did you come from, brother?' Tzimiskes pointed. A servo-skull hovered in the air, its optic sensors fixed on the battle below. Bile laughed. 'Of course.'

Tzimiskes tapped his chest with two fingers. Bile nodded. 'I fully agree, Honourable Tzimiskes. It is past time to evacuate. Lead the way.' He looked at Savona. 'Still eager to indulge yourself?'

She smiled. 'The only thing more pleasurable than a beautiful death is living to die another day.' She set her maul on her shoulder.

'Lead on, Lieutenant Commander Fabius.'

CHAPTER TWENTY-ONE

Shatter-Song

The sound of the Kakophoni accompanied them as they fought their way towards the plaza. The song was deafening. It had hijacked every frequency, drowning out the demands for support and the calls to withdraw that otherwise occupied it. As Bile led his small band through the crooked lanes of the craftworld, their numbers swelled by stragglers from other, failed breach points, hard-pressed by the eldar, or lone warriors, separated during the confusion of battle.

Bile was struck by the familiarity of the moment. He recalled similar retreats, other grand failures. The broken exodus from Skalathrax, the flight from Canticle City... a litany of last stands and defeats, stretching back as far as his memory went. Somewhere along the way, the Emperor's Children had become more familiar with defeat than victory. And yet, they continued to strive towards perfection. Was it idiocy, or simply sheer bloody-minded tenacity that drove them? The will to succeed, whatever the cost.

A will that could be shaped, and reforged, into something great once more. He recalled the vision he'd seen in the grove of himself, of Lieutenant Commander Fabius, clad in purple and leading a renewed Legion to war. Irritated, he flicked the thought aside. A fancy, nothing more. And now was not the right time for fancies.

By the time they reached the outskirts of the plaza, they had been joined by over a hundred warriors, most of them Renegade Astartes. A solid fist of ceramite, capable of punching through almost any enemy battle line. But the eldar seemed content to snipe from a distance. They harried the makeshift column from rooftops and windows, containing them to the central boulevard. The detritus of battle marked their path. Fires raged out of control through the craftworld, and weird shapes danced in the ruins: Neverborn, indulging themselves even as they grew thin and returned to the audient void from which they'd sprung, or human followers of the Lord of Pleasure, seeking entertainment at the expense of self-preservation.

Over it all, the song of the Kakophoni grew louder yet. Chunks of masonry tumbled down from the heights above, and it felt as if the entire craftworld were about to shake itself to pieces. Perhaps that was the plan. If so, Bile hoped they'd refrain until he could enjoy it from a safe distance, preferably aboard the *Vesalius*, heading out of system.

They arrived at the plaza proper in time to witness the fall of Blessed Lidonius. The monstrous Joybound was surrounded by a number of eldar constructs – tall, vaguely eldar-shaped devices, crafted from wraithbone, with blank faceplates that reflected the fires raging about them. Their bulky weapons turned the few unlucky warriors fighting alongside Lidonius inside out, reducing them to scattered motes of cinder and ash. As they approached, Lidonius sent his thunder hammer scything into an eldar war machine. The construct crumpled, but the others turned their weapons on Lidonius, silencing his roars for good.

As one, the constructs turned. Bile grimaced, realising why their advance had been unhindered. A solid wall of constructs stood arrayed before them, backed up by a number of eldar guardians, preventing any entrance to, or escape from, the plaza. But two could play that game. Bile raised his hand. 'Tzimiskes – make us a path, if you please.'

Tzimiskes motioned and his battle-automata charged forward, weapons pounding. The hulking robots tore a hole in the line, hurling the eldar-sized constructs aside, or else using them as makeshift weapons against their compatriots. The constructs turned their full attentions on this immediate threat, as Bile had hoped, leaving their eldar masters to face the advancing Emperor's Children alone. 'Go, leave them to it,' he said, extending his sceptre. 'Keep moving, fools.' He swatted an eldar aside, and brought the rod down on the ground, causing the wraithbone deck to buckle and split. Eldar were knocked from their feet.

'Master – you live.'

Bile turned and saw Oleander hurrying towards him, sword in hand, followed closely by the Joybound called Merix. Bile recognised the Radiant's relic-blade as Oleander lifted it, and wondered where his former student had found it. The Apothecary led a phalanx of Emperor's Children in a steady advance across the rubble. There weren't many of them, but enough to make the eldar think twice about getting close. 'Lidonius?' Oleander asked, as he reached Bile. 'He was leading a sortie...'

'Dead,' Bile said. 'As we'll be, unless we find cover.'

'None to be had, I'm afraid,' Oleander said. 'The whole plaza is coming apart.' As if to emphasise his point, the ground shuddered. A distant tower cracked and tilted on its base, slowly toppling towards the street below. Walkways were shattered as it smashed through them. A wave of dust and smoke swept through the streets.

Eldar shot forward, using the dust as cover. Clad in segmented green armour, they resembled some deadly species of insect, and elongated protrusions on the sides of their helmets spat needles of white fire. Bile blocked the sweep of a chainsword, and caught a thin wrist, twisting a shuriken pistol aside as it fired. The eldar was surprisingly strong, but not strong enough. He snapped its wrist, as the chirurgeon's limbs struck. A bone-drill pierced the eldar's visor, spearing into its skull with a wet sound.

More of the green-armoured eldar darted through the disorganised ranks of the Emperor's Children, isolating warriors and dispatching them with ruthless grace. 'Back to back,' Bile shouted, amplifying his vox-circuits to carry his voice over the increasing commotion of the Kakophoni. 'Don't let them separate you.'

'I think I've heard this song before,' Oleander said, as his blade hissed down against an eldar's sword. 'The words are different, but the melody is the same. How comforting.' He spun aside, allowing Arrian to surge past him, falax blades thrust outwards. The eldar, taken by surprise, was caught in the torso by the twin blades. Arrian's shoulders twitched and the eldar came apart in a welter of gore.

'Comforting is not the word I'd use,' Arrian said. At the far end of the plaza, the Noise Marines were congregating.

'Whatever they're doing, they'd best make it quick.' He glanced at the weapon in Oleander's hand. 'New sword?'

'A keepsake.' Oleander looked at Bile. 'You arrived just in time for the end of the performance, master. How timely of you.'

'Enough wit. What are Ramos and his kin up to?' Bile said.

'I daresay we're about to find out – listen!'

The scream of the Kakophoni rose up and up, impossibly high in its crescendo. Too high, even, for the enhanced senses of a Space Marine to discern. But the craftworld could. As the piercing sound spiralled up into inaudibility, the tremors grew worse. The ground began to buck and heave beneath their feet. Wraithbone peeled away, exposing flickering patches of circuitry which soon burst into flames of an uncanny hue. The towers groaned and walkways vibrated loose from their supports. The plaza had become the epicentre of a great reverberation, which rippled outwards. The dome above cracked, venting atmosphere. An eldar staggered, wailing as its spirit stone burst from the sonic rhythm.

With a resounding shriek, a tower exploded. And then another, and another. A fourth, a fifth. Cascades of rubble tumbled down to strike the plaza with the force of a god's fist, and cast up a cloud of dust. Eldar and Space Marines alike were knocked sprawling, or buried beneath tonnes of rubble as the upper levels of the dome collapsed inwards.

And then, for a moment, all was silence.

Bile struggled to his feet, coughing. His armour's respirators had become clogged by dust and particles of wraithbone. His head ached with the echoes of the pulse. 'I think – I think it is definitely time to leave,' he said, searching for the others. He saw Arrian and Oleander, their armour coated in filth. Knots of Emperor's Children made their way through the rubble, seeking to consolidate their vastly dwindled ranks, and to escape from the trap they'd cheerfully walked into. 'Get to the Dreadclaws.'

He heard a soft laugh. He turned, muscles weighed down by fatigue and the sludge of fading stimulants and battle-drugs, to catch a glimpse of green and gold and black. He saw a familiar colourful figure race out of the dust, blade held low. With belated comprehension, he recognised the Harlequin who'd attacked him on Sublime. But he wasn't its target, not this time. He saw Oleander whirl, but slow – so slow, compared to his death.

And then Tzimiskes was there, a bull of iron charging into the fray. His vox-grille throbbed with a wordless roar, the first sound Bile had ever heard him make. The Harlequin spun on its heel, altering course on the instant. Its blade flashed, and Tzimiskes' roar was cut short. The chain-axe fell from his grip as he sank to his knees. The Harlequin stepped back, hesitating just for a moment at this unforeseen occurrence. Oleander jerked forward, his sword licking out. The troupe master's high-crested head bounced away, into the swirling dust.

The remainder of the troupe retreated, fading into the dust as swiftly as they'd appeared, their colours flickering out like motes of light. Bile looked around. Tzimiskes wasn't the only casualty. More than half of the Emperor's Children who'd been nearby were down or dying. Savona and Merix were still standing, but both were wounded. The survivors were firing into the dust, wasting what little ammunition remained in a vain attempt to bring down the Harlequins.

'Cease fire, you fools, cease fire,' Bile said. He slammed the haft of his sceptre down, sending ripples of red light spreading out into the dust. One by one, the boltguns fell silent.

'The jaws that bite, the claws that catch,' a voice sang from on high. Bile looked up. The Harlequin Shadowseer sat on the slope of the pillar, leaning against its staff. Shadows and dust congealed around it like a shroud. The silvery mask looked down at him. 'One is as good as another, I suppose.'

'Chief Apothecary,' Arrian began. The World Eater was tense, like a hound straining at the leash. He raised his weapons, and tapped them together.

Bile gestured. 'Hold. See to Tzimiskes.' He looked at the eldar. 'You survived the daemon? How unexpected.'

'This is not the story of my death,' the Shadowseer said, simply. 'Nor is it yours, if you heed me, Lieutenant Commander Fabius. Master of the Apothecarion. True son of Chemos.'

'Are you offering to surrender?' he asked.

The Harlequin gripped its sides and cackled, legs kicking. Echoing laughter rose up from the rubble. The other members of the troupe hadn't gone far. Bile frowned. He heard a groan and turned. Oleander had lifted Tzimiskes up, as Arrian probed the wound. The World Eater glanced up and shook his head. Bile's jaw tightened, and he felt a tooth crack.

'Tzimiskes,' Oleander said.

Tzimiskes wheezed and caught at his shoulder. 'B– brother,' he said, simply, in a voice like a crackle of static. Then his head sagged back, and he was nothing but dead weight. Oleander closed his eyes, and bowed his head, only for an instant. He looked up at the Shadowseer.

'You tried to kill me.'

'Count Sunflame is *supposed* to die, Apothecary, that is the way the role is written,' the Harlequin said, rising to its feet. 'The King of Feathers sets aside his rags and returns to his throne, renewed and ready, but Count Sunflame perishes at his feet, killed in his moment of triumph. His death galvanises the King of Feathers and enables him to take his rightful place. Thus goes the tale.'

'Then it's a poor one,' Bile said.

'Maybe so. But the play is done. The Radiant King is deposed, his followers in disarray, and the throne vacant for another.' The Harlequin turned its silvery gaze on Bile. 'Take your place, King of Feathers.'

'It's right,' Oleander said. 'Put down the bloody scalpel and take up the gods-be-damned sword.' He spun his sword about, extending the hilt towards Bile. Bile reached out and tapped his fingers against Kobeleski's pommel, just for a moment, before pushing it aside.

'Ah. The game becomes clear at last,' Bile said. 'I wondered what you were up to with all that talk of Legions and brotherhood, Oleander. But this was artfully done. All sides and none, attacking the problem from every angle.' He felt tired. More tired than he had felt since Terra. As if the weight of his sins were bearing down on him all at once. 'I must congratulate you.'

'I did only as you taught me. Only as I must, for the good of the patient.'

'What have you done, brother?' Arrian said, rising from Tzimiskes' body.

'Isn't it obvious, Arrian?' Bile said. 'He's made a deal with these devils. He's bargained us away to these chattering clowns. And now they've come to collect.'

'Traitor,' Savona snarled. She made to lunge, but Merix gripped her and shook his head. She subsided at a look from Bile.

'Of course I made a deal with them,' Oleander said. 'Through their witchery, they saw this attack coming years ago, centuries perhaps. Or the possibility of it at least.' He looked at Bile. 'I told you the Radiant was charismatic. In a few hundred years, he'd have been unassailable, with a fleet capable of shattering this flimsy half-world. But now he's gone the threat to the eldar passes, and I get the remains of an army in search of a new leader. A leader who pulls them from the fire, saves them from extinction. Who shows them a better way.'

'You,' Arrian said.

'No, brother. *Him.*' Oleander pointed Kobeleski at Bile. 'It has to be you, master. You're the only one left who can do it. With this army at your back, you can start putting the pieces back together. You can heal us, Chief Apothecary. You can make us whole again. This was all meant for you.'

'And whose idea was that?' Bile said, thinking of what he'd seen and heard in the grove of crystal seers. 'Yours, Oleander – or theirs?'

'I don't know,' Oleander said. He looked around. 'Does it matter? All I do know is that you have a chance now... a chance to rebuild what has been lost. Canticle City doesn't have to be our epitaph, master. Here – now – you have the seeds of new life. The Twelfth Company still lives, battered and bleeding, but alive. With it at your back, we can gather the others. We can rebuild the Third Legion. Make whole what has been broken. Think of all you could accomplish, if you just take up the burden...'

'Ha,' Bile said. 'And there it is. The trap.'

From above came the sound of the Harlequin's laughter. It clapped its hands and said, 'Not a trap, Fabius, but a role. Your destined role, the role of a lifetime. Will you, won't you, play the part?'

'What is it talking about?' Saqqara said.

'The trap,' Bile said. 'The burden of leadership. It would take everything I have left to rebuild, to heal the Third. And all that I have worked for would be consumed in the doing of it. As it almost was the last time.'

'Master–' Oleander began.

'I believe I told you not to call me that.' Bile caught hold of Oleander's throat. 'If it was up to me, I would rewrite every blood-soaked page of our history, so that it might be perfect,' he hissed, as he lifted his former student. Ceramite cracked in his grip, and the chirurgeon breathed a warning into his ear. 'But that is not possible. You cannot perfect what is dead. You only waste your time.'

He looked over his shoulder, and saw a flash of green. The Harlequins were massing, perhaps for another assault, perhaps to merely watch what came next. They didn't want him dead, after all. He glared up at the creature perched on the fallen column. 'And that is what this is about,' he said, extending Torment. 'You want me to waste my time, what little I have left, in trying to resuscitate the dead.'

'Is that not what an Apothecary does, mon-keigh?' the Harlequin asked, with a brittle laugh. 'Were we mistaken? Have you fallen so far now that you do not recognise your purpose when it finds you? We offer you life, and you call it death.'

'I know my purpose better than you, clown.' Bile laughed. 'You saw a future in which poor Kasperos murdered this world. What, I wonder, did I accomplish in that distant time that so frightened you, that you would seek to shackle me to old duties?' He flung Oleander to the ground and raised his hands. 'No, don't answer, I already know. I will build a better tomorrow on the bones of today, even if it means my ultimate extermination. There is no other possibility.'

'There are always possibilities,' the Harlequin said. All humour was gone from its voice now. All traces of laughter banished. Bile realised suddenly that he had committed that most grievous of sins – he had gone off script. He met the silvery, impenetrable gaze with a malicious smile. Satisfaction surged within him. He had never been one to follow the well-trod path.

'Not for me.' Bile let his hand drop to the grip of his needler. Stimulants pulsed through his system, the chirurgeon whining in what might have been apprehension. He ignored it. He needed them, just for a moment more. 'Let the galaxy burn. I will survive. My work will survive. Humanity will survive, through my art. But you, I fear, shall not.'

He whipped the needler out with chem-enhanced speed and fired. The Harlequin leapt upright with a startled shriek and plunged away out of sight. He could not say for certain that he'd hit it, but it didn't matter. He heard screams of rage from the dust and rubble. The rest of the troupe would be upon them soon.

'What have you done?' Oleander said.

'I have done as I have always done. Chosen my own fate.' Bile gestured to a nearby Dreadclaw. 'We go – now. Stay or come, as it pleases you,' he said, looking at Savona and Merix. 'The Radiant is gone, and your fellows are either dead or beyond caring. Gather those you can, if you wish. But we must retreat now, and swiftly, if any of us are to survive.'

Gunships swooped over the ruined plaza, trading fire with the eldar, and Dreadclaws grumbled to life, disengaging their anchor-hooks. He suspected that few of the battle-maddened Emperor's Children would survive the retreat. But some would. Enough, perhaps, to salvage something from this affair.

'And what of me?' Oleander said, levering himself to his feet, with the help of his sword. He faced Bile, sword in hand. 'Will you deny yourself the throne I have won for you, merely because I obscured the truth?'

'By rights, I should kill you here and now,' Bile said, raising his needler. 'You have cost me the life of a valued servant, and set enemies on my trail. I told you before that mercy has its limits, Oleander. You have reached mine. But in recognition of past service, I shall leave you to find your own fate, as I will find mine.' He lowered the weapon and turned away, striding towards the nearest Dreadclaw.

'Master... Chief Apothecary,' Oleander said.

Bile stopped on the Dreadclaw's ramp. He did not turn around. He waited.

'It was good to work beside you again, Chief Apothecary.'

'Goodbye, Oleander,' Bile said.

As the Dreadclaw's bay began to close, he saw Oleander heft the Radiant's sword, and raise it in what might have been farewell. Or perhaps a salute, as a soldier for his commander. Then he saw nothing but the bay doors.

The withdrawal from Lugganath was a nightmare of screaming engines and shuddering decks. Many in the assault force had ignored the order to retreat, and had instead redoubled their attempts to hold their positions. They died, but their efforts were most appreciated by those wily enough to make good use of the distraction. Barely more than a hundred Space Marines in all made it back to the ship, including a number of eerily silent Noise Marines, Ramos among them.

As he strode down the Dreadclaw's ramp, he staggered. Arrian caught him. 'Lean on me, Chief Apothecary,' he said, softly. Bile barely heard him. He clutched at his chest, fighting for breath. The pain was worse than it had been. The gnawing ache had been replaced by a frenzied agony. His body was starting to shut down.

'Benefactor, you are hurt.'

He looked up and saw Igori hurrying towards him, followed by her pack. She caught him, helping Arrian to hold him up. 'I thought I told you to return to the *Vesalius*,' he said. His voice was barely a croak. The ship shuddered, as fire raked it. There was still a battle going on outside. Even if the *Quarzhazat* managed to break contact, it would be easy prey unless it could put some distance between itself and Lugganath.

'You did,' Igori said. 'I did not. I knew the route you would use to return. I intended to be here to greet you. I ordered Wolver to take the *Vesalius* out of system, and away from the battle. The eldar never even noticed them.'

'Good,' Bile said. His breath rasped in his lungs as he forced himself erect. The last batch of stimms was wearing off, and everything hurt. Alarms screamed bloody murder, and the ship shook again. He heard the dull boom of something exploding, and he could smell fire. The *Quarzhazat* screamed in agony.

'What now?' Savona said. Her face was charred in spots,

and blood dripped freely down her chin. 'What of us?' The lights flickered, casting her in shadow.

'What about you?' Bile said, through clenched teeth. He pushed away from Arrian and Igori, trying to ignore the weakness in his limbs. 'There is no uncertainty here, woman. You serve or you die. Those are your choices.' Bile studied the surviving Joybound. 'I can always use a few strong arms or few more spare parts. I shall leave it up to you, to choose which you would rather be.' The deck shuddered. The air was thick with smoke and the smell of fire.

'We must depart this system before the eldar can mount a proper pursuit,' he said. 'We must rendezvous with the *Vesalius*.' He gestured to Arrian. 'Go to the command deck and take charge of this abomination and get it going in the right direction. I must rest.'

He left them there and made his way slowly to the Radiant's chambers. The ship, which had once seemed full to bursting with horrors, was cavernous and empty now. The crew hid in their stations, watching him with wary eyes, or shrieking in brute terror at every direct hit.

He felt the deck tremble beneath his feet as he reached the Radiant's quarters, and knew the great engines were firing, bringing the Luna-class cruiser about and away from the wounded craftworld. He stumbled through the doors as they irised open. There were no daemons present now. Without the Radiant to amuse, they had departed for the Outer Dark, leaving the chamber in silence.

Bile looked around, studying the rotting tapestries and corroded trophies. The detritus of a wasted life. He picked up a battered helmet, studying the Imperial eagle moulded onto its front. 'We were the chosen. We were the light and the future, and now we are nothing but cold ashes, scattered across history's desolation,' he said. His voice echoed through the cavernous chamber. He tossed the helmet aside. Oleander had not been wholly wrong. It was up to him. It had always been up to him. There was no one else who possessed the clarity of foresight, who understood as he did. But he was not a leader of men.

'Physician heal thyself,' Bile said, softly. He wondered who he was talking to. Maybe he was simply trying to convince himself. He sagged back onto the Radiant's throne and passed palsied fingers through his thinning hair. It came away in clumps. The chirurgeon hissed softly, and he scanned its readings.

This body was almost done. He would need a new one soon. And then another and another, a parasite in his own borrowed flesh.

He was so tired. But he could not rest. Not now. He must live.

He must.

Fabius Bile closed his eyes.

'Until my work is done.'